ONE NIGHT

SIZZLING ATTRACTION

MAISEY
YATES

ANNIE
WEST

CARLA
CASSIDY

MILLS
BOON

Published in Great Britain 2017
By Mills & Boon, an imprint of HarperCollins*Publishers*
1 London Bridge Street, London, SE1 9GF

ONE NIGHT: SIZZLING ATTRACTION © 2017 Harlequin Books S.A.

Married for Amari's Heir © 2015 Maisey Yates
Damaso Claims His Heir © 2014 Annie West
Her Secret, His Duty © 2014 Carla Cassidy

ISBN: 978-0-263-93192-1

09-0318

ONE
NIGHT

SIZZLING
ATTRACTION

ONE NIGHT OF
CONSEQUENCES COLLECTION

October 2017

November 2017

December 2017

January 2018

February 2018

March 2018

MARRIED FOR
AMARI'S HEIR
MAISEY YATES

To Limecello, for sharing the picture on twitter that sparked the idea for this story. And for knowing I needed to see it!

Maisey Yates is a *USA TODAY* bestselling author of more than thirty romance novels. She has a coffee habit she has no interest in kicking, and a slight Pinterest addiction. She lives with her husband and children in the Pacific Northwest. When Maisey isn't writing she can be found singing in the grocery store, shopping for shoes online, and probably not doing dishes. Check out her website, www.maiseyyates.com.

CHAPTER ONE

You will meet me at The Mark at 1:30 p.m. You will
wear the dress that was sent this afternoon. In this
bag is the lingerie you will wear beneath the dress.
This is nonnegotiable. If you do not comply, I will
know. And you will be punished for it.
—R

CHARITY WYATT LOOKED at the very high-end shopping
bag that was sitting on the hall table in her entryway. It
was a deep gray color, innocuous, except for the famous
lingerie label printed on the side. It had matching slate
tissue paper inside, and underneath the very first fold of
paper was a thick white envelope with a card inside. She
knew, because she had opened it. Opened it and read
the instructions that were printed on it while her cheeks
burned with rage.

The card was now tucked safely back into the bag. She
didn't want to read it again. Once was enough.

The Mark. A clever location to ask for a meet up, since,
six months ago, that was what *he* had been to her father.
And to her.

A mark, part of a con. A mark who now had her utterly
and completely at his mercy. She hated that. Hated being
on the losing end. Hated being at a disadvantage.

She should have sent her dad packing when, after nearly a year of no contact, he'd breezed back into her life.

One more, Charity. Just one more.

Just one more and it would all be golden in the end. How many times had she heard that? Always with his signature wink and smile, the charm that got him everywhere in life. Oh, how she'd craved the chance to be in his circle. To be a part of him. To be valuable enough to him that he would take her everywhere. No more time spent on her grandmother's couch, wondering when her dad would be back. No more terrifying nights alone in an empty apartment while he went out and "worked."

It would all end, once he had the perfect score.

He was so good at spinning golden stories out of straw. And she wanted to walk down into the glittering world he always spoke of. Where things were easy. Where they would be together.

But it always took just one more job.

All her life, her dad had promised there would be rainbows after the storms. So far all she'd ever seen was the thunder and lightning. She had yet to get her rainbow, and this time was no exception.

In this instance, he had left her standing in a puddle, holding a lightning rod.

The minute her father had left town she'd known she was up a creek. But she'd stayed. Because she didn't have anywhere else to go. Because she had a life here. Had some friends. Had a job. And she'd been certain she would avoid detection. She always had.

Six months of silence. Six months of her life going on as it always had. Six months to get over her father's betrayal. Six months for her to forget that she had made a powerful enemy.

And now this.

This demand.

It came one day after he'd made contact for the first time. A call to her cell phone from an untraceable number.

She knew what he looked like. Rocco Amari was famous, the media's favorite businessman playboy. He had model good looks, shiny cars, shinier girlfriends. Basically, everything you needed to capture the attention of the public.

She had seen him before in print images, but she had never heard his voice. Until yesterday. Until he'd made contact. She'd realized quickly that she couldn't outrun him, that she couldn't hide from him.

Not without pulling up stakes and disappearing into the night. Leaving her little apartment, her restaurant job, her small group of friends. Becoming a vapor, as she'd been in her childhood. Invisible. With few enough things to stuff them all into one bag so she and her dad could run quickly if they needed to. Then her dad could drop her at his mother's for "a while" at a moment's notice.

No. She hadn't been able to face becoming that person again. A ghost in the human world, never allowed to touch anything. Never allowed to be a part of anything.

So she'd stayed.

Which meant pulling a much more brazen con than she would like. One that would hopefully end this thing with him, and see her on her way. Free and clear. She had to go to him, convince him of her innocence.

But he hadn't been playing by her rules. And then he'd finally called.

"Charity Wyatt?"

"Yes?"

"We've never spoken before, but you know who I am. Rocco, Rocco Amari. You have something that belongs to me, my pretty little thief." His voice was deep, his Italian

heritage evident in each syllable. It was the kind of voice that seemed to have a flavor all its own, something smoky, like Scotch and cigars. It curled itself around her, around her throat, made it difficult for her to speak.

"I am not a thief," she said, injecting a note of ringing conviction into her voice. "My father is a con man and he—"

"And you are his accomplice," he said, the certainty in his voice squashing the false ring of conviction in hers.

"I need to explain. He lied to me. I didn't know what I was doing!"

"Yes, yes. Very nice, hysterical cries about your innocence. However, I find myself unmoved."

She bit her lip, trying to force herself to feel persecuted, to call up everything she'd felt when her father had left. So that he could hear a truth that wasn't there. "But I didn't mean to steal anything from you."

"And yet, I find myself short a million dollars. And your father is nowhere to be found. Things must be made right."

"If I could get hold of my father, I would see that he returned the money." Even though she knew it had been put into other assets by now.

"But you can't get hold of your father, can you?"

No. No she couldn't. Even if she could, she doubted he'd be on hand to bail her out of trouble by putting his own neck on the chopping block. He'd left her to deal with this on purpose.

"However," Rocco continued, "I find that I have a suggestion for you...a deal."

"A deal?"

"Yes, but I do not discuss important business on the phone. You will receive instructions tomorrow. Follow them, or I will change my mind. And I will press charges. And you, Ms. Wyatt, will spend quite a few years in jail for fraud and theft."

* * *

And that was how she found herself here. With these instructions, with this bag, with the dress that was still sitting in its garment bag, because she was afraid to look at it.

But then, ignoring it wouldn't make it go away. Ignoring Rocco wouldn't make him go away. Wouldn't remove the threat that had been placed on her freedom.

She would have to go to the meeting. She would have to comply with his instructions.

And after that, she had no idea what she would do. Her eyes fell to the lingerie bag again. A shiver of disgust wound down her spine. She didn't know what his offer would be, but a suspicion was starting to form. One that didn't sit well at all. One that, now it had entered her mind, would not be removed.

It was silly, of course, because she couldn't imagine why he would want *her* in lieu of a million dollars or justice. But there was lingerie. That fact remained.

No matter what her concerns, she had no choice but to comply.

It was either that or jail.

And as terrifying as the bag of lingerie was, an orange jumpsuit was far, far scarier. There were enough courtroom dramas on TV painting law and order as a great equalizer that Charity knew most people must see the justice system as something that protected them.

She never had.

Her father had talked about Robin Hood. Twisting tales where thieves were heroes and anyone in uniform was out to shore up the impossible walls built around the rich and elite. Walls that kept people like them down and out.

Yes. The law was nothing but evil. Jail, the worst fate that could befall someone like them because they could disappear in there. No one on the outside cared about people like them. The ones on the bottom rung of society. They had to take care of themselves, because no one else would.

There was a very large part of her that still clung to those teachings, was still shaped by them.

But she'd talked her way out of worse.

She just had to find her angle.

And once she found it, she would exploit it to the best of her ability. And her abilities on that score were pretty damn good.

Rocco might think he had the upper hand…and she would allow him to continue thinking that.

The dress was so tight that Charity could barely breathe. Sheer layers of black lace that clung to her curves and revealed hints of skin beneath. There had been shoes in the bag which, somehow, fit her, just like the dress. Just like the lingerie. The heels were tall, and given the brief hemline of the garment, lengthened her legs and showed a whole lot more skin than she was comfortable with.

Which was, in many ways, going to work to her advantage. The fact that she was uncomfortable in these clothes would help. She could use it, and use them.

Charity took a deep breath and walked through the black entryway doors of The Mark, her impractical heels clicking loudly on the black-and-white-striped tile. She walked through the lobby area into the entrance of the restaurant, feeling her face heat when the hostess appraised her.

The woman's expression remained neutral, and yet, somehow, Charity sensed a hint of disdain beneath it.

She could well imagine that women in tight, tiny dresses only served one purpose in an establishment like this. If Rocco had intended to humiliate her, he was doing a very fine job.

Yet again, not necessarily a bad thing. Because she could embrace that. Go ahead and welcome the heat she could feel spreading in her face, the slight trembling in her legs. All the better to play the part of shivering ingénue.

All the better to appeal to his humanity.

"I'm here to see…Rocco Amari," she said, placing a slight hesitation before his name. Getting into character already.

This earned her a slight smile. "Of course, miss. Mr. Amari keeps his own private table in the back of the dining room. He has not arrived yet, but I'm happy to show you to your seat."

The hostess turned and began to walk into the dining room, and Charity followed. Her high heels sank into the plush carpet, her ankle rolling slightly with each step. She put all of her focus on walking in a straight line and not breaking a bone.

She hadn't worn shoes like this in a while. The mangled sidewalks that ran through the ancient New York neighborhood she lived in certainly weren't practical for this kind of footwear. And in her line of work, she rarely wore anything fancier than black slacks and a black polo shirt. Along with some very sensible sneakers that allowed her to stand on her feet all day.

Her waitressing job, at a restaurant that was much less posh than this one, was the first real job she'd ever had. After her dad had left last year she'd wanted to get out of their "family business." She was old enough now to understand that running cons wasn't just a job, and that, no matter how rich or terrible the people you conned were, it wasn't any way to live your life in the long term.

But then he'd come back, all beguiling smiles and laughter, the kind she'd missed since he'd been gone, and he'd asked her to help him again.

Just one more time...

She could stab her own arm with the salad fork. She was such an idiot. She was a con who'd been conned by a con. And now she was in too deep.

"Can I get you anything to drink?" the hostess asked.

Charity weighed her options. On the one hand, sobriety would definitely be an asset when dealing with a man like Rocco. On the other hand, she needed something to help her get a handle on her nerves. Sometimes wine made conversation flow a little more smoothly.

"White wine," she said. She didn't have to drink it after all. But it would be there if she needed it.

"Of course, miss." The hostess disappeared, leaving Charity sitting alone.

Charity glanced at the menu, not really bothering to read the descriptions of the food. Everything would be good at a place like this, but she was feeling a little nervous. Her stomach always got funny when she was lying. Which was inconvenient when you had to lie a lot.

While she was skimming the menu a hush fell over the restaurant. Or, perhaps the restaurant had already been hushed and something else in the atmosphere changed. Grew thicker, tighter.

Whatever it was, there was a change.

She looked up, just in time to see a man walk in. He was arresting, and she wasn't the only one who found him so. It seemed that almost every eye in the restaurant—male and female—was on him. He was tall, sleek like a panther. His black hair slicked back off his forehead, trim physique encased in a black suit that was tailored perfectly to the stark, lean lines of his body. But it wasn't his clothing, or the handmade Italian shoes on his feet, nor the impossibly expensive gold watch on his wrist and the no doubt overpriced sunglasses he pulled from over his eyes as he walked deeper into the restaurant, that held everyone's attention.

It was something deeper. Something more. A magnetism that could not be denied.

Everything about him was designed to capture and hold the attention of an audience.

And as he drew closer she could see that he was extraordinarily handsome. Olive skin, high cheekbones, a strong, straight nose. And his lips… She couldn't remember ever noticing a man's lips before, but she certainly noticed his.

Rocco Amari was even more beautiful in person than he was in the glossy pages of a magazine. So annoying. Why couldn't he be a sad disappointment?

"Ms. Wyatt," he said, that voice as affecting now as it had been over the phone. "I am pleased to see you made it. And that you found the dress to your liking."

That comment made her wish her wine was already here, so she could throw it in his face. He had given her no choice, and he knew it.

Don't let him get to you. You have to get to him.

"It is a very good fit," she said. "As we have never met before, I was a little bit surprised by that."

"Oh, I had you investigated. Very thoroughly." He took a seat in the chair opposite her, undoing the button on his jacket as he did, and suddenly several members of staff seemed to materialize out of nowhere. "We will have what the chef recommends," he said.

The staff melted into obscurity after that and Rocco turned his full attention to her, his dark eyes blazing with a kind of sharpness that seemed to cut through her. It was disconcerting to say the least.

A new waitress, one she had not seen before, set her white wine down in front of her. Charity grasped the stem, needing something to keep her hands busy.

"Hopefully that pairs well with the meal," he said, looking pointedly at her drink.

"I will say, that is not my primary concern at this point."

"It is always a primary concern of mine. I appreciate life's luxuries. Good food paired with good wine, good Scotch and beautiful women. Which, I must say, Ms. Wyatt, you are." He practically purred the last bit of his sentence, the roughness in the words rippling over her skin, making her break out in goose bumps.

What was wrong with her? She didn't play this game. Didn't go for flirtations and teases. She always had to keep her wits sharp, and that meant no melting around sexy men.

"I suppose I should say thank you, but I'm not going to. Because I feel like you're only putting off the inevitable conversation we must have."

"Perhaps I am," he said. "They serve very good food here. I should hate to spoil the meal."

Charity looked to the left and noticed a table full of upscale Manhattanite women staring at them. Likely wondering what a woman like Charity was doing with a man like Rocco. Just as those women read upper class from their perfectly coiffed hair down to the tips of their designer shoes, Charity read low-class pretender. Even a couture dress couldn't fix that. She had all the hallmarks of a woman who was here on her dining partner's dime.

She knew these things because her father had made a study of the upper class. Had learned their every mannerism, in order to inveigle his way into their midst. All the better to steal their money.

Charity hadn't spent much time playing those parts. Especially when she'd been young, her function in her father's schemes had been to play the part of wide-eyed ragamuffin. A downtrodden innocent who desperately needed help.

It was the role she would be reprising tonight. And while she wouldn't thank her dad for abandoning her to face the music alone, she would thank him, albeit silently, for giving her the tools to fix the broken mess he'd left.

"The meal was spoiled for me before I came," she said, injecting a healthy bit of conviction into her tone.

Rocco didn't seem moved by it. He extended his hand, brushing her cheekbone with the back of his knuckles. She was so shocked, all she could do was sit frozen, a flash of heat radiating from her cheek downward. She looked at the table of women again, saw their sneers and looked down at her wine.

Of course they assumed she was a call girl. Sitting there in that dress in the afternoon. Either a call girl or a kept woman, although there were few differences. They thought they were better than her. Because they were born with what she couldn't even earn.

But she was used to that.

"Come now. I do not want a difficult lunch partner."

"You knew people would think this," she said, her voice low, vibrating with manufactured emotion. "You knew they would think I was your...whore." She made sure to meet his gaze. "I'm not that kind of girl."

She nearly cringed at that overbaked line. But she was having a very easy time accessing this justified rage. *She* almost believed that she was nothing more than a wronged innocent. Almost.

He moved his hand back to her, and caught her chin with his thumb and forefinger, holding her face steady. And suddenly all her false anger was forgotten. "But, *cara mia*, that is what you are. You are here because I have offered you something. You are here because I've offered you a deal. And, do not forget, I bought everything you are wearing."

He was a horror. Nothing seemed to shake him up. He was heartless. Which might be problematic.

She jerked out of his hold, and he lowered his hand. "Just tell me what you want."

The waitstaff appeared again, placing food in front of them, and Charity's stomach turned. She needed this to be over, soon. The longer this stretched out, the less likely he was to bend.

Rocco had no such issues with the meal. He ate slowly, in silence, relishing each bite. The minute stretching out longer, every second a torture. She didn't want to say too much, and she really didn't want to say too little. He seemed fine sitting in silence, letting her feeling of being a mouse caught in a trap intensify beneath the study of his dark gaze.

Worse, the longer he looked at her, the more acutely aware she became of the feeling of the soft, expensive lingerie that was beneath her dress. It was something about the way he looked at her. The fact that he *knew*.

She could see it in his eyes. That he knew exactly what she was wearing, and that he knew what she might look like in the items he had sent.

He was looking at her as if she was a possession, as if he owned her already.

And the fact was, he might. The longer she sat there, the longer she'd had to fully understand her potential fate and the circumstances she found herself in. She didn't know what he would demand of her yet. But she knew the alternative.

Yet another thing he had accomplished by bringing her here. He highlighted the difference in their stations.

She was a waitress; she was a woman. Her ties to criminal activity were irrefutable, though she had never once been arrested. Her father was gone with the money he had taken from Amari Corporation, and he likely wouldn't resurface even if Charity were brought to trial. Actually, if Charity were brought to trial he would be less likely to surface than ever. Because Nolan Wyatt would not stick his neck on the chopping block for anyone. Not even his only daughter. Not when it was between a life of luxury— albeit a temporary one—or life in prison.

Charity would be made the example. She would be brought to court, a scarlet woman who had stolen from a man who worked hard for his money. And she would go to jail. She could see it playing out now.

But he was prepared to offer her a deal. One that would mean avoiding jail.

Realistically, she wasn't sure she could turn it down no matter what it was.

Even if it was the worst.

In that moment she hated herself for being such a coward. For entertaining the idea of selling herself in exchange for avoiding time spent in prison. But she was afraid. Jail was the big bad. Growing up, the law had been a terrifying prospect, men in uniform the enemy.

It was a fear that was bred so deeply into her that just thinking about it now made her break out into a cold sweat. She was afraid of the unknown, and while both options she was entertaining in her mind were unknown, one would be over much faster.

You don't know that's what he wants.

No, she didn't know. But he had sent lingerie, and that said an awful lot.

And she wasn't naive about men. Her father was a liar and a manipulator. And both in word and by example, he'd taught her how to identify other liars and manipulators. Charity wasn't naive about anyone or their motivations.

She liked to be prepared for the worst. And in this case... Well, in this case it meant that Rocco had dressed her for the job he intended her to perform.

Another waiter appeared as soon as Rocco had cleaned his plate. "Dessert, Mr. Amari?"

"No—" the words left Charity's mouth before she could reconsider them "—no dessert."

"Please have dessert and coffee sent to my suite," Rocco said, as though she hadn't spoken. "Ms. Wyatt and I are ready to retire."

"Of course, sir." The waiter inclined his head, his bland expression not betraying any thought whatsoever, and scurried away to do Mr. Amari's bidding.

Charity's stomach sank to her toes, a sick feeling overtaking her. He wanted to take her somewhere private. He wanted to get her alone. Nothing good would come of that. "Are we going to discuss the deal?" She didn't want to leave the dining room. She needed him to change his mind here.

"Of course. Up in my room. And this is the part where I will discover if you heeded my warning."

Her heartbeat sped up, her pulse beating rapidly at the base of her neck. "What warning?" she asked, her throat dry. Because she knew which warning. She *knew*.

"If you are not wearing the lingerie I sent, I am about to find out."

"I haven't agreed to anything," she said, her eyes meeting his. She tried to remind herself to dial it back. To appeal to him on an emotional level.

Challenging a man like him wouldn't get her anywhere. He was all alpha male. If she tried to go at him head-on, he would push back. But if she played the weak, simpering female, she might just be able to arouse his protective instincts. She had to remember that. She had to stay in character.

"You will agree to whatever I ask. Because if we go to court, I will win. You know that to be true."

She swallowed hard, not bothering to disguise it. She wanted him to see her every nerve. Every flicker of fear in her eyes. Being brave wouldn't win any points with him. "I don't understand how this would benefit you."

"But you see, *cara*, that is not for you to understand. I do not have to explain myself to you. I merely have to present you with your options." He put his hands on the table, his large fingers splayed over the pristine white cloth. "So you tell me, would you rather come to my suite or go to jail?"

Charity looked down at her untouched lunch, her lips cold. "If those are my options I would rather go to your suite," she said, determination washing through her like a tide.

She could still turn this around. She would make him see that she was just a victim. She repeated the mantra over and over again. If she said it enough times, she might believe it. And if she believed it…all the better to make him believe it, too.

"Very good." Rocco stood and walked toward her, extending a hand as though he were the perfect gentleman seeing to his companion. She didn't accept the hand, standing up on her own, taking the hard glitter in his eyes as a personal triumph.

"I very much appreciate a strong-willed woman. But I also require compliance when it is demanded." He straightened his cuffs, buttoned his jacket, then raised his focus to her, his dark gaze locking on to her. "I hope very much that you have given it where I have commanded. Otherwise, you will find my threats are not empty." He held out his hand, and this time she took it. "Now, come, *cara mia*. It is time for us to adjourn to my room."

CHAPTER TWO

THE SUITE WAS BEAUTIFUL. There were massive windows that overlooked Central Park, letting a generous amount of natural light in, bathing everything in warmth, in sunlight. For a moment, she simply stood in the doorway, pretending she was only taking in the sight of a beautiful room. One that was well out of her price range, one she would typically never even get to look at.

Unless she was running a con.

That's all this is. You're just running a con. And on the other side, lies freedom. You never have to do it again. You can be done.

She took a deep breath and kept examining the room, delaying the moment this became real. The floors were marble, rugs stationed throughout, beautifully appointed matching furniture with solid wood detail in the seating area, with a bed that boasted a matching frame in the bedroom. It was a large bed, with rich purple velvet coverings, and more pillows than she had ever seen in one place before.

For a moment, it was nice to look at. For a moment, it seemed innocuous.

But only for a moment.

Then Rocco came to stand behind her, the heat from his body intense, energy radiating from him and throwing everything inside of her out of alignment. As if he'd reached into her chest and moved everything around.

He had certainly reached into her life and done that. Moved everything around, put things on their ends.

"Dessert should be here shortly," he said, breezing past her and walking into the room. "Make yourself at home."

As if that was going to happen. "It's difficult for me to feel at home here."

"Oh yes, I imagine it is quite different to your little apartment in Brooklyn."

Charity froze. Of course he would know all about her. He had sent the clothes to her home, after all. But hearing the details of her life spoken about by a perfect stranger just didn't sit comfortably.

"Do you have to imagine?" she asked, her tone crisp. "Don't you happen to have full walk-through photographs of my home available for your perusal? You seem to know a lot about me."

"The art of war. One must know their enemies. Or so I have read."

"And I'm your enemy?"

He closed the distance between them, curling his fingers around her arm, pulling her close. The contact of his skin against hers struck her like lightning. "You stole from me. People do not steal from me," he said, his face close to hers, his tone deadly.

She could sense then that he was every inch the predator she had feared. And whatever she had been afraid he might ask of her, it would likely be that and more. Because there was no softness in him. No compassion.

He was the sort of man who only understood one thing. The cutthroat, black-and-white nature of revenge. Of killing or being killed, hunting or being hunted.

That would limit her ability to manipulate. But her strength would lie in him underestimating her.

He thought she was his prey. But he didn't know that beneath this lacy monstrosity beat the heart of a beast. She had been brought up in a hard environment, with instability and poverty and all the rest.

She hadn't survived by being weak.

"My father lied to me," she said, putting her hand on her chest, feeling her heart beating hard beneath her palm. "I really thought he had finally gotten honest work. I had agreed to help him garner investments from reputable companies. I did not know he was going to take that information and siphon money out of your accounts. I promise I didn't know." The lie came easy, even looking into those flat, dark eyes. Because protecting her own skin was second nature. Was the most important thing. The only thing.

"Your name is on the wire transfers. Your name is connected to the bank account the money went into."

"Because I agreed to help him set the accounts up." And she knew, even as she tried to explain, that it was going to do nothing to move him. But she wasn't going to simply stand here and allow him to level accusations at her. Not when they weren't true. Not while she still had a chance to get him to understand.

"Then you are a fool. Because everything I can find about Nolan Wyatt says that he is a con man. Now and always."

"He is," she said, her throat tight. "But I—"

There was a knock on the door to the suite and Rocco released his hold on her, stalking to the entryway.

"Room service, Mr. Amari," the man on the other side of the door said. "Where would you like me to put the tray?"

"I will take the tray." Rocco took control of the tray

and closed the door, wheeling the coffee and two pieces of chocolate cake to the center of the room.

If she couldn't eat a light meal of vegetables and salmon, she was hardly going to be able to eat this.

"Haven't you ever wanted to believe the best of someone?" She hoped he had. She hoped he did.

"Never. I only want the truth."

"I'm giving it to you. And I can only explain away the fact that I helped my father by saying I wanted to believe the best in him when I shouldn't have. He's the only family I have. I just wanted him to be telling the truth this time."

She found herself very convincing. She would be shocked if he didn't.

"So much that you were willing to take a chance on helping him with another fraud?"

"My dad is small-time. I didn't expect anything like this from him." That much was true. She'd had no idea his designs were quite so grand. A million dollars. He'd overplayed his hand. The idiot. Anything smaller and Rocco wouldn't have noticed, much less pursued her like this. "Yes, he's stolen fairly large amounts of money before, and I know it. I didn't live with him most of the time I was growing up, but when I did, we would always have times where we would move, and then we would have something for a while. A house, food, money, clothes. But it would always disappear very quickly. We would find ourselves dodging landlords, dodging police. Then, we would move again. Dad would get *jobs*, he called them. Then we would move again, and have things for a while. And the cycle would repeat. Eventually, he stopped taking me with him when he moved."

"I see. Is this meant to make me feel sorry for you?"

"I only want you to understand…I'm a person like you

are," she said, a pleading note lacing her voice. "I made a mistake in who I trusted. Surely you understand?"

He chuckled, a hollow sound that echoed in her chest. That made goose bumps spread over her arms. "The problem with trying to appeal to my humanity, Charity, is that I don't have any. I can understand why you would assume differently. But let me be the one to inform you definitively that I'm not burdened by conscience. Nor am I burdened by compassion. Every cent I have, I have earned. Getting to this position in life cost me in blood and I will not allow myself to be taken advantage of. I will set an example if I must." He moved to her again, not touching her this time, merely standing so close she could feel the heat coming from his body. "I will make an example of you if I must. Do not think I will lose sleep over throwing a beautiful woman like you in prison when it is deserved."

"So, is this my last meal?" she asked, indicating the food on the tray.

Overdramatic, perhaps, but she was starting to feel desperate.

"Either that or it is fuel to help you keep up your strength for the next couple of hours. You might find you need it."

Adrenaline spiked through her blood. "So, you get off on forcing women into bed?" The words came out slightly harsher than intended.

A smile curved his lips. "Absolutely not. I never force women into my bed. I will not force you. You will come to me, because you want me."

"How would you know I wanted you? When it's you or a jail cell it seems as though my choices are limited."

"I'm comfortable with that," he said, his smile growing wider. He looked like the Big Bad Wolf, ready to devour her. "Would you like some coffee?"

"No."

"Very well. Then it is time for me to see if you have kept your end of the bargain."

She swallowed hard, her hands shaking, her fingers cold. "The lingerie?"

"Did you do as you were instructed, *cara mia*?"

She couldn't believe it. She had lost.

Her stomach sank into her feet, the intense weight of defeat crushing her before she was able to process all the implications in front of her.

This was the moment of truth. Either she threw the coffee on his face and stormed out of the room, and took what came, later—charges, an arrest, a trial.

Or she did this.

She took control. She pushed him as he was pushing her. Called his bluff.

She would not stand here and wait to be undressed.

Before she could think it through, her shaking fingers found the zipper to her dress and began to tug it down.

He would stop her. He would stop this. She was sure of it. And it was that certainty that kept her going.

She could feel the fabric separating, exposing skin. Could feel the dress getting loose in the bodice. Then the top fell exposing her breasts, clad only in the whisper-thin lingerie. It was the same color as her skin, a kind of milky coffee color. It made her appear almost bare.

She knew, because she had spent a fair amount of time looking at herself in the mirror wearing this, that he would be able to see the shadow of her nipples beneath the fabric.

No man had ever seen this much of her body before. She didn't know if she was in shock, if she was still convinced he would put an end to it, or if the moment was simply too surreal for her to absorb it all. But she felt cushioned by something, by a gauzy curtain that had been pulled around her vision, making things seem hazy. Making them seem a little less harsh.

Whatever it was, whatever magic this was, she needed it. Because the character, the nervous ingénue, wasn't a refuge here. Not now.

It was too close to the bone.

Too close to who she was in this setting.

In life, she had very little in the way of innocence. But here? In the bedroom? She'd never trusted a man enough to be this intimate with him. Had never wanted to.

And she didn't trust him. But she didn't need to. For some reason, right now, she realized trust didn't matter. This was all about power. And he had underestimated hers.

She finished pulling the zipper down the rest of the way and pushed the dress down her hips so that she was standing there in nothing but the high heels and the matching bra and panty set. The panties were as sheer as the bra, and she knew he could see the shadow of dark hair at the apex of her thighs.

She stared straight ahead, not looking at him, her eyes fixed on a blank spot on the wall. She was still in this chess game and her new revelation was adjusting her strategy. Putting her in view of Rocco's queen.

Power. Control. That was the game here. It wasn't sex.

All she had to do was take his control.

"Look at me," Rocco said, his voice laced with steel, the command impossible to ignore.

She redirected her gaze, her eyes clashing with his, and all the breath rushed from her lungs.

There was an intensity to his dark gaze that was unmatched by anything she had ever seen before. It could never be said that Rocco looked passive, at least not in her very brief experience of him. But this was different. There was a fire burning beneath this that set something ablaze low and hot inside of her.

He moved toward her, reaching out and touching the silken strap of the bra, sliding his thumb and forefinger over the fabric. "You were a very good girl. I must confess I am surprised." He never took his eyes off hers, and the heat inside of her intensified.

What was happening to her? Why was he touching her? Not her skin, but beneath it? Why was he making her feel all this heat?

She could still leave. She could still pick up her dress, put it back on and go.

But she didn't. Instead she stood, frozen, as fascinated as she was terrified by what might happen next.

He leaned in slowly and she held her breath. He pressed his lips against the curve of her neck, just beneath her ear, and a shiver went through her body.

She wasn't cold at all anymore. But she was still shaking. And it wasn't from fear.

"I will make you beg for me," he said, his voice a dark whisper that wrapped itself around her mind.

She angled her head slightly, pushing down every bit of insecurity. She hated this man. This beautiful, horrible man. And she didn't care what he thought about her. She didn't care what he thought of her body. What he thought of her soul.

He was her enemy and after today she would never see him again.

For some reason that realization sent a shock wave through her. Confidence, pleasure, a rolling feeling of satisfaction that she couldn't have explained if she wanted to.

She leaned in, her lips a breath away from his. "Not if I make you beg for me first."

His lip curled and he leaned in, tracing the line of her

jaw with his forefinger. "Do you think you could make me beg?"

"Can you walk away?" she asked, taking the roughness in his formerly smooth and cultured voice as evidence of the effect she was having on him. "Right now, could you leave this room?"

"I am not finished with you yet," he ground out.

She forced a smile to curve the corner of her mouth. "I guess that says it all. You're the one who can't walk away. And I don't even have prison to threaten you with."

He gripped her chin tight, and she stared him down. His dark eyes were blazing and she was certain hers matched. Then he slid his thumb across the edge of her lower lip.

And closed the distance between them.

The fire in her stomach ignited, sending flames roaring through her. It was no longer contained, no longer content to merely burn in the hearth. And she realized her fatal mistake too late. She might have taken his control, but hers was gone, too. Whatever this heat was had taken over everything, threatening to reduce all that she was to ash.

She'd never been kissed like this. Had never been held close to a man like this, his arms so tight around her, his body hard and muscular against hers.

This was the last thing she had expected. For him to kiss her as if he was a man dying of thirst and she was an oasis. She had expected him to be cool. She had expected him to hurt her, humiliate her. She hadn't expected him to make her want.

Make her feel.

Wanting him was almost scarier than the alternative. Because she was only here for one reason, for him to extract the debt she owed from her body. She meant nothing to him beyond that. In fact, he *hated* her. Saw her as an enemy.

She had a feeling that right at that moment, neither of them had the control. She wasn't even sure if they were fighting for it. If each brush of his lips against hers was a press for more dominance, or if they'd both given up altogether.

She was forgetting. Forgetting everything but his lips against hers.

He shifted, cupped her face, tilting his head and deepening the kiss, his tongue sliding against hers. The delicious friction sent a shiver through her. It shocked her, sent a wave of pleasure through her and, for a moment, she could only process how good it felt.

How could he touch an enemy like this? How could he hate her and taste her so deeply? With such care?

No one else ever had. Only this man. This man who despised her.

That should make her want to run, but she didn't. She stayed. Rooted to the spot. Anchored to him.

When they parted, he was breathing hard, his fingers going to the knot of his tie, loosening it with startling efficiency, before casting into the ground. "Yes, you are a very good girl indeed," he said, his voice ragged.

He pulled her back to him, kissing her again. She wanted to fight him. Wanted to fight this. The way it felt as if he was stripping her bare without ever touching the silken undergarments that covered her skin.

But she couldn't. She felt so small, but she didn't feel weak. She felt protected. And as things started to crumble and fall inside her; as the walls, the anger, the fear, started to crack, in the deep, empty well that lived inside of her, an insatiable and hungry thing that had craved this simply opened up and allowed itself to be filled.

Oh, it hadn't been sex she desired specifically. But touch, attention. To have someone look at her as though she mattered. As though it had to be *her* standing there in front of them and no one else.

To have someone pay attention to what she wanted, what she liked. To have someone lavish pleasure on her. Because that was the only way she could think of it. She was entirely bathed in sensation, the singular focus of this large, powerful man.

He wasn't handling her roughly, not with anger. He was in supreme, complete control and he was exercising that control to make her feel…good.

It wasn't what she had expected and it made her feel vulnerable. Strange.

No one had ever wanted her. No one had ever needed her.

And even if it was naive, she felt in this moment that Rocco *needed* her. And it made her want to give in to him. It made her want to give him everything.

He hates you. And you are trading your body to keep yourself out of jail.

You can't do this.

She could still leave. She could walk out the door and damn the consequences. He wouldn't physically stop her. She was confident in that.

But you don't want to.

No. Because she'd never had the courage to touch a man like this. To kiss a man like this. And now there was nothing holding her back. Nothing stopping her. Why not have this? Why not have him? She pressed her palms to the hard muscle of his chest, and leaned in deeper for the kiss.

Rocco growled, tightening his hold on her waist, and backing them both across the room, and to the bed.

Yes.

This wasn't about money, or jail, or freedom or fear. This wasn't about control. Not now. This was about him.

About everything she'd spent her life too afraid to grab. She was so tired of it. So tired of herself. Of being a ghost that no one could touch or connect with because she was hiding her past.

He was touching her. And he knew her past. He knew it and hated it and he still wanted her. That meant it didn't matter what she did now. Didn't matter that she was a virgin who had no clue what she was doing.

She slid her hands to his shoulders, and down his back, exploring the feel of him, the sheer breadth of him. So different to her. To her body.

He moved one hand to her thigh, lifting her leg and bringing it around his own, opening her center to him. He pressed himself against her, the hard length of his arousal making contact with the source of her desire, sending a shot of pleasure through her body.

It was happening so fast, and yet she found not fast enough. She couldn't think anymore, couldn't reason. Couldn't work out why she had been so afraid of this being the outcome. Because this wasn't scary. And it didn't hurt.

It felt wonderful.

And everything melted away. Who she was. Who he was.

He wasn't a mark. And she wasn't a con artist.

He was a man. And she was a woman.

And *they* wanted.

He tore his mouth from hers, kissing the line along her collarbone, to the edge of the lace bra that she knew had cost more than a month of her wages. He traced the scalloped edge of the delicate garment with the tip of his tongue, and she shook, sliding her fingers through his hair, holding him tightly to her.

"You are delicious," he said, forcing one of the lace cups down, exposing the entirety of her breast to him. Then he lowered his head, taking her nipple into his mouth and sucking deeply. "Delicious," he said, turning his focus to the other breast and repeating the motion.

He slid a thumb over one of the tightened buds, his eyes rapt on her body, watching as it tightened further while he teased her. He pinched her gently and she gasped, arching against him, bringing the heart of her body into contact with his hardness again.

"I did not anticipate wanting you so much," he said. "You are so responsive."

Was she? She wanted to ask him if she was especially responsive, but she couldn't speak. Couldn't do anything but feel.

"Responsive," he said, kissing the valley between her breasts, "and very delicious. I mentioned that, but it must be said again. And I must taste you again." He moved lower, kissing her stomach, and lower still, his lips hovering above the waistband of her panties.

He couldn't mean to…he wouldn't. Because somewhere in the back of her mind she thought that this was a self-less act. One that would mean giving to her, and revenge wasn't selfless. Revenge wouldn't allow him to give that.

But then he was pulling those expensive panties down her legs and forcing her thighs apart, opening her to him. And he looked. More than looked, he stopped, frozen for a moment, and gazed as though she was a work of art in a museum, and he was poring over her every detail.

She could hardly breathe, her heart beating so hard she thought it might burst through her chest.

Then he leaned in, his eyes never leaving hers, his tongue trailing a line along the sensitive skin of her inner thigh. Then he moved close to…to…

A burst of insecurity broke over her. "I don't…you don't have to…"

He growled and pushed his hands beneath her bottom, tugging her close to his mouth, his eyes still on hers. "I will have whatever I like."

He closed the distance between them then, laving the sensitive bundle of nerves with the flat of his tongue. And she stopped pushing at him. Instead, her fingers curled into claws, dug into his skin. For a moment she was afraid she was hurting him, but he let out that low, feral growl again and pulled her more tightly against his mouth, tasting her even deeper, and that thought, along with every other thought she'd ever had, fled from her mind.

She found herself flexing her hips in time with his tongue, pushing herself closer to the edge of climax. She'd never done this with a man before, but she was familiar enough with how her body worked. Though, it was different when someone else had so much of the control. Wilder. More exciting.

He shifted, and she felt his finger slide through her slick flesh, testing the entrance to her body. She tensed, unsure of what to expect next. He pressed into her, the sensation unfamiliar, but not at all painful.

She let out the breath she'd just brought in, and relaxed into the new rhythm, into the feeling of being filled by him. Pleasure started building again, harder, faster. And then it broke over her, a wave that pushed her out to sea, tumbling her in the surf before bringing her up short, spent, and breathless.

She forgot everything. Why she was here. That he was a stranger. That he was her enemy.

How could he be a stranger when he had just touched her more intimately than anyone else ever had? How could he be an enemy when he had taken greater care for her pleasure, her needs and her comfort than anyone else in her life ever had?

And for a moment, just for a moment, he moved up so
their bodies were aligned, and he held her in his strong
arms, against his solid chest, so that she could rest her
head against him and feel the raging of his beating heart,
and she felt...she felt home.

Safe.

Cared for.

More for him, more in his arms than she'd ever felt
before.

He moved his hand down between her thighs, then
leaned in, kissing her neck as he teased her clitoris with
his fingers, arousing her again, much more quickly after
her orgasm than she would have imagined possible.

She wanted to beg. But somewhere in her mind she remembered him saying she would. And so she bit her lip
to hold it back.

Then he lowered his forehead against hers, sweat bead-
ing on his skin. She could feel his arousal pressed against
her inner thigh, so close. So close to what she knew they
both wanted.

"Per favore." He whispered the broken words in Italian, and his need was the final bit of fuel on the flame.

She released her hold on what was left of her control.

"Yes," she said, her voice a sob. "Please. Please take
me." She was desperate, and she didn't care if he knew it.
And it wasn't just for pleasure, but for a connection. For
an answer to the deep, unending emptiness inside her she
hadn't been aware of until this moment.

"You want this?" he whispered, the words frayed. "You
want me inside you?"

"Yes," she moaned, arching against him.

He kissed her lips before moving away from her, opening the drawer of the nightstand by the bed and producing
a little square packet.

A condom.

Oh yes, they weren't done. This was it. She was going to lose her virginity now. To him. And she couldn't even muster any fear. No shame. No doubt. Because she just wanted. More of what he'd given her only moments ago, more of being skin to skin with him. More of his lips against hers, his body *in* hers. She wanted more.

She wanted it all.

He worked the buckle on his dress pants and shoved them partway down his lean hips before positioning himself over her, and tearing open the condom. He was still almost entirely dressed, and she saw nothing but the deft movements of his hand as he rolled the condom over himself.

But when he moved to her entrance, she felt the blunt head of him, stretching her, tearing the thin barrier she'd never before given much thought about. She tensed, squeezing her eyes shut tight as the burning pain reached its peak, then dissipated slowly after he'd buried himself to the hilt.

She gritted her teeth, fought to keep from crying out, but she wasn't successful. A whimper escaped her lips and she shivered beneath him as pain laced its way around all the beautiful pleasure she'd felt only a moment before.

He swore, violent, rough against her ear, and pushed himself up, dark eyes blazing into hers. But he said nothing.

Instead he angled his face and kissed her, long and deep, as he withdrew slowly from her body before sliding back home. It didn't hurt at all that time, and as he established a steady rhythm to his thrusts, discomfort faded to a kind of neutral fullness, and from there grew, expanding to a deep, pulsing pleasure that was unlike anything she'd ever felt before.

She arched against him, as she'd done when he'd gone down on her, meeting his every thrust, the motion sending little sparks of heat through her, a familiar tightness coiling low in her stomach.

She felt him start to shake, felt the control in his movements start to slip. A groan escaped his lips, and he bucked hard against her, freezing above her, pushing them both over the edge to oblivion.

When she came back to herself, she was lying on her back, starting at an unfamiliar ceiling, with his warm, protective weight covering her. As if she was something precious.

Except…he wasn't protective. And she wasn't precious.

She was nothing more than a criminal, who had tried to make good for a while and failed. And he was…he was…

She tried to push away the reality that was crowding in. Tried to ignore the truth she would have to face eventually. She didn't want to. Not now. Not while pleasure was still buzzing through her. Not while she still felt so good.

The power she'd felt only a few moments before was slipping through her grip like sand through an hourglass and there was no way for her to turn it back over and start again.

Then he was up, moving away from her, turning and walking into the bathroom, slamming the door shut behind him.

And she could only lie where she was, still staring at that ceiling. At the way the molding formed different tiers and textures. She listened to the sounds of the streets outside filtering up, audible even through the closed windows.

Life was moving out there, and yet, in here, in this room, in this moment, she was frozen.

The bathroom door opened and Rocco reappeared, his shirt buttoned, his pants redone. Except for the lack of tie, he looked exactly as he had done when he'd first walked into the restaurant. As though nothing had happened. As though past minutes hadn't existed.

They might have just shared cake and coffee, instead of their bodies.

"I have a meeting to get to," he said, his voice as unaffected as his exterior. "You may stay here if you wish. The room is paid for through the night."

"I...I..."

"That is all I will be requiring from you. Though, I confess, I didn't expect you to give in quite so easily."

His words were cold, distant, and she tried to recapture the feeling she'd had moments ago, of feeling close to him, and found she couldn't. She would wonder if it had all been in her mind except she was still naked, on the bed.

She sat up, holding her hands over as much of her body as she could. Trying to reclaim some modesty, some dignity, some...something.

"I would have taken a lot less from you, *cara mia*, but you played the part of whore so well, who was I to stop you?"

She felt as if she'd been slapped, a sick, cold feeling of shame trickling through her veins. And she had no mask to recall. None to put in place and hide her nakedness, her vulnerability. "But you...I..."

"Speechless?" He arched a dark brow. "It was quite good, I'll give you that. But, regrettably, I don't have time for seconds." He bent and picked up his tie, tying it quickly before buttoning his jacket.

He was untouched. Invulnerable. And she was still stripped. Of everything.

"As I said, I require nothing more from you. Consider your debt paid." He turned away from her. "The sex was... incredible. But I'm not sure it was worth a million dollars.

I think, in the end, you got the better part of the deal." He strode away from her, pulling the door open and pausing, turning to face her. "I want you to remember something, Charity."

He waited. Waited until her heart was thundering so hard she was certain he could hear it. Waited until she was certain she would be ill. Waited until she couldn't hold the question back any longer.

"What?" she asked, her throat dry.

"That it was just as I said. I made you beg for it." Then he walked through the door, and let it close firmly behind him.

Charity just sat there in the center of the bed, tugging her legs up to her chest. She looked down at the white bedspread and saw a smear of blood and the full horror hit her.

A tear slid down her cheek, a sob shaking her body.

Dear God, what had she done? What had he made her into?

She'd never been a "good girl." Never been honorable or honest. How could you be when the first skill you learned was tricking strangers into thinking you needed money so you could bring it back to your father? How could you ever be good when you'd been straddling the lines between right and wrong from the beginning?

But there were lines she had never crossed. She had never used her body like this.

And now...

The room is paid for...

No. She wouldn't stay here. She couldn't. And she wouldn't let that damned lingerie touch her skin ever again.

Another tear slipped down her cheek and she wiped it away, anger fueling her now. She could fall apart later, but for now, she needed to handle this.

She had made a mistake. A terrible mistake. She had

revealed herself to him. Her real self, not just her facade. You didn't show yourself to a mark, ever.

He was still a mark. That was all. And she would never make such a mistake again.

She picked up the phone that was by the bedside and dialed the front desk. "Yes," she said when the woman on the other end answered. "I'm in Mr. Amari's room. I need a pair of sweats and a T-shirt. Medium. Some sneakers. Size eight. And a bra. Thirty-six B. Just charge it to the room."

She hung up and sat back down on the bed. She wasn't touching that dress, those shoes, or the lingerie again.

The sweats were a fair trade.

It was the last thing she would ever take from Rocco Amari. The very last thing.

After this, she would forget about him. About this hotel room. Where she had lost her pride and her virginity all at the same time.

From this moment on, Rocco Amari was dead to her. She would leave this experience here, over and done.

She'd used her body to escape, so she would damn well see that it was an escape. No more cons. No more helping her father out with one last thing.

She would leave here, and go into her new life, with a fresh start.

After this, she would not speak of him. She would not think of him. She would take nothing from him ever again.

CHAPTER THREE

ROCCO AMARI WAS a bastard. In every sense of the word. He'd been aware of that from an early age. From the time he'd first been teased by other neighborhood children for not having a father to the moment he'd watched his mother, a grim look of wounded pride on her face, accept money from an employee of the man who'd sired him, to help them keep the modest house they called home. Provided they never made contact with him.

Yes, he had known, then and always, that he was nothing more than an illegitimate child born to a rich man's unwanted mistress. And as time had gone on he had learned that playing the part of the bastard in the colloquial sense served a man well in his ascent to success.

Though, in his case, the role had become his reality. There was no place in his life for conscience, no place for compassion. He had learned, long ago, that a man had to look out for himself because when push came to shove no one else would.

Venture capital was not the sort of business that lent itself to being sentimental or soft. Yes, it was about building businesses, but you had to be willing to cut dead branches. And Rocco was more than willing.

A man had to protect what was his, because other men wouldn't hesitate to try and claim it for themselves.

And given that he was a bastard, and given that he took a dim view of compassion, he found himself irritated by the fact that the conscience he had no place for felt seared by his encounter with Charity Wyatt.

He had never meant for it to go so far.

The plan had been to bring her into the hotel room, strip her bare, humiliate her and leave. Perhaps, not an overly sympathetic plan, but nowhere in his planning had he imagined he would actually... No. Trading sex for his stolen money had never been a part of the plan. Yes, he had intended to flirt with the line. He had always intended to do that. But Charity was a thief, and in his mind she was just lucky he didn't believe in more medieval forms of punishment.

But things had not gone according to his plan. He had lost control.

Which was, perhaps, the most unforgivable part about it.

The rest he could have forgiven himself for. But not the loss of control.

By taking her to his room, by commanding her to strip, by making her beg for him, he had been proving to her that she was in over her head. That he commanded the situation, as he did all things. But her rich, dark eyes had met him in challenge as she'd taken the expensive, overtly sexual clothing off her body, revealing the perfection beneath. And something had flipped. He had not proven his control. She had *broken* it. Yes, he was certain he had humiliated her, but at what cost? At what cost to his own pride?

It had been nearly two months since their encounter, yet at night he still woke up drenched in a cold sweat, dreaming of soft delicate fingertips trailing down his stomach. Of rich, dark curls spread out over his chest. Coal-black eyes looking up at him with wonder.

It was the wonder that got him. Because it wasn't anything he had never seen before. Certainly, women had looked at him with desire, with satisfaction, but never with the kind of awe he had seen in Charity's eyes. And he knew why.

He clenched his hand into a fist. He shouldn't care. What did it matter if a woman had made love to a hundred men, or one? It didn't. It shouldn't. Not to a man like him.

And yet it mattered.

It made his sin feel that much greater, when he didn't wish to feel as though he had sinned at all. Normally, he lived his life exactly the way he chose to, conducting affairs with women as he saw fit, spending his money as he chose, drinking as much as he desired. He didn't answer to anyone, least of all the archaic idea of black-and-white morality. Life on the streets of Rome had taught him early on that morality was only for the middle class.

Those who had nothing couldn't afford it, and those with billions could pay to bypass it.

And yet here he was, regretting a sexual encounter with all the guilt of a choir boy. Concerning himself over the virginity of a woman who had been far from *innocent* regardless of her past sexual experience.

It was unacceptable as far as he was concerned. As it was unacceptable that the woman was still taking up so much space in his mind. It was also unacceptable that he was still without his money.

He had not intended to let her off the hook on that score, either.

But as he had deviated from his plan, he had yet to regroup and decide what he would do now.

He could not pursue prosecution now. As he had promised absolution in exchange for sex. However, he'd never intended to actually have sex with her.

But he had. And that limited his options.

That damned conscience again. Where the hell had it come from? He should have no qualms about either one of those things.

His intercom buzzed and he pressed it, annoyance coursing through his veins. "What?"

"Mr. Amari—" his secretary, Nora, sounded harried "—there is a woman here who refuses to leave."

Rocco gritted his teeth. This was not the first time, nor, he imagined, would it be the last. It was either Elizabeth, a woman he'd ended his association with a little over three months ago, or it was someone entirely random, hoping to fill the currently vacant position of mistress in his life.

Too bad for whoever it was he didn't enjoy being pursued. He liked to be the one directing the pursuit.

"Tell her I am in no mood."

"I did. She is still sitting here."

"Then have security remove her."

"I thought I should call you before I resorted to that," Nora said, her tone conveying that she found the idea of having a woman forcibly removed from the building distasteful. He didn't find it distasteful in the least. If she didn't want to be carted out, then she should have obeyed the command to leave in the first place.

"Next time don't bother. Have security remove her as a matter of course. You have my permission."

He heard a muffled shout, and response from Nora. She must have put her hand over the receiver. And then she was back. "Mr. Amari, she says her name is Charity Wyatt, and she says you will want to see her."

His blood ran cold. Rage following closely, thawing out the ice.

He didn't want to see Charity Wyatt unless it was in hell.

Of course, in many ways he felt he was already there.

Put there by his very own fallen angel. Who had now crawled back into the pit to pay him a visit.

"Send her up," he said, shutting off the intercom. He would regret this. And yet, he couldn't resist the temptation. To see her one more time. To shove her skirt up around her hips and take her again, bent over his desk this time. To prove that she was just as helpless in the face of this attraction as he was. Prove that he wasn't weak.

He stood from behind his desk and began to pace the room, pausing as soon as he heard a knock on the door. A timid knock. Clearly, Charity Wyatt was not quite so defiant as she had been the last time they met.

She wasn't defiant for long. She melted quickly enough beneath your touch.

He gritted his teeth and willed his body back into submission. "Come in."

The door opened, and the sight that greeted him was a surprise. It was Charity, but not as he had ever seen her before. Gone was the beautiful, sleek siren he had taken to bed in the hotel suite. Instead, standing in front of him was a woman wearing black pants and a T-shirt. Her dark wavy hair was pulled back into a ponytail that looked as if it would suit a schoolgirl better than a woman in her early twenties.

The only makeup she appeared to be wearing was a smear of gloss over her lips, the rest of her face bare. There were dark circles under her eyes, as though she hadn't slept.

One thing was certain; she was not here to conduct a seduction.

He fought against the hard punch of disappointment that slammed into his gut. He shouldn't care. He would listen to whatever it was she had to say, and go out and find the nearest socialite and drag her back to his penthouse.

That was his problem. He had been working himself into the ground since his encounter with Charity, and he had not had a chance to be with anyone in the time since. Nearly two months was far too long for a man like him.

Still standing there looking wide-eyed and wounded, she made his gut twist hard. She was not supposed to be here, this woman who had destroyed his control.

He needed her gone.

"Well, obviously you aren't here to screw me. Which makes me feel very short on patience," he said. "You had better speak quickly."

She met his gaze, completely unintimidated by his attempt at scaring her away. "I am certainly not here to… That," she said, her tone haughty.

He let out a heavy sigh, looking down at the paperweight on his desk. Straightening it before looking at her again. "I find myself growing more impatient. Either get on your knees for me or get out."

"There are no circumstances on earth that would find me on my knees for you. Not begging you, not pleasuring you. That is my firm promise."

Anger cut through his veins like a knife. "We will see about that, or do you forget that I hold your future in my hands?"

She crossed her arms beneath her breasts and tilted her head to the side, that ridiculous ponytail tilting with her, glossy dark curls sweeping over her shoulders. "Before you start making threats you should know that I carry *your* future in my womb."

Charity hadn't meant to impart the news quite that way.

She had intended to come over slightly more vulnerable. That was the entire point behind coming in her waitressing outfit. The entire point to not dressing up, to show him the way that she really lived.

Maybe it was stupid to try and engender his sympathy, for a second time, but she needed him to understand that she wasn't living large with his money. Because his money was exactly what she needed.

For her new life. For her.

For the baby.

It was still so surreal. More surreal than sleeping with a stranger at all, was the realization that she had created a life with one. That there would be a person on earth who would share DNA that belonged in part to her, and in part to him. It didn't seem fair, really. Not to her, not to the child. She didn't much care if it was fair to Rocco.

There were certain things she could never provide for a child, not with her income. And really, she shouldn't be ashamed. This was a sacrifice of her pride, to ensure that her child was taken care of. To ensure the child had everything it deserved.

She didn't want him to play the part of daddy, and try to make a happy family with her. Far from it. She just needed his money.

But, she felt she had a legitimate claim on it, considering.

She ignored the slight jab in her conscience that reminded her she had already taken some of his money.

But I don't have it. And so neither will the baby.

She needed the baby to have it. Otherwise, what could she offer? It was either life with the server's wages, or life that looked a lot like hers had when she'd been growing up. Moving from place to place, running cons.

She didn't want that for her child. She wanted better. She wanted the best. She wanted to try and figure out how to be a good mother. She wanted to figure out how to be something other than a thief.

It had been nearly thirty seconds since she had dropped her bombshell, and Rocco still hadn't spoken. Charity didn't feel obligated to fill the silence. He deserved to feel the same shock she had felt when she had taken the test. When she had seen the little pink lines that had changed everything.

Yes, they had used a condom, but she knew enough to know that they did fail sometimes. And anyway, no amount of arguing that point with the universe would take back what had been done.

Still, she couldn't help but feel she was being punished for the way she'd handled things. Had she refused him, she would simply be in jail rather than expecting a baby.

That thought almost made her laugh. Just because it was so absurd. Just because she could hardly feel any regrets over sidestepping prison. No matter what else had happened since.

In some ways, she had arrived in a hopeful place about the baby. That this would be a true stepping-stone into something different. Into a different life.

"Was that your way of making an announcement?" Rocco finally spoke, his tone hard.

"I suppose it was. That wasn't exactly the plan, but then I didn't expect you to be so horrible. I suppose that was my first mistake. We have met after all."

"We used protection," he said, the words cold. Blunt.

"Yes, and I did speak to the universe about that when I realized my period was late. However, it didn't seem to care."

"How do I know you didn't rush out and bed the first man you found after we parted? A little bit of revenge? Trying to pass his baby off as mine?"

Charity embraced the genuine, righteous anger that burned through her. "How dare you? You, who blackmailed me into sex. You took my virginity in payment for money my *father* stole, money that I never touched." That much was true. She'd never had her hands on the money for a moment. "You are every inch the villain in this scenario, Rocco Amari. I will not lie down and take these accusations. I will not allow you to stand there looking superior when the simple fact is you all but forced me into having sex with you, and you don't deserve to comment on my character when you were the one who led things between us."

Rocco drew back as though he had been slapped. But when he recovered, she could feel the rage radiating from him in waves. "Perhaps I did some of those things. But I did not force you into bed. Do not deny that in the end you *begged* for me. You said yes. Yes *please*. And I gave you what you wanted."

She looked away, her cheeks heating. "I was a virgin. It was never going to take much to make me lose my head. I wouldn't let it go to your ego." She needed him to feel responsible. And she needed him to feel annoyed. So he would get rid of her, but also offer her money.

"You cannot play the victim now. I would never have gone so far with you had you not asked."

"Are you honestly going to say that you didn't intend for it to end in sex?"

He paused, his dark eyes flat, his jaw clenched tight. "I did not. All I really wanted was for you to beg. But you were much more convincing than I anticipated."

The admission seemed to cost him, and she had no idea why. If it should hurt anyone to hear that, it was her.

She had overpaid. And now, she would keep on paying.

She gritted her teeth. "Don't forget you begged, too."

"I didn't have to beg for long, did I?"

"I *hate you*," she said, and she found she meant every word, even though she was speaking it as part of her role. As part of the indignant, downtrodden waitress who found herself alone and pregnant.

That's exactly what you are.

She swallowed hard, her throat tightening, genuine emotion overwhelming her. "What have you done to us?" she asked.

"Inexperience will not cover your actions in this. Do not put the blame on me entirely."

"Oh, you don't want all the blame? Then perhaps you shouldn't swan around as though you are the God of the universe. You cannot be both all-powerful and without fault. You threatened me, you made me feel as though I had to fall into line or I would be put in jail. Yes, I acknowledge that in the end I consented. But had I not been coerced in the first place I would never have been in your room. Obviously, I have spent my life staying away from men's hotel rooms, and yours would have been no exception."

"Fine. I was an absolute monster. Is that what you want to hear? Does that ease your pain? It shouldn't, as it doesn't change the situation."

"I'm surprised you would admit to the fact that you're a monster," she said, anger pouring through her.

"Being considered a nice man has never been a concern of mine. I don't particularly care whether or not I acted with the highest moral standards. That is not what drives me. I wanted success. I have achieved it. And I will keep it. Everything else is incidental. I will have what's mine, and that is my utmost concern."

"I can't get you your money back. I don't know where my father is. If I did, count on it, I would be the first person to turn him in. I'm not protecting him. I'm not that self-sacrificial. In fact, I'm not self-sacrificial at all. I slept with you to keep myself out of trouble because you wouldn't listen to me. I would have turned him in to you a thousand times over to avoid that." The only problem with turning her father in was that he would talk. And then her proclamations of innocence wouldn't mean much anymore. Because he would confirm her involvement and she didn't want that. Even though Rocco didn't believe her innocence she couldn't bring herself to confess her guilt, either.

"All of this is beside the point," he said, waving his hand, as though to brush her concerns out of the air as if they were nothing more important or substantial than cobwebs. "What do you want?"

"I wanted to give you the chance to know about the baby. Because I wanted to give you the chance to make a choice about whether or not you wanted to be in its life."

He only stared at her, dark eyes flat. "And what part would you expect me to play in the life of a child?"

"The part of father I would imagine, as that is the role you played in its conception." He wouldn't accept it. And she knew it. But she had to ask. She'd never known her mother, and her father had been distant. She would give Rocco this chance.

But he would turn it down. And she would be grateful. Because while she needed to give him a chance to be involved with his child, the last thing she wanted was for him to have any involvement with her.

Beyond the financial support he would no doubt offer, and which she and her baby would desperately need.

"I would not know the first thing about being a father. I didn't have one."

"Well, I don't have a mother, and yet it seems I'm about to become one. Apparently, lacking a particular parent isn't an effective form of birth control. Who knew?"

"I do not see why you would want me to participate in the child's life."

She was surprised by the depth of anger she felt when he said those words. Surprised by the deep, elemental rage that started down low in her stomach and flowed outward. Because she was only just wrapping her head around this motherhood thing, and that she should have an instinct, of any kind, was shocking. Especially because her ultimate goal was definitely not to have him involved.

But hearing him say it—it affected something in her she hadn't even known was there. It cut too close to the bone. Too close to her own childhood. So full of indifference, abandonment, regret…

She gritted her teeth. "Then don't. But you will pay child support. I'm not raising your child in poverty while you eat in fine dining establishments and…and…prop your feet up in your giant Italian villa."

"I most certainly will pay child support. If it is mine."

"It *is* yours. I haven't been with another man. Ever. My first time was in your godforsaken hotel suite, and it was my only time." She swallowed hard. "And you know that. I *know* you do. You, on the other hand, have been with so many women I bet you don't even know the official number. I made sure to get a panel done when I went in for my blood test to confirm the pregnancy. To make sure that I didn't catch anything from you."

His lip curled into a sneer. "I always use protection."

"And obviously it isn't always effective."

His expression went flat again. Unaffected. "Do you need money for medical care?"

She blinked. "I will. Unless I can get on some kind of assistance…"

"How soon can you get a paternity test done?"

She clenched her hands into fists, starting to feel lightheaded. "Not for a few weeks. And from what I've heard there's a miscarriage risk."

"Your choice. Discuss it with your physician at your appointment, and I will leave that decision to you. But, if you do take assistance from me during the pregnancy and upon delivery of the child the test is done and I discover it is not mine, you will owe me for the care you received."

She gritted her teeth. "I will probably take option two, as I'm completely confident in what the results will be. I'm not worried about owing you a damn thing."

"Excellent," he said, as though they had just solved a particularly tricky business issue. "I will arrange for an account to be set up for your medical needs. After the delivery of the baby, after we have legally established paternity, we can work out some sort of child support agreement."

This was it. She had won. He was agreeing to child support. It was going to get her what she needed, give her and her child the best life possible. And he wasn't going to be involved.

For some reason, the victory was so much more hollow than she had imagined it might be. For some reason, she didn't feel victorious at all. She just felt dizzy, dazed.

Maybe because she was in shock. She very likely had been from the moment she'd first taken the pregnancy tests. The first one, at home, and the follow-up blood work at the free clinic. She had probably been in shock the whole time she was formulating this plan. A way to make sure everything was taken care of, without having Rocco in her life.

It was difficult to feel victorious when everything about this just felt frightening. Strange.

"I suppose you know how to contact me," she said.

"And you know how to contact me. Clearly."

"Is that everything?"

He shrugged and went to sit behind his desk. "Unless you have any further concerns. Or, have any information on the whereabouts of your father."

She shook her head, feeling numb. "No."

"That is a shame. Do let me know when the results of the paternity test are in."

"You mean when your child is born."

"I imagine the timing will coincide," he said, looking away from her now completely. As though she was already gone.

"I'll call you. Someone. Your secretary," she said, turning away from him and walking out the door.

She managed to hold it together until she was halfway through the lobby. But then, just as she was passing the receptionist's desk, a sob worked its way through her frame, catching her breath, making her pause. Her chest burned, her whole body shaking. She didn't know why this hurt so much. Didn't know why it mattered whether or not he cared about the child. She didn't want him to, dammit. Why was she feeling guilty now?

Because you know how much it hurts. You know it hurts forever.

Yes, she did know. Knew that the pain of abandonment, of complete disinterest, didn't ease.

She hated that her child would be starting out life the way she had started hers. And it was a strange and terrifying thing to know that, already, the needs of her child felt so much more important than her own.

She pressed on through the lobby, sucking in a gasp of fresh air as soon as she was outside. She blinked against the harsh light of the sun, staring up at the cloudless blue sky that seemed to mock the state of her life with its beautiful perfection.

But somehow, while part of her felt angry about the

beauty of the day, another part of her took comfort in it. Things were changing in her life, faster than she could process them. But everything around her was the same.

It wasn't the end of the world. It was just the start of a strange, new one. And no, her child wouldn't have a father. But she knew from experience that a father who sucked was probably worse than no father at all.

And her child would have a mother. There was no question about that.

It was scary. Terrifying. She was a twenty-two-year-old waitress who didn't feel as if she'd started her life yet. She didn't know how to be normal. Her moral compass skewed from childhood. But she would have to change the way she saw things now, change the way she did things. Because she didn't want to carry on the legacy that her father had tried to instill in her. A legacy she had been taking part in because she hadn't known what else to do.

She still didn't know what to do. But with the financial support coming from Rocco, she wouldn't even be tempted to engage in cons anymore. Maybe she would get a house in the country. Maybe she would make friends with other mothers. Maybe she would make up a story about where she was from, and what happened to her baby's father.

Maybe that could be her last con. One that she lived in. One that she stayed in. Something normal, something happy.

The thought of it made her smile.

Things were going to change. But she needed that. Desperately. *She* needed to change. Maybe this was her chance to finally have real connections. To love someone the way she wanted to. Without reserve. With love in return.

A love neither she nor her child would ever have to earn. No *just one more con* looming overhead. A mythical destination that would supposedly fix all, but would never arrive.

She closed her eyes and wiped away the tears that had fallen down her cheeks. She didn't need Rocco Amari to be happy. Neither did her child.

This whole thing with her dad had started out as one of the biggest mistakes of her life. But maybe out of it something amazing would happen.

Either way, it was a new chapter. She was done with her father. She was done with the life they'd led. Done with cheating people.

And she was done with Rocco, except when it came to the financial support he would offer. It was a new life, a new beginning.

And now that she had taken care of the hard part, she was ready to start.

CHAPTER FOUR

THE ROOM WAS EMPTY. Everything was gone. Nothing to identify who might live in this tiny little house in Rome. No toys to show that a child played here. No pots or pans in the kitchen to prove that there was a mother who lived here. A mother who had cooked dinner every night, regardless if the meal was comprised of the most modest portions.

Even the blankets that were usually fashioned into a nest in the corner of the living area were gone.

And there were strangers standing there. Strangers who were smiling although there was nothing to smile about.

His toys were gone.

But worst of all, his mother was gone.

No matter how many times he asked where she was, no one would answer. He asked until he was hoarse, until his voice was gone, and still there was no answer. Only smiling, and strange assurances that everything would be fine, when he knew nothing would ever be fine again.

The room was empty, and he couldn't find anything that he needed.

Rocco woke up, his body drenched in sweat, his heart hammering so hard he feared it might burst through his chest. His bedroom was, of course, not empty. He was sleeping on a king-size bed with lush blankets and pillows covering every square inch. In the corner, he could see his dresser, and mounted to the wall the flat-screen TV. Everything was here, just as it should be.

Most importantly, he was not a small crying child. He was a man. And he was not helpless.

Yet for some reason, in spite of the realization that he had been having his usual dream, the unease didn't let up. His chest still felt as though it was being squeezed tight, a large hand wrapped around his throat.

He got out of bed and walked over to the bar that was next to the door. He needed a drink, and then he could go back to sleep.

He flipped on the light and reached for a bottle of Scotch, pouring himself a generous amount, his hands shaking. As he lifted the glass to his lips, he replayed the dream in his mind. And suddenly the face of the child changed. It wasn't him any longer, but a child with her mother's defiant expression and wavy black hair.

He swore and slammed the glass down onto the bar top. There was no reason for him to take part in the life of the child Charity was carrying. The odds that she was truly pregnant were slim. The odds that she was carrying his child slimmer still. It was a tactic to use him. She was a con woman, just like her father, and he knew it.

Yes, she had been a virgin, he knew that, too. But perhaps she had not been. Perhaps it was all part of her elaborate ruse. He couldn't be sure.

He should forget this. Forget she had ever come to see him. It would be easy for him to send a certain amount of money to her every month, money he would never even look at. She would be cared for, as would the baby, and he could go on as he always had.

Yet again, his mind was filled with large, sad brown eyes. He looked down into the Scotch as though it betrayed him, then lifted the glass and hurled it at the wall, watching it shatter. It left a dark blot behind, a spray of liquid clearly visible, and shards of glass on the floor. He didn't care.

And he shouldn't care about Charity Wyatt and the baby she might or might not be carrying.

You would abandon your child? Is this what you have become?

He did not hear the questions in his own voice, but a voice from far in the past. His mother. Who had left luxury with his father to give birth to him. Who had, before that, sold all of her jewelry, all of her clothes. A mother who had worked nights at a factory, walking a dangerous route home in the early hours, alone.

His mother had given her all, until she had lost her life in pursuit of caring for him.

And he was going to leave his child with nothing more than an automatic deposit once a month.

He ignored the uncharacteristic guilt that wound itself around his lungs, making it difficult to breathe. He didn't believe in guilt. It was useless. It accomplished nothing. He believed in action.

So take action.

What action could he take? Would he keep the child for himself? Take Charity as his wife? Make a family with the woman who had defrauded him out of a million dollars?

The woman who had tested his control and found it wanting?

Unacceptable.

All of it. He owed her nothing. He didn't even owe her child support all things considered. He was still half convinced she had his money tucked away somewhere. A million dollars of his ferreted away into an account to use at her discretion.

In truth, he was being generous offering her anything. Yes, he was generous.

He took another glass from the bar and poured himself more Scotch. He would not think of this again. He would place his assistant in charge of arranging Charity's medical appointments. She would receive the best care available. Another token of his generosity.

He had made the right decision. And he would not question it again.

He downed to the rest of his Scotch and went back to bed.

Charity felt like hell. She had for the past two weeks. Everything she ate seemed to disagree with her, and she had no energy at all. She had missed so many shifts at the restaurant that her financial situation was getting dire.

But, the unavoidable fact was that nobody wanted a clammy, pale waitress serving them food.

And today was her first official doctor's appointment that had been arranged at the clinic chosen by Rocco. It was a strange thing, going to a clinic that had been selected by the man who was so intent on keeping himself separate from all of this.

Well, she was willing to bet that Rocco himself hadn't actually selected the clinic. More likely he had had his assistant do it. Which, actually sat a bit easier with her.

The place was certainly upscale, a far cry from the free clinic where she'd gone to get her blood work done in the early stages of the pregnancy. Instead of plastic chairs, cracked tile floors and water-stained ceilings there was plush carpet, a comfortable seating area designed to look more like the living room of a nice home and chilled bottles of water offered upon entry.

It was amazing what could be achieved with a little bit

of money. Or a lot of money, in this case. She could almost see why her father was so driven to join the elite class and enjoy the fruits of their labor.

Of course, Charity had discovered that it wasn't really worth the risk. Too little too late, however.

"Ms. Wyatt?" A woman poked her head through one of the doors that partitioned the waiting area off from the patient rooms.

Charity picked up her water bottle and stood, following the woman back to a scale, where her weight was taken, then to a restroom, where a sample was taken. And from there, to one of the little rooms that had a white gown neatly folded on a chair and a large cushioned exam table at the center.

"The doctor will be in to see you shortly. Remove your clothes, and put the gown on," the woman said.

Charity nodded, feeling slightly numb again. The baby stuff was all fine in theory, but when things got real like this she started to retreat inside herself again.

She went through the motions, removing her clothing, putting the thin nondescript gown on. She sat on the table, her hands folded in her lap, unease pooling in her stomach.

There was a knock on the door. "Come in," she said.

A smiling woman in a lab coat walked through the door, and Charity smiled back. And then a man followed her, dressed in a perfectly fitted black suit, his black hair combed off his forehead, his dark eyes glittering with some sort of intense emotion she could not readily identify. One she didn't want to identify. Any more than she wanted to identify the man himself.

Rocco was here. And she felt as though she had been punched.

"Well, now that the father is here, I suppose we're ready to begin," the doctor said.

"Such a surprise," Charity said, her hackles rising. "Rocco," she said, his first name strange on her lips, "I didn't expect you."

"I would imagine not. *I* didn't expect me. And yet, here I am." He didn't sound very happy about it.

She smoothed the gown down, ensuring that it covered as much of her legs as possible. "I don't really see how it's possible for you to surprise yourself."

She was shocked, but she was doing her best not to let him see it. She promised herself she wouldn't give him any more of who she was. He didn't deserve it. A mark never did. And he had already had enough of her.

"We live in strange and interesting times," he said, taking a seat in one of the chairs that sat opposite the exam table.

The doctor looked from her to Rocco, and back to her.

"Everything is fine," Rocco said, not bothering to look at Charity. "Just a little spat."

Charity snorted. "Yes, a lover's quarrel." What a joke. She and Rocco could hardly be called lovers. They'd had sex. At its most base level. Love hadn't come into it. Like hadn't even been involved. He had used her. Humiliated her.

"So what is it that we are waiting for?" Rocco said, looking around as though he was expecting something grand, as though she was going to deliver the baby here and now.

The doctor blinked, then turned to the computer, entering a password, and bringing up Charity's chart. "Well, Charity, your weight looks good. And everything was normal with the urine sample."

Ridiculous, considering Rocco had seen her naked, but the mention of *fluids* made Charity's cheeks heat. "Well, that's good to know."

"And, now we're just going to try and see if we can hear a heartbeat. If we can't get it on the Doppler, it could just be because it's so early. So there's no need to be concerned. But it is nice to try and establish viability this way if we can."

Rocco was staring at her, hard. Maybe this was what he was here for. The chance to hear the heartbeat. To see if she was telling the truth. Though, she would have thought that he might send a lackey to ascertain this sort of information. She could just picture his secretary sitting here, waiting to report back. She would find that less disconcerting.

The doctor stood and put on a pair of rubber gloves. "Could you lie down please?"

Charity shot a look over to Rocco. "Please come and stand up by my shoulders."

"You did not conceive the baby on your own," he said, his tone laconic. "We both know I've seen it before."

Even the doctor blinked at him in shock. "You will have to forgive him," Charity said. "He was raised by wolves. They did a terrible job."

Rocco shrugged, a rather wolfish smile crossing his features. "The founder of Rome was also raised by wolves. I consider myself in good company."

Charity rolled her eyes. "Oh, great Caesar, come and stand up by my shoulders."

She was surprised when he complied. But maybe he was just tired of the delay. He moved up to the head of the exam table, and she lay down. The doctor retrieved a sheet from beneath the cabinet and laid it over Charity's lap.

The doctor adjusted the gown, then squirted some warm gel onto Charity's stomach. She took a small wand and placed it over the gel, sliding it around, a strange, watery sound filling the room. She moved it lower, and lower still. And suddenly a pulsing sound rose up over the baseline noise.

"That's it," the doctor said, her tone bright. "That's the baby's heartbeat."

Charity looked up at Rocco, then immediately wished she hadn't. She didn't care what his reaction was. At least, she shouldn't care. But truly, she had imagined he would have no reaction at all, and that was clearly not the case.

His face had turned to stone, as hard and immobile as a statue.

He was truly beautiful, and it was an inconvenient moment to think of it. But he was the father of her baby and that realization made her study his features that much more closely. The golden tone to his skin, the hard, angular lines of his cheekbones, his jaw. The sensual curve of his mouth.

Her child would be half of him. Would he have the same sulky expression? Dark straight hair like his father? Or a riot of black curls like her?

Rocco's frown deepened. "It does not sound like a heartbeat," he said, the mocking edge smoothed from his voice. He sounded…strange. Uncertain.

"It does to me," the doctor said, clearly not at all intimidated by Rocco.

There was an odd light in Rocco's dark eyes, something she couldn't put a name to. "It's very fast," he said, and if Charity wasn't so cynical about him, she might have thought she heard concern in his voice.

"Normal," the doctor said. "Strong, and absolutely nothing to worry about." She directed her focus to Charity.

"She is pregnant," Rocco said, not a question.

The doctor's brows shot up again. "Absolutely."

A deep groove formed between his dark brows. "I see," he said, his tone stoic now. "And I hear."

For a while, no one spoke at all. There was only the

sound of the baby's heartbeat, and on the monitor, a wavy line that moved with each beat. A band that seemed to stretch between Rocco and herself, tightening a bond between them she hadn't realized was there.

Charity wished it would go away.

"Do you have any questions for me?" the doctor asked, breaking into Charity's internal monologue.

Charity shook her head, suddenly unable to say anything. Unable to think at all.

"Then I'll see you in four weeks for your next appointment. Everything seems right on schedule. Nothing to worry about." Charity could think of about fifty things to worry about without even trying.

The doctor removed the wand from her stomach and wiped away the gel with the sheet that was over her lap. "I'll leave you to get dressed."

And then she left, leaving Charity and Rocco alone.

"Would you go please?"

"Why?" Rocco asked, sitting back down in the chair he had been in before. Any softening, any humanity she thought she might have glimpsed a moment ago was gone now.

"I need to get dressed."

He put his hands behind his head and leaned back. "You're being so charmingly modest. We both know you possess quite a bit more boldness."

"Fine. If you're looking for a show, enjoy." She stood from the exam table, letting the sheet fall to the floor. The gown covered her until she turned her back on him, and she knew she was revealing everything to him then. She untied the top of the gown and let it fall completely. Then she set about getting dressed.

She was too angry to be embarrassed. She didn't care

if he looked. He was right, he had already seen her. He had touched her. He was the reason things were like this.

Once all of her clothing was on, she turned to face him. He was staring at her, dark eyes glittering. "I should've charged admission for that," she said.

"I found the ingénue much more charming. Perhaps you could revert back?"

"Oh, I think you and I both know that I can't play the ingénue now. I seem to have lost my innocence somewhere."

A half smile curved his lips. "And so you have. Though, I'm starting to think that virginity is not necessarily innocence."

She shrugged. "I won't argue with you there."

"Is this an admission of guilt?"

"Certainly not. I'm only saying my innocence is unconnected to whether or not I've slept with a man."

"You really were a virgin, weren't you?"

She lifted her chin, staring him down. "Is it important?"

He looked back at her, and for a moment she thought she saw something in his dark gaze, something that looked strikingly like guilt. But then it was gone, replaced with the smooth, impenetrable expression she'd come to expect from him. "Not particularly. If I had a conscience, I suppose it might be a little dented by the realization. Happy for both of us I don't. Though, it might bear weight on how convinced I am that this is my child," he said, directing his gaze at her stomach.

"It is your child. There was no one else before you, and no one else after you." She watched his expression carefully for more clues. And was disappointed. So she pushed harder. "Makes it difficult for you to vilify me, doesn't it?"

"You might find this strange," he said, his tone hard. "But I'm not here to vilify you."

"Well, you certainly aren't here to shower me with flowers and compliments. So why are you here?"

"I've changed my mind."

"What do you mean you've changed your mind?"

He stood, pacing the room. "I have decided the child support isn't enough. I have decided that I want my child." He paused, dark eyes boring into hers. "Not only do I want my child, I want you."

CHAPTER FIVE

HE HAD SUCCEEDED in shocking her. She was simply staring at him, her large, dark eyes wide, her lush lips parted.

"Was there something confusing about what I just said?" he asked.

He felt a twinge of something in his stomach. A slight bit of... Had he been any other man he might have thought it was insecurity. But that was impossible. Still, he was questioning his methods. He did not seem to be winning her over to his side with his current tactic.

But he despised the need to try and woo her. Especially considering that he still believed her to be a thief. But, perhaps treating her so harshly was not helpful.

He decided to try something slightly different. "What I mean to say is, I am keeping the child. And I am keeping you as well, as I find the idea of our child being without a mother unacceptable. I am still missing a million dollars. I do not feel as though keeping you in exchange is unreasonable."

Her expression contorted, this time anger replacing shock.

He had the feeling he had not selected the proper method.

"You can't...keep me. What does that even mean? You cannot *keep* a person."

He frowned. "Certainly I can. I have a villa on the Amalfi Coast. And I intend to take you there."

"You cannot be serious."

"I am serious. I'm very serious. In fact, I intend to take you at once."

"I can't leave," she said, her dark eyes shifting to the left. "Who will feed my cat?"

"You have a cat?"

She met his gaze again, her expression ferocious. "No, but I could."

"There, you have no cat. There is no issue. It's settled. You are leaving with me. Now."

She blinked rapidly. "What about my job?"

"What about your job?" he said, waving his hand. "You are a waitress. And as the mother of my child, you will never have to wait tables again."

"I don't understand. Just a couple of weeks ago you sent me away, promising me no contact, and money." She sounded desperate and angry.

Yes, he had said all that. But at the time he'd been knocked so flat by her revelation his reaction had been... much less than gracious. And he'd decided he didn't believe her, because it was easier. She couldn't be pregnant, not by him. Not when he'd used a condom.

He had decided that she probably wasn't pregnant at all. But then the dreams of that wide-eyed little girl had continued to plague him. And so he'd decided to come down to the doctor's appointment and prove it.

But Charity had been at the appointment. And then... and then the heartbeat.

And he had known in that moment it was his child. Had believed that, in this instance, she spoke the truth.

But he didn't want her to be too confident in that just yet. Not while he was still sorting through his feelings.

"And you seemed to want me in the child's life."

"I don't need you in the child's life," she said, "I only need child support."

"I disagree."

"You said that you didn't want to be a father," she said.

"And yet, it seems I'm going to be one. *Want* has nothing to do with it. But for stronger scruples or a stronger condom, we wouldn't be in this mess. But alas, we had neither. Still, I think the situation can be salvaged."

"I felt it had been salvaged rather well already."

"Why? Because you got my money?" Perfect, chilled rage, rushed through his veins. "What do you plan to do with the child? Farm it out to relatives? An elderly aunt? No doubt while you continued to collect my money."

"No, I intend to raise my baby. But I don't need you to do it," she said, lifting her chin, her expression defiant.

"I have as much right as you. I am the child's father."

"And, not to put too fine a point on it, I hate you."

He chuckled. "Am I supposed to be bothered by that? You are not the first woman to hate me, and I daresay you will not be the last. However, you are the first woman to carry my child. And I will have you both. This is nonnegotiable."

"Or else?" she asked, crossing her arms beneath her breasts, her dark eyes glittering.

"Prison is still an option," he ground out.

She blinked rapidly. "You wouldn't really send me to jail."

"They take very good care of pregnant women in prison." He looked at her, watched as the fear took hold of her. Good. Let her understand that he wasn't giving hollow threats. He was not a man to be trifled with. Most especially by a woman who had wronged him. "I would hate to explain to our child that its mother was a criminal, but I will do what I must."

"You bastard," she said.

"Guilty. And you might want to be careful throwing that term around, as technically, our child is a bastard, too."

Her dark eyes glittered. "How dare you?"

"That is the reality of the situation we find ourselves in, *cara mia*. If you do not like it, take steps to change it."

"What steps?"

He lifted a shoulder. "You could always marry me," he said.

It was the most extreme version of his plan, but not one he was entirely uncomfortable with. He saw no reason why marriage should affect his lifestyle in any way. Or hers. But it would at least provide a comfortable framework for his child's life. That was something he had lacked growing up, and he didn't want his child to lack in the same ways.

It was part of his growing obsession.

Ever since that night, the night after she had come to tell him about the baby, he had been plagued by the same nightmare over and over again. The empty house, the searching child. The child that eventually became his.

And he had known then what he had to do.

He had grown into an entirely selfish man over the years. He knew that. He had not connected with a single person since the death of his mother. The homes he had bounced between offered him nothing—no comfort, no love. And when he had gone into the workforce, he had approached things with a single-minded ruthlessness. Life on the street had taught him early on that you had to look out for yourself, because no one else would.

His mother's fate had taught him that you had to be the most dangerous person in the alley, or you would become a victim.

Rocco Amari refused to become a victim.

And yet, he felt connected to this child. The child in his dream. He had no way of knowing if it was a vision of some kind. In fact, he was certain it wasn't, because he didn't believe in such things. But he didn't feel he could ignore it, either.

His sleeplessness had driven him here. To confirm the pregnancy, to confirm what he must do. The moment the sound of the baby's heartbeat had filled the room, he had known. No matter the cost, he would create a family. A stable environment.

He was determined.

"Are you insane?" she asked, taking a step back.

"No."

"You say that with a lot of confidence, for someone I'm pretty certain is insane," she said, shaking her head, a curtain of glossy curls swirling around her. She truly was beautiful. It was a shame she was a criminal.

"You don't need to answer that now. But you will come back to the island with me now."

"Or prison?"

He smiled. "Or prison. Yet again, I feel it's a fairly easy choice."

"I should have run."

"Before or after the con?"

She paled, an ashen tone running beneath her cream-and-coffee skin. "I don't want to talk anymore," she said.

"Too close to the bone?"

"I don't have a choice, do I?"

He advanced on her, closing the space between them. And as the air shrank, his chest tightened, his blood running harder, faster. There was something about her, something that called to him. Something elemental. He could not fathom it.

"Did we ever?" They were not the words he meant to speak, and yet he found it was an honest question.

He wondered if there had ever been a choice where she was concerned. If, rather than being the woman he was certain had been a part of stealing his money, he had spotted her in a crowded bar, they would have ended up in bed together.

If, no matter the circumstances, their connection would have been forged.

"I didn't," she said.

"You made your choice when you agreed to help your father steal my money. And now I am the one making the choices. You will come with me. Now. I do not make empty threats, and I think you know that."

"Well then," she said, her voice strangled. "Perhaps you should show me to your private jet."

"I will. Make no mistake, *cara*, you are mine now. And by the end of next week, I will decide what exactly I am going to do with you."

For the second time Charity found herself looking at a set of written instructions, and a garment bag.

She still felt as if she was dreaming. Only, it wasn't a particularly good dream. They had left the doctor's appointment, only to get on a plane and fly overnight to Italy. Rocco had spent the entire flight ignoring her, which suited her just fine. She'd slept most of the way, and she assumed he had been working, or whatever it was he was doing on his computer. Possibly looking at pictures of women in bikinis. She didn't really care.

He'd continued his silence on the car ride through the city and up a winding mountain road. Charity had tried to appear blasé about the whole experience. From the moment they had boarded his private plane, until they had touched down in a country she had never even dreamed of visiting. But she'd found it was impossible. Especially when faced with the beauty of Italy.

The narrow streets, tall buildings, cluttered balconies and brightly colored flowers on climbing vines were too beautiful for her to ignore. She'd pressed her nose to the glass of the limo they were riding in and watched as the road widened, the buildings became more sparse, stared in awe at the intense jade ocean down at the bottom of the rocky cliffs.

And once the expansive villa had come into view, she'd had to fight to keep her mouth from dropping open.

Now she was inside, installed in her bedroom, which was larger than the New York hotel suite Rocco had seduced her in. It was expensive, light and airy, with white curtains and flowing white linens cascading over the wrought-iron frame of the bed.

And yet, there was a heaviness in her chest that she could not shake.

And now the note.

You will join me for dinner. You will wear the dress that I have provided. We have much to discuss.
—R

This scenario felt far too familiar for her liking. And the worst part was, much like the first time, she was in no position to refuse him.

She blinked, her eyes feeling gritty. The time change and restless sleep on the airplane was starting to catch up with her. She took her shirt off, and her skirt, then unzipped the garment bag to find a bright yellow dress made of a light fabric that looked as if it would be comfortable in the heat.

She had expected a corset and garter belt, so it was a pleasant surprise.

She slipped the dress on over her head and turned to look at herself in the mirror. Unfortunately, she looked as tired as she felt. Deep purple circles marked the skin beneath her eyes, and she was certain that there was a permanent line etched in her forehead that had not been there BR.

Before Rocco.

She sighed and took her hair out of its clip, running her fingers through the glossy dark curls that she had always imagined were a gift from her mother. A thick, unruly gift that made getting ready a chore. A fitting present from a woman who had never once bothered to check on the child she had given birth to.

She reached down and picked up her purse, taking out her bright pink lipstick and smearing a bit over her lips. The effect brightened her face some, made her look less tired. Made her look less worn down. She needed that. That little bit of armor in place so that he didn't just think he had won. So that he didn't assume he had the upper hand.

She arched one dark brow at her own reflection. "You are in his villa, in a foreign country. A country where you don't speak the language. He's a billionaire. And you are not even a thousandaire. There is no question who has the upper hand."

She sighed and turned away from the mirror.

She didn't know how she was going to get out of this, but she would be damned if she betrayed herself to him.

She opened the door to the bedroom, running a countdown in her mind as she walked slowly down the hallway that led to the sweeping curved staircase. She put her hand on the polished wooden banister and let her fingers glide across the smooth, cool surface as she made her way down to the opulent entryway.

Ten. Nine. Eight.

She was strong. She would hold her own.

Seven. Six. Five.

He might have brought her here, but he did not control her.

Four. Three. Two.

All of the vulnerability he had made her feel back in the hotel room was over now. She was impervious to it. Impervious to him.

One.

She stepped off the bottom stair and looked up. Rocco was there, his dark eyes clashing with hers, his hand extended toward her.

She sucked in a sharp breath, her heart hammering hard, her stomach twisting.

"So pleased you could join me," he said, appraising her slowly. "I knew that color would suit you."

"You can't imagine how relieved I am that you approve of my appearance. I was deeply concerned."

"Come now, must everything be a fight?" He kept his hand extended. "Take my hand."

"No thank you, I can walk just fine. Probably better without you leading me off a cliff. Oh, look. I suppose everything does have to be a fight."

He arched a brow and lowered his hand. "Dinner is back this way on the terrace. And while it does overlook a cliff, I have no desire to walk you off it."

"You expect me to trust you? I don't trust anyone," she said, following him through the expensive living area, her shoes loud on the marble floor.

"I see. And why is it that you don't trust anyone? Because I find that a curious stance for someone like yourself. I could understand a victim of yours no longer trusting people."

"I don't have victims," she said, her tone crisp. "They're called marks."

"Admitting something?"

"No," she said, looking away, her heart beating a bit faster, "I'm not."

"You will not convince me of your innocence. You might as well drop the denial."

She rolled her eyes. "So I should give you a full, signed confession?"

"You could start by simply answering my question."

"Why don't I trust people? Because I see what happens when you trust people. My father is a con man. He always has been. The quality time I remember with my dad consisted of running scams that required playing on people's sympathy for children. Not exactly a weekend at the ballpark. Why would I trust people?"

He pushed open the double doors that led outside to an expansive terrace that overlooked the ocean. He turned to face her, his lean figure backlit by the sun. "You shouldn't trust people. At least not in my experience. Certainly don't trust me."

She followed him outside, to a table that was set for two. There was a Mediterranean platter including olives and various other Italian delights, a basket of bread, a glass of wine for him and water for her.

"Oh, I don't trust you."

He pulled her chair out and indicated that he wanted her to sit. "Good. I don't need you to trust me. I simply need you to stay with me. Sit."

She kept her eyes on his and she obeyed his command, deciding that in this instance, it wouldn't do any good to push against him. "What do you mean you want to keep me?"

"I have done some thinking. I want to be in my child's

life. And I want you to be in the child's life. You see, I was denied both my parents at a very early age. I cannot knowingly do the same to my own flesh and blood."

"Well, I…I feel the same way. At least as far as I'm concerned." It was the truth. Growing up without a mother, it had never been an option for her to give her child up. Knowing that her mother had left her with a con artist for a father and never bothered to contact her again, had caused Charity pain all of her life. Doing the same to her own child was unthinkable.

"Then it is decided. Shall we set a wedding date?"

"I am not marrying you."

He waved a hand. "Marriage is not necessary. I'm flexible on that score. But I do think we should share a household, don't you? It would only be jarring for the child to bounce back and forth between your tiny apartment and one of my homes."

"Are you suggesting we live together?"

"If you refuse to marry me, cohabitation works just as well."

"But…I don't understand. You can't possibly want a relationship with me."

"Of course I don't." He tossed the words out casually, no venom in his tone at all. "I don't care about you at all. Except in the context of what you mean to our baby. Even if we were to marry we would continue to conduct our lives separately."

"I don't want to marry you."

"I did not say I *wanted* to marry you," he said, taking a seat across from her. "Only that I feel it is an option."

She studied him hard. "You believe me. About the baby?"

"Yes."

"And you want the baby. You want to be a father."

"I am going to be a father. That means I…have to be one," he said, sounding slightly less confident than he typically did.

"Why did you change your mind?"

"I lived in Rome when I was a boy." He leaned back in his chair and picked up his glass of wine, swirling the liquid inside slowly. "We lived in a very poor neighborhood. I never knew my father. I woke up one morning and the house was empty. Everything had been taken. And there were strangers there. My mother was gone. And I kept asking them where she was, but no one would answer me. I found out later that she was killed on her way home from work. I assume the landlord took all of our possessions and left me alone. But I don't know the details, and things like that are always difficult to sort through. Childhood memories. The recollections of a five-year-old are not always clear. But I know what it means to be alone. I know what it is like to feel lost." There was a faraway look in his dark eyes, a deep well that she could not see the bottom of. So different to the flatness that was usually there. "I do not wish that for our child. I wish for them to have a full house. I wish for them to have both of us. If he wakes in the middle of the night I do not want him to be alone."

Her chest tightened to the point of discomfort. She looked down at her plate, picked up an olive and rolled it in between her thumb and forefinger. Emotions made her uncomfortable. Especially the emotions of other people. In her experience connecting was dangerous. Empathy was dangerous. It had made it impossible to do what her father asked growing up. Because if she started to think too deeply about what other people would feel when they discovered they had been cheated, she had to contend with her conscience.

And if ever she connected with people, it only dissolved once the con ended and she had to run.

It was why she could never engage herself. Why she had to play a character wholly and completely, so that she was wrapped in it, so the real her was protected.

But she found that she was not protected now. She was not distant. Because it was too easy to picture a lonely boy in an empty house. Because she had felt that, too.

"Some nights," she said, questioning the words even as she spoke them, "my father would go to events, and he could not bring me with him. He would tell me to lock the doors, not open them for anyone. We had a password. So when he came home in the early hours of the morning, he would say it, and I would know not to be afraid. But sometimes he didn't come home. And I would be by myself all night. Normally I would sleep through it, but sometimes I would wake up, go get a glass of water, something like that. And the house was so empty. It's a very scary feeling late at night." She met his gaze. "I don't want that for our child, either. I want what you want."

Her stomach twisted hard. She didn't really want to deal with him, because he frightened her. Because he had used her. Because he had scraped away the layers of rock she kept between herself and the world, made her vulnerable to him. Exposed her to him. She could not forget that.

"He will have it," Rocco said, a certainty in his voice that she found oddly comforting. "It is a terrifying thing as a child. Being alone in that way. I am...sorry that you were alone. I know that feeling. It is... I avoid it at all costs now."

She swallowed hard, an unexpected wave of emotion washing over her. "Thank you."

Then, as though he had not just softened for her, he straightened, his eyes unreadable again. "Then it is settled. We are staying here for the foreseeable future."

"Why?" Her heart was pounding fast, fluttering in her chest like a panicked bird.

"Because I don't trust you. I do not trust that you will not find a way to make off with my money and my baby. Your word has limited value to me."

His words cut close to the bone, because there was so much truth to them. Because initially she had intended to take his money and go. Because she was a liar, and she had proven herself to be. And she could not even find a shred of righteous indignation to throw back at him. "I am being honest with you," she said. It was all she could say.

He looked at her, his gaze hard. "I cannot read you, and I find that disturbing. Are you a practiced con woman? Are you an innocent virgin? Are you a tough girl from the wrong side of the tracks forced into criminal activity because of your circumstances and your upbringing? I don't know. Because I have seen you play all those roles. And you play them all very well."

"Maybe I'm all of them." She reached down and put her fingers on her water glass, turning it in a circle. "And what about you? Who are you? A lonely boy without a mother? The wicked predator who blackmailed me into bed?"

"I am definitely the second. I decided long ago to move past where I began. Feeling guilty doesn't benefit you, Charity. You make decisions—you must own them."

"So, you don't think I should feel guilty about the money my father took and the part I played in it?"

He took a sip of his wine. "If I were you? I wouldn't feel guilty in the least. However, I am not you. I am me, and I had to ensure that you paid for what you did."

"With sex."

"I already told you," he said, his eyes meeting hers. "That was not part of the plan."

"And I already told you I don't trust people. I'm not sure why you think I should take you at your word."

"Because I have no reason to lie to you. Not on that score."

Charity laughed and took a piece of bread from the basket at the center of the table. "Who is going to teach our child morals? It seems that you and I both lack them."

How was she supposed to teach a child right and wrong? How was she supposed to enforce consequences for wrong behavior when she'd spent so much of her life dodging consequences.

When she'd been a thief for so long.

For the first time she wondered if she deserved to go to prison. She didn't want to. But she was guilty of all she was accused of.

She clenched her hands into fists, a sick feeling settling in the pit of her stomach. She couldn't go to jail. Then her child wouldn't have a mother.

She could be better, though. Something was changing in her. For the first time she didn't just *know* that stealing from him was wrong. She *felt* it.

Rocco frowned. "We should get a nanny."

Charity was about to disagree, but then realized he was probably right. She didn't know the first thing about babies, after all. Someone was going to have to show her how to change a diaper.

"We...we probably should."

"We will worry about that a little bit later. For now, I suggest we get used to dealing with each other."

"Do we have to?" she asked, picking up her glass of water. "We could always just ignore each other."

"I would much rather sleep with you again."

She sputtered. "What?"

"Why not? We are attracted to one another. And you will be here indefinitely. It could benefit us both."

"Yeah. No." She picked up another piece of bread and ate it. "I spend most days feeling a lot like I just licked the underside of a shoe. So I can honestly tell you that sex is the furthest thing from my mind. In fact, I'm a little bit angry at sex. I blame sex."

He shrugged, looking completely unconcerned by her refusal. "Fair enough."

She was slightly wounded that he didn't press. Which was ridiculous. She should not be wounded. She should be thrilled. Or something. She didn't want to sleep with him again. He hated her. He had only brought her here because she was having his baby.

Come to that, *she* wasn't that fond of *him*.

Yes, in that hotel suite, in the heat of the moment, with a veil of fantasy drawn around them that had begun with that note and that lingerie, something had caught fire between them. But here, with the brine from the ocean playing havoc with her sensitive stomach, the cool breeze blowing across her skin, raising goose bumps on her arms, things felt all too real.

Still, the rejection stung a little bit, even if she didn't know why. Some sort of previously unknown feminine sexual pride that had been uncovered by their indiscretion.

Just another bit of evidence to prove that sleeping with him in the first place was incredibly stupid.

"So that's it then?"

"Did you think I was going to pine after you?" He looked her over, his dark eyes conveying a kind of dismissiveness that cut deep. "I'm used to much more experienced women, *cara mia*, and while your innocence had a certain charm I prefer a partner who understands the way a man's body works."

Heat assaulted her cheeks. "You were the one who propositioned me."

"Because it made sense. I'm not a man prepared to go without sex. I'm hardly going to be celibate, so the decision is yours. Either I sleep with you or I will find someone else."

A ball of rage lodged itself in her chest. She couldn't quite work out why. She had refused him, so, by that logic, he should be free to share his body with whoever he wanted. But she didn't feel that he should be. His body belonged to her. At least, that was what it felt like. He was the only man she had ever touched like that. The only man who had ever been inside her. How could that not feel significant to him? It didn't seem fair.

But she would not show him her feelings. She would not reveal herself. "Do what you want. I'm not bothered. Just don't touch me."

"I always do what I want. But your gesture of offering permission was cute." He stood, picking up his glass of wine and swallowing the rest of the contents before setting it back on the table. "And on that note, I believe I will go out and do what I please. Have a good evening."

He turned and walked off the terrace, leaving her sitting there. Alone.

She picked up another piece of bread and bit into it with no small amount of ferocity. She didn't care what he went to do. She did not own him. She did not own his body, in spite of her earlier thoughts on the subject.

She didn't want to go out. She wanted to sit here. And eat. Go to bed early.

Master of the Manor aside, the house was beautiful, and she should just enjoy being here. The money her father had stolen would never gain him admittance into a place like this. To a man like Rocco a million dollars was a drop in an endless sea.

So, she would sit here and enjoy the fact that, although her father had abandoned her and left her to take the fall, she was the one sitting in a villa in Italy.

With a man who had blackmailed her into bed. And had got her pregnant. And was headed out to undoubtedly have sex with another woman.

So, except for all those things, she would sit here and enjoy the fact that she was in an Italian villa. She would ignore the other things. For as long as she could.

CHAPTER SIX

ROCCO WRENCHED HIS tie off and cast it down to the marble floor in the entryway of his home. He had gone out, and he had stayed out all night. He had found a beautiful woman, and he had bought her a drink. However, when it had come time for him to take the beautiful woman to bed, he had changed his mind. He had not even kissed her, not even tried to seduce her. He had bought her a drink, chatted with her and realized that his body had no interest in her.

He wasn't entirely certain what to do with that realization. She was a beautiful woman, and there was no reason for him to do anything but take her to bed. However, he found he simply lacked the desire. And so he had spent the rest of the night drinking, attempting to get himself into a place where he might not be so aware of the woman he wanted to seduce. But still, as he had approached a blonde later in the night, Charity—her dark curls, beautifully smooth skin, like coffee and cream—swam before his vision, the pale beauty before him washing out into insignificance.

He had ended his time out as the sky began to turn gray, the sun preparing to rise over the sea, walking through the city using the frigid early-morning air to help sober him up.

And then he had walked back to the villa. He would send someone for his car later.

But, though his head was clear, he was not in a better mood.

He did not understand why he had been immune to those women.

He started up the stairs, unbuttoning the top couple of buttons on his shirt, and the cuffs, pushing the sleeves up to his elbows.

As he made his way down the hall toward his bedroom he heard a thump and a groan.

He paused, turning in the direction of the sound. It was coming from Charity's room.

He did not stop and think; rather he charged toward the door and pushed it open, just in time to see her crawling on all fours into the bathroom. He frowned and strode across the room. In the bathroom, he saw her kneeling in front of the toilet, retching.

He walked in behind her, lifting her hair from her face, until she was finished being sick.

"Go away," she said, her voice pitiful.

"No, I will not go away. You are ill."

"I'm not," she said, sputtering, before leaning back over and being sick again. He made sure her dark curls were pulled away from her face, his fingers making contact with the clammy skin on her forehead, the back of her neck.

"Yes, you are." She slumped backward, her limbs shaking, a shiver racking her frame. "Are you finished?" he asked.

She nodded feebly, and he scooped her up into his arms, conscious of how cool her skin felt, even though it was beaded with perspiration. "Water," she said.

"Of course, but let me get you back into your bed."

"You getting me into bed is what caused this in the first place," she mumbled.

"This is because of the pregnancy?" He set her down at the center of the bed, debating whether or not he should put a blanket over her.

"Well, it isn't food poisoning."

"I have no experience with pregnant women," he said, feeling defensive. "I knew that pregnancy could make you ill, but I did not realize how severe it might be."

She drew her knees up to her chest, curling into a little miserable ball. "Mine is quite severe."

"You seemed well yesterday."

"It usually only does this in the morning."

"Are you cold?"

She shivered. "No, I'm hot."

"You are shivering."

"Okay, now I'm cold."

Rocco didn't know the first thing about caring for another person. He had never done it before. Since the death of his mother he had spent his life renting out connections. Foster families that never kept him for longer than a couple of months, lovers who lasted a couple of nights. In his experience, the only thing that was permanent were the things he could buy. So he invested in things. In brick, and marble. In cars and land. People were too transient in nature. Too temporary.

He remembered—a hazy image—that when he had been ill as a child his mother used to bring him a drink. With a lemon. Or maybe it wasn't a real memory at all. Maybe it was just something his mind had given him, something he had created for his mother's image to replace the more concrete memories of her looking desolate, tired.

Either way, he imagined Charity might like tea.

* * *

Charity watched as Rocco turned wordlessly and walked out of the room. She hadn't really expected him to leave without a word, but all things considered she was relieved. Having him walk in while she was throwing up had to be one of the most humiliating experiences of her life. Vomiting was bad enough. Vomiting in front of Rocco was even worse.

She did not want him seeing her when she was so low. He didn't deserve it.

She crawled to the head of the bed and slipped beneath the covers, exhaustion rolling over her in a wave.

Dimly, she registered that he was wearing the suit he had been wearing last night, though he did not have his tie or jacket on. So that meant he had gone out all night. Very likely, he had slept with someone else.

Misery joined the exhaustion, and she shivered. At least when he'd come into the bathroom he hadn't been cruel. He'd held her hair. Had carried her to bed. It had almost been as if he cared about her comfort.

Which was silly. Because he didn't care about anything. Least of all her.

A few moments later, Rocco reappeared, carrying a tray, his black hair disheveled, his shirt open at the collar, revealing a wedge of tan skin and dark chest hair. His sleeves were rolled up past his elbows, the weight of the tray enhancing the muscles of his forearms. And the strength of his hands.

He really did have wonderful hands.

She liked his hands much better than she liked his mouth, though that was beautiful, too. His hands had only given her pleasure. His mouth did a lot to administer pain.

"What are you doing?" she asked, as he set the tray, which she now saw had a teapot, a cup, a small plate with toast and a little jar of jam, down on the bed.

"This is what you do when people aren't feeling well. Isn't it?"

"Well, it can't hurt." She readjusted herself so that she was sitting, leaning back against the nest of pillows that were on the bed, and the headboard.

Rocco picked up the teapot and the cup, pouring a generous amount for her before handing it to her. "Careful," he said, the warning strange and stilted on his lips, "it's hot."

She lifted the cup to her lips and blew on it gently, before looking over the rim at her delivery service. "Why are you being so nice to me?"

He cleared his throat, a wrinkle appearing between his brows. "I'm not being nice. I am being practical. It does not benefit either of us for you to die."

She sighed heavily into the sip of her tea. "I don't know. If I died you wouldn't have to deal with any of this. You wouldn't have to face fatherhood."

His expression turned grim. "I have dealt with quite enough loss, thank you. I should like to keep you alive. And the baby."

She looked into her tea. "Sorry. That was gallows humor at its worst."

"I think you believe I'm a bit more of a monster that I really am." He said the words slowly, cautiously.

"Probably. But can you blame me, considering our introduction?"

"Can you blame *me*, considering our introduction?" His dark gaze was level, serious. And that guilt, that newfound guilt she felt deep down, bit her.

"I suppose not." She didn't really know what to say to that. Because she couldn't justify her actions, not anymore. She had spent a lot of years doing just that. Because from the cradle, her father had educated her in an alternate morality that was not easy to shake. But the older she got, the more difficult it had become to justify what she knew was stealing.

It had been easy to hold on to righteous indignation where Rocco was concerned because of what had happened between them.

"I'm sorry," she said, before she could fully think it through.

"Why are you apologizing?" he asked, his lips thinning into a grim line.

"Because we stole from you. It was wrong. You can dress things up...you can call them cons. You can call your victims marks. You can pretend it's okay because they have money and you don't. But at the end of the day it is stealing. And regardless of the fact that there was a time when I truly didn't know better, I do now. But...if you knew my father, you would understand how easy it is to get sucked into his plans. There is a reason he is able to talk people into parting with their money, Rocco. He's very convincing. He has a way of making you think everything will be okay. He has a way of making you think that somehow, you deserve what it is you're going after. Regardless, my involvement was wrong. And I'm sorry."

Hopefully, he wouldn't have her thrown in jail.

But she felt that these things had to be said before they could move forward. Or maybe she was just half-delirious because she still didn't feel very well. Or maybe his little gesture with the tea had meant a little bit more than she should let it. Either way, here she was. Confessing.

And she wasn't just confessing to him, but to herself.

Suddenly, she felt drained. Dirty. Desolate.

Acquiring a moral compass was overrated.

"Do you suppose there's a place in life where you become past the point of redemption?" she asked.

"I've never considered it." He sat down on the edge of the bed. "But then, that could be because I never imagined I had the option of redemption."

"I probably don't either then."

"Is it so important? What's the purpose, anyway? Is it that you want to be considered *good*?" he asked.

"I…I never really thought very much about whether or not I was good or bad. I remember asking my father one time why we were afraid of the good guys. The police. Because, even I knew from watching TV that they were supposed to be good. And people who ran from them were bad. So, I asked him if we were bad. He said it isn't that simple. He said sometimes good people do bad things, and bad people do good things. He said that not everyone in a uniform is good. But I just wanted to know if we were good. Maybe I still do."

"Does it matter?"

"Doesn't it? I don't know that anybody aspires to be one of the bad guys. And…I want to teach our child to be good so…I should be, too."

"I suppose you can only really be a good or bad guy in your own life, at least, in my experience. There are a great many people who would characterize me as a villain, though I have never broken the law. However, I have accomplished what I set out to accomplish. I have created the life for myself that I always wanted. What does being good have to do with any of that?"

Charity frowned. "I don't know. But I'm not sure I really know who I am. How can I know if I'm good or bad if I don't know the answer to such a simple question?"

"Do you suppose if we get a nanny she can help us with these sorts of questions?"

Charity laughed, in spite of herself. "You mean, do you

suppose she would mind helping a couple of emotionally stunted adults?"

"I suppose you and I don't make the most functional pair."

"Are we a pair?"

"Only in the sense that there are two of us, and we will be raising this child. Though, in what capacity I'm still not certain."

She wanted to ask him about last night. Wanted to ask him if he had slept with someone else. But it seemed strange, and not her business. Since she had made a grand declaration about the fact that she would not be sleeping with him again.

Though, right now she felt less resolute in that. Possibly because she felt less resolute about everything. Because as soon as she had spoken the words about not knowing who she was, she realized that they were true. She knew how to put on masks, how to play parts. Even when she had decided to step away from her father, from the con games, all she had done was put on the mask of waitress, woman in her early twenties. She hadn't made real connections with anyone, hadn't made friends. Had not assigned any kind of depth to the persona she had been playing for the past couple of years.

For a moment, she was worried that was all there was. That she had played too many parts on too shallow a level to ever find anything beneath them. What kind of mother would that make her? What did that mean for the rest of her life?

No wonder it had been so easy for her mother to leave her. No wonder it had been so easy for her father to detach from her in the end. There was no substance in her to hold on to.

That can't be true.

At least, she wouldn't let it continue to be true. And she'd...she'd felt the implications of what she'd done. She still did. That had to mean something.

She needed dreams. She hadn't let herself have any, not since the last con. Because, she was afraid that her dreams would outstrip her means, and that she would fall back into the same behavior she'd been raised in. But she couldn't live like that. For the sake of her child, she had to be more.

Of course, she had no idea what her future held, because it seemed as though Rocco was currently clutching it in his palm. For those brief moments outside of his office, back in New York, she had imagined a life blissfully raising her child, alone. That had seemed satisfactory. But once again everything had been uprooted. Her fantasies proving impossible.

"Don't worry about whether or not you are good or bad," he said, finally. "What you really need to focus on is making it to a day where you don't vomit in the morning."

"Oh, Rocco. You do fill a girl with hope and butterflies."

He frowned. "I am trying to help."

"But you aren't being nice," she said, a small smile curving her lips. "According to you."

He shook his head. "No, I am being practical. My mother used to bring me tea."

Charity's chest tightened. Imagining Rocco as a little boy, a little boy she knew had ended up alone. It made her ache for him. And it made her feel swollen with emotion. Because, this one bit of tenderness he seemed to know, he had chosen to pass on to her. Whether he called it practicality or kindness, it didn't change the fact that he was giving some to her.

"Well, I appreciate it. I really do." She cleared her throat and picked up one of the pieces of toast, neglecting the

jam, because she wasn't certain her stomach could handle
it yet. "Though, you don't need to come and hold my hair
when I'm… It's gross."

"I find nothing gross about it. You are sick. You are
sick because of my baby. It seems only fair that I should
take care of you."

"Is that what this is? You're going to take care of me?"

"I confess, I hadn't really thought it through."

"Somehow, I feel like that's the story of every single
interaction you and I have had, indirectly or directly," she
said.

"Probably. Had one of us been thinking more clearly
at any stage of this, things could've turned out quite differently."

"Yes, we should begin that soon."

"I'm thinking quite clearly now."

Charity opened the small jar of jam and began to spread
a little bit onto the piece of toast, feeling slightly more em-
boldened as she had taken three or four bites and not felt
her stomach turn once. She lifted the toast to her lips, a
little bit of bread crumb getting on her thumb, sticking to
where some jam had made contact with her skin.

"I'm glad to hear it," she said.

Silence settled between them and she looked up at him,
meeting his eyes. He was watching her, a strange softness in his expression. At least, if it had been any other
man she might have thought it was softness. With Rocco,
it never was.

"What?" she asked.

"I'm thinking," he said.

"About?"

"The fact that I will probably try and seduce you."

She sputtered, putting her toast back down on the plate,
crumbs still sticking to her fingers. "I'm sorry, what?"

"I'm going to seduce you," he said, his tone decisive. "I will succeed. We both know that."

She spread her hands wide. "I just threw up in front of you, and I'm now lying in bed covered in jam. How could you possibly be thinking about seduction? And you really think I'll agree to…be seduced?"

"Yes," he said, turning away and walking toward the door.

"Where are you going?"

"I thought I would wait to seduce you until you felt better. Do you require anything else?"

She felt as if she'd been hit over the head with something very heavy. "No."

"You seem confused."

"How did we get from tea and toast to…seduction?"

"I want you," he said. "I have, from the first moment I saw you. I am…used to having what I want."

"But I'm a woman and not a Ferrari. So you can't just come down to the lot and plunk down cash. I have a say."

"I know," he said. "And I want you to say yes. I value the yes, Charity. It means nothing if you don't want me, too. Which is why I plan to seduce you, not simply take you. We will talk later." Then he stood and walked out, leaving her with a promised seduction, tea and toast.

Seduction really was the most logical course of action. Because he had not been able to force himself to get excited about any of the women he had encountered last night. And he needed to prove to himself that he could take control of whatever this thing was that seemed to take him over whenever he was around Charity.

And when he'd been sitting there, looking down at her he had felt…a strange warmth in his chest. And it had pulled at him. Called to him. And she had asked "what."

What he was thinking, he assumed, and his mind had been blank.

He hadn't been thinking. He'd been feeling.

Then for some reason seduction was the first thing that came out of his mouth.

But really, it made sense.

That day in the hotel she had challenged everything he had ever known about himself. He did not lose control, and yet, with her he had. So he could continue to avoid her, which would keep her in possession of his control, or he could stoke the fire of the things that burned between them, bring them under his command.

Yes, that was definitely the better idea.

The only other option was allowing his beautiful little thief to claim total control over his libido and that was not acceptable.

He strode through the villa, wearing a different suit to the one he had been wearing last night, feeling reinvigorated. He had not slept at all since coming home, but in lieu of sleep, his new plan would do just as well.

He moved through the living area and onto the terrace, taking in the grounds. He had not encountered Charity in the house, and he wondered if she was still sick in bed. Her feeling sick would be an impediment to his plan.

His plan had begun to seem very important, as he doubted he would find another means to get his interactions with her on track. Not as long as he was distracted by his desire for her body.

He could nearly taste her again. Those sweet, dusky-rose lips and the honey between her thighs. He was hard just thinking about it. How long had it been since he'd wanted one woman specifically? Had he ever?

He wanted sex, women in a general sense, but never specifically. Art, cars, *things*, he craved with a ferocious specificity, but never women. He craved *beauty* so that he could collect it, keep it.

He craved things because the more he owned, the more there was of him. The more evidence there was of his power. Never had he felt more helpless than as a boy with nothing. And so, he had become a man with everything.

It was why he had built a house into a carved mountainside that gazed out at the sea, owning a piece of what was wild. Taming it.

He wanted to tame her. Keep her. Make her his.

The epiphany was utterly disturbing, and yet he realized, standing there scanning all that he owned, it was her he was searching for. And no amount of awareness about the nature of his attraction would stop him searching for her.

She had him. And he had to reverse that ownership.

He saw a faint splash coming from the courtyard, from the large infinity pool that overlooked the sea. His gut tightened. It was her. He knew it was her.

He moved away from the terrace and back into the living room, striding out the double doors that led to the walled-in garden. There was an outdoor living area, with a bed and gauzy curtains, perfect for those times when he simply couldn't wait to get a lover indoors. The pool and its glass wall faced the sea and a completely private beach, if he enjoyed the feeling of putting on a show without actually having an audience.

And Rocco had to confess, without any shame, that he did.

He looked at the pool and saw barely a ripple. Then, her sleek, dark head resurfaced. She had her back to him, her black curls tamed by the water. She pushed her hands back over her hair, droplets sluicing down over her hair, her arms.

"The view from here is very nice," he said.

She whirled around quickly, her eyes wide, her mouth open. His eyes fell to the low cut of the bathing suit she was wearing—one that must have been provided by his staff, as he had requested sometime last night that they see to it that his guest had clothes. It was a one-piece suit. Out of deference to her pregnancy, he imagined. And yet it was still incredibly sexy.

He couldn't tear his eyes away from her breasts. They were average size, he supposed, but incredible. Perfectly round with lovely, caramel nipples that had set his body on fire. He was obsessed with tasting her again. Everywhere.

"I thought so," she said, offering him a strained smile. "You picked a great location for the pool."

"I wasn't talking about the ocean."

Her cheeks darkened. "Oh."

He moved closer to the pool, closer to her. He couldn't help himself.

With her, he could never seem to help himself. "You are beautiful, *cara mia*, surely you know that."

She lifted a shoulder, a water droplet rolling down her skin. "I don't think about it often."

"Not at all?"

She shrugged again and began to walk toward the steps of the pool. Slowly she rose from the water, revealing her body inch by delectable inch. He could not yet see any changes from the pregnancy, though she was nearly at the three-month mark by now. She was still slim, the rounded curves of her body pure perfection. He could remember clearly what it had been like to run his hands over all that bare skin...

"It doesn't mean anything to me. In my position in life either you use your beauty to manipulate, or you don't. Until I met you, I'd never used my body. Not even for a con."

"I am curious," he said, and he found he was, "when did you stop helping your father? And why did you go back?"

She let out a heavy sigh and walked over to the chair that had a white towel folded and placed in the center. She picked it up and started to dry herself, wrapping it tightly around her hips. "When I was about seventeen I told him I didn't want to play the game anymore. He wasn't happy, but I was basically taking care of myself anyway. A lot of what I did was facilitating corporate scams and charity frauds." She lowered her eyes. "It was bad. But I'd always done it and…I just didn't think much about it. He used to say that there was no amount of hard work that could ever get regular people like us to the top. He said if people weren't smart enough they didn't deserve to keep their cash. 'A fool and his money are soon parted' was always one of his favorite phrases. Of course, it never applied to him and how fast he went through whatever he got."

"Naturally not," Rocco said, keeping his voice neutral.

"But there was a point when I realized it was…not something I wanted to do. So I stopped. And he left town about six months later. I got a job waitressing. I'd been doing that for about three years when he came back. I hadn't heard from him at all for the last year. And I was struggling and it sounded so easy. More than that…my dad was back. I've never been able to say no to him because I just want to be…I want us to be a family. He's all I have. And it was just one more job—hit AmariCorp, get them to invest in us, roll out with the money. I swear I didn't know it would be so much. And…look, it was wrong," she said, dark eyes blazing, "I know it was. Old habits and stuff. I got tempted to cut corners and I didn't hold up to the temptation. I did it because I knew that I wouldn't make that much in a year of work and I was tired of struggling. And then he took off, and I felt like crap and I just…well,

I never saw any of the money we took from you. It took us a couple months to organize the scam, another one for me to realize my dad left me in the lurch and another three for you to find me. And you made me pay, Rocco. You made me pay enough that I know I'll remember the cost if I'm ever tempted again. Nothing is free."

Her words sat uncomfortably in his gut. "I made you pay. With sex?"

"Among other things. I don't know if I ever truly understood how wrong it all was until I met you and it...it hurts."

"I feel I have asked too much of you," he said, moving to close the distance between them. "I am...I regret the way things passed between us."

"You're sorry?" she asked, tilting her head to the side.

He frowned. "I would not go that far."

"I feel all warm inside, Rocco. I really do."

He moved to her, wrapped his arm around her waist and tugged her up against his body. His heart was raging, his hands shaking and he didn't have any idea why.

"I am not sorry," he said, his voice rough, "because I cannot regret wanting you. I cannot regret having you. Even though I should."

He raised his hand to her cheek and slid his thumb over her lip, slicking up a drop of water that remained there. She was the epitome of beauty, a living embodiment of all the things he surrounded himself with. All the things he tried to collect. All of the things he wanted to own. And she didn't want him.

It enraged him, that she was so close to him, and yet so far from him in so many ways.

No, it was unacceptable. He would not endure it.

"I'm cold," she said, shivering.

"I could make you warm," he said, his voice rough.

"Why?" she asked, her eyes searching his.

"Because I want you," he said, tracing the perfectly shaped line of her upper lip before sliding his fingertips over her sculpted cheekbones. Learning her face. Taking possession of it.

"But I don't understand *why* you want me. You've given me every indication that you hate me. You humiliated me in New York. You used me. And whether you want to talk about it or not, you paid for my body. It doesn't make sense."

"None of this makes sense. When you walked into that hotel in New York I had every intention of humiliating you. I wanted to leave you in that hotel room aching and begging for me. I didn't think I would want you. How could I want a thief?" He gripped her chin between his thumb and forefinger. "I don't think you understand, Charity. Nobody steals from me. What I have earned is precious to me in ways very few people comprehend. I despised you before I laid eyes on you. I was not supposed to want you."

"So why do you?"

"There is no reason. Except for chemistry. This is truly potent chemistry, *cara*, and I certainly don't know how to fight it. The fact is, I don't want to. I spent many years deprived of human contact, living with families who showed me no affection. I spent a great many years without the things that I truly craved. And I do not believe in denying myself, not now. Now I have the power to deliver to myself everything I desire. I have no practice at it and restraint. And no need for it. And so I underestimate you, and where the attraction to you would lead. And now I find that I'm aware of how powerful it is, I want to explore it."

"I don't see why I should sleep with a man who despises me."

"You did it once."

She looked down, her expression stricken. "I'm not proud of it."

"Why?" He tightened his grip on her chin, forcing her to look back at him. "Why aren't you proud? You nearly brought me to my knees. You made me weak with wanting. You forced me to deviate from my plan, and no one does that, Charity, *no one*. You could bring me to my knees now if you would promise to let me taste the beauty between your thighs. How can you not feel some pride in that?"

"I suppose," she said, her voice trembling, her cheeks flooded with dark color, "I suppose it's because I have never put much stock in sexual attraction. I've never really felt that before you, not in a specific sense."

"Sex drives the world. There is very little that is more powerful." He laughed, though he didn't feel anything was particularly funny. "Perhaps money. And our interactions have been fueled by both. Is it any wonder we are so potent together?"

"I don't want this," she said, her voice a whisper.

"You don't want my attentions? Or you don't want to feel this attraction?"

"I don't want to feel this," she said, not looking at him.

"But you do," he said, his voice fierce. "You do."

"Yes."

"I do not despise you," he said, the words a rough whisper. "I recognize something in you."

"What?" she asked.

"Hunger. You are so empty. So hungry. Like me." She nodded, emotion flashing bright in her dark eyes. "Let me fill you."

She nodded and it was all the consent he needed.

He dipped his head and captured her lips, a raw sound rumbling in his chest as he did, the relief that flooded him unlike anything he had ever known. He was so hungry for this, so hungry for her, and he had not realized until the taste of her dropped onto his tongue. Only then did he realize just how intense the craving was.

He coaxed her mouth open, sliding his tongue against hers, tasting her deeply, drinking her in as he would do a fine brandy, savoring her, letting the heat flood every part of him, warming the deep places that were always cold.

But she went deeper than any alcohol could ever burn, touching a part of his soul he had not realized still lived.

Wanting her became the physical ache, a drive that he could not fight, a drive he did not want to fight.

She was far too stiff in his arms for his liking. He slid his hand down to the curve of her bottom, pulling her tightly against him, against his growing arousal, showing her exactly how she affected him, exactly how much he wanted her. And she began to soften in his arms, a sound of capitulation on her lips, as she tasted him as deeply as he had been tasting her. As she allowed herself to get drunk on him, as he had been doing on her. And he felt her grow languid, felt her melt against him, her breasts pressed against his chest, an eroticism he didn't think he had ever fully paused to appreciate before.

He was a jaded man, a man with too much experience. Kisses had long since ceased to thrill him. But this kiss was everything. It was more than any kiss. More than he had ever imagined a kiss could be.

"I must have you," he said, wrenching his mouth from hers so that he could speak the words that were burning in his chest. "I need you, Charity, I need you."

It vexed him, even now, that she could make him want so deeply. With all of himself. This little thief who had reached inside of him and stolen the very thing he prized the most: his control.

Right now, he was not even certain if he wanted it back. The only thing he was certain of wanting was her.

He gripped the straps to her swimsuit, pulling them down her arms and revealing her breasts. He lowered his head, taking one nipple into his mouth, sucking her in deeply and groaning as he relished the taste of her. She was everything, everything he had remembered and more.

"We shouldn't do this," she said, breathless, as lost as he was.

He traced the shape of her with the tip of his tongue reveling in the difference in texture between her creamy skin and the tightened bud. "We shouldn't," he said, breathing hard. "We absolutely should not. But you and I are notorious for doing things we shouldn't. I see no reason to change now. Not when this feels so good."

She said nothing, but she wove her fingers through his hair, held him to her as he continued to indulge his craving for her. He shaped her curves with his palms, absorbing every bit of her softness, committing this to memory. In case this was the last time. Because he would take nothing for granted with her, ever. He could not predict her, and in his life finding something so unpredictable was rare. He enjoyed it as much as he feared it. Another rarity.

He rolled her wet suit down her hips, and she stepped out of it, kicking it to the side. He raised his head and kissed her lips deeply again, before turning around so that she was facing away from him, wrapping her hair around his hand and pressing down gently on her shoulders with his other hand, so that she was leaning over the outdoor sofa.

He traced the elegant line of her spine with the tip of his finger, all the way down, until he was teasing the damp entrance to her body, testing her readiness. She was wet,

wet and ready for him. He leaned in, pressing a kiss to the back of her neck, and she shivered beneath his touch.

He freed himself from the confines of his trousers and positioned himself at her damp core, bracing himself by holding more tightly to her hair, and gripping her hip, as he sank into her softness slowly. She tugged against his hold, turning her head so that her eyes met his, her lips parted, her eyes wide. He flexed his hips forward so that he was buried inside of her to the hilt, and a raw sound escaped her mouth.

"Good?" he asked, the word strained.

She nodded slightly, encountering resistance thanks to the tight restraints he'd placed on her. He withdrew slightly, before thrusting back home, establishing a steady rhythm designed to drive them both to the brink. He slipped his hand forward, placing it between her thighs, teasing her clitoris with his movements.

Release started to build in him, far too soon—he wanted this to last, wanted her screaming his name before he took his own pleasure. He gritted his teeth, increased the pressure on the bundle of nerves he was focused on. He heard her gasp, and he took it as approval. He continued to tease her, pushing her closer and closer. Could feel her internal muscles tightening around him, could feel the climax building inside of her. He leaned forward, still stroking her, and grazed the side of her neck with his teeth. A hoarse cry escaped her lips and she dropped over the edge.

And then he stopped holding back. He pounded into her heat, chasing his own release, his blood roaring in his ears as he came hard, the sound of his own release mingling with hers.

When the storm subsided, he moved away from her, breathing hard. The outline of his fingers red on her hip, the evidence of his passion left in the slight impressions on the delicate skin of her neck, stood out like beacons in the night, irrefutable proof of his lack of control. And yet, he could not bring himself to regret it.

She was trembling, and he swept her up into his arms, an echo of their first time together back in New York. But this time, he would not be leaving her. This time, she would spend the night in his bed. With him.

CHAPTER SEVEN

CHARITY ROLLED ONTO her back and stretched, raising her hands above her head, her knuckles cracking against the hardwood headboard. A headboard she did not have at her apartment in Brooklyn.

She opened her eyes and looked around the room. Late-afternoon sunlight was filtering through gauzy white curtains. Because she wasn't in Brooklyn, she was in Rocco's villa. Though, the late-afternoon sunlight was a little bit more confusing.

She sat upright, the sheet falling down to her waist. She was naked. She supposed she shouldn't be surprised.

Then a host of images filtered through her mind, memories of the way they had spent the majority of the day. And she *knew* she shouldn't be surprised by her nudity.

Just then, Rocco came walking into the room from the bathroom, as naked as she was. And clearly a lot less self-conscious about it.

"So, all of that…happened." She reached down and gripped the edge of the sheet, drawing it back up over her breasts.

A smile curved his lips. "Yes. More than once."

"What time is it?"

"Nearly six."

So they had been in bed all day. Which was one way

to while away the hours when she felt wretched. Have orgasms instead. Really, it was kind of a no-brainer. Climaxes were better than vomiting.

She didn't feel sick at all right now. In fact, she felt hungry. Starving.

"Dinner will be sent up shortly." It was as if he could read her mind. Disconcerting, but handy in this particular situation. And in others.

When it came to what she wanted in bed he seemed to be able to read her mind better than she could. She was so inexperienced that until him she hadn't really known what she might want. But he was showing her. With great skill.

He was every bit as commanding between the sheets as he was out of them. And it turned out she quite liked it.

Less so when they were vertical than when they were horizontal, but they would work on that.

She had no idea what this arrangement between the two of them was supposed to be. They were having a baby. They were, as of a few hours ago, sleeping together. But she was still the woman who had stolen his money, and she doubted that he had forgotten that along the way.

He was still the man who had forced her to come to Italy with him. Still the man who had held the threat of prison over her head, who had sent her that note, and the lingerie.

That hadn't changed. But for some reason, it felt as if the air between them had. Which was silly. People didn't change, not really. They only put on new masks. New costumes. She knew that better than anyone. She had spent her entire life doing it. She had proven it when she'd hopped right back into the con ring the moment her father had shown up and offered her a chance at taking the easy road again.

She'd shed her waitress uniform quickly enough and fallen back into old patterns. She couldn't imagine a future where she wouldn't do it again. No matter how settled she thought she might be.

If she hadn't managed to change before, why would she be able to do it now?

"What sort of dinner?" she asked, because it was an innocuous question, which felt necessary right now. And because she was interested in food.

"I didn't specify. Beyond that it be easy to eat in bed." He crossed the room and sat down on the edge of the mattress, and her stomach turned over, her heart rate increasing. Being close to him again made her want things. Already. Again.

"You don't think we should get up for a while?" she asked.

"I think that sounds like a terrible idea. I would rather stay in here all day." He looked at her, and for once his dark eyes weren't flat. They weren't filled with anger or mockery of any kind. They were warm. And it made her feel warm. A flame that started at the center of her stomach and radiated outward.

He adjusted his position and moved toward her, placing his hands on either side of her as he leaned in for a kiss. It was a brief meeting of their mouths, nothing to get too excited about. And yet, for all that it was so brief it was that much more exciting.

"That seems...decadent."

He arched a brow. "Decadent? An interesting choice of words for a woman such as yourself."

"What's that supposed to mean?"

"I had imagined you had tasted your share of real decadence. Given that..."

She shifted uncomfortably, her throat tightening. "That we stole money."

He slid his thumb over her cheekbone. "I did not mean it like that."

She wasn't sure if she should deflect or opt for a little bit of honesty. Which seemed silly in a lot of ways, as they were sitting here naked with each other. And a certain degree of honesty should be implied by that. But while they had shared their bodies, she wasn't certain they had shared anything deeper than that.

"Sometimes it was like that." The words came out rusty, rough. "When my dad ran a con and things went well, there was a lot of sitting back and enjoying the spoils. Of course I didn't realize that's what I was doing. But you know, we would have weeks of going out to dinner every night. And they sort of made up for the weeks where we hadn't had food at all. Weeks spent with my dad smiling and laughing and…being with me. Yes, that was decadent to me." She looked down at her hands. "As I got older I realized exactly what we were doing. And I struggled with it. But my father is a con man. And he does a good job of spinning a story. He did a good job of spinning one about us. About what we were doing. About how we were just working like anyone else. The people we stole things from were too rich to notice what was missing. And if they did notice, then they deserved it for being stupid enough to let us get hold of it." She repeated her father's words, almost verbatim. He always said them with a smile. As though he were partly joking. As though none of it were real.

Just make-believe. A game. A game that happened to be a crime. A game that happened to be immoral. But a game nonetheless.

"I see," he said, a strange light in his eyes.

"Like I told you. He's small-time. What he did to you is the biggest job he's ever pulled. At least as far as I know. If he has money like that, other than yours of course, stashed anywhere he certainly never told me about it. And considering he seemed more than willing to let me take the fall for this and leave me without money…"

"You truly do not have it."

She shook her head. "I don't. I never did. I helped him get it but…I don't have it."

"I believe you," he said.

Her stomach twisted. "So much for family. So much for decadence, too."

"So would you say I'm your first taste of decadence?" he asked, his voice positively wicked now.

Heat speared her stomach, blooming outward, flooding her cheeks. "You know you're the first man I've been with."

"Yes," he said, his voice rough and gentle at the same time. "And I am intrigued about that. Would you care to elaborate?"

"Well, I had never had sex before. Then I met you. And I had sex with you."

He angled his head and leaned in, biting her lower lip. The sharp shock of pain faded quickly, ending on a sizzling burst of pleasure that flowed through her entire body. "That is not what I meant." There was something that looked a lot like humor in his eyes, and she wasn't really sure what to do with that.

But she liked it.

"Sex seems like an awful lot of stripping. A good con woman doesn't like to remove her masks. I know I don't. So I was never in a hurry to get that close to anyone. I mean, I could have been with someone if I'd wanted to. But I would've been playing a role. And that never sat well with me."

"And with me? With me in the hotel room, back in New York. And with me now? Are you yourself?" He leaned in, pressing a kiss to her jawline. "Or are you still wearing a mask?"

His gaze met hers, his dark eyes boring into hers, and she had to look away. "I don't know. I have no idea who I am. I've spent every day of my life playing a part. Even the waitress…the version of myself that was supposed to be good. Supposed to be honest—that was a role. I was only *pretending* to be normal. Slipping on the costume. But at the end of the day I would take it off and…I just felt like me again. I didn't feel different. I'm always pretending."

"And with me?"

She took a deep breath, her heart thundering hard. "That's what terrifies me most." It was the truth. And she didn't know why she was admitting it. Didn't know why she felt compelled to offer him the kind of honesty she'd rarely even given to herself.

"What? What terrifies you, *cara mia*?"

"That the day we made love in New York was the most honest I've ever been. With myself. With anyone." She swallowed hard. "I'm not sure I liked her." She said the last part slowly, heat assaulting her cheeks.

"And why didn't you like her?"

"Because she…" She was starting to feel stupid talking about herself in the third person. "I…I slept with you. And I didn't even know you. And I liked it."

"And that's a problem?"

She looked down, her voice muted. "For a lot of people, yes, it would be."

"It isn't for me." He shifted his position so that he was sitting next to her. "I spent too many years *wanting* things. So I don't now. I *take*. I *have*. I don't *want*."

"I do. That's pretty much all I do." That was true, too. Another thing she wasn't certain she should've shared.

"Not anymore. Not with me. I can give you anything

you want. I can give our child anything they might want.
Anything they might need. And I will do the same for you.
I promise, with me it will only ever be feast, Charity. You
will never have to live through famine again. I swear it."
His voice was fierce, his dark eyes intent on hers. "I can
give you decadence. You will never want for it again."

She wanted to take him up on that promise. She wanted
to sink into it. To sink into him, to cling to him and make
him promise never to let her go.

It was then she remembered that he'd never promised
her fidelity. And he had never promised a relationship. He
was only promising things.

And he had gone out last night.

He might have slept with someone else less than twenty-
four hours ago.

The idea made her skin crawl.

"You went out last night," she said, conscious of the
insecurity in her tone.

He paused for a moment, his dark eyes flat. "Yes, I
did."

"Did you sleep with someone else?" Her chest tightened painfully.

"No," he said, his tone definitive.

The knot loosened slightly, her heart pounding hard.
"Don't lie to me. Not about that."

"I have no reason to. You know that."

"Don't," she said, her voice a whisper. "Don't lie to me.
And don't sleep with anyone else."

He put his palm on her cheek, his dark brows drawing
together. "Forever, *cara mia*? That's an awfully long time.
I doubt either of us can predict the future quite that well."

She couldn't imagine ever wanting another man. But
then…she was inexperienced. He was not. She couldn't
fathom it now—but maybe someday.

But she doubted it. "Then at least not while you're sleeping with me."

"I promise," he said, his tone grave.

It was enough for her. It was enough for now. So she leaned in and kissed him, leaning in to his lips, to his promises, to his decadence. Because she was tired of wanting.

And in Rocco there was satisfaction. So she was determined to seize it.

For as long as possible.

Rocco was certain he had left some of his sanity back in that bed. Back beneath the covers with Charity. And for some reason he couldn't bring himself to be disturbed by that.

He had promised her fidelity.

Granted, he didn't think he could make his body respond to another woman even if his brain wanted him to. Hell, he *knew* he couldn't. He had tried. He had failed.

Even so, he didn't promise such things to women. Because he knew they might start thinking that they had a more permanent place in his life than they did. Though, if any woman had a permanent place in his life it was Charity. Not as his lover, certainly, but as the mother of his child.

As his lover... She was incredibly beautiful. Incredibly responsive. And right now he couldn't imagine preferring anyone over her. But sex was all about satisfying the immediate need. And he had no idea how his immediate needs might shift over the course of the next few weeks. He had never practiced long-term commitment. And he didn't intend to start now.

But he would honor his promise. His promise not to take anyone else to bed, as long as she was in it.

He didn't want to hurt her. Which brought him back to his missing sanity.

He couldn't even regret it. She was too beautiful. But it was more than beauty. There were many beautiful women in the world, and he had been with a good percentage of them.

It was everything she was. Her inexperience, combined with her enthusiasm. The smooth perfection of her coffee-colored skin, a confection so sweet he could lick every inch of it and never be satisfied.

He wanted to buy her something. A necklace. He could envision it now. Something with a heavy pendant that would settle in the valley between her breasts. He could picture her wearing that and nothing else.

Damn, he was obsessed.

And he was beginning to think he might want to bring her to the gala he was attending this weekend. He never brought dates to such events. It was a chance to find a woman for a night of fun, not come shackled.

But he was well and truly shackled, so he might as well embrace it. He had always enjoyed showing off his new things, after all.

A new car, a new villa, new suit and tie even. He liked those outward shows of power. Those claims to his new life that couldn't be taken from him. And he liked others to see them.

Perhaps it would do him well to show Charity off, as well. His newest acquisition.

For some reason the idea of it sent a wave of satisfaction through him, a sharp adrenaline rush that always came from adding another thing to his collection. The kind of rush he never experienced over a woman, because sex, while enormously satisfying, was cheap and easy to come by. The woman never mattered, only that he got what he wanted.

Though, Charity mattered. If only because she was the mother of his child. Really, he could not come up with another reason why she should. Unbidden, his thoughts flashed back to the afternoon he'd spent in bed with her. It was difficult to pretend that didn't matter. The taste of her, the scent of her. Every damn thing about her. The way her black curls tumbled over his pillow, as untamed and wild as she was.

Just thinking about her got him hard.

He shifted, adjusting his position at his desk. She had him acting like a schoolboy. It was disturbing. But delicious in its way. If only because he couldn't remember enjoying anything quite so much at any other point in his life.

Yes, he would bring her to the gala. And he would take her out today to find a dress. She said she had had a lack of decadence in her life, and he would see to it that it was rectified.

He would mourn the lost time with her in the bedroom. But she had scarcely been out of the villa since they'd arrived in Italy, and he wanted her to have a chance to experience the beauty of his home country. A smile curved his lips. He would make a private appointment at a boutique in town. That way if he had a desire to remove every gown after she tried them on, they would not be disturbed.

He reached toward his phone, his decision made.

Adrenaline fired through his blood as he thought of what it would be like to walk into the gala with Charity on his arm. A clear and outward sign of his possession. And yes, he did want to possess her. There were a few things he was uncertain about these days, but at the moment that wasn't one of them.

She would be his. On that score there was no uncertainty.

Charity had been surprised by Rocco's abrupt announcement that they were going out. Mainly because every time he had walked into the room over the past couple of days it had ended, not in them going out, but in them getting naked and satisfying their need for each other on the nearest available surface. Not that she was complaining.

It was a strange thing, to have shared so much physically with someone while exchanging so few words. To exchange such deep, intense intimacies without the common intimacies you could simply speak.

Even so, it was more than she had with anyone else in her life. More than she had ever had. And he was doing strange things to her heart, twisting it around, cinching it in tight, making her feel as though she couldn't breathe.

She was surprised when today he hadn't taken her clothes off. He had ushered her into his car instead. And now he was driving them into the heart of the village that was down the mountain from the villa. She had done absolutely no exploring of their surroundings, not since he had driven her up to his home at the beginning of the week.

He maneuvered the car effortlessly through the narrow cobblestone streets, coming to a stop in front of a shop with an unassuming facade. Red brick and the wooden trim all painted in black with a round sign hanging above the door.

"We have an appointment," he said, putting the car in Park and killing the engine before getting out. He rounded to her side of the car and held the door open for her, the show of chivalry unexpected and dangerous to her already-vulnerable heart. A sense of warmth joined the squeezing feeling.

"To do what? You realize that you have been very cagey. Possibly more cagey than I am on a daily basis. And that's saying something."

He smiled, something he was doing with more and more frequency these days. "It's a surprise."

Her stomach tightened, hope mingling with fear. Because things just didn't come through in her life. Surprises had never been anything good. And she was afraid to hope now that they might be.

She didn't understand this relationship she'd found herself in. Didn't understand what was happening to her at this moment in time. But she wasn't even sure if she wanted to. She just wanted to close out the world, the future, the reality, and keep living in it.

"Trust me," he said, extending his hand.

"You know I don't trust anyone," she said, her voice breathless even to her own ears.

"Okay then, right now. Trust me right now."

She reached out and took his hand, and his fingers closed around hers, his grip strong. "I can do that."

He tugged her forward, leading her into the shop. Inside they were greeted by a petite Italian woman dressed all in black, her hair pulled back into a severe bun, her lips painted a bright red.

"Mr. Amari," she said, inclining her head, "I have set aside a few selections based upon your description of both the event and your friend here," she said, gesturing to Charity. Charity was not sure how she felt about being called Rocco's friend in quite that tone. She was not his friend. She was his lover. Though, she imagined the woman meant escort or something. But Charity wasn't that, either.

Are you really his lover, though? What are you really?

She gritted her teeth and met the other woman's eyes, forcing a smile. She was not a shrinking violet. That much she was sure of. If she had one legacy from her father that she would claim and use, it was the ability to shine in any situation, at least outwardly.

"Charity Wyatt," Charity said, extending her hand. "It's nice to meet you."

The shopkeeper was clearly surprised by the introduction, but she took Charity's offered hand and shook it, and Charity could tell she had won a bit of grudging respect.

"If you don't mind," Rocco said, "we will continue to the back to begin trying things on. Now that you have seen Charity, perhaps you have a few other selections to recommend?"

The woman could tell she had been dismissed, but because Rocco was so darn rich and powerful, it was also clear that she wouldn't argue, even though she wanted to. "Of course, Mr. Amari. Everything is set up in the back, and if you need anything at all just let me know."

"We will," Rocco said, tightening his hold on Charity's hand and leading her toward the back of the store, into an alcove that was furnished with plush chairs, a three-way mirror and a little changing area that was partitioned off from the rest of the room by a thick velvet curtain.

"And are you going to tell me what's going on now?" she asked, abruptly realizing that she had no idea what she was doing here.

"I have a gala to attend tomorrow night. I thought you would like to be my guest," he said, sitting down in the chair and sprawling out, his long legs stretched out in front of him, his elbows positioned on the armrest, fingers tented beneath his chin, his gaze watchful.

She blinked. "You've only just decided you want to take me?"

"I never bring women to such events. This is some sort of charity thing—I'm not sure for what. I don't really care. I'll throw money in the box, and it's good for my name."

"Why do you want to bring me?"

He frowned. "What sort of question is that?"

"You don't normally take women to these sorts of

things, you just said. Now you want to take me. And I'm wondering what changed."

"I decided I didn't want to meet a woman at the event and take her home with me. That is the beginning and end of why I don't bring dates to these sorts of things. But you are the only woman I want to go home with, so it stands to reason you should come with me."

Some of the warmth in her chest was squashed by his words. "Oh."

He looked away, as he often did when she started getting personal or emotional. "Were you expecting something else? I am not a sentimental man, *cara mia*. You should have realized that by now. Honest, yes. Sentimental? No. I can fully satisfy your carnal desires, but your finer feelings will have to be dealt with elsewhere. Perhaps watching romantic movies?"

It made her angry that he did that. That he minimized then what had, for a brief, shining moment, become such a large thing in her mind.

A chance to be brought into his world. A chance to be part of it. A part of him.

So she didn't feel so alone.

"You're assuming I have any finer feelings," she said, turning and walking into the dressing room, shutting the velvet curtain behind her. "I'm only a con woman after all. It's very likely I don't have them."

She turned and saw an array of dresses hung there, waiting for her. She was having a flashback to that moment in her apartment, when she had realized that she was caught. When she was staring at a lingerie bag, a dress and a demand.

But this was different. This time, she had her choice of dress.

She reached out and touched the hem of one of the

gowns, the fabric soft, finer than anything she could have afforded under normal circumstances. She touched each one of them, settling on the one in emerald green, the softest to the touch.

"I never said you didn't have feelings," he said, his voice coming from a much closer place than it had been only a moment before. He was standing right on the other side of the curtain, she could tell.

"But it's what you think, isn't it?"

"I may have a difficult time understanding feelings, or connecting with them, Charity. However, I never said you didn't have them. And I certainly didn't say it was because you were a con woman. You are the one who seems hellbent on identifying yourself as such as often as possible."

"So neither of us forget." She tugged her shirt up over her head, then made quick work of her pants, before taking the green dress off the hanger and undoing the zipper, stepping into the waterfall of rich silk.

"I am not likely to forget as it is the thing that brought us together. What a wonderful story for us to tell our child."

She pulled the dress up, holding it against her breasts, reaching behind her and trying to get a hold of the zipper tab.

She managed to get it partway up, but could not get the fabric to meet more than midway up her back. She arched, trying to contort herself so that she could get it up the rest of the way, rustling against the curtains as she did so.

"Let me help you," Rocco said, his voice softer, richer, darker than the crushed velvet that separated them.

"I'm fine."

"Don't be so damned stubborn," he said.

And then she felt his hands on the fabric of the gown, one braced on the base of the zipper, the other on the tab, as he quickly did it up. A lightning bolt of need shot through her as his knuckles brushed against her bare skin, only a fleeting touch, but it was enough. And not nearly enough all at the same time.

"There," he said, "it's much easier when you aren't stubborn, isn't it?"

She looked over her shoulder and was surprised by how close he was, his lips a whisper from hers now. "Easier, maybe. But it's not as much fun."

A smile curved his lips and she suddenly found herself being pushed deeper into the dressing room, his hold tight on her hip as he turned her to face him, pressing her back against the mirror. "You think this is fun?" He pressed his body against hers, and she could feel the hard length of his arousal against her stomach. "A little challenge?"

"What is life without a challenge?"

"Death," he said, leaning forward, scraping the sensitive skin of her neck with his teeth. "As long as we struggle we know we're still alive."

There was no doubt that she felt alive now. Her heart was thundering hard, her pulse racing, her core aching for something only he could give her.

"We can't do this here," she said, her voice strangled.

"I'm paying a lot for this room. I've paid less for hotel suites. All things considered, I can do whatever the hell I want here." He kissed her just beneath her jaw.

"This is a nice dress," she said.

"It would look nicer crumpled up on the floor."

"That won't help me choose," she said.

"I like your lips," he said, leaning in and kissing her hard, deep. When they parted, they were both breathing hard. "But I like them much better when they are wrapped around my dick."

Desire shot through her like an arrow, hitting its target straight on, the ache inside of her intensifying. But this was how things always went with him. He demanded; she acquiesced. He pushed and she gave way.

But not now. She would make him wait. She would make *him* beg.

"I have shopping to do," she said, leaning forward and taking his lower lip between her teeth, nipping him gently. "And you need to go sit out there and behave yourself. And tell me which dress you think looks best."

He growled, tightening his hold on her and pulling her firmly against his body. "Is that what I have to do?"

"Yes," she said, keeping her tone firm.

He released his hold on her and took a step back, his dark eyes glittering. "Have it your way." He turned and walked out of the dressing room, and for a moment she was afraid he had walked out altogether. Until she heard him settle in the chair.

She moved away from the mirror and turned to face it, so that she could get a look at the gown for the first time since she'd put it on. It was beautiful. Elegant. And not *her* at all.

Which was a strange thought to have, because she had only just been thinking that she wasn't certain who she was. But she was not this dress. That was all she knew.

She managed to unzip it on her own, and then stood in her underwear appraising the other garments that were available to her.

She reached out and touched one that looked like molten gold, the fabric shimmering as it moved beneath her fingertips. It was definitely flashy. Not something she would have gravitated toward under normal circumstances. Not unless she was trying to draw attention to herself for a con. But then, standing there, looking at all the dresses, she found she liked that one best. There was no reason for her to like it best. No brief that she was filling, except for her own.

And because there was no reason for her to like it other than that she simply did, she decided to try it next.

She removed it from the hanger and slipped it on. This one was strapless too, but the zipper was a little bit more cooperative. She removed her bra. The support built into the gown was all that was needed for her curves.

She looked up at her reflection in the mirror and her breath caught in her throat. Even without makeup, and without her hair done, she almost looked like a different person in the shimmering golden wonder. It lit up her complexion, catching the warmth in the brown tone of her skin and eyes.

She shifted and the light caught hold of the fabric, lighting the small space with a shower of sparkles. She tilted her head to the side and placed her hand on her hip, shifting her weight to her left leg. The fabric parted, revealing a high slit that ended well above her knee.

She liked this. And that hidden bit of daring meant that Rocco would probably like it, too.

She turned toward the curtains and walked out of the dressing room. Rocco was sitting in the chair, his posture casual, his manner disinterested. Until he lifted his gaze and saw her standing there.

Then his focus sharpened, his expression going as hard as stone.

"What do you think?" she asked. But she already knew what he thought. And it made her feel hot all over. Such an amazing thing, to be able to read the thoughts of another person so clearly. To be close enough to someone to be confident that she knew what he wanted.

And to know that what he wanted was her.

"You look very expensive," he said, his voice measured.

"There isn't a price tag on the dress. Which means it must be."

"That is not what I meant. The dress doesn't look expensive." He pushed against the arms of the chair and stood. "You look expensive. There are not many things I can't afford, Charity. But you look like you might be one of them."

"Is that a compliment, Rocco?"

He cupped her chin, tilted her face upward. His dark eyes were burning with the dark flame. "How could it be anything else?"

"Some women might not like the implication that they can be bought."

"That isn't what I was talking about. I like expensive things," he said, tracing her lower lip with his thumb. "Not because they represent status but…a certain amount of security. Stability." He moved his hand, pushing his fingers through her curls. "It shows that you are not…weak. Not helpless. I am a man who has spent his whole life collecting things. To show that I am no longer a boy in an empty house. A boy with no power. I am now a man who has all the power. All the wealth that one could possibly want. There is nothing I cannot have…but you. You are far beyond me. Beyond any man who will be at the gala tonight." He slid his palm over her cheek. "*Expensive* is perhaps… not the right word. *Priceless*. You look priceless."

Charity tried to breathe and found that she couldn't. Something shifted inside of her, an empty space filling. A part of her that had always felt reed thin, insubstantial and easily broken felt strengthened, wrapped up in his words as though they were spun gold, reinforcing her. Shielding her.

She had never felt valuable. From the first moment she could remember she had felt like a drain. Because her father had made it clear that having her cost him.

That she had to earn her keep. She didn't add to his life, she took away.

To have Rocco look at her and say that she had value… it was altering in a way she'd never imagined she needed.

"If I'm so costly…am I worth the trouble?" She knew she sounded insecure, desperate even… Right now she didn't care. She was testing this newfound strength inside of her. Seeing if it could grow even more. Seeing if he might build it up or knock it down. Seeing if she could withstand it either way.

"Everything worth having in life is trouble. It comes at high cost, at high risk and with much work. Easy things are for those too weak to mine life for all its richness. At least that's my take on it."

"I'll take this dress," she said, leaning in and pressing a kiss to his lips. "It had the exact effect I was looking for."

"It made me want you? Believe me when I say, I want you in or out of the dress, Charity. It doesn't matter what you're wearing."

"That isn't what I meant. It makes me feel special. It makes me feel like me. I like that. But you said some nice things, too."

A smile curved his lips. "As far as I'm concerned, that was damn poetry, woman."

"Noted. And appreciated." She closed her eyes and kissed him again, letting the feeling of closeness, the feeling of—if not camaraderie—not being at each other's throats, wash over her. "I guess we're done here then."

"Not quite." That smile of his turned wicked. "I was thinking perhaps you'd like a chance to choose some of your own lingerie, too."

CHAPTER EIGHT

THE GALA WAS a glittering affair. From the high-gloss marble floors to the pristine white pillars, to the chandeliers dripping with crystal hanging low from the ceilings. But nothing glittered brighter than the woman on his arm. Charity was the loveliest thing he had ever held in his possession. And he only realized as he walked into the crowded ballroom, filled with other people, how desperate he was to take her back home and lock the door. To put her up on a shelf in his home for safekeeping, so that no one and nothing could touch her.

He had recognized her value. And now that he had put her on display like this, so would everyone else. So would every other man here. And that made him feel... It made him feel as though something that was his was under threat of being stolen. And there was nothing on earth that filled him with greater anxiety than that. Even as they walked deeper into the room, it grabbed him by the throat like the jaws of a hungry wolf and shook him hard. Because it took him back. To helplessness and empty rooms. And the loss he could never quite recover from.

No, that won't happen. That's the whole point of gaining power.

The ballroom came back into focus, and it was only then that he'd realized darkness had been crowding around the edges of his vision. He tightened his hold on Charity's waist, moving his hands down around her hip, drawing her closer to him. She turned her head to look at him, her expression questioning.

She was so sensitive. Always looking for things in him that weren't there. Though, in this instance, he supposed they were. But, he was hardly going to confide in her. He was barely going to allow the thoughts to take hold in his own mind, let alone speak them out loud.

"Are you all right?" he asked, because turning it around her was infinitely preferable to examining himself.

"I'm fine," she said, her dark eyes moving to search the room. She was exquisitely made up tonight, compliments of the hair and makeup person he had brought in to help style her for the evening. She had been shocked, and slightly offended, but ultimately she had agreed, and the results were beyond anything he had imagined they might be.

Charity was always beautiful. Whether dressed in clothing sent by him to humiliate, or in her waitress uniform, with her face bare. But tonight, she was somewhere beyond beautiful. He had told her yesterday that she was expensive. Had added *priceless* in order to make her understand. But that had been closer to the truth than he'd realized. She *was* beyond price. Something a man could sell all of his possessions for and never hope to buy.

The makeup artist had used shades of gold and orange around her eyes, the color enhancing their deep brown. Her cheeks seemed to glow, her lips looked slick, the color of juicy citrus in the sun. Begging him to take a bite. Begging him to allow them to satisfy his thirst.

Her black hair had been tamed into sleek waves, left loose around her shoulders, one diamond pin keeping back a few curls, sparkling beneath the lights.

And that was to say nothing of the golden dress. It

looked like solid metal that had been melted down and
poured over her curves, conforming to her skin, moving
with her, the skirt billowing around her legs, the slit baring
a tempting amount of tanned, toned thigh. All he wanted
to do was grab her and pull her into a darkened corridor
so he could take the gown off her and undo all the expert
hair and makeup.

But, he supposed that ran counter to coming here in
the first place.

Damn it all.

But he did need to stop her before they went out into
the center of the room. Because he had one more thing for
her. He almost didn't want to give it to her now, because
she was perfect as she was, and he was afraid that adding
to it might ruin the effect. Or worse, steal what was left
of his control.

All the more reason he had to give it to her. To prove
that he had not, by any stretch of the imagination, ceded
any of his control to her.

"I have something for you," he said, bringing them both
to a halt.

She looked up at him, surprise and something unreadable moving through her dark eyes. An answering emotion echoed in his stomach, and even while he felt it, he
found he couldn't put a name to it. "You have something
for me?" She looked down. "Don't I have enough from
you? You've bought me all these clothes. You're paying
for the medical care…"

"I'm not keeping a tally," he said, his voice harder than
he would've liked. "At least, not beyond the million dollars your father stole from me."

"So, you are keeping a tally?"

"Only that one. This is not on it. Neither is the dress.
And certainly the health care that you're receiving for the

pregnancy, for our child, is not. Stop making me out to be more of a monster than I am."

She looked up at him again. "More of a monster? That seems to imply that you are a bit of one."

"You know as well as anyone that I am. A bit of one, anyway. And I have a gift for you." He reached into the interior pocket of his jacket and took out a slim, long velvet box. Charity's expression morphed from surprise to concern. "It is not a venomous serpent of any kind," he said.

"I didn't think it was."

"Then why are you looking at me like that?"

"No one has ever given me a gift before. And no, the lingerie you had sent to my house back in New York does not count."

"I would never have suggested it did." He frowned. "Surely someone has given you a gift before."

"Who would have?"

He had nothing to say to that. He had spent much of his childhood lonely. Without a mother. But he had had one for a while. And she had certainly given him presents. Yes, a great many of them had ended up being taken from him. But the act of her giving them to him... That could never be taken. Long after the things were gone, the gesture remained.

Charity had never even had the gesture. And so she was forced to receive it from him. A man who was not qualified in any way to be responsible for the emotional well-being of another person.

His stomach twisted, and he opened the box quickly. "It's just a necklace," he said. He wanted to minimize the gesture now, so she would stop looking at him that way. Expectantly. As though she expected him to know what to do now. As though she expected him to know what to say, as though she expected him to have some sort of remedy for the things that hurt her.

"It's beautiful," she said, her voice a whisper, her eyes soft.

He wanted to tell her to stop doing that. And yet, at the same time he wanted her to look at him like that forever.

None of it made any sense. And he didn't have the time to sort through it now, in a crowded ballroom.

"You should wear it," he said, taking it out of the box and undoing the clasp.

"Okay. If you think it goes with my dress," she said, wringing her hands in front of her as though she were nervous.

"I chose it to go with the dress," he said. "Of course it goes with the dress."

He turned to face her, holding the necklace out and placing it gently around her neck. He kept his eyes locked with hers as he worked on the clasp until he was certain it was secured.

He had chosen a heavy, teardrop-shaped emerald, one he had known would settle perfectly between her breasts once the dress was removed. He had lied about it being chosen to go with the dress. He had chosen it to go with her body. With her skin.

He had chosen it because of how she would look later, wearing only that.

But he had a feeling if he said that, the look of wonder and gratitude would slide right off her beautiful face, and he didn't want to see that happen. If he mentioned it, he would wait until it was dark. Until he couldn't see. Or, he would wait until he had her mindless with pleasure.

He reached out and slipped his fingers beneath the gem, testing its weight in his palm, before placing it gently back against her skin.

"Perfect," he said, taking a step back.

She was. Indescribably so. Of course, now he had ensured that he would not be able to think of anything else but her, bare and wearing only that necklace. But then, the odds were high that all he would have been thinking about was her naked whether or not he had given her the necklace.

"Thank you," she said. She was so sincere. And he wasn't sure what to do with that. Sincerity usually skimmed right over his hardened veneer of cynicism, but hers had managed to find cracks he had not realized were there. He didn't like it. But his liking it didn't seem to be a factor.

"You're welcome," he said, knowing he sounded less than gracious. "Shall we?" He extended his arm, looking away from her and at a crowd of people at the center of the room.

He felt delicate fingers curled around his forearm, and he swallowed hard, using every bit of his strength to keep from looking at her. He led them both down the stairs and into the center of the room. And it didn't take long for the devils in suits to notice that he had dropped a particularly beautiful angel in their midst.

But she was not for them. None of the assholes in here were worthy of her. Hell, he wasn't worthy of her. But if anyone was going to defile her sweetness it was going to be him. Because she belonged to him.

He tightened his hold on her as they moved deeper into the crowd.

Leon Carides, a businessman from Greece who Rocco had had vague dealings with in the past, locked his eyes onto Charity, then looked back at Rocco, a slow smile spreading over his lips as he separated himself from the group he was talking to and made his way toward them.

"Amari," he said, his focus now firmly back on Charity, "nice to see you here. And you've brought a guest. You normally come to these events alone."

"Not tonight," Rocco said.

"Clearly. Leon Carides."

"Charity Wyatt," she returned, holding out her hand as she had done to the woman in the boutique yesterday. Really, the only time he had ever seen her betray any signs of weakness was with him. And he was under no illusion that initially she had been using it to try and manipulate him. But later, when she had come to tell him about the pregnancy, when he had gone to see her in the doctor's office, she had shown him her vulnerability. And he was only just now realizing how rare that was.

"Pleasure," Leon said, holding on to Charity's hand much longer than Rocco would have liked. In fact, he was contemplating separating the other man's hand from his wrist when he finally released his hold on her.

"Did you have business you wanted to discuss, Carides?"

"Not particularly," the other man said, his eyes still fixed on Charity. "Though, I must say, I'm surprised that you brought a date. You seem to prefer stealing mine at the end of the night to bringing your own."

For some reason Rocco bristled at the mention of his past behavior. He didn't want it brought out in the open in front of Charity. Which was stupid. Especially since she knew exactly what manner of man he was, both because of his own words and because of the deeds he had committed against her.

Still, he didn't appreciate Leon trotting it out for her examination.

"If you think you're going to return the favor, Carides, think again."

"That would be up to your guest, don't you suppose?" Leon asked, his eyes glittering as he appraised Charity.

"His guest who is standing right here," Charity said, her tone crisp. "And thank you for the offer, if it was indeed an offer. I'm flattered."

"Oh, it was," said Leon. "Do you have an answer for me?"

"No," Rocco said. "Her answer is no."

He felt Charity stiffen beneath his touch. But he didn't really care if she was angry with him. All that really mattered was that Leon understood that Charity belonged to him and would be going home with no one else.

"I can speak for myself," she said.

"You didn't speak fast enough," he said, his voice hard.

"Rocco…"

"Trouble in paradise—a shame," Leon said. "If you have a different answer than your minder here," he said, directing the words at Charity, "do come and look for me before you leave." He turned and walked away, leaving Rocco standing there vibrating with rage.

"I don't need you to answer for me," Charity said, her voice low.

"I gave you a gift, I can do whatever I like," he said, knowing he was being unreasonable and not caring at all.

"I will give it back if that's how you see things. It was my understanding that gifts came without strings attached."

"How would you know, as this is the first one you have ever received?"

For a moment, he saw hurt, deep and raw flash through her dark eyes before she put her mask back on, leaving her face smooth, unreadable. "I regret telling you that," she said.

He wanted to tell her not to regret it. He wanted to apologize. But he didn't know what that would accomplish. Only a few moments ago she had looked at him as though she wanted something from him, something emotional and deep. And just now he had proven he was not the man to give her that. It was for the best.

Decadence he could give her. Pleasure he could give her. Clothing, jewelry, he could give her. As for the rest? He didn't even know what the rest was.

"I wish I could give you something more substantial than that regret," he said, and in this instance he was being truthful. "Sadly, I feel if you're looking for anything more than physical satisfaction with me, regret is all you will find."

"I'll keep that in mind. I wonder if it's the same for Leon. Something to consider, as I seem to have an open invitation."

Rocco slid his hand up her spine, taking hold of the back of her neck. "Tell me, *cara*, do you want the father of your child arrested and sent to prison for murder?"

Her eyes flared wide. "No."

"Then do not tempt me to kill Leon Carides." Charity opened her mouth to speak, but he decided he was done talking. "Shall we dance?"

"That is…not what I expected you to say next."

"Does it matter what you expected? Come and dance with me. It is not a request. Or have you forgotten that I still hold the power in this arrangement?" He was being an asshole, and he knew it. But he couldn't seem to moderate his own behavior at the moment, and that was disconcerting.

"How could I forget, as you're so good at reminding me?"

She was angry with him, but she allowed him to lead her to the dance floor. Allowed him to pull her close, so that her breasts were pressed against his chest. She even wrapped her arms around his neck, feigning compliance. But he knew that it wasn't real. Knew that she was only pretending to be brought to heel. Probably so she could get close enough to him to strangle him.

He slid his hand down the curve of her lower back, to her ass, pushing her more tightly to him, allowing her to feel the arousal that was coursing through his body in spite of his anger. He was hard for her. But then, he was always hard for her.

She drew her head back, anger glittering in her eyes, even while her pupils expanded, her desire for him evident, as evident as her anger. Fine. He didn't care if she liked him. He only needed her to want him.

"You don't seem to care," he said, moving them both in time with the music.

"Of course I care. A prisoner can never forget she's in jail."

The light of challenge in her eyes spurred him on. "But you are not in jail, my dear, or have you forgotten? You could be. But you are not."

She lifted her chin, her expression haughty. "Am I supposed to get on my knees and thank you?"

"It all depends on what you intend to do while you're down there."

"Ensure that you're incapable of fathering any more children?"

"Oh, we both know you won't do that. That part of my body is far too valuable to you. As you have proven over the past week. Repeatedly." He leaned in and pressed a kiss to her lips. "You might not like me, Charity. But you can't resist me." He was driven to push her now, to strike out at her because the whole experience with Leon had burned him deep down in his chest and since he had no idea how to heal that pain, he had decided to keep on burning everything until he went numb.

"Keep talking. A few more well-placed phrases and I bet I'll be able to resist you permanently."

"We both know that isn't true. If you couldn't resist me that day at The Mark, you won't be able to resist me now." He said it as if it was a certainty, but really, it was a question. And he hated himself for feeling the need to ask it.

But he needed to know that he had her. That no matter what, she wouldn't turn away from him. That he was as irresistible to her as she was to him.

"You seem determined to push me until I can."

"Does it seem that way? That is not my intent." Or perhaps it was. Something, anything to get a handle on his control.

Why did this woman test it? Shatter it?

"Then maybe you could try being nice for a while," she said.

"I don't know how to be nice," he said. "I've never had to be."

"You can start by not making death threats to men we meet at parties. And then you can finish by not behaving as though you have the right to control my actions."

"I don't think you understand, *cara*. You are mine." He raised his hand and cupped her cheek. "And when someone tries to steal what is mine I do not respond kindly. Leon was treading on dangerous ground."

"But I'm not an object, Rocco. He isn't going to just pick me up and make off with me."

"He might. He is a wealthy man. He would have a lot to offer you."

"I thought I was priceless, Rocco. Why are you acting as though I can be bought?"

"You seemed interested," he bit out.

"I'm not. Not in a man who won't hold my hair when I throw up the morning after he's spent the night holding me in his arms. And I'm insulted that you would think I might be tempted to go with him."

He looked past her. "Why would I ever think differently? I don't know you."

"That's insulting," she said, her voice soft. Wounded. It touched him somewhere down deep, and he realized he was not yet numb. No matter how much he wished he were. "You know me better than anyone."

Her words hit him with the force of a slap. "Do I?"

"How can you ask that? You're the only man I've ever been with. You know that."

"In my experience sex has nothing to do with how well you know someone."

"Maybe not to you. But it does to me. I already told you why I was never with another man. I told you…I feel like you've been standing by watching as I discover who I am. How could you not know me?" Her eyes were luminous, filled with emotion.

Her words grabbed ahold of something inside of him and twisted hard. "I want to show you something."

The open emotion transformed into a near-comical scowl. "If it's your penis I'm going to go ahead and say no thank you."

He laughed, somewhat reluctantly. He wasn't sure how he could be so angry, aroused and amused all at once. He was not sure how he had wound up here, feeling like this, with a woman he had intended to hate. "Well, I will probably offer to show you that after. But that is not what I meant." He didn't know why he was making this offer, except perhaps as some kind of desperate last attempt to undo the damage he had done over the past half hour. To try and recapture the look on her face when he had given her the necklace. The look he had never deserved, the look he had proved he didn't deserve only moments afterward.

Truly, feelings made no sense. And he was getting tired of having them.

"Okay, you can show me something," she said, her expression softening. "Anything."

Her words flooded his chest with a burst of warmth. "We'll just finish this song then."

And for the rest of the dance, he held her close. And they didn't say anything. And for a few moments at least, he thought she might not just want him, but she might like him, too.

Charity wasn't sure what had transpired between her and Rocco at the gala tonight. Yes, they had fought, but in some ways she felt closer to him now than she had before they had left the house. He had given her a gift. He had insulted her. He had made her feel things. Had made her angry, had made her happy, had made her sad. Like a miniature relationship ecosystem all contained in the ballroom of a hotel.

And now they were back at the villa. And she wasn't sure what was going to happen next. There had been something strange in his tone when he'd told her he had something to show her. Strange enough that she'd been an idiot and tried to defuse the tension with humor.

Because she was still uncomfortable when things got close to the bone. When things got real, authentic. She was so accustomed to slipping on different masks, using them to shield her from anything unpleasant, that she seemed to default to it easily.

"What is it you want to show me?" she asked, pausing in the vast entryway.

"My things," he said, the bland note in his voice betraying more than outward emotion. Because he was like her. He put a mask on most especially when he was feeling deeply. And that was what he had done the moment they had walked inside.

This was important to him.

She frowned. "What things?"

"All of them. Of course, you've been living in my home for the past week. So you have seen some. But…just come with me."

He walked on ahead of her, down a hallway she had never gone down before. Because she had had no reason to. She wrapped her arms around her waist to try and keep herself warm. Because for some reason she felt an unaccountable chill.

Rocco stopped in front of a set of double doors. He turned to face her, a muscle ticking in his jaw. There was a keypad by the door and he entered in a series of numbers quickly, and she heard a lock release.

"Internal security?"

"Yes," he said. "I told you, no one steals from me."

Of course, that was very like her father. To rip off a man who clearly had more than just your average issue with being stolen from. But on the heels of that thought came another one. One that ripped through her like a ravenous beast. There was a reason for this.

She flashed back to what he had told her about when his mother died. When they had taken him from his home, when they had taken all of his things… She looked up at him, a wave of horror washing over her. He looked away from her and pulled the doors open.

She moved behind him, wrapping her arms around his waist and resting her head between his shoulder blades. She was shaking, and she hadn't even seen what he was about to show her. "You don't have to," she said, her heart thundering fast now.

She wasn't sure if she was trying to spare him, or her.

Because when she saw, once all of the pieces that she had been collecting of him were complete, once she was able to fit them all together, the vague yearning that was in her chest would be complete, too. Would turn into something else. Something she didn't want to think about.

"I want to show you," he said, his voice rough.

He released his hold on the door and stepped out of her embrace, walking into the room.

There was framed art on the wall, figurines in glass cases, vases. Coin collections, swords mounted onto the wall. Basically anything that could be considered collectible was here, except for cars. Though, she knew he had his share of those in his garage. She wasn't sure what she had expected, but it wasn't this.

"I collect things," he said, "expensive things. Any expensive thing really. I told you already, when my mother died I lost everything. I spent most of my life with nothing that belonged to me. My bedrooms were shared with other children. And more than that, they were temporary. I had no family. I had nothing. I felt helpless. Like there was nothing keeping me from drifting out to sea. As I became more successful, I realized that I could fix that. I bought myself a house. Now I own four houses. And I have my own bedroom in all of them. And nobody sleeps in them but me."

Charity realized then that she had never spent time in his room. Always when they slept together it was in her room. Her stomach twisted. And he continued.

"And I began to collect things. Things to replace what I lost. To make me feel like I was here." His dark eyes met hers. "I protect what belongs to me."

She kept thinking of what he had said at the gala. That she was his. That she belonged to him. It had seemed offensive, dismissive and minimizing. But she could see now that to him it meant something much deeper than it would to anyone else.

These things, these things that belonged to him, he protected above everything else. He prized them.

She turned in a circle, trying to take in the vast collection. "It's amazing," she said.

"Is it?" he asked. "I confess, I don't enjoy what I have in here very often. Though, I frequently check to make sure it's all still here."

His words made her feel as if someone had reached into her chest, grabbed her heart and squeezed it tight. She could barely breathe. She looked at the far corner of the room and saw a pedestal, with a glass case over the top. But she couldn't tell what was underneath it.

She took a step forward, her breath catching when she recognized what was beneath the glass case. Army men. Little green plastic army men that had no value. At least not monetary value.

"Rocco..."

He looked away, color staining his cheeks. "They were my favorite. They were the things I missed the most. Except for my mother. But...they were what I missed the most that I could replace." He looked back at her, his dark eyes hollow. "So, now you see."

"Yes," she said.

And she was certain they weren't just talking about the collection.

"Rocco..."

He closed the distance between them, his expression fierce, pulling her hard up against his body, cupping her cheek with his large warm hand. "Don't."

"Don't what?"

"Whatever you were going to do. Kiss me instead."

So she did. She rose up on her tiptoes and kissed him with everything she had in her. He sifted his fingers through her hair, holding her tightly to him as he kissed her deep, hard. He was shaking, and she was sure that she was, too. He moved his hand down to cup her chin briefly, then trace the line of her throat with his fingertips, before they came to rest on the jewel at the center of her necklace.

"Perfect," he said, his tone intense. "And mine." And she realized, through the haze of her arousal, that he didn't mean the necklace. "If only I could keep you here as securely as I do everything else I possess."

Her heart fluttered in her chest, fear joining the desire that was roaring through her. She had a feeling he was sincere. That he would lock her in a glass case if he could, and yet, she didn't want to run from him. Because that would mean being without him. And she didn't want that, either.

She had been right about understanding him. Had been right about what it would make her feel. Or rather, understanding him had given her a name for her feelings.

She was afraid that she loved him. And worse than that, she wanted him to love her back.

She was a stupid girl. She had wanted her father to love her, had wanted the love of her mother, a mother who had never even been there. Wanted too the love of a grandmother who had only ever taken her in sporadically so that she wouldn't end up sleeping alone on the streets.

For so much of her life, she had craved the love of people who wouldn't give it to her. And now, she was adding one more to the list.

Rocco.

The father of her child. Her lover. The only man who knew her at all.

Her heart suddenly felt too big for her chest, her eyes

stinging with tears she refused to shed. Her head ached, her body ached.

Maybe none of them love you back because you don't deserve to be loved back.

She gritted her teeth and closed her eyes against the insidious voice that was shouting loudly inside of her. Finally putting into words what she had always believed in her heart to be true.

Surely if she were lovable, someone would've loved her by now.

She was a thief. She was guilty. She had stolen from this man who prized his possessions above all else. This man who had lost quite enough.

He could never possibly feel the same for her as she did for him, not knowing the extent of what she was.

No. She wouldn't think of that now.

Anyway, this moment wasn't all about her. This was about him. He had given her so much of himself in this moment. And she had to honor that gift.

"I'm sorry," she said, words pouring out of her now. "I'm sorry I stole from you. I had no right to take anything from you. And I have no excuse. I can't hide behind my father. I can't hide behind my upbringing. Because I knew it was wrong, and I did it anyway. I'm sorry," she said, repeating the apology over and over again.

She didn't care if he could use this against her. Didn't care if she was giving him evidence to put her in jail forever. All that mattered now was that she make it right. In the only way she could. She couldn't return the money, but she could admit what she'd done. Could confess it all to him, lay herself bare, as he had just done for her.

"I know it was wrong," she said, more for her now than for him. "And I'm not going to do it again. I've changed.

I really have." She had to believe it. She needed to say it, because she needed it to be true.

"I know you stole the money," he said, his dark eyes meeting hers. "It doesn't matter."

"Yes it does," she said.

He cut her words off with a fierce kiss, still holding the gem on her necklace. "No," he said, resting his forehead against hers, "you are not a con woman. You have done dishonest things. I believe that you have conned people. I believe you conned me. But those cons…they are just things you've done. They are not *you*."

She swallowed hard, her throat so tight she could barely breathe. "I don't deserve that."

"Life is nothing but a series of things we don't deserve. Both good and bad. I say we take the good when it comes, because God knows the bad is never far behind."

"I don't…"

"Just accept it. Accept this," he said, kissing her again.

She squeezed her eyes shut, kissing him back, drowning in him, in this. In the atonement that he offered. He was right, after all. Nothing of life was fair. She had accepted that in terms of the bad, and this was good. So she should take it. While it was here. Touch some of the brightness before it all slipped back into shadow.

Rocco gripped his tie and loosened it, and she helped him pull it through his collar, casting it down onto the floor. Her fingers went to the buttons of his shirt, clumsily undoing two of them, her hands shaking.

She didn't know what the future held, but she knew she wanted this. She knew that she loved him. And she knew that she wanted this moment. Beyond that, she didn't care.

He lowered them to the rug that covered the marble floor, not breaking their kisses as he did so. He settled over her, her skirt falling back, the split parting, revealing her leg. Rocco placed his hand on her thigh, the warmth of his touch burning through her skin, through her entire body.

"I have a fantasy," he said, "of seeing you wearing nothing but this necklace."

His words heated her body further, filled that empty place inside of her that was so hungry for someone to care. For someone to want her. She was his fantasy.

You're mine.

And she knew now what that meant to him. Knew now that it was not meant to lessen the connection between them, because she had seen for herself just what a claim of ownership meant to him.

"It's an easy fantasy to see realized," she said, kissing him just below the line of his square jaw.

He reached behind her and tugged on the zipper of her dress, pulling the garment that would have cost a couple months of her waitressing wages down and discarding it in a molten gold ball on the floor. She wasn't wearing a bra, nothing other than a black thong that was little more than a sheer whisper of lace, framing her body more than it concealed it. He curled his fingers over the waistband of her panties, rough skin brushing the most sensitive part of her as he dragged them down her legs.

"Yes," he said, his breath hissing through his teeth, dark eyes intent on her body. "This is exactly what I wanted." He reached up and touched the necklace, weighing it in his hands. "This is exactly how I thought it would look." He let it fall between her breasts, the jewel warm from his touch. "I like having you here, with my collection. You are mine, Charity."

She lifted her hand and pressed it to his chest, over his shirt, and she could feel his heart raging beneath her palm. "Mine," she said, the word even more feral on her lips than it had been on his. "If you think you can take possession of me, then I will damn well take it of you."

"You have it," he said. "Though, I'm not sure why you would want it."

"Is that a gift?"

"Yes." He kissed her neck, the curve of her breast. "It is."

"I'm up to two then."

He straightened, undoing the rest of the buttons on his shirt and discarding it. Then he put his hands on his belt, working it free as he took his shoes and socks off, making quick work of his pants and underwear, so soon he was as bare as she was. "All of this is yours, if you want." She looked at him, his broad shoulders, his hard, well-defined muscles. His dark, intense eyes. "Say you want me," he said, a note of desperation in his tone.

"You know I do," she said.

"I need you to say it. Because the first time you felt like you had to strip for me. Now I want you here, naked, because you want to be."

"I do. I want you."

It was all the permission he needed. He groaned and kissed her, covering her body with his, easing her thighs apart as he settled between them. He moved his hand to palm her breast, squeezing her nipple between his thumb and forefinger. A sharp shock of pleasure rocked her, curling itself around the emotion that was expanding in her chest, until they were inextricably linked. She would never be able to separate the two again. Pleasure like this would always belong to Rocco, would always be part of the love that she felt for him. The love that she craved from him.

He bent his head, sliding his tongue around one tight bud, then drawing it deeply into his mouth. "Mine," he said. Then he kissed her lower, beneath her rib cage, beneath her belly button, moving lower still until his lips were hovering over the most sensitive part of her. "Mine," he said again, the word nearly a growl.

He lowered his head, tasting her deep, teasing the sensitive bundle of nerves at the apex of her thighs before delving deeper still, penetrating her damp core with his tongue. She gasped, arching into him, moving in time with him.

He lifted his head, turned and bit her inner thigh, the sharp jolt of pain rocking her, pushing her closer to climax.

"Mine," he said. "All of you. All for me."

He moved back to her mouth, kissing her deeply, the evidence of her own arousal there on his lips.

He thrust deep inside her and she gasped, his possession pushing her over the edge, pleasure roaring through her as she lost herself in this, in him.

In being his.

He kept his eyes locked with hers as he chased his own release, clenching his jaw tight, the fingers of one hand buried deeply in her hair, the other hand holding firmly to her hip.

"Mine, Charity, all mine," he said, the words ending on a harsh groan as he gave himself up to his own pleasure. He closed his eyes, his body shuddering out its climax, his shaft pulsing deep inside of her as he gave up his control utterly, completely.

He had taken possession of her, but he had given her some of himself.

He had given her a gift.

He was the only one who ever had.

She wrapped her arms around his neck and held him close. The carpet was starting to feel scratchy beneath her back, possibly because her skin was raw from the intensity of their lovemaking. And he was starting to get heavy, his skin hot against hers, slick with sweat. But she didn't want him to move. She wanted to freeze this moment forever.

It was the happiest moment of her entire life. She realized that with the harsh, sudden force of a blow.

In this moment her entire future stretched out before her, and in it, she wasn't alone. Because right now, with Rocco as close to her as she could possibly be to another human being, it was impossible to imagine being alone. Right now she had him and their baby. She had security. She had passion.

She had more right now—or at least the promise of more—than ever before. And she was treasuring this moment of possibility more than she could have ever fathomed treasuring anything.

After a long while he shifted position, pulling her against him, wrapping his arm around her waist, his chin resting on her shoulder. She could have stayed like that forever. Barring that, she would take it for the next few hours.

She didn't sleep. She simply lay there in Rocco's arms, trying to will the sun to stay sunken into the sea. Because as long as the darkness was drawn over them like a blanket, it felt as if time was standing still.

And when the sky started to turn a lighter shade of gray, she closed her eyes, so she could pretend again.

But inevitably, she knew the time would pass. She knew this moment would pass. And all of the incredible possibilities would dissolve, as future became the present.

But not now. Right now, she was in Rocco's arms.

And that was all she would think about.

CHAPTER NINE

CHARITY'S PHONE RANG at about three in the morning. Rocco opened his eyes and looked through the dark, his eyes focusing on the ceiling. But he didn't move. Beside him, she groaned and stirred, and he felt the mattress depressing as she sat up.

"Hello?" Her voice was gruff, sleepy, and he found it unaccountably sexy. "What do you want? Why are you calling me?" Abruptly, her voice sharpened. He felt her get out of bed, and he remained motionless.

"I could be in jail for all you know," she said, her tone a fierce whisper now. "Not that you bothered to check."

Her father. It had to be her father. He didn't move. He wanted her to stay in the room, to keep talking. Mostly, he wanted to take the phone out of her hand and yell at the man on the other end.

And it wasn't so he could get his money back.

For some reason, in this moment, Rocco was angry because that man had left his own daughter to take the fall for his actions.

And you made sure it was quite a fall.

His stomach twisted, guilt turning over inside of him.

"You would have seen it on the news? That's nice."

The door to the bedroom opened, and Charity's voice became fainter.

He rolled sideways, swinging his legs over the edge of the mattress and standing. Then he made his way to the door, keeping his footsteps silent. She had left it open a crack, and he took full advantage of that, lingering in the shadow as he did the best he could to catch the rest of her conversation, filtering in from the hallway.

"You have to return the money," she was saying now.

His breath caught in his chest, settling there like a rock. If her father returned the money, much of his leverage would be gone.

Certainly, legally he would still have a claim, but the entire goal was to see the return of his property. At least, in the beginning it had been. And Charity knew that.

The simple fact was, he would not have her thrown in jail. Not now. He would protect her, no matter what. But, if she *knew* that, she might not stay. And that was unacceptable.

He needed his leverage.

"He knows. He knows who I am." There was a pause. "I'm with him now." Another pause. "None of your damn business what I'm doing with him."

He assumed her father was speaking again. "Yes, as a matter of fact I am sleeping with him. Again, not that it's your business." She paced a few steps. "His whore? That's rich coming from you. You're a thief. And you're really trying to take the moral high ground? Return the money. Because if there's one thing I can't do, it's protect you from him. He'll do what he wants. I don't have any control over it."

She must have hung up, because a moment later she put her hand down to her side and he heard her whisper a short, sharp curse.

Rocco turned away from the door and got back into bed, waiting for her to return.

"Who was that?" he asked, waiting to see what she would say.

"No one," she said, getting into bed beside him.

Disappointment gripped his throat, and he wasn't sure why.

Maybe he was disappointed because, as far as he could tell, there had been no reason for her to keep the phone call a secret. Except that she didn't trust him.

"Wrong number?" he asked.

"Yes," she said, her voice muted. "No," she said abruptly, rolling over to her side. "It was my father. I'm sorry, lying to you seemed easier."

A rush of relief flooded him. "I know, I was eavesdropping. In the spirit of honesty," he said, "I figured I should confess, too."

"Oh. You were going to let me get away with lying?"

"Yes."

"He didn't tell me anything. He wanted to see if you had found out. And I told him you had. He says he doesn't have the money anymore. And, as I'm sure you could tell from my tone, he isn't sorry at all that he left me to fend for myself. He had some choice names for me, actually."

"You are not my whore," he said, anger like a ball of molten steel in his chest. "And I am sorry that I ever used the word in connection with you. I am sorry I called you that. I was angry, and I was trying to hurt you. And I knew that those words would be hurtful. Especially after what I had done." He paused. "I know what it is to be at a disadvantage in life. The fact that I ever put you in that position, where you felt you had to trade your body for your freedom... It was unconscionable. Though I confess freely that I'm a man who has been out of touch with his conscience for a great many years. But I never thought I would become one of those men who took advantage of women in quite this way."

"Thank you," she said, burying her face in his shoulder. "Thank you."

He was sorry. And he regretted the way he had started things between them, and yet he couldn't regret the place they were in now. And he also couldn't let her go. An impossible situation.

"I'm not sure I deserve to be thanked."

"Well, you were wrong. And you were a...a...an absolute beast. And sometimes you still are. But I was hardly an angel. I stole from you. And I lied to you. And I played as innocent as I could in order to make you feel sorry for me. And then, when we went to your hotel room...I forgot everything. I know it started out...like it did. But once we were there...once you kissed me...I forgot everything but wanting you. You didn't force me. You know you didn't."

"I never get tired of hearing that." He laughed, a hollow, humorless sound. "So, the fact that you have to tell me that says an awful lot about my character."

"We went over this already. Neither of us had the best of characters when we first met."

"I disagree," he said. "You're a very strong woman. You have made some bad decisions, but I think your character was always strong. To survive the childhood you did..."

"I admit it wasn't all roses and daffodils. But plenty of people go through hard times and never end up turning to a life of crime."

"And plenty of people have money stolen from them without blackmailing the thief into bed."

"I can't get your money back," she said, her voice wound tight with regret. "I don't even know where he is."

"Then you must stay with me. Marry me." He had not intended to propose, but the words came out of their own accord, and the moment they did, he realized how very badly he wanted her to say yes. And so, he did what he did best; he took away her choice. "You must. It is the only way you can make restitution for what you took from me."

"Is this a proposal, or more blackmail? It's very hard to tell with you."

"It's a little of both."

"It didn't sound like it was a question."

He wrapped his arms around her and pulled her close. "It wasn't."

"What's the benefit of marriage?"

"I told you, Charity. You are mine now." He closed his eyes, gritting his teeth against the intense wave of feelings that were coursing through him. He wasn't used to this. To wanting quite so fiercely. Not anymore. He had got himself to a position in life where he didn't want anymore. He had. He possessed. He was unaccustomed to feeling as though he was lacking something, but he did now. For some strange reason, he felt as if he was back at square one, scrabbling alone in a dark empty room desperately seeking purchase.

And it made no sense, because he was holding Charity in his arms right now. And yet he could feel something was missing.

It should be simple. As easy as buying a beautiful painting, but it wasn't. Because even with her here and now, physically, he felt that it wasn't complete. It should all fit together. It should all make sense, and yet it didn't.

"Marriage seems like a good way of making it permanent," he said finally.

Making her his wife. That would solve it. Turning the lock, ensuring she couldn't simply leave. More insurance.

"Okay," she said.

"Is that your answer?"

"It wasn't a question. You already said that."

"No," he said, confirming it yet again. "It wasn't." And

yet, he couldn't shake the feeling that a yes from her lips would have been much sweeter than forced compliance.

But if he asked the question, he had to accept the fact that her answer could be no.

He was not prepared to take that risk.

"When do you want to get married then?" she asked.

"Before the baby is born," he said.

The sooner they made it official the better. It might do something to ease the panic that was rioting through him.

"I suppose I'll need a dress."

Some of the pressure in his chest eased. "Well, as it happens I know where you can get one of those."

He closed his eyes again, relishing the warm weight of Charity's hand on his chest.

Soon she would have a ring to go with her necklace. And the entire world would know that she belonged to him.

Charity was having her fitting for her wedding gown, and Rocco was not allowed to attend. Which meant he was planning on going anyway. Currently, he had been banished from her room until the seamstress was finished with the fitting.

It would be a small wedding. They had already decided. It wasn't as though Rocco had any friends to invite. Though, there were business associates who would be terribly offended if they weren't allowed to attend.

The media would, whether they wanted them to or not, make a big song and dance about the legendary playboy Rocco Amari settling down and committing for life, so they would have to at least make a show of a genuine wedding anyway. Inevitably, the truth about the baby would come out, too. Particularly since Charity was beginning to show, and three weeks from now when the ceremony was actually held he imagined the evidence of her pregnancy would be even more significant.

He could no longer wait to see her. And he was a man who never did what he didn't want to do. He turned and headed back toward her bedroom, flinging the doors open wide without knocking.

Charity looked up, her dark eyes wide with shock, and so did the woman who was kneeling at the hem of Charity's dress, tugging pins out of the fabric.

Charity's dark curls were loose and wild, a couple of wildflowers tucked into her glossy mane, bright pink lipstick highlighting her beautiful mouth. The dress was simple, a light flowing fabric that skimmed the increasingly full curves of her body. The dress was tight just beneath her breasts, then looser around her stomach, beautifully displaying the changes that had taken place in her body over the past weeks.

There was something highly sensual about it, and it sent an elemental heat firing through his blood.

His woman, in a wedding gown, pregnant with his child.

All of it increased the intensity of the word that was constantly echoing inside of him, whenever he looked at her. *Mine.*

"Beautiful," he said, because it was all he could say.

"You weren't supposed to come in," she said, clearly annoyed with him.

"We do all kinds of things out of order. Why would we be expected to observe tradition in this?" he asked, moving deeper into the room.

"Maybe because I asked you not to?" She arched a brow, her tone full of censure.

"I do not take direction well, Charity, a fact you should know by now. Are you finished?" He directed the question to the seamstress.

"Yes, but I will need to take the dress so that I can make the alterations."

"I will help her undress. You are dismissed," he said.

The woman nodded and stood, making her way out of the room quickly.

"Well, you are in an extra autocratic mood today."

He shrugged a shoulder. "Am I different than usual?"

"I guess not."

"I did not want her in here while I gave you this. Neither did I want to wait to give it to you." He reached into his jacket pocket and pulled out a ring box. "Speaking of things we have done out of order." He opened it and revealed the ring inside. An emerald that did, indeed, match her necklace.

Charity just stood there staring at him, blinking slowly. "Am I supposed to just take it?"

"Do you want me to put it on you?" He found, that as soon as he said the words, he wanted very much to take her hand in his and slip the ring onto her finger himself.

"It isn't necessary," she said, reaching out and taking the ring between her thumb and forefinger. He gritted his teeth against the disappointment that assaulted him. She slipped it onto her fourth finger, and held it out in front of her. "It's beautiful," she said. "You have very good taste in jewelry."

"Yes, well, I am a connoisseur of nice things. That was a compliment by the way."

She arched her dark brows. "Was it?"

"You do not seem happy with me," he said.

"Do I not? I am. I'm fine."

"Do not lie to me. I'm tired of dishonesty between us."

She let out an exasperated breath. "All right, I'm a little bit dazed. This is all happening very quickly."

"It has to happen quickly. You said you wanted to get married before the baby was born."

"I never actually said I wanted to get married," she said, her words hitting him with the force of a slap.

"And I do not recall asking," he said, his words hard.

"No, you didn't."

He turned away from her and began to pace the length of the room. "But you want this."

"Does it matter?"

He whirled back around. "What are your other options? To go back to your hovel in Brooklyn? To go to prison?"

"I don't have other options," she said, her tone grave.

For some reason a piece of memory hit him. Strangers picking him up, carrying him out of his house.

"Everything will be fine," he said, almost in time with the strangers in his head.

Everything will be okay.

But nothing was ever okay again.

"I'm sure it will be," she said, her dark eyes blank.

"What is wrong with you? You were fine last time we spoke about this. You were fine this morning."

"It all feels very real now."

"So the past few weeks of living with me, carrying my child, sharing a bed, did not feel real?"

"You know what I mean. This feels permanent." She blinked more rapidly now, her brown eyes getting glossy. "In some ways I can't really believe the past four months have happened at all. And I can't believe... Never mind."

"No. Tell me."

"Or what? You'll have me thrown in prison?"

"If I were you it would be a very real concern."

"But it isn't a concern. Because I'm doing what you ask."

Her words landed in that hollow place inside of him,

that empty void that he seemed to be becoming more and more aware of. A void that had been hiding for years, one that he had hidden beneath his status, his collections, his possessions. Things that he could see now had done nothing to actually fill that void.

"See that you continue to do so." He turned away from her, and she reached out and put her hand on his forearm, her fingers curling into the sleeve of his shirt. "What?" he asked.

"Do you want to marry me?" He turned to look at her, and was hit full on with the force of the emotion in her dark eyes. "I mean, do you want to be with me? Or is this just you doing what you can to keep control?"

"Of course I want control."

"Are you going to be faithful to me?"

He hadn't specifically thought about it, not since their initial conversation when he had said he would continue to behave as he had always done. But, the truth was he had no desire to be with anyone else.

"Yes, and you will be faithful to me," he said.

"Another edict?"

"It damn well is," he said through gritted teeth.

"You didn't answer my first question, though. Do you *want* me?"

He lifted his hand and cupped her cheek, tracing her lower lip with his thumb. It was so soft. *She* was so soft, all over. And he could not imagine a time when he didn't crave her. When his body didn't ache for her. "I have you."

And with that, he turned and walked out of the room.

Charity watched Rocco walk out, leaving her standing there with a hollow feeling in her stomach. Her legs began to shake, and she crumpled onto the floor, her dress billowing out around her.

She looked down at her hand, at the ring that Rocco had just presented her with. He had not put it on her finger. Of course, she hadn't allowed him to. But honestly, what good was it to have a man put a ring on your finger when you had to ask him to do it? He should have wanted to do it. In an ideal world he would've wanted to.

But this was not an ideal world. And their relationship wasn't real. Not to him.

She had to keep reminding herself that their relationship had started with a bag of lingerie and a threat. But it was so hard to remember that now, now when she felt so close to him. Now when she felt as if her next breath depended on having him with her.

The problem was she wanted more. She didn't want his ownership. She wanted his love. It felt nice at first, him saying she was his. Because no one had ever given her even that much. She had been a burden, not something anyone desired. But she was coming to realize that his wanting to possess her was not the same as him loving her.

And she wanted him to love her. She didn't want this desperate obsession, this compulsion he seemed to have to hang on to what he felt was his.

She wanted emotion. She wanted desire.

She had wanted to be loved all of her life, and she didn't want to spend the rest of it wishing for the same thing and getting nothing in return.

But she was trapped.

Unless she changed something.

Which was not going to happen while she sat here on her knees like someone in the throes of an emotional breakdown. Well, okay, so she kind of felt like someone in the throes of an emotional breakdown, but she wasn't helpless. And behaving like a helpless person was unacceptable.

She pushed herself up off the floor and adjusted her skirt, walking out of her bedroom and looking both ways down the corridor, searching for Rocco. She didn't know why, but she had the feeling he had gone to his room. He had never invited her into his room. It was one of his sacred spaces, and she was discovering he had a few of them.

Another bit of evidence that he didn't love her. There were too many parts of his life that he kept secret from her. That he kept only for himself.

Another thing that was about to end.

She walked down the hall, in the direction of his room, her teeth gritted in determination.

Thankfully, he did not have a keypad installed on his bedroom door. She turned the handle and pushed the door open, letting herself in with no announcement at all. Rocco was standing by his bed, undoing the cuffs on his shirt-sleeves. He lifted his head and turned to face her when she walked in, his expression fierce.

"What are you doing in here?"

"I didn't come to vacuum," she said, keeping her tone even.

He crossed his arms over his broad chest. "Speak."

"What if I told you I didn't want to get married?"

"I would tell you that's too damn bad." He dropped his arms back down at his sides. "Is that all?"

"I don't want to get married," she said, injecting as much steel into her voice as she could.

"Why are you telling me this now? While you're wearing your dress? It all looks a bit late for protesting, don't you think?"

Her heart burned in her chest, screaming at her to stop. Because she did want to get married. She wanted to marry him. She wanted to spend her life with him. But not under these circumstances. Not as a part of his plan for revenge, or possession, or restitution, or whatever this was. She wanted him to marry her because he wanted her. Because he loved her. Because he wanted to make a life with her.

"I don't think it's too late to protest until the marriage vows have been spoken." She took a deep breath. "With things as they are now, I don't want to marry you."

"You do not have a choice, *cara mia,*" he said, lifting his hand and undoing the cuff that was still buttoned, rolling his shirtsleeves up to his elbows. "The decision has been made. And unless you want me to press charges…"

"So we're still at threats then, are we?"

"If that's what it takes."

"But I am your prisoner. Not your fiancée. I need you to understand that."

He reached out and grabbed hold of her wrist, lifting her hand in the air so that the light caught on the gem sparkling on her finger. "This suggests otherwise."

"But a fiancée can leave whenever she wants without the threat of jail time hanging over her head. A prisoner cannot. Don't lie to yourself, Rocco. Don't pretend this is something it isn't. Things haven't changed. On your end, they haven't changed. They are exactly the same as they've been from the beginning. You making demands, making threats if I don't comply with them. Even though I want you, it's always going to be colored by that. It's always going to be colored by the fact that I don't have another choice. So I'm telling you now, I do not want to be your wife."

He tugged her forward, lowering his head and kissing her, deep, hard. And she kissed him back, pouring every ounce of emotion into the kiss, her anger, her love, letting him have it all. And everything she gave, he took.

When they parted, they were both breathing hard. "It does not matter what you want. You will be my wife. That is final. Now, get out of my room and do not return here unless you're given an invitation."

Charity swallowed the lump made of grief and misery that was rising in her throat. "Okay. As long as we have an understanding."

"You are the only one who needs to understand."

She nodded once, and then turned and left him alone in his room. A wave of sadness, combined with an intense feeling of finality stole over her. And she had no idea what she felt at all. Because she wanted to be with him, and she had accomplished that.

But she wanted him to feel differently. And she couldn't force him to.

She was starting to think that a life with Rocco, with his emotions firmly cut off from her, would be much lonelier than a life without him.

But she would never find out. Because she did not have a choice. Or rather, she did. She could leave and test him, make him prove that he would send her to prison. But as much as she believed he wouldn't…could she risk it? She was guilty, and there was no denying it.

And if she were in prison what would it mean for her baby?

She couldn't leave, she wouldn't. But she wanted him to be certain of what he was doing.

What she had said to Rocco was true. He didn't really want a wife. He wanted a prisoner.

And he seemed intent on her serving a life sentence.

CHAPTER TEN

I DON'T WANT to be your wife.

Charity's words rang in his head as he stalked to his gallery, pain twisting his stomach like a knife stabbing him deep, sharp, deadly. He needed to be surrounded by his things.

He didn't know why she was suddenly fighting against him. Why she was making him feel as if he was a prison guard, keeping her in a leg shackle, when she had been treating him like a lover for the past few weeks. When she knew as well as he did that she responded to his every touch, his every kiss. He was not her enemy.

He had given her a ring. He had promised her his fidelity.

And this was how she repaid him, by standing there in the dress that he was buying for her and telling him she did not want to marry him.

She was *his*. She was his and there would be no negotiation on that score.

He turned and his eyes locked onto the army men that were on display in the corner of the room. It was a childish thing, he supposed, to keep those here among all of this priceless artwork. But he had liked the idea of having them. Of having something of his childhood returned to him.

The army men had been a gift from his mother, though not these exact toys, but toys just like them. Even after he had lost them, he had remembered them. Remembered the moment his mother had given them to him.

He gritted his teeth against the painful memories, memories it seemed were very close to the surface these days, and he couldn't quite fathom why. Memories of that horrible emptiness, of loss.

It made no sense. Charity was here, as secure as all of the things in this room. She couldn't leave him.

So why did it feel as though he had lost her?

Because you can't own a person. They have to choose you.

He didn't know where those words came from. He didn't know why this moment was blurring, images from the past intruding, taking over.

No one had chosen him. He had gone from family to family, each one keeping him for a set amount of time out of obligation, to collect their stipend from the government for taking part in the foster care system. But no one had chosen him.

He had aged out of the system without ever once having someone express interest in keeping him forever. Plenty of people had had legal claim over him during his growing-up years, but no one had chosen to keep him.

Mama chose you. Even though it cost her pride, her wealth, all the luxury she'd grown accustomed to. Her life.

He covered his eyes with his palms, digging the heels of his hands in hard. Trying to ease the ache that had taken up residence in his head.

What was the difference between those two things? He felt as if he was so close to it, so close that he could almost grasp hold of it. But it was hard, hard when he had spent so many years trying not to feel things. When he had spent so many years pretending emotions didn't matter.

Love.

No. His entire body rejected that. Because love was so painful. Love was devastating.

You couldn't buy it. You couldn't make it stay with you. You couldn't replace it.

But the effect of the gift remains…

He growled, turning back to the glass display case that contained the green plastic figures. It had never been about them. But about what he'd felt when she'd given them to him. About trying to recapture that, when he'd known he could never recapture her.

It was never about the *things*.

The emptiness was never about the loss of the toys.

But it would be so much easier if it were. Because he could buy things. He could replace things. But he could never replace the love that he'd had for the first five years of his life, and never again.

You can't make Charity love you by forcing her to stay with you.

The empty chamber inside his chest echoed now, pain radiating through his entire body. Because he knew it was true.

These things in this room had never given him anything. They were nothing but dead artifacts. Void of power, void of life. He had told himself that they would fix things, that they would make the emptiness go away. He had thought that by filling his house he would move farther and farther away from that small boy he had been, standing there in an empty hovel in Rome.

But all they had done was mask the loss.

He couldn't replace his mother with art, with cars, with money.

And he couldn't make Charity love him by forcing her to stay with him. She was right; she would never be anything but a prisoner as long as he made her stay.

You have to let her walk away. You have to give her the choice.

Everything inside of him rebelled against that. He wanted to lock her up. He wanted to keep her in this room, this room that was kept shut and secure with a code that only he knew.

But then everything between them would be empty. None of it would be real.

None of it was real at all until she made the choice.

She might say no.

He ignored that voice and walked out of the room, into the corridor. Yes, she might say no. But he had never given her the chance to say yes. And if she said yes...

He needed her to say yes.

He walked down the stairs and prowled through the main part of the house, unsure as to where he might find Charity. She had been avoiding him since their confrontation after the dress fitting, but only because he had been allowing it. He was not allowing it anymore.

And you are back to behaving as though you own her.

He gritted his teeth. Old habits die hard, especially when he didn't want to break them. But he had to. Because this was not about him anymore. It was about her.

He looked out onto the terrace and saw her standing there, her elbows rested on the balustrade. She was wearing a short, bright blue dress, her dark curls blowing in the breeze. She had never looked more beautiful. He had never felt a greater sense of her importance in his life.

And he was about to offer her freedom.

He was a fool.

He strode through the living area and out onto the terrace. "I will not send you to prison," he said, the words coming out clipped, rushed.

Charity looked up, whirling around to face him. She said nothing, her lips parted slightly, her brows raised.

"You are free. What I mean is you are free from any threat I have made to you. I will not press charges against you for the con you and your father ran. I do not care if he returns the money or not. You don't have to marry me. We will work out a custody deal with the child. I will pay child support. We will work out visitation. You have nothing to fear from me."

"You're letting me go?"

"Yes. I am letting you go." He swallowed hard, heavy, leaden weight settling deep in his chest. "You have nothing to fear from me."

"I don't have to stay?"

The way that she said it, the words she had chosen hit him with brutal force. "Of course you do not have to stay."

And he realized then that her answer was no. She didn't want to stay with him. And why would she? He had strongarmed her into this from the very beginning. Had made sure she knew that the only alternative to him was a jail cell. Why would she want him? He was a monster.

He had gone into all of this feeling as though he were the victim and she the criminal.

But he could not see it that way now.

"I thought you wanted to get married?"

"I do."

"Then why do you want to marry me?" she asked.

"Because," he said, his voice hard. "I am a possessive bastard. I don't want anyone else to have you."

"Is that all?"

Pain roared through his chest, a sharp tearing sensation rending through his heart. No, of course that wasn't all. But he didn't know what else there was. He didn't know how to say it. All he knew was that his head was pound-

ing with pain, and that great, suffocating terror was gnawing at his throat. It all felt like trying to use a limb that
was broken, mangled beyond repair. He knew in so many
ways what he should do, what he should say, but he didn't
have the strength.

Didn't have the strength to want something so fiercely
again and be denied it.

And so he gave the only answer he could.

"There is nothing else."

She nodded slowly. "Okay. I'm going to pack my things.
And I need for you to arrange for me to return to New
York."

"That's it?"

"Yes," she said, her voice strangled. "If that's all you
can say to me."

"I can't give you anything more," he said, hating himself because it was a lie. Hating himself because what it
came down to was that he was simply too afraid to give
anything more. And yet, he didn't know how to fight it.
He didn't know how to be stronger.

Because everything that was rising up inside of him
felt bigger than he was. Stronger. It was like a great, angry
beast that had been kept locked down so deep he hadn't
even realized it was there. And now that it had woken up
it was starving, enraged and incapable of being satisfied.
And he didn't want to try and satisfy it. He just wanted it
to go away. Wanted the numbness he had felt for so many
years to return.

And yet, right now he feared that would be impossible.

"Goodbye, Rocco. Please do get in touch about the custody arrangement."

"I will be there when you give birth," he said.

She nodded silently. "Okay."

"Is this it then?" It seemed wrong. It was far too quiet

an ending for something that had begun with so much fire. Yes, it had been a fire born of anger, but there had been passion, too. It'd been more than he had felt in years. And now it was simply ending. A dying flame, not ended dramatically with torrential downpours and wind, but with a slow and final suffocation.

"There was never really anything to end. Just a little bit of blackmail, right?"

"I suppose so." No. It had never only been blackmail. Not from the moment he'd first laid eyes on her. From that very moment it had been bigger than that, bigger than him.

And still he couldn't say it.

He felt like a little boy again, strangled by grief, strangled by fear, unable to speak the words that he so desperately needed to say.

"Then we'll be in touch."

"Yes, I daresay we will."

And so he stood there, as immovable as stone, his expression set, his jaw firmly clenched, while he screamed inside and watched Charity walk out of his life.

Charity managed to keep from breaking down until she was safely ensconced in Rocco's private plane.

But as soon as the doors to the aircraft closed and she looked around the empty cabin a sob escaped her lips, and tears started falling down her cheeks. She didn't want to leave. That was the worst part. She wanted to stay and accept whatever he was willing to give. Even though it wasn't what she wanted. Right now, she was wishing that she had decided to stay and take his crumbs, even though she needed more.

Because anything had to hurt less than this. A lifetime of knowing she was part of his collection, and only a possession to him, had to be better than a life without him. A life of knowing that he was sleeping with other women. That she would never fall asleep in his arms again. That he would never kiss her again.

They weren't going to be a family. That little part of herself that had—for the first time in years—let herself dream, felt like it was dying.

Unless he comes after you.

He could. He could still come after her. He wouldn't let her leave. Not after everything that had passed between them. Not after he had held her so close and told her she belonged to him. She had seen the way he kept his things, so secure, so safe. If she were one of his things, there was no way he would let her go.

He would come after her.

She waited while the minimal crew prepared the cabin for departure. Waited while the engine began to hum. And her tears fell harder, faster. And she realized that he was not going to come after her.

He can't.

And suddenly, she realized. Realized that she was an idiot. Realized what he was doing.

He was letting her go because he didn't see her as a possession. Not anymore.

He might not love her. He might never love her. She hated to think of that. Hated to face it. He was changing. This was a step for him. So far from the man who had sent that lingerie, that note, that demand. And that mattered.

She didn't want to be in love alone. But this was a test of that love, and she was failing it.

Love wasn't supposed to be this selfish.

No, her life hadn't been easy. But neither had Rocco's. She was learning, she was changing, and she was doing it faster than he was. But he had a harder climb. And if she wasn't standing at the top of the mountain waiting for him when he got there, then what good was her love?

It wasn't any better than the fickle parental love her father had often said he felt for her. He had only given it when it had suited him. And then, he had left her easily. Left her when she needed him most.

As she was doing to Rocco.

She was stronger than this. She wasn't going to run away like a coward when it got hard, when it got painful. She was going to fight. She was going to make demands, because damn it all, she was worth it.

She had spent all of her life waiting for someone to love her, but she had never once asked for love.

And now she wasn't just going to ask for it. She was going to demand it.

"Stop the plane." She realized that the staff couldn't hear her over the roar of the engine. "Stop the plane!"

Rocco had closed himself in his personal museum when Charity had gone off to pack.

He had been standing here, counting everything, taking mental inventory of everything for the past few hours. Everything was present. Nothing was missing. And yet his house felt empty. His body felt empty. As though Charity had torn something essential out of him and taken it away with her.

And none of these things helped. They didn't fill the emptiness.

Because you love her. And you were too much of a coward to say it.

The realization sent a searing bite of pain through his body. Yes, he did love her. But love was the most terrifying thing he could think of. Something he'd had for a mere five years before it had been torn from his life.

But the gift remains.

He pushed his hands through his hair, walking across the room and over to the display that held one of his vases. And then he pushed over the column that held it up, smashing both the glass case and the vase itself. He didn't feel any worse.

He turned and knocked over another display case, shattering the figurine that was beneath it. That was two things gone from his collection, and he didn't give a damn. Nothing mattered. None of it mattered.

These things that he had been protecting so jealously for so long, meant nothing. They offered no protection, no security. He was exposed. He was raw and wounded. And none of these *things* stopped the pain from roaring through him, savaging him.

She was all that mattered, and he had let her go.

She didn't choose you. You had to let her choose.

There was no reward in being virtuous. He laughed, the sound hollow, echoing in the room. He had spent so much of his life being decidedly unvirtuous because he had always known that there was no point to it. And truly, he had just now confirmed it.

He had done the right thing. And he felt no better for it. He certainly didn't feel enriched.

Now he would see his child whenever he was in New York. And what if she married someone else? Another man would be playing the part of father, living in the same household as his son or daughter. Another man would be sleeping with his woman.

Because whether or not he had let her go, he could not get rid of the feeling that she was his.

Always.

She might be gone, but the changes she'd made in him would stay.

He looked at the fractured glass on the floor, glittering against the marble. Those vases really didn't matter. These things didn't matter. He didn't need them.

That was new. It was different. It was because of her.

And no, he wouldn't have Charity. At least not now. But he would be a good father to his child. And without her, without having her in his life, he would not have been able to. Only a couple of months ago he had been prepared to never see the child. And now, that was unthinkable.

Yes, he had changed.

Though he certainly didn't feel very rewarded for it now, he knew he would be in the future. If for no other reason than that he would be able to have a relationship with his child. It was his chance to have love.

He walked across the broken glass, the pieces grinding beneath his shoes as he did so. He opened the doors and walked out into the main part of the house, then went up the stairs. He needed to shower. He needed to clear his mind. Figure out where to go from here.

He paused when he walked into his room and saw a bag sitting in the center of the bed.

He moved toward it, his heart pounding heavily. No one came in his room except for his staff. And even then, it was only when they were scheduled to be here. And no one was scheduled to be here now.

There was tissue paper in the top of the bag, and nestled in between the folds was an envelope. He picked it up, opened the flap and took out the note that was inside.

You will meet me on the terrace. In this bag you will find my engagement ring. If you have any interest in going forward with the wedding you will put this

ring on my finger. And you will get down on one
knee. There is no other option.
—C

With trembling fingers he took the tissue paper out of
the bag and revealed the ring box sitting in the bottom.
He picked it up, opened it. Inside was her ring. And she
was here. She wasn't gone. She was on the terrace waiting for him.

He wrapped his fingers around the box, squeezing it
tight in his palm as he walked out of the room and hurried down the stairs. When he reached the living area he
froze. She was there, out on the terrace. She was there just
as she had said she would be.

And he wasn't empty anymore.

She had *chosen* him.

He had to will himself to step forward. He was never
nervous. He was always decisive. And yet, in this moment he found he was nervous. Still decisive. But nervous. Charity had the ability to turn his life upside down.
Now and always.

He stopped in the doorway, taking a moment to admire
her beauty. Taking a moment to relish her presence. He
would never take it for granted. Never after this.

"You came back."

She lifted her head, a smile on her lips. "I didn't get
very far. They started the engine of the plane and I started
screaming and telling them to stop. I think they were concerned I was having some kind of medical episode."

"But you weren't."

"No. I just realized I was making a mistake."

He tightened his hold on the ring box. "Why? You
seemed very sure when you left."

"I was waiting for something. But I hadn't given you

anything. I wanted you to give me a reason to stay, but I hadn't given you a reason to ask. I'm going to give you one now." She met his gaze, her eyes bright, fierce and wonderful. "I love you. And I do want to be your wife. What I didn't want was to be married to you only to have you ignore me, only to have you treat me like I'm simply a possession you can lock away for safekeeping. But I didn't even give you a chance. And I never told you. I never asked you to love me. So I'm telling you now. I'm asking you now. Because if I don't give you a chance, well…what kind of love is that?"

His heart beat faster, each thump painful, shocking. Had she truly said she loved him? Did she love him? "More than I deserve. I didn't give you a reason to give me a chance."

"Yes, you did. Things didn't start out very good between us. But you've changed. I've changed."

"I *have* changed. You have no idea how much."

"I do."

"No, you don't. Because I haven't told you everything. I haven't told you how I feel." He took a deep breath. "Charity, I love you. I should have told you earlier. But the very idea of love… It terrified me. Because I loved my mother, and I lost her. And I spent almost thirty years without love in my life. Sometime during my time being passed around foster homes I just decided I wouldn't need it anymore. But in order to force yourself into a place where you don't think you need love you have to forget what it feels like. You have to forget why it's good. In order to escape the bad emotions you have to turn off a lot of good ones, too. That was what I did. Until you."

"Rocco…"

"No, let me finish." He drew an unsteady breath. "There was a void in me. A void in my life. There has been ever since I lost my mother. And it was so much easier to pretend that the things, the house, all of those material items were a part of that void. Because they were replaceable. And so I pretended that my money, that my collections were taking steps and fixing that, but they were only masking the real problem. That there was no love in my life, in me. But my mother sacrificed everything to take care of me. To raise me for as long as she did. I forgot that sacrifice. I forgot the importance of her love because it was too painful. And I became something... Something she would not have been proud of. But I want to change that. I want to be a good father to our child. I want to be a good husband to you. I want to stop being afraid. Because I don't think love and fear can exist in the same heart."

"Rocco, I love you, too," she said, closing the distance between them and kissing his lips. The most profound sense of relief, of peace washed over him. Happiness. Such a strange thing to feel happy after so many years of pretending it didn't matter.

"Such a strange thing, Charity. You are in so many ways my very worst nightmare. You stole my money from me, and you know what an offense that was to a man like me. Then, you stole my heart. The thing I protected above everything else. And yet, I am so grateful you did."

"Yes, well I am sorry about the money. Less so about your heart."

"I'm not sorry about either one. Seeing as it brought us together."

"What are we going to do when our child asks how we met?"

He laughed, and for the first time in a long time, there was humor in the sound. "We tell him the truth I suppose. That I met a beautiful thief and whisked her away to my private island where we fell in love. He will not believe us, naturally. Which is why, in this case, I believe the truth will serve us well."

"When you put it like that it all sounds very romantic."

"Is it not? I was under the impression it was." He opened his hand and looked down at the ring box in his palm. "At least, it will be if the rest of this goes well." He sank down to his knee in front of her, and he found it was the most natural thing in the world. "Will you give me your hand?"

"Of course," she said, her voice thick with tears.

He took her left hand in his, and this time, he placed the ring on her finger. "Charity, will you marry me?"

"Yes," she said.

Finally, she had said yes to him.

Finally, she had chosen him.

He stood and pulled her into his arms, kissing her deeply, fiercely. "I love you," he said. "And I will be a terrible husband. At least at first. Because I am changing, but you know it has been slow. I will make mistakes. It's going to take me some time to understand all of these new feelings. But I want to. Because you are more important than protecting myself. And you are certainly more important than my pride. Than anything in my collection. I broke a vase."

Her dark eyes went wide. "You didn't."

"I did. I broke two of them."

"Rocco, why would you do that?"

"Because I was angry. And because they didn't matter. The only thing that mattered was you. And you are not a thing. I cannot collect you. I cannot own you. And the truth of the matter is I don't want to. Because I like it when you fight me, I like it when you disagree with me. I like your mind as well as your body. I don't want to subject you—I want you to stand equal with me. I don't want to change your life more than you've changed mine."

"Before I met you I didn't feel like I knew myself. I felt like each and every thing I did was just another role I was playing. I felt so thin…so insubstantial. But you looked at me and you told me I was priceless. You told me I mattered. When everyone else made me feel like I made their life less…you made me feel like that couldn't be true. Not if I was worth so much in your eyes. And I know who I am now. And I know what I want. More than that…I know what I deserve."

"And what is that, *cara mia*?"

"To be loved. And to have you. I want you."

"Anything else?" he asked, kissing her again.

She waved her hand. "Oh, there's a whole list of things. But we can sort that out later."

"Can we?"

She fluttered her lashes at him. "I want a pony."

He chuckled. "We'll discuss it," he said.

"Why don't we discuss it after we go upstairs for a while? I have a feeling you'll be in a better mood by then."

"I have been in a better mood since the moment you walked into my life."

"Really?"

"Well, not every moment of it."

She smiled. "Good. I would hate to become predictable."

"Now that is one thing I think we will never have to worry about."

"Yeah, a reformed con woman married to an Italian billionaire. One thing is certain—our lives will never be boring."

EPILOGUE

CHARITY WAS RIGHT about that. She was right about a great many things over the next fifteen years, but the fact that their lives wouldn't be boring was chief among them. It was impossible to be bored with four children.

Even more impossible now that they were all either teenagers, or edging into their teenage years. No one could say that their household was lacking in drama.

In fact, there was a healthy amount of drama happening about ten feet down the coast from where she and Rocco were currently standing.

Lilia, their oldest, was currently being tormented by Marco, the youngest, and a piece of seaweed, while the middle two, Analise and Lucia, looked on in a state of amusement.

Charity glanced over at her husband, who appeared as amused as the children. "You should stop him," she said.

"Probably," Rocco said, turning and smiling at her.

That smile never failed to make her knees weak. Still. After all this time.

"You aren't going to."

"I didn't have siblings, but I like to think that if I did I would have done things very similar to the way Marco does them. He's a smart boy. The only boy, so he must make the most of that."

"He's a handful."

"I think he gets it from you, actually."

Charity laughed. "You think I'm a handful?"

Rocco leaned in and kissed her neck, and a shiver went through her body. "You do fit my hands perfectly."

It was funny now to think back on how they had met. To think about finding out she was pregnant with Lilia. How terrified she had been. How angry she had been when Rocco had insisted he be a part of the child's life.

If she had only had a window into how things would be in the future, she never would have hesitated.

She could remember clearly that moment when she had told Rocco about the baby, and when she had left his office. How, even in her misery, she had thought that at least she had the possibility of a new start.

She had been right about that at least. She just hadn't been right about the details.

She could never have fathomed this much happiness. Could never have imagined that her life would be so full of love.

She had gone twenty-two years feeling as if no one loved her. And in the fifteen years since she had met Rocco she had never gone a day without feeling loved. Without *knowing* she was loved. She never felt as if she was standing on the outside. She was wrapped in it.

"You know, I'm very glad I stole your money," she said.

He tilted his head to the side. "What brought that on?"

"I was just thinking about how we met. How you changed my life."

"Well, I'm very glad I caught you."

"I'm glad you caught me, too."

"More than that, I'm glad you decided to stay caught."

"Me, too."

"You know, as much as I don't like to think about what

an ass I was back when we first met, I was thinking the other day about what I said to you in the hotel that first day."

"Were you?"

"Yes," he said, his tone grave. "I told you that you got the better end of the deal. Seeing as I had spent a million dollars on sex."

She rolled her eyes. "Oh yes, how could I forget?"

"You can't. I was horrible. But, I was thinking now, knowing what I do, I should have given you everything then and there."

"Because having a wife and children has proven to be so expensive?" she asked, smiling broadly.

"No, because you are priceless. I know that now with a depth of certainty that surpasses all else. Years of watching you, growing with you, loving you, have only strengthened my love. And I would give everything, then and now, to have you in my life forever." He cupped her cheek, bending down and kissing her on the lips. "All I have is worth nothing if I don't have you."

She looked up at her husband, warmth, love, flooding through her. "You have me. Forever."

* * * * *

DAMASO
CLAIMS HIS HEIR

ANNIE WEST

For Ana Luisa Neves.
With heartfelt thanks for your patience and
Portuguese language expertise.

Annie West has devoted her life to an intensive study of tall, dark, charismatic heroes who cause the best kind of trouble in the lives of their heroines. As a sideline, she's also researched dream-worthy locations for romance, from bustling, vibrant cities to desert encampments and fairytale castles. It's hard work, but she loves a challenge. Annie lives with her family at beautiful Lake Macquarie, on Australia's east coast. She loves to hear from readers and you can contact her at www.annie-west.com or at PO Box 1041, Warners Bay, NSW 2282, Australia.

CHAPTER ONE

DAMASO SAW HER and his breath snagged in his lungs.

He who'd had women dancing to his tune well before he made his first million.

How long since one had quickened his pulse? He'd known divas and duchesses, models and Madonnas. In the early days there'd been tourists by the armful, and one memorable tango dancer whose sinuous body and blatant sexuality had made his teenage self burn with need. None had affected him the way she did—without effort.

For the first time she was alone, not laughing with her coterie of men. He was surprised to see her crouched, photographing flowers on the rainforest floor. She was so engrossed, she didn't notice him.

That was new for Damaso. He'd grown used to being watched and avidly sought after.

It pricked him that she was oblivious to him while he was hyper-aware of her. It infuriated him that his eyes strayed to her time and again, yet she had done no more than gift him with the dazzling smile she awarded so indiscriminately.

Damaso moved closer, intrigued. Was she really unaware or was she trying to pique his curiosity? Did she know he preferred to be the hunter, not the prey?

Beautiful blondes were commonplace in his world. Yet from the first day, watching her radiant face as she'd emerged drenched but undaunted from white-water raft-

ing, Damaso had felt something new. A spark of connection.

Was it her unbounded energy? The devilment in her
eyes as she risked her pretty neck again and again? Or that
sexy gurgle of laughter that clutched at his vitals? Perhaps
it was the sheer courage of a woman that didn't baulk at
any challenge on a trek designed to spark the jaded interest of the world's ultra-wealthy.

'Marisa. There you are. I looked for you everywhere.'
Young Saltram blundered out of the undergrowth to stop
beside her. A computer geek who looked about eighteen,
yet was worth upwards of seven figures annually, he was
like an over-grown puppy salivating over a bone.

Damaso's jaw tightened as Saltram ate her up with his
eyes—his gaze lingering on the delectable peach ripeness
of her backside as she squatted with her camera.

Damaso stirred, but stopped as she turned her head.
From this angle he saw what Saltram couldn't: her deep
breath, as if she'd mustered her patience before turning.

'Bradley! I haven't seen you for hours.' She gave the
newcomer a blinding smile that seemed to stun him.

That didn't stop him reaching out to help her rise, though
it was clear she didn't need assistance. Damaso had never
seen a woman so agile or graceful.

Saltram closed his hand around her elbow and she
smiled coquettishly up at the youth.

Amazingly, Damaso felt something stark scour his belly.
His fingers twitched as he resisted the urge to march across
and yank the boy away.

She was laughing, flirting now, not at all perturbed that
Saltram was breathing down her cleavage.

She wore shorts and hiking boots and her toned legs
drew Damaso's gaze like a banquet set before a beggar. He
swallowed, tasting his own hunger and the sharp, pungent
tang of green apples.

Scowling, he recognised it was her scent filling his nostrils. How could that be? Standing in the shadows, he was too far away to inhale her perfume.

She turned and let Saltram guide her down the track, her long ponytail swaying across her narrow back. For a week Damaso had wanted to stroke that shining fall of gold and discover if it was as soft as it looked.

Yet he'd kept his distance, tired of dealing with fractious women who wanted more than he was prepared to give.

But she wouldn't make demands, the voice of temptation whispered. *Except in bed.*

For Princess Marisa of Bengaria had a reputation with a capital R. Pampered from birth, living carelessly off inherited riches, she was a party girl extraordinaire. The tabloids branded her wilful, reckless and as far from a demure, virginal princess as it was possible to get.

Damaso had told himself he was sick of high-maintenance women. Yet a week in her vicinity had given him a new perspective. She might be feckless but she wasn't needy.

She'd flirted with every man on the trek. Except him. Heat drilled through his belly as the significance of that hit.

She was *exactly* what he needed. He had no interest in virgins. A little wildness would add spice to a short vacation liaison.

Damaso smiled as he sauntered down the track after her.

Marisa turned her face to the waterfall's spray, grateful for its cooling, damp mist in this sultry heat. Her blood pumped fast and her limbs felt stretched and shaky from fatigue and adrenalin as she clung to the cliff face.

Yes! This was what she wanted. To lose herself in the challenge of the moment. To put aside all the—

'Marisa! Over here!'

She turned her head. Bradley Saltram watched her

from a perch well away from the waterfall. His grin was triumphant.

'Hey, you did it! Great going.' Bradley had confided his fear of heights. Even his relatively straightforward climb was a momentous achievement. No wonder he wore full safety harness and had Juan, their guide, in close attendance. 'I knew you could do it.'

But it was hard meeting his bright eyes, almost febrile with excitement and pleasure.

A hammer blow struck her square in the chest and she clutched at her precarious handhold. When he smiled that way, with such triumph, she remembered another smile. So radiant it had been like watching the sun's reflection. Eyes so clear and brilliant they'd been like the summer sky. Happiness so infectious it had warmed her to the core.

Stefan had always been able to make her forget her misery with a smile and a joke and a plunge into adventure, making a nonsense of the joyless, disapproving world that trapped them.

Marisa blinked, turning away from the bright-eyed American who had no idea of the pain he'd evoked.

A lump the size of Bengaria's cold, grey royal palace settled in her chest, crushing the air from her lungs and choking her throat. Her breath was a desperate whistle of snatched air.

No! Not now. Not here.

She turned back to Bradley, pinning a smile on her features. 'I'll see you at the bottom. I just want to check out the falls.'

Bradley said something but she didn't hear it over the drumming pulse in her ears. Already she was moving, swinging easily up, shifting her weight as she found new foot- and hand-holds on the slick rock-face.

That was what she needed, to concentrate on the challenge and the demands of the moment. Push away everything but the numbness only physical exertion brought.

She was high now, higher than she'd intended. But the rhythm of the climb was addictive, blotting out even Juan's shouted warning.

The spray was stronger here, the rock not merely damp but running with water.

Marisa tuned in to the roar of the falls, revelling in the pounding rush of sound, as if it could cleanse her of emotion.

A little to the left and she'd be at the spot where legend had it one brave boy had made the impossible dive into the churning pool of water below.

She paused, temptation welling. Not to make a name for herself by a daredevil act, but to risk herself in the jaws of possible oblivion.

It wasn't that she wanted to die. But dicing with danger was as close as she'd come lately to living, to believing there might possibly be joy in her life again.

The world was terminally grey, except in those moments when the agony of grief and loneliness grew piercingly vivid. Those moments when Marisa faced the enormity of her loss.

People said the pain eased with time but Marisa didn't believe it. Half of her had been ripped away, leaving a yawning void that nothing could fill.

The pounding of the falls, like the pulse of a giant animal, melded with the rapid tattoo of her heartbeat. It beckoned her, the way Stefan had time and again. When she closed her eyes she could almost hear the teasing lilt in his voice. *Come on, Rissa. Don't tell me you're scared.*

No, she wasn't scared of anything, except the vast aloneness that engulfed her now Stefan was gone.

Without thought she began climbing towards the tiny ledge beside the fall, taking her time on the treacherously wet rock.

She was almost there when a sound stopped her.

Marisa turned her head and there, just to her right, was

Damaso Pires, the big Brazilian she'd been avoiding since
the trek had started. Something about the way he watched
her with those knowing dark eyes always unsettled her, as
if he saw right through what Stefan had dubbed her 'party
princess' persona.

There was something else in Damaso's gaze now. Something stern and compelling that for a moment reminded her
of her uncle, the all-time expert in judgement and condemnation. Then, to her amazement, he smiled, the first genuine smile he'd given her.

Marisa grabbed at the cliff as energy arced through her
body, leaving her tingling and shaky.

He was a different man with that grin.

Dark and broodingly laconic, he'd always had the presence and looks to draw attention. Marisa had surrepti-
tiously watched the other women simper and show off and
blatantly offer themselves to him.

But when he smiled! Heat slammed through her in the
wake of a dazzling blast of raw attraction.

His dark hair was plastered to his skull, emphasising
the masculine beauty of his bone structure. Tiny streams
of water ran from his solid jaw down his strong throat.

It was only then that Marisa realised he wasn't wearing a safety helmet.

It was the sort of thing Stefan would have done in one
of his wilder moments. Did that explain the sudden tug of
connection she felt?

The Brazilian jerked his head up and away from the
falls, his ebony eyebrows rising questioningly.

Following his gesture, Marisa remembered Juan telling
them about a lookout beyond the falls and a rough track
that curved down from it to the valley floor.

She met those fathomless eyes again. This time their
gleam didn't disturb her. It beckoned. Her body zinged with
unexpected pleasure, as if recognising an equal.

With a nod she began to clamber up and away from the

sheer plunge of water. He climbed beside her, each movement precise and methodical, till in the end she had to make
a conscious effort not to watch him. Weary now, Marisa
needed all her concentration for the climb. The spurt of
energy that had buoyed her had abated.

She was almost at the top, her vision limited to the next
tiny hold, her breath ragged in her ears, when a hand appeared before her. Large, well-kept but callused, and bearing the silvery traces of old scars, it looked like a hand you
could rely on.

Arching her neck, Marisa peered up and met liquid dark
eyes. Again she felt that jolt of awareness as heat poured
through her. Heat that had everything to do with the sizzle
in Damaso Pires's gaze as he stood above her on an out-
crop of rock.

Marisa hesitated, wondering what it was about this man.
He was different from the rest. More…real.

'Take my hand.'

She should be used to that rich accent now. It was a week
since she'd arrived in Brazil. But, teamed with Damaso's
dark, velvet voice, the sultry seduction of it made something clutch inside.

A quiver rippled through her. She ignored it and made
herself reach for his hand, feeling it close hard around her
fingers. His strength engulfed her. As she watched, his lips
curved in a smile of pure satisfaction.

Awareness pulsed through their joined hands and Marisa
knew something like anxiety as his expression sharpened.
For a moment he looked almost possessive. Then he was
hauling her up, not waiting for her to find the purchase of
another foothold.

His display of macho strength shouldn't have made her
heart hammer. When she'd been in training she'd known
plenty of strong, ultra-fit men.

But not one of them had made her feel as feminine

and desirable as she did now, standing, grubby and out of
breath, before this man.

His eyes held hers as he deftly undid her helmet and
drew it away. The breeze riffled her damp hair, tugging
strands across her face. She knew she looked a mess, but
refused to primp. Instead she returned his stare, cataloguing achingly high cheekbones set aslant an arresting face
of dark bronze, a long nose with more than a hint of the
aquiline, a firm mouth, unsmiling now, and heavy-lidded
eyes that looked as if they held untold secrets.

The way he looked at her, so intent, so direct, made her
feel like he saw *her*—not the celebrity princess but the
woman beneath, lost and alone.

No man had ever looked at her like that.

His gaze dropped to her mouth and her lips tingled.
She swallowed hard, unprepared for the sexual need that
swamped her as she inhaled his scent—clean, male sweat
and something else—soap, perhaps—that reminded her
of the sea.

'*Bem vinda, pequenina.* Welcome, little one. I'm glad
you decided to join me.'

She stood, looking up at him, her chin tilted, revealing the
slender line of her pale throat. Her eyes, the purest azure
he'd ever seen, held his, unblinking. And all the while
his body tightened, impossibly aroused by the touch and
sight of her.

How would she taste?

The question dried his mouth and set his libido spinning.

'Is this the lookout Juan spoke of?' She didn't move
away but slipped her hand from his as she turned to admire the view. It was stupendous, the sort of thing people
travelled continents to experience. Yet Damaso suspected
she used it as an excuse to avoid him.

Too late for that. He'd felt the throb of mutual awareness.

He'd recognised desire in her eyes even as she'd clung like a limpet to the vertical rock.

There would be no more avoiding what was between them. The time for that was past.

'What were you doing, over by the falls?' The words shot out—an accusation he hadn't intended to voice. But the memory of fear was a sharp tang on his tongue. It had sent him swarming up the cliff face without bothering with safety gear.

There'd been something about the way she'd climbed— a determination—as she'd headed for the exposed, most dangerous part of the cliff that had sent a chill scudding down his spine.

What *had* she been up to?

The shadowed, almost dazed look in her eyes when she'd turned to face him on the cliff had shot a premonition of danger through him. Growing up where he had, Damaso had a well-honed instinct for danger in all its forms. He hadn't liked what he'd read in the princess's eyes.

She shrugged. 'Just looking.' Her tone was off-hand, as if she hadn't just risked her life on one of the country's most notoriously treacherous climbs. 'I remembered Juan talking about that boy's dive into the pool.'

Anger stirred at her recklessness. Damaso opened his mouth to berate her then noticed the taut muscles in her neck and her rigid posture. She was like a guard on parade.

Or a princess deflecting impertinent questions?

She had a lot to learn if she thought he'd be so easily dismissed.

He lifted a hand and stroked long, golden strands from her cheek and back over her shoulder.

Her hair was as soft as he'd imagined.

She said nothing, didn't even turn, but he watched with satisfaction as she swallowed.

'The forest seems to go on for ever.' Her voice had a husky quality that hadn't been there before. Damaso smiled.

She was out of danger now and she was here with him. Why probe what she clearly didn't want to talk about?

'It would take days to walk out, and that's if you didn't get lost along the way.' He couldn't resist reaching out to sweep a phantom lock of hair off her cheek. Her skin was hot, flushed with exertion, and so soft he wanted to slide his fingers over all of her, learning her body by touch before testing it with his other senses.

A pulse throbbed at the base of her neck, like a butterfly trapped in a net.

Heat drove down through Damaso's belly as he imagined licking that spot.

Her head jerked around and he was snared by her electric-blue gaze.

'You know the forest well, Senhor Pires?'

She sounded like a courtier at a garden party, her tone light with just the right amount of polite interest. But the cool, society veneer merely emphasised the hot, sexy woman beneath. The fact she was dishevelled, like a woman just risen from her lover's arms, added a piquant spice.

Damaso was burning up just looking at her.

And she knew it. It was there in her eyes.

Awareness sizzled between them.

'No; I'm city bred, Your Highness. But I get out to the wilderness as often as I can.' Damaso always allowed himself one break a year, though he took his vacation checking out one of his far-flung companies. This year it was an upmarket adventure-travel company.

He had a feeling the adventure was just about to start.

'Marisa, please. "Highness" sounds so inflated.' A spark of humour gleamed in her bright eyes. It notched the heat in his belly even higher.

'Marisa, then.' He liked the sound of it on his tongue, feminine and intriguing. 'And I'm Damaso.'

'I don't know South America well, Damaso.' She paused

on his name and a shiver of anticipation raced under his skin. Would she sound so cool and composed when he held her naked beneath him? He didn't know which he'd prefer, that or the sound of her voice husky with pleasure. 'I haven't visited many of the cities.' She reached out and picked a leaf off his open collar. The back of her fingers brushed his neck and his breath stalled.

A tiny smile played at the corner of her mouth. Her eyes told him the lingering touch had been deliberate. Siren!

'My birthplace isn't on anyone's must-see list.' Now *there* was an understatement.

'You surprise me. I hear you're something of a legend in business circles. Surely they'll be putting up a sign saying "Damaso Pires was born here"?'

He plucked a twig from her hair and twirled it between his fingers. No need to tell her no one had any idea where exactly he'd been born, or whether there'd even been a roof for protection.

'Ah, but I wasn't born with a silver spoon in my mouth.'

She blinked, her mouth thinning for an infinitesimal moment, so that he wondered if he'd blundered in some way. Then she shrugged and smiled and he lost his train of thought when she took the twig from his fingers, her hand deliberately caressing his. That light touch drew his skin tight across his bones as lust flared.

'Don't tell anyone,' she smiled from under veiled eyes as if sharing a salacious secret. 'But silver spoons aren't all they're cracked up to be.'

With a quick twist of the wrist he captured her hand in his. Silence throbbed between them, a silence heavy with unspoken promise. Something kindled in her eyes. She returned his hungry look, not resorting to coyness.

'I like the way you face challenges head-on,' he found himself admitting, then frowned. Usually he measured his words carefully. They didn't just shoot out.

'I like the fact you don't care about my social status.'

Her hand shifted in his hold, her thumb stroking his. It pleased him that she didn't pretend disinterest, or lunge at him desperately. The sense of a delicate balance between them added a delicious tension to the moment.

'It's not your title I'm interested in, Marisa.' Her name tasted even better the second time. Damaso leaned forward, eager for the taste of her on his tongue, then stopped himself. This wasn't the place.

'You don't know how glad I am to hear that.' She planted her palm on his shirt and his heart leapt into overdrive. It felt as if she'd branded him.

Tension screwed his body tight. He wanted her *now* and, given the way her fingers splayed possessively on him, her lips parting with her quickened breathing, she felt the same.

He wanted to take her here, hard and fast and triumphantly. Except instinct told him he'd need more than one quick taste to satisfy this craving.

How had he resisted her for a whole week?

'Perhaps you could tell me on the way back down exactly what you *are* interested in, Damaso.'

He snagged her hand in his again and turned her towards the rough track leading away from the cliff. Her fingers linked with his, shooting erotic pleasure through him that felt in some strange way almost innocent. How long since he'd simply held a woman's hand?

Marisa towel-dried her hair while looking out at her private courtyard in the luxurious eco-resort. A bevy of butterflies danced through the lush leaves.

She tried to focus on how she'd capture them on film but all she could think about was Damaso Pires. The feel of his hand enclosing hers as they'd clambered down the track. The wrench of loss when he'd let her go as they'd approached the others. The way his burning gaze had stripped her bare.

No wonder she'd avoided him.

But now she craved him. She, who'd learned to distrust desire!

Yet this was something new. With Damaso Pires she
sensed a link, a feeling almost of recognition, that she'd
never experienced. It reminded her a little of the very different bond she'd shared with Stefan.

Marisa shook her head. Was grief clouding her thoughts?

Physical exertion, even danger, didn't ease her pain.
Since Stefan's death she'd been shrouded in grey noth-
ingness, till Damaso had reached out to her. Could she do
it? Give herself to a stranger? Excitement and fear shivered through her. Despite what the world believed, Marisa
wasn't the voracious sexpot the press portrayed.

Then she remembered how she'd felt trading words with
him, their bodies communicating in subtle hints and re-
sponses as ancient as sex itself.

She'd felt happy. Excited. That aching feeling of isola-
tion had fled. She'd felt alive.

A knock sounded on her door, reverberating through her
hollow stomach. Second thoughts crowded in, old hurts.
Marisa glanced in the mirror. Barefoot, damp hair slicked
back from a face devoid of make-up, she looked as far from
a princess as you could get.

Did he want the real woman, not the royal? She wa-
vered on the brink of cowardice, of wanting to pretend she
hadn't heard him. She'd taken chances on men before and
been disappointed. More, she'd been eviscerated by their
callous selfishness.

The knock came again and she jumped.

She had to face this.

With Damaso, for the first time in years, she dared risk
herself again. That tantalising link between them was so
intense, so profound. She *wanted* to trust him. She wanted
desperately not to be alone anymore.

Her heart pounded as she opened the door. He filled
the space before her, leaning against one raised arm. His

eyes looked black and hungry in the early-evening light. Her stomach swooped.

With a single stride he entered the room, closing the door quietly behind him, eyes holding hers.

'*Querida.*' The word caressed her as his gaze ate her up. If he was disappointed she hadn't dressed up, he didn't show it. If anything his eyes glowed warm with approval. 'You haven't changed your mind?'

'Have you?' She stood straighter.

'How could I?' His smile was lop-sided, the most devastating thing she'd ever seen. Then one large palm cupped her cheek and he stepped close. His head lowered and the world faded away.

CHAPTER TWO

'*MALDIÇÃO!* WHAT YOU do to me.' Damaso's voice rumbled through her bones, his hands gripping tight at her hips as his mouth moved against her ear. Marisa shivered as her hyper-aware nerve endings protested at the sensory overload.

She'd never felt so vulnerable, so *naked*. As if their love-making had stripped her bare of every shield she'd erected between herself and a hostile world.

Yet, strangely that didn't scare her. Not with Damaso.

Marisa clutched his bare back, sleek and damp, heaving slightly as he fought for breath. His chest pushed her down into the wide mattress and she revelled in the hard, hot weight of him, even the feel of his hairy legs imprisoning hers.

All night Damaso had stayed, taking his time to seduce her, not just with his body but with the fierce intensity he'd devoted to pleasing her. He was a generous lover, patient when unexpected nerves had made her momentarily stiff and wooden in his arms. She'd been mortified, sure he'd interpret her body's reaction as rejection. Instead he'd looked into her eyes for an endless moment, then smiled before beginning a leisurely exploration of every erogenous zone on her body.

Marisa shivered and held him tight. Holding him in her arms felt...

'I'm too heavy. Sorry.'

Before she could protest, he rolled over onto his back,

pulling her with him. She clung fast, needing to maintain the skin-to-skin contact she'd become addicted to in the night.

Marisa smiled drowsily. She'd been right: Damaso *was* different. He made her feel like a new woman. And that wasn't merely the exhaustion of a long night's loving speaking.

'Are you all right?' She loved the way his voice rippled like dark, molten chocolate in her veins. She'd never known a man with a more sensuous voice.

'Never better.' She smiled against his damp skin then let her tongue slick along the solid cushion of his muscled chest. He tasted of salt and that indefinable spicy flavour that was simply Damaso.

He sucked in a breath and her smile widened. She could stay here, plastered to him, for ever.

'Witch!'

His big hand was gentle on her shoulder, lifting her away. After lying against the furnace of his powerful body, the pre-dawn air seemed cold against her naked skin. She opened her mouth to protest but he was already swinging his legs out of bed. She lifted a hand to catch him back then let it drop. He'd be back once he'd disposed of the condom. Then they could drowse in each other's arms.

Marisa hooked a pillow to her, trying to make up for the loss of Damaso. She buried her nose in its softness, inhaling his scent, letting her mind drift pleasurably.

They had another week left on the tour. A week to get to know each other in all the ways they'd missed. They'd skipped straight to the potent attraction between them, bypassing the usual stages of acquaintanceship and friendship.

Anticipation shimmied through her. The promise of pleasure to come. Who'd have thought she could feel so good when only yesterday…?

ANNIE WEST

23

She shook her head, determined to enjoy the tentative optimism filling her after so long in a grey well of grief.

Marisa looked forward to learning all those little things about Damaso—how he liked his coffee, what made him laugh. What he did with his time when he wasn't looking dark and sulkily attractive like some sexy renegade, or running what someone in the group had called South America's largest self-made fortune.

A sound made her turn. There, framed in the doorway, stood Damaso, watching her.

The first fingers of dawn light limned his tall body, throwing his solid chest, taut abdomen and heavy thighs into relief. The smattering of dark hair on his chest narrowed and trickled in a tantalising line down his body. Marisa lay back, looking appreciatively from between slitted eyes. Even now, sated after their loving, he looked formidably well-endowed. As if he was ready to…

'Go to sleep, Marisa. It's been a long night.' The dark enticement of his voice was edged with an undercurrent she couldn't identify.

Shoving the spare pillow aside, she smoothed her arm over the still-warm space beside her.

'When you come back to bed.' She'd sleep better with him here, cradling her as before. It wasn't sex she craved but his company. The rare sense of wellbeing he'd created.

Damaso stood, unmoving, so long anxiety stroked phantom fingers over her nape. Almost, she reached out to drag up the discarded sheet. She hadn't felt embarrassed by her nudity earlier, when he'd looked at her with approval and even something like adoration in his gaze. But this felt different. His stare was impenetrable, that tiny pucker of a frown unexpected.

The silence lengthened and Marisa had to clench her hands rather than scoop up the sheet. She'd never flaunted herself naked but with Damaso it had felt right. Till now.

He prowled across the room with a grace she couldn't

help but appreciate. He stopped at the edge of the bed, drawing in a deep breath. Then he bent abruptly to scoop something off the floor—his discarded jeans. He dragged the faded denim up those long thighs.

Surely he had underwear? she thought foggily, before the implication struck.

Her gaze met his and rebounded from an impenetrable black stare. Gone was the spark of excitement in his gaze, the wolfish hunger that should have scared her yet had made her feel womanly and powerful. Gone was the sizzle of appreciation she'd so enjoyed when they'd sparred verbally.

His eyes held nothing.

'You're leaving.' Her voice was hollow. Or was that her body? Ridiculously, she felt as if someone had scooped out her insides.

'It's morning.' His gaze flicked to the full-length window.

'Barely. It's still hours till we need to be up.' How she spoke so calmly, she didn't know. She wanted to scuttle across the bed and throw herself into his arms, beg for him to stay.

Beg… Marisa had never begged in her life.

Pride had been one of her few allies. After years facing down family disapproval and the wilder accusations of the ravenous press, she'd been stripped of everything but pride. Now she was tempted to throw even that away as desperation clutched at her.

'Exactly. You should get some sleep.'

She blinked, confused at the hint of warmth in his voice, so at odds with his unreadable expression. She felt like she'd waded into knee-deep water and suddenly found herself miles out to sea.

More than ever Marisa wanted to cover herself. Heat crept from her feet to her face as his hooded gaze surveyed her. Was that a flicker of regret in his eyes?

'It's best I go now.'

Marisa bit down a protest. Perhaps he was trying to protect them from gossip, leaving her room before even the
staff were up. But since the pair of them had missed dinner last night it was probably too late for that.

'I'll see you at breakfast, then.' She sat up, pinning a
bright smile on her face. There would be time enough to
spend together in the next week.

'No. That won't be possible.' He finished the buttons
on his shirt and strode to the bedside table, reaching for
his watch.

'It won't?' She sounded like a parrot! But she couldn't
seem to engage her brain.

He paused in the act of wrapping his watch around his
sinewy wrist.

'Listen, Marisa. Last night was remarkable. *You* were
remarkable. But I never promised you hearts and flowers.'

Indignation stiffened her spine, almost dousing the chill
dread in her veins. 'I hardly think expecting to see you at
breakfast has anything to do with *hearts and flowers,* as
you so quaintly put it.'

Damn him! She leaned down and grabbed the sheet,
pulling it up under her arms. At least now she wasn't quite
so naked.

'You know what I mean.' The hint of a growl tinged his
deep tone and Marisa felt a tiny nub of satisfaction that
she'd pierced his monumental self-assurance. For that was
what it was—that unblinking stare from eyes as cool and
unfeeling as obsidian.

'No, Damaso, I don't know what you mean.' She regarded him with what she hoped looked like unconcern,
despite the fact she was crumbling inside.

'I gave no commitment.' As lover-like statements went,
this one hit rock bottom.

'I didn't ask for any.' Her voice was tight.

'Of course you didn't.' Suddenly he looked away, intent

on his watch. 'You aren't the type. That's why last night was perfect.'

'The type?' Out of nowhere a chill crept over her bare shoulders.

'The type to cling and pretend a night in bed means a lifetime together.'

His eyes met hers again and she felt the force of desire like a smack in the chest. Even as he rejected her the air sizzled between them. Surely she didn't imagine that? Yet the jut of his jaw told her he was intent on ignoring it.

There she'd been, daydreaming that this might be the start of something special. That, after a lifetime of kissing frogs and finding only warty toads, she might actually have found a man who appreciated her for herself.

She should have known better. Such a man didn't exist.

Marisa's stomach plunged, reopening that vast chasm of emptiness inside.

'So what did it mean to you, Damaso?' She clipped the words out.

'Sorry?'

He looked perplexed, as if no woman had ever confronted him like that. But Damaso was an intelligent man. He knew exactly what she was asking.

'Well, clearly you don't want me expecting a repeat of last night.' Even now she waited, breathless, hoping she was wrong. That he *did* want to spend more time with her, and not just for sex. Marisa wanted it so badly that she discovered she'd curled her hands into hard fists, the nails scoring her skin.

'No.' He paused, his face very still. 'This can't go anywhere. There's no point complicating things further.'

Complicating? Now there was a word. The sort of word men used to denigrate what made them uncomfortable.

'So, out of curiosity…' She kept her voice even with an effort. 'What was last night to you? Did you make a bet with the others that you could get me into bed?'

'Of course not! What sort of man do you think I am?'

Marisa raised her eyebrows, surveying his shocked expression with a dispassionate eye even as hurt carved a channel through her insides. 'I don't know, that's the point.'

She'd vowed never to be burned again. Yet here she was, regretting the impulse that had made her open herself to him.

Marisa had been so sure that this time she'd found a man who at least had no hidden agenda. How many times did she have to learn that particular lesson? Bitterness soured her tongue.

'So it was the princess thing, was it? You'd never done it with a royal?'

He loomed over her, his jaw set.

'Why are you being deliberately insulting?'

And it wasn't insulting, the way he was shoving her aside once he'd had what he wanted, without as much as a 'good morning' or a 'thank you' or even a 'see you later'?

Bile burned in the pit of her stomach and she swallowed hard when it threatened to rise. She wouldn't give him the satisfaction of seeing how he'd hurt her. She'd finally reached out to someone, trusted herself with a man…

Marisa bit her cheek, cutting off that train of thought. She'd been right to hesitate when he'd held out his hand to her on the climb. If only she'd followed her instinct and not touched him.

'I merely want to get it clear in my mind.' She rose and wrapped the sheet around her. She still had to look up at him but at least she wasn't sitting like a supplicant at his feet.

'It was sex, great sex. That's all.' Suddenly there was fire in his eyes and a frisson of angry energy sparked from him. 'Is that what you needed to hear?'

'Thank you.' She inclined her head, wondering how she'd managed to invest simple animal attraction with such significance.

Because she was so needy?

Because she was so alone?

What a pathetic woman she was. Maybe her uncle was right after all.

'Marisa?'

She looked up to find Damaso frowning. This time it was concern she read on his features. He'd even moved closer, his hand half-lifted.

Marisa stiffened. She didn't need anyone's pity, especially this man who'd seen her as perfect for just a night, no strings attached. No doubt, like too many others, he saw her as a woman who wouldn't mind being bedded then shunned.

Her skin crawled and pain stabbed hard between her ribs. It was all she could do not to clutch at her side, doubled up at the force of what she felt.

'Well, if we've finished here, you might as well go.' She looked past him to the bathroom. 'I have a yearning for a long, hot shower.' She wished she could scrub away the hurt that welled as easily as she could wash away the scent of his skin on hers. 'And don't worry; I won't look out for you at breakfast.'

'I won't be here. I'm leaving.'

Marisa blinked and looked away, making a production of gathering up her robe where it had been discarded last night.

So there'd never been a chance for them at all. Damaso had always planned to leave and hadn't had the decency to tell her.

That, as nothing else, clarified exactly what he thought of her. She'd never felt so bruised by a man, so *diminished*. Not since the night Andreas had admitted he'd bet his friends he could get her into bed.

Pain swelled and spread, threatening to poleaxe her where she stood. She had to get away.

Marisa drew herself up and headed for the bathroom.

She paused in the doorway, clutching it for support, and looked over her shoulder.

To her surprise, Damaso hadn't moved. He watched her with a scowl on his face. A scowl that did nothing to reduce the magnetism of his honed features.

He opened his mouth to speak and Marisa knew she couldn't bear to hear any more.

'I wonder if that makes me a notch on your belt or you a notch on mine?' Her voice was a throaty drawl, the best she could manage with her frozen vocal chords.

Then, with a flick of the trailing sheet that only long hours' practice in a ball gown and train could achieve, she swept into the bathroom and locked the door behind her.

'It's a pleasure to have you visit, sir.' The manager smiled as he led the way.

Damaso strode through the lodge, his gaze lingering approvingly on the lofty spaces, the mix of local stone, wood and vast expanses of glass that gave this mountain eyrie an aura of refined, ultra-modern luxury. He'd been right to build it, despite the problems constructing on such a site. Even after a mere six months the place had become a mecca for well-heeled travellers wanting to experience something different.

Beyond the massive windows the vista was stunning as the setting sun turned the jagged Andean peaks and their snowy mantle a glowing peach-gold. Below, even the turquoise surface of the glacier-fed river was gilded in the last rays of light.

'Your suite is this way, sir.' The manager gestured Damaso and his secretary forward.

'I'll find it myself, thanks.' Damaso's eyes remained fixed on the remarkable view.

'If you're sure, sir.' The manager paused. 'Your luggage has been taken ahead.'

Damaso nodded dismissal to both men and headed into

the main lounge. Something about the stillness and the feeling of being up above the bustle of the world drew him. Not surprising, given he'd worked like the devil for the last month, his schedule even more overloaded than usual.

Yet, no matter how frenetic his days or how short his nights, Damaso hadn't found his usual pleasure in managing and building his far-flung empire.

Something niggled at him. A sense of dissatisfaction he hadn't the time or inclination to identify.

He looked around, surprised to find the vast room empty. Turning, he strolled towards a door through which came the hum of voices. The bar was this way. Perhaps he'd have a drink before dinner. He had a full night ahead with his laptop before tomorrow's inspection and meetings.

Laughter greeted him as he stepped across the threshold, halting him mid-stride. Rich laughter, infectious and appealing. It coiled through his belly and wrapped tight around his lungs.

His pulse gave a hard thump then took off.

He knew that laugh.

Damaso's neck prickled as if delicate fingers brushed his nape, trailing languidly and drawing his skin tight with shivering awareness.

Marisa.

There she was, her golden hair spilling around her shoulders, her smile pure invitation to the men crowded close. Her eyes danced as she spoke, as she leaned towards them as if sharing some confidence. Damaso couldn't hear what she said over the thunder of blood pounding in his ears.

But there was nothing wrong with his eyes. They traced the black dress that hugged her sinuous curves. The hemline hovered high above her knees, making the most of the contrast between sparkly black stretch fabric and shapely legs that would make grown men sit up and beg.

He should know. He'd spent hours exploring those legs along with every inch of her delectable body. Everything about her had enthralled him, even the long, curving sweep of her spine had been delicious. *Was* delicious.

A wave of energy surged through him. He found himself stepping forward until his brain clicked into gear. Did he mean to stalk across and rip her away from her slavering fans? What then? Throw her over his shoulder and take her to his room?

A resounding *yes* echoed through his whole being.

That stopped him in his tracks.

There'd been a reason he'd left her so abruptly a month before.

Left? He'd run as fast as he could.

It had nothing to do with business commitments and everything to do with the unprecedented things she'd made him *feel*. Not just desire and satiation, but something far bigger.

He'd got out of her bed with every intention of returning to it then had realised for the first time in his life there was nowhere else he wanted to be.

The idea was utterly foreign and completely unnerving.

That was when he'd decided to order a helicopter back to the city. Not his finest moment. Even with his date-them-then-dump-them reputation, he usually displayed far more finesse in leaving a lover.

Even now part of him regretted leaving her after just one night. What they'd shared had been amazing.

Marisa's gurgle of laughter floated in his ears. Damaso swung round and walked back the way he'd come.

Once was enough with any woman. This...reaction to Princess Marisa of Bengaria was an anomaly. He didn't do relationships. He couldn't. Nothing would ever change that.

He strode up the stairs and along a wide corridor to the owner's suite.

She was nothing to him. Just another party girl. Had she even gone home after the rainforest vacation? Probably not. She was probably whiling away a couple of months in exclusive resorts at her nation's expense while trying out some new lovers along the way.

His teeth ground together and his pace picked up.

There was a tap on the conference-room door before a concerned-looking staff member entered.

'I'm sorry to interrupt.' Her eyes shifted from the manager to Damaso, his secretary and the other senior staff at the large table.

'Yes?' the manager asked.

She shut the door behind her. 'One of the guests has been taken ill on the slopes. They're coming back now.'

'Ill, not an accident?' Damaso heard the note of worry in the manager's voice. Illness was one thing; an accident under the supervision of the lodge's staff was another.

'It sounds like altitude sickness. She only arrived yesterday.'

'She?' Damaso surprised himself by interrupting.

'Yes, sir.' The woman twisted her hands together, turning back to her boss. 'That's why I thought you should know. It's Princess Marisa.'

'You've called a doctor?' Damaso found himself standing, his fists braced on the table.

'Don't worry, there's one on staff,' the manager assured him. 'Only the best for our clients, as you know.'

Of course. That was what set Damaso's hotels apart—attention to detail and the best possible services.

'The doctor will be with her as soon as she arrives,' the manager assured Damaso, nodding dismissal to the staff member, who backed out of the door.

Damaso forced himself to sit but his focus was shot. For the next half hour he struggled to concentrate on profits, projections and the inevitable glitches that arose with any new enterprise. Finally he gave up.

'I have something to attend to,' he said as he stood and excused himself from the meeting. 'You carry on.'

He knew he was behaving inexplicably. Since when did Damaso Pires delegate anything he could do himself? Especially when he'd crossed the continent to take these meetings personally.

Five minutes later he was stalking down a quiet corridor, following a nervous maid.

'This is the princess's suite, sir.' She gestured to the double doors with their intricately carved rock-crystal handles. Tentatively she knocked but there was no answer.

Damaso reached for the door and found it unlocked. 'It's okay,' he murmured. 'I'm a friend of the princess.' Ignoring her doubtful gaze, he stepped inside and closed the door behind him.

'Friend' hardly described his relationship with Marisa. They didn't *have* a relationship. Yet curiously he hadn't been able to concentrate on the business that had brought him here till he checked on her himself.

The sitting room was empty but on the far side another set of double doors was ajar. He heard the murmur of a woman's voice followed by the deeper tones of a man.

'Is it possible you're pregnant?'

CHAPTER THREE

'No!' THE WORD jerked out in shock. 'I'm not pregnant.'
Still shivery from nausea, Marisa squinted up at the doctor.

Her? A mother? Why would she bring a child into the
world when she couldn't get her own life on track?

She could just imagine her uncle's horror: impulsive,
unreliable Marisa who frittered her time away with un-
suitable interests rather than knuckling down to the role
she was born to. Not that he had faith in her ability to perform that role.

'You're absolutely certain?' The doctor's gaze penetrated and she felt herself blush as she hadn't since she'd
been a teen.

She waved one hand airily. 'Technically, I suppose
it's possible.' She drew a slow breath, trying to ease her
cramped lungs as images she'd fought hard and long to
obliterate replayed in her head. 'But it was just one night.'

'One night is all it takes,' the doctor murmured.

Marisa shook her head. 'Not this time. I mean we...he
used a condom. Condoms.' The blush in her cheeks burned
like fire. Not from admitting she'd been with a man; after
all, she was twenty-five.

No, the scorching fire in her face and belly came from
the memory of how many condoms they'd gone through—
just how insatiable they'd been for each other. Until Damaso had said he wanted nothing more to do with her.

'Condoms aren't a hundred per cent effective, you

know.' The doctor paused. 'You're not using any other contraceptive?'

'No.' Marisa's mouth twisted. All those years on the Pill while she'd been in training and now... Should she have kept taking it?

'Forgive me for asking but how long ago was this night you're talking about?'

'Just over a month ago. A month and a day, to be exact.' Her voice sounded ridiculously husky. She cleared her throat, telling herself to get a grip. Her periods weren't regular—the time lapse meant nothing. 'But I've had no other symptoms. Surely I would have? It has to be altitude sickness. That's what the guide thought.'

Even now the room swooped around her when she moved.

The doctor shrugged. 'It could be. On the other hand, your nausea and tiredness could indicate something else. It's best we rule out the possibility.' He delved into his bag and held something out to her. 'Go on, it won't bite. It's a simple pregnancy test.'

Marisa opened her mouth to argue but she was too wrung out to fight. The sooner she proved him wrong, the sooner he'd give her something to make her feel better.

Reluctantly she took the kit and headed to the bathroom.

Damaso stood unmoving, staring blindly at the sunlight pouring across the richly carpeted floor.

He didn't know what stunned him more—the possibility of Marisa being pregnant, or the fact he'd been her only recent lover.

When he'd left her in the rainforest he'd expected her to find someone else to warm her bed. The way she'd teased those guys in the bar just last night—pouting and showing off that taut, delectable body—he'd been certain she'd ended the night with a man.

If the press was to be believed, she had no scruples about sharing herself around.

Yet she'd been so certain there'd only been him.

That was why Damaso had stayed where he was during the conversation. Eavesdropping wasn't his style, but he was no fool. His wealth made him a target for fortune hunters. It had seemed wiser to wait and hear what she admitted to the doctor in case she tried to bring a paternity suit.

His mouth tightened. He was no woman's easy prey.

But then he recalled the raw shock in her voice. She wasn't playing coy with the doctor—that much was clear. She'd been speaking the truth about the date. If anything there'd been a tremor almost of fear in her voice at the thought of unplanned pregnancy.

A month and a day, she'd said. So precise. Which meant that if she *was* pregnant it was with Damaso's baby.

Shock rooted him to the spot. He was always meticulous about protection. Inconceivable to think it had failed this time.

Even more inconceivable that he should have a child.

Alone almost from birth, and certainly for as long as he could remember, Damaso had turned what could have been weakness into his greatest strength—self-sufficiency. He had no one and needed no one. It had always been that way. He had no plans for that to change.

He plunged his hand through his hair, raking it back from his forehead. He should have had it cut but this last month he'd thrown himself into work with such single-minded focus there'd been no time for fripperies.

A month and a day. His gut churned.

A murmur of voices dragged his attention back to the other room. In two strides he was there, arm stretched out to open the door.

Then his arm fell as the unthinkable happened.

'Ah, this confirms it, Your Highness. You're going to have a baby.'

* * *

Marisa wrapped her arms around herself as she stared out at the remarkable view. The jagged peaks were topped with an icy covering that the setting sun turned to candy pink, soft peach, brilliant gold and every shade in between. Shadows of indigo lengthened like fingers reaching down the mountain towards her, beckoning.

Realisation struck that this was one invitation she couldn't take up. No more climbing for her, no skydiving or white-water rafting if she was pregnant. All the activities she'd used to stave off the grimness of her life were forbidden.

For the hundredth time Marisa slipped her palm over her belly, wonderment filling her at the fact she was carrying another life inside her.

Could the doctor be wrong?

Marisa felt fine now, just a little wobbly and hollow. She didn't *feel* as if she was carrying a baby.

She'd head to the city and have another test. After all, the kit wasn't infallible.

Marisa didn't know whether to hope it was a mistake or hope it wasn't—she was too stunned to know how she felt.

One thing she was sure of, though—she wouldn't be raising any baby of hers within sight of Bengaria's royal palace. She'd protect it as fiercely as any lioness defending her cub.

'Excuse me, ma'am.' Marisa turned to find a smiling maid at the open door from the suite out to the private terrace where she sat. 'I've brought herbal tea and the chef has baked some sesame-water crackers for you.' She lifted a tray and Marisa caught the scent of fresh baking. Her mouth watered. She hadn't eaten since breakfast, worried about bringing on another bout of nausea.

'I didn't order anything.'

'It's with the hotel's compliments, ma'am.' The maid

hesitated a moment then stepped out onto the terrace, putting her laden tray on a small table.

'Thank you. That's very thoughtful.' Marisa eyed the delicate biscuits and felt a smile crack her tense features. The doctor must have organised this.

Leaving the edge of the balcony, she took a seat beside the table. An instant later the maid bustled back, this time with a lightweight rug.

'It's cooling down.' She smiled. 'If you'd like?' She lifted the rug.

Silently Marisa nodded, feeling ridiculously choked as the downy rug woven in traditional local designs was tucked around her legs. How long since anyone had cossetted her? Even Stefan, who'd loved her, had never fussed over her.

She blinked and smiled as the maid poured scented, steaming tea and settled the plate of biscuits closer.

'Is there anything else I can get you, ma'am?'

'Nothing. Thank you.' Her voice sounded scratchy, as if it came from a long distance. 'Please thank the chef for me.'

Alone again, Marisa sipped the delicately flavoured tea and nibbled a cracker. It tasted divine. Or perhaps that was simply because her stomach didn't rebel. She took another bite, crunching avidly.

She needed to make plans. First, a trip to Lima and another pregnancy test. Then... Her mind blanked at the thought of what came next.

She couldn't bear to go back to her villa in Bengaria. The memories of Stefan were too strong and, besides, the villa belonged to the crown. Now Stefan had gone, it belonged to her uncle and she refused to live as his pensioner. He'd demand she reside in the palace where he could keep an eye on her. They'd had that argument before Stefan had been cold in his grave.

Marisa drew the rug close. She'd have to find a new home. She'd put off the decision for too long. But where?

ANNIE WEST 39

Bengaria was out. Every move she made there was reported and second-guessed. She'd lived in France, the United States and Switzerland as a student. But none were home.

Marisa sipped her tea and bit into another biscuit.

Fear scuttled through her. She knew nothing about being a mother and raising children. Her pregnancy would be turned into a royal circus if she wasn't careful.

Well, she'd just deal with that when and if the time came, and hope she was more successful than in the past.

'Marisa?'

Her head swung round at the sound of a fathoms-deep voice she'd never expected to hear again. Her fingers clenched around delicate bone china as her pulse catapulted.

It really was him, Damaso Pires, filling the doorway to her suite. He looked big and bold, his features drawn in hard, sharp lines that looked like they'd been honed in bronze. Glossy black hair flopped down across his brow and flirted with his collar, but did nothing to soften that remarkable face.

'What are you doing here?' She put the cup down with a clatter, her hand nerveless. 'How did you get in?'

'I knocked but there was no answer.'

Marisa lifted her chin, remembering the way he'd dumped her. 'That usually means the person inside wants privacy.'

'Don't get up.' He stepped onto the terrace, raising his hand, as if to prevent her moving.

She pushed the rug aside and stood, hoping he didn't see her sway before finding her balance. The nausea really had knocked the stuffing out of her.

'I repeat, Senhor Pires, why are you here?' Marisa folded her arms. He might top her by more than a head but she knew how to stand up to encroaching men.

'Senhor Pires?' His brows drew together in a frown that

made her think of some angry Inca god. 'It's a little late for formalities, don't you think?'

'I *know*,' she said, stepping forward, surging anger getting the better of her, 'that I've a right to privacy.'

Her stomach churned horribly as she remembered how he'd made her feel: an inch tall and cheap. She'd have thought she'd be used to it after a lifetime of not measuring up. But this man had wounded her more deeply because she'd been foolhardy enough to believe he was different.

He digested her words in silence, his expression unperturbed.

'Well?' Marisa tapped her foot, furious that her indignation was mixed with an unhealthy dollop of excitement. No matter how annoyed she was, there was no denying Damaso Pires was one fantastic looking man. And as a lover...

'Let me guess. You discovered I was here and thought you'd look me up for old times' sake.' She drew a quick breath that lodged halfway to her lungs. 'I'm afraid I'm not interested in a trip down memory lane. Or in continuing where we left off.'

She had more self-respect than to go back to a man who'd treated her as he had.

She stepped forward. 'Now, if you'll excuse me, I'd like to be alone.'

Her steps petered out when she came up against his impassable form. His spread legs and wide shoulders didn't allow space for her to pass.

Dark eyes bored into hers and something tugged tight in her belly. If only she could put it down to a queasy stomach but to her shame Marisa knew she responded to his overt, male sexuality. A frisson of awareness made her nape tingle and her breasts tighten.

Surely a pregnant woman wouldn't respond so wantonly?

The thought sideswiped her and her gaze flickered from his. Today's news had upended her world, leaving her feeling adrift and frail. What did she know about pregnancy?

'Marisa.' His voice held a tentative edge she didn't re-member. 'Are you all right?'

Her head snapped up. 'I will be when I'm allowed the freedom of my own suite, *alone.*'

He stepped back and she moved away into the sitting room, conscious with every cell in her body of him loom-ing nearby. Even his scent invaded her space, till she had to focus on walking past and not stopping to inhale.

She was halfway across the room, heading for the en-trance, when he spoke again. 'We need to talk.'

Marisa kept walking. 'As I recall, you made it clear last time I saw you that our…connection was at an end.' Val-iantly she kept her voice even, though humiliation at how she'd left herself open to his insulting treatment twisted a searing blade through her insides.

'Are you trying to tell me you thought otherwise?'

Her steps faltered to a halt. If she'd truly been unaffected by his abrupt desertion, she wouldn't be upset at his return, would she? She certainly wouldn't show it. But it was be-yond even Marisa's acting powers to pretend insouciance. The best she could manage was haughty distance.

She needed him out of the way so she could concentrate on the news she still had trouble processing. That she was probably pregnant—with *his* child.

Marisa squeezed her eyes shut, trying to gather her strength. She'd face him later if she had too. Now she needed to be alone.

'I didn't think anything, *Damaso.*' She lingered over his name with dripping, saccharine emphasis. 'What we shared is over and done with.'

Her fingers closed around the door handle but, before she could tug it open, one long arm shot over her shoul-der. A large hand slammed palm-down onto the door be-fore her, keeping it forcibly closed. The heat of Damaso's body encompassed her, his breath riffling her hair as if he was breathing as hard as she.

'What about the fact you're carrying my child?'

She gasped. *How did he know?*

Marisa stared blankly at the strong, sinewy hand before her: the light sprinkling of dark hairs; the long fingers; the neat, short nails.

She blinked, remembering how that hand had looked on her pale breast, the pleasure it had wrought. How she'd actually hoped, for a few brief hours, she'd found a man who valued her for herself. How betrayed she'd felt.

'Marisa?' His voice was sharp.

She drew a jagged breath into tight lungs and turned, chin automatically lifting as he glowered down at her from his superior height.

The sight of him, looking so lofty and disapproving, stoked fire in her belly. She'd deal with him on *her* terms, when *she* was ready.

'I don't know what you think gives you the right to come here uninvited and throw your weight around. But it's time you left. Otherwise I'll have the management throw you out.'

Damaso stared into blazing azure eyes and felt something thump hard in his belly. Energy vibrated off her in waves. Just meeting her stare sent adrenalin shooting into his bloodstream.

His body tensed, his groin tightening at the challenge she projected.

She tempted him even as her disdainful gaze raked him. But it wasn't only dismissal he read in her taut features. The parted lips, the throbbing pulse, the fleeting shadow in her bright eyes gave her away.

He aroused her. He sensed it as surely as he recognised the symptoms in his own body. He hadn't got her out of his system even now.

Without thinking, he put his hand to her face, cupping her jaw so that a frantic pulse jumped against his skin. His fingers brushed her silk-soft hair.

She felt every bit as good as he remembered. Better than he'd allowed himself to believe. He leaned towards her, lowering his head. Discussion could wait.

Sudden pain, a white-hot flash of agony, streaked up his arm.

Stunned, Damaso saw she'd fastened on to a pressure point in some fancy martial arts manoeuvre. He sucked in a breath, tamping down his instinctive response to over-power her. He'd never learned to fight by any code of rules. Where he'd grown up, violence had been endemic, brutal and often deadly. In seconds he could have her flat on her back in surrender. He forced himself to relax, ignoring the lancing pain.

'I'm calling the management.' She breathed heavily, as if it was she, not he, in agony.

'I *am* the management, *pequenina*.'

'Sorry?' Her fierce expression eased into owlish dis-belief.

'I own the resort.' Damaso tried to move his fingers but another dart of pain shot through him. 'You can let me go,' he said through gritted teeth. 'I promise not to touch you.'

'You own it?' Her grip loosened and he tugged his hand free, flexing it as pins and needles spread up his arm. For an amateur, her self-defence skills were impressive.

'I do. It was my team of architects who designed it. My builders who constructed it.'

'The staff report to you?' Her tone was sharp. 'That explains a lot.' Her mouth tightened. 'I don't see why the doctor should run to you with news of my health, even if you employ him. What about patient confidentiality?' She didn't raise her voice but the way she bit out the words, as if chipping off shards of glacial ice, spoke volumes.

Damaso shook his head. 'He didn't breathe a word.'

At her frown he explained, 'I was here, in the suite, when he confirmed your test results.'

She stared up at him, her eyes bright as lasers, and just

as cutting. Damaso felt his cheeks redden, almost as if he blushed under her accusing stare.

It was impossible, of course. Embarrassment was a luxury denied those who'd survived by scavenging off others' refuse. Nothing fazed him, not even the shocked accusation in her glare. He didn't care what others thought.

Yet he looked away first.

'I'd heard you were ill and came to see how you were.'

'How very considerate.' Her hands moved to her hips, pulling the fabric of her designer T-shirt taut over those delectable breasts. Belatedly, Damaso tore his gaze away, only to find himself staring at her flat stomach. She cradled his baby there. The shock of it dried his throat. He wanted to slip his hand beneath the drawstring of her loose trousers and press his palm to the softness of her belly.

The snap of fingers in front of his face startled him.

'Being the owner of this place doesn't give you the right to pry into my private life.'

'It was unintentional. I was coming to see you.'

'That's no excuse for spying on what is my affair.'

'Hardly spying, Marisa.' Her flashing eyes told him she disagreed. 'And this *affair* affects both of us.'

Colour streaked her cheekbones, making her look ridiculously young and vulnerable.

He softened his voice. 'We need to talk.'

She shook her head, her bright hair slipping like spun gold across her dark shirt. With quick grace she turned and crossed the room to the vast windows framing the view of the Andes. She stood rigid, as if his presence pained her.

'A month and a day, remember, Marisa? This is as much my business as yours.'

She didn't move, not so much as a muscle. Her unnatural stillness disturbed him.

'When were you going to tell me?'

Still she said nothing. Damaso's skin tightened till it felt like hundreds of ants crawled over him.

'Or weren't you going to? Were you planning to get rid of it quietly with no one the wiser?'

Damaso grimaced at the pungent sourness filling his mouth. Had she decided to get rid of his child?

His child!

He'd been stunned by the news he was to be a father. It had taken hours to come to grips with the fact he'd have a child—blood of his blood, flesh of his flesh.

For the first time in his life, he'd have family.

The idea astounded him, scared him. He, who'd never expected to have a family of his own. Yet to his amazement part of him welcomed the idea.

He didn't know exactly how he expected this to play out. But one thing was absolutely certain: no child of his would be abandoned as he'd been.

No child of his would grow up alone or neglected.

It would know its father.

It would be cared for.

He, Damaso Pires, would make sure of that personally. The intensity of his determination was stronger than anything he'd known.

He must have moved for he found himself behind Marisa. Her hair stirred with each breath he exhaled. His fingers flexed, as if to reach for her hips and pull her to him, or shake her into speech.

'Say something!' Damaso wasn't used to being ignored, especially by women he'd known intimately. Especially when something as profoundly important as this lay between them.

'What do you want me to say?' When she turned, her eyes were wide and over-bright. 'No, I hadn't planned an abortion? No, I hadn't decided when I'd tell you, if at all? I haven't had time even to get my head around the idea of being pregnant.'

She jabbed a finger into his sternum. 'I don't see this being as much your business as mine.' Her finger stabbed again. '*If* I'm pregnant, I'll be the one carrying this baby. *I'll* be the one whose body and life and future will change irrevocably. Not you.'

Her finger wobbled against his chest; her whole hand was shaking, Damaso realised. He wrapped his hand around hers but she tugged loose from his hold and backed away as if his touch contaminated her.

Too late for that, my fine lady.

Marisa watched his harsh mouth curve in a smile that could only be described as feral. He looked dangerous and unpredictable, his eyes a black gleam that made her want to step back again. Instead she planted her feet.

How had he turned the tables, so his intrusion on her privacy had become a litany of accusations against *her*? Enough was enough. She was tired of being bullied and judged.

'Obviously you've had time to jump to all sorts of conclusions about this pregnancy, if there is one.' She fixed him with a stony gaze.

'You deny it?' He scowled.

'I reserve judgement until I've got a second opinion.' She braced her hands on her hips, refusing to cower before his harsh expression. 'But obviously you've gone beyond that stage.'

'I have.' His gaze dropped to her stomach and she felt a hot stirring inside as if he'd touched her there. Abruptly, his dark eyes locked on hers again. 'There's only one sensible option.'

'Really?'

'Of course.' His brooding features tightened, a determined light in his eyes. 'We'll marry.'

CHAPTER FOUR

MARISA COULDN'T PREVENT the ripple of laughter that slipped from her mouth.

'Marry?' She shook her head. Astonishment punctured the bubble of tension cramping her chest. 'You've got to be kidding. I don't even know you.'

His downturned mouth and furrowed brow told her he didn't appreciate her levity. Or maybe he didn't like the panicked edge that see-sawed through her laughter.

Marisa didn't like it either. She sounded, and felt, too close to the edge.

'You knew me well enough for us to create a baby together.' His deep voice held a bite that eradicated the last of her semi-hysterical laughter. It brought her back to earth with a thump.

'That's not knowing. That's sex.'

He shrugged, lifting those broad shoulders she'd clung to through their night together. She'd dug her nails into his flesh as ecstasy had consumed her. She'd never wanted to let him go and had snuggled against his solid shoulder through the night.

Until he'd made it clear he wanted nothing more to do with her.

'You've changed your tune.' Did he hear the echo of hurt in her tone? Marisa was beyond caring; she just knew she had to scotch this insanity.

'That was before there was a child, *princesa*.'

She stiffened. 'There still may not be one. I won't be sure till I've had another test. It could have been a false positive.'

Damaso tilted his head, as if examining a curious specimen. 'The idea of a child is so horrible to you?'

'No!' Marisa's hand slipped to her stomach then, realising what she'd done, she dropped her arm to her side. 'I just need to be sure.'

He nodded. 'Of course. And when we are sure, we'll marry.'

Marisa blinked. Why did talking to Damaso Pires feel like trying to make headway against a granite boulder?

'This is the twenty-first century. People don't have to marry to have children.'

He crossed his arms, accentuating the solid muscle of his torso beneath the pristine business shirt, reinforcing his formidable authority. Wearing casual trekking gear, he'd been stunning, but dressed for business he added a whole new cachet to the 'tall, dark, handsome' label.

If only she didn't respond at that visceral, utterly feminine level. She couldn't afford to be distracted by such rampant masculinity.

'We're not talking about *people*. We're talking about us and our child.'

Our child. The words resonated inside Marisa, making her shiver. Making the possibility of pregnancy abruptly real.

She put out a hand and grabbed the back of a nearby settee as the world swam.

Suddenly he was there before her, his hand firm on her elbow. 'You need to sit.'

It was on the tip of her tongue to say she needed to be alone but she felt wobbly. Perhaps she should rest—she didn't want to do anything that might endanger her baby.

And just like that she made the transition from protest to acceptance.

Not only acceptance but something stronger—something like anticipation.

Which showed how foolish she was. This situation had no built-in happy ending.

Marisa let Damaso guide her to a seat. The pregnancy no longer felt like a possibility, to be disproved with a second test. It felt *real*. Or maybe that was because of the way Damaso held her—gently, yet as if nothing could break his hold.

She lowered her eyes, facing the thought of motherhood alone. Learning to be a good mother when she had no idea what that was. The only things she'd ever been good at were sports and creating scandal.

Marisa bit down a groan, picturing the furore in the Bengarian royal court, the ultimatums and machinations to put the best spin on this. The condemnation, not just from the palace, but from the press.

In the past she'd pretended not to feel pain as the palace and the media had dealt her wound after wound, slashing at her as if she wasn't a flesh-and-blood woman who bled at their ferocious attacks.

'I'll get the doctor.' Damaso crouched before her, his long fingers still encircling her arm.

'I don't need a doctor.' She needed to get a grip. Wallowing in self-pity wasn't like her and she couldn't afford to begin now. More than ever she had to find a way forward, not just for herself, but for her child.

'You need someone to care for you.'

'And you're appointing yourself my protector?' She couldn't keep the jeering note from her voice.

For the first time since he'd shouldered his way into her suite, he looked discomfited. Eventually he spoke.

'The baby is my responsibility.' He spoke so solemnly, her skin prickled.

'Sorry to disillusion you but I don't need a protector. I look after myself.' She'd learned independence at six, when her mother had died. Now she only had vague memories of warm hugs and wide smiles, of bedtime stories and an exquisite, never-to-be-repeated certainty she was precious.

'Reading the press reports about your activities, I can see how well you've done that.'

Marisa's chin shot up, her furious gaze locking with his. 'You shouldn't believe everything you read in the press.'

Except everyone did, and eventually Marisa had given up trying to explain. Instead she'd been spurred to a reckless disregard for convention and, at times, her own safety.

That stopped now. If there was a baby...

'So I should give you the benefit of the doubt?' He leaned closer and her breath snared in her lungs. Something happened to her breathing when Damaso got near.

'I don't care what you think of me.' In the past that had worked for her. But with Damaso things were suddenly more complicated.

'I can see that. But I also see you're unwell. This news has come as a shock.'

'You're not shocked? Just how many kids do you have littered around the place?' Marisa strove for insouciance but didn't quite achieve it. Absurdly, the thought of him with a string of other women made her stomach cramp.

'None.'

Ah. Maybe that explained his reaction.

'Let me propose an interim arrangement.' He sat back on his haunches, giving her space.

It was a clever move, she realised, as her racing pulse slowed.

'Yes?'

'You want a second pregnancy test. Let me take you to the city and arrange a medical examination. Then, if the results are positive, we talk about the future.' He spread his hands in a gesture of openness.

Yet the glint in his dark eyes hinted things weren't so simple.

But what did she have to lose? He only proposed what she'd already decided. And, as owner of the lodge, he could get her out of here quickly, without waiting for a scheduled flight.

'No strings?'

'No strings.'

Doubt warred with caution and a craven desire to let someone else worry about the details for once. If he tried to trample her, he'd learn he was messing with the wrong woman.

'Agreed.' She put out her hand, using the business gesture to reinforce that this was a deal, not a favour. A tiny bubble of triumph rose at his surprised look.

But, when his hand encompassed hers, engulfing her in its hard warmth, her smile faded.

Marisa twisted in her seat as the helicopter's rotors slowed. Damaso saw anger shimmer in her eyes as she glared at him. 'You said we'd go to the city.'

'São Paolo is inland, not too far away.'

'You lied to me.' Her mouth set in a mutinous pout that made him want to pull her close and kiss those soft, pink lips till all she could do was sigh his name.

Damaso stared, grappling with both his urgent response and surprise at her vehemence.

'I said I'd take you to have your pregnancy confirmed.' Even now, after a day to absorb the news, he felt a pooling of emotion at the thought of the baby they'd created.

'In a city. That's what we agreed. That's why I agreed to come to Brazil with you. I thought when we transferred from the plane we were going into São Paolo.'

'I've organised for a doctor to visit you here, in my private residence.'

Marisa's gaze roved the view beyond his shoulder, past the ultra-modern mansion looking over a pristine beach and aquamarine water to the tangle of lush forest rising up the slope beyond. 'It's secluded,' he murmured. 'I own the whole island.'

'You think that's a recommendation? I have no interest in your *private* estate.' Her jaw clenched, as if she read what he'd tried to suppress—the physical hunger that still plagued him.

From the moment he'd seen Marisa, he'd wanted her. One night in her bed had only sharpened his appetite, and not just for her lithe body. He wanted to possess all of her: her quicksilver energy; her laughter; her earthy, generous sexuality and that feeling she shared some rare, exquisite gift with him. Even arguing with her was more stimulating than sealing a multi-billion-dollar deal.

This craving disturbed him. Usually he found it easy to move on from a woman. But then, he'd never had one carry his child before. That must be why he couldn't get her out of his head.

'Lots of women would give their eye teeth to be here.'

She looked at him with a supercilious coolness that made him feel, for the first time in years, inferior. 'Not me.'

The smack to his lungs, the hot blast of blood to his face, shocked him to the core.

He was Damaso Pires, self-made, successful, sought after. He bowed to no one, gave way to no one. He'd banished the scars of childhood with the most convincing cure of all: success. Inferiority was a word he'd excised from his personal lexicon years before.

'You're not impressed, *princesa?*'

Her eyes widened a fraction. Because he'd called her 'princess', or because he'd growled the words between gritted teeth?

'It's not about being impressed.' She spoke coolly. 'I simply don't like being lied to.'

Damaso drew a slow breath and unclicked his seat belt. 'It wasn't a lie. I often commute to the city from here.' He put up his hand before she could interrupt. 'Besides, I thought you'd appreciate the privacy of my estate, rather than go to a clinic or have an obstetrician visit you in a city hotel.' He stared into her sparking blue eyes. 'Less chance of the paparazzi getting hold of the story, since my staff are completely discreet.'

He watched her absorb that: the quick swallow, the rushed breath through pinched nostrils.

Ah, not so superior now. Obviously she didn't want news of her condition made public.

'Thank you.' Her quick change of tone surprised him. 'That's thoughtful of you. I hadn't considered that.' She fumbled at her seatbelt so long, he looked down and saw her hands were unsteady. He wanted to reach out and do it for her but her closed expression warned him off.

At last the seatbelt clicked open and she pushed it away. 'But don't ever lie to me again. I don't appreciate being lured here under false pretences.'

It was on the tip of Damaso's tongue to say he wasn't interested in luring her anywhere. But that was exactly what he'd done, because it suited his purposes. Much as it went against the grain to admit it, she had a point.

'Very well. In future you will be consulted.'

Her perfect dark-gold eyebrows arched. 'In future,' she corrected in a voice of silk-covered steel, 'I *decide*.'

In one easy movement she swung her legs out of the door, held open by one of his staff, and strode away from the tarmac of the landing pad without waiting to see if he followed.

She walked like a princess, head up, shoulders straight, with a firm gait that wasn't a stride but somehow conveyed her absolute confidence that the world would rearrange itself to fit her expectations.

He told himself she was spoiled and wilful. Instead, he found himself admiring her. He wasn't used to having his arrangements questioned.

Her thanks for his thoughtfulness had surprised him.

Her firm insistence on making her own decisions was
something he understood.

He watched the cream linen of her trousers tighten
around her shapely backside with each step, watched the
way her hair, a thick curtain of gold, swung between her
narrow shoulder-blades.

In future he'd remember to take the time to convince
Princess Marisa to agree to his decisions before he put
them into action.

Damaso's mouth curved in a rare smile as he got down
from the chopper and followed her. Persuading Marisa presented all sorts of interesting possibilities.

Marisa strode from the house mere moments after the doctor had left her. Not just any doctor, but the region's best
obstetrician, apparently, and a woman to boot. Damaso had
thought of everything.

No doubt he was closeted with the doctor, receiving
confirmation of the pregnancy.

Marisa's step quickened till she reached the soft, white
sand of the beach where she tugged off her sandals.

She wanted to sprint down the beach till her lungs
burned, swim out into the impossibly clear depths of the
bay till she was totally isolated from the luxury mansion
full of staff. Climb the rocky headland that jutted at the
far end of the beach.

Anything to feel free again, if only briefly.

Marisa sighed. She needed to be more cautious now she
was pregnant. She could sprint, of course, but the security
guard trailing her would think she was under threat. If she
explained, he'd feel obliged to race up the beach beside her,
destroying her enjoyment.

Reluctantly she looked back and there he was: a bulky
figure trying, ineffectually, to blend into the foliage just
above the beach.

Even in Bengaria she'd had more freedom!

Marisa waded into the warm shallows till she was up to her calves, letting the tiny waves lap against her legs. She breathed deep, trying to feel at one with the gentle surge and wane of the water, focusing on slowing her pulse.

It was years since she'd practised the techniques she'd used to prepare herself for a gymnastics competition. If ever she'd needed to feel grounded, it was now.

She was going to be a mother.

Joy, mingled with fear, spilled through her veins. Despite the circumstances, she couldn't regret the child she carried. Did she have what it took to raise it and care for it the way it deserved?

She had no one to turn to, no one to trust, but Damaso: a stranger who saw this baby as a responsibility.

Fleetingly, Marisa thought of the others who'd claim a say in her child's future.

Her relatives. She shivered and wrapped her arms around her torso. No matter what it took, she'd keep her child safe from them.

The advisors of the Bengarian Court. No, they'd simply follow her uncle's lead.

Her friends. Marisa bit her lip. She'd given up seeking real friends long ago—after the few she'd had were ostracised by the palace for being too uncultured and common for her to mix with.

Which left her alone.

Her smile was crooked as she gazed towards the mainland. She'd always been alone, even when Stefan had been alive. There was only so much he'd been able to do to support her. He'd had his own troubles. She'd been lucky—as a mere princess, she was window dressing, for she'd never inherit the crown. Poor Stefan, as crown prince, had borne the brunt of everyone's expectations from birth.

'Marisa.'

She swung around to see Damaso at the water's edge. In lightweight trousers and a loose white shirt, sleeves rolled up past his elbows, he looked too sexy for her peace of mind.

Her heart crashed against her ribs and her lungs tightened, squeezing the air from her body till she felt breathless and light-headed. Her skin tingled as his dark gaze slid over her. She was burning up, a pulse throbbing between her legs.

'We need to talk.'

'You don't waste time, do you?' She crossed her arms. 'What do you mean?'

'You've come straight from the doctor, haven't you?' He'd said they'd find out if she was pregnant then they'd talk about the future. 'Can't you give me some breathing space?'

She hadn't meant to say it aloud but she felt hemmed in by news of the pregnancy, by the security guard, by the fact she'd have to tell her uncle. Above all, by this man, who for reasons she didn't understand made her *feel,* right to her core.

'I'm not going to hurt you.'

Marisa sucked in a breath. 'I'm not afraid of you, Damaso.' How dared he even think it? She, who'd never turned from a physical challenge in her life.

'No?' She supposed that tightening of his mouth at one corner was supposed to be a smile. She didn't see anything funny about the situation.

'Absolutely not.' Facing down a sexy Brazilian with an ego the size of Rio's Sugarloaf Mountain was nothing compared with what she'd dealt with before.

Yet she didn't move to join him. Instead he waded out to meet her, the water covering first his bare feet then soaking his trousers. Marisa's mouth dried as if she hadn't tasted water in a week.

He stopped a breath away, his scent mingling with the salt tang of the water.

'How do you feel?'

'Fine.' It was true. She'd been sick again this morning but tea and dry toast in bed and a slow start to the day had made the nausea easier to handle.

'Good. We need to talk.' His intent scrutiny made the hairs stand up on the back of her neck. Some sixth sense told her he wasn't here to continue an argument about marrying for the baby's sake.

'What is it?' She'd received bad news before and, attuned after Stefan's recent death, she knew Damaso would rather not break this news. 'Is it the baby?' Her voice was a hoarse whisper. 'Did the doctor tell you something she didn't tell me?'

He took her elbow as she lunged towards him, her heart pounding frantically. 'It's not the baby. Nothing like that.'

Instinctively Marisa planted her hand on his chest, needing his support. She felt the steady thud of his heart beneath her palm and managed to draw a calming breath. She pushed down a moment's terror that there'd been something the doctor hadn't shared.

'What, then? Tell me!'

His mouth thinned to a grim line. 'It's the press. There's been a report that you're pregnant.'

'Already?' Her head swung towards the multi-level residence commanding the half-moon bay.

'It wasn't one of my staff. No one here would dream of going to the press with a story about a guest of mine.'

'How can you be sure?' Something passed across his face that Marisa couldn't fathom. 'For the right sort of money...'

He shook his head. 'My people wouldn't betray me.'

Fleetingly, Marisa wondered what bond could possibly be so strong between a billionaire and his paid staff.

'It was someone from the hotel in Peru. One of the kitchen staff. They overheard my request for something to settle your morning sickness.'

'*Your* request?' Marisa dragged her hand back from his

chest as if scalded. She'd thought the doctor had ordered tea and crackers for her.

The thought of Damaso leaving her room and heading to the kitchens to make a personal request on her behalf made her still. It didn't fit with the way he'd treated her. But, now she considered it, since learning of her pregnancy he'd been intent on looking after her.

She'd been too annoyed at his high-handed actions to acknowledge it, possibly because his way of helping was to try taking control.

'It was a new staff member. Now an ex-staff member. They won't work in any of my enterprises again.' The steely note in his voice made Marisa feel almost sorry for whoever had thought to profit from gossiping to the press.

'I thought I'd have a little more time before it became public.' She tried for nonchalance, though an undercurrent of nerves made her body tense. Once the news was out...

'It's an unconfirmed rumour. Nothing they can prove.'

'I suppose I've weathered worse.'

Memories rose of being pilloried at just fifteen. Someone on the gymnastics squad had leaked the fact that Marisa was on the Pill and it had been splashed across the press, along with photos of her partying.

No one had been interested in the fact she'd been prescribed the medication to help deal with periods so painful they'd interfered with her training, or that the parties were strictly chaperoned. Everything had been twisted. Innocent glances in photos turned into lascivious stares, smiles into wanton invitations. They'd portrayed her as a little slut, precocious, uncontrollable and without morals.

Once typecast by the paparazzi, there'd been no way to turn the tide of popular opinion.

The palace had been ineffectual. It was only years later she'd begun to suspect the palace had left her to fend for herself—a brutal lesson in dancing to her uncle's tune or else. Eventually, after years fighting the tide, Marisa had given up and begun to take perverse pleasure in living down to expectations.

She breathed deep and stepped back, registering anew the gentle swish of water against her legs.

'At least I don't have to worry about the press here.' She pasted on a smile. 'Thank you, Damaso. It seems you were right. If I'd stayed in a hotel, I'd be under siege.'

Was it her imagination or did his gaze warm a fraction? 'In the circumstances, I'd prefer not to have been right.'

It was tempting to bask in the fragile sensation of being looked after. But she couldn't afford to get used to it.

They walked side by side up the beach, scooping up their discarded shoes and turning towards the house.

They'd just stepped onto the cropped emerald turf when a white-coated servant appeared and spoke to Damaso in swift Portuguese.

'What is it?' Marisa sensed the instant change in him.

'A message for you. You had a phone call and they're calling back in fifteen minutes.'

'Who was it?' But already Marisa felt her stomach plunge like a rock off a precipice. She knew exactly who it had been.

His words confirmed her fears. 'The King of Bengaria.'

CHAPTER FIVE

DAMASO PACED THE shaded loggia, the tray of coffee and his laptop forgotten. Through the full-length glass he had a perfect view of Marisa.

He'd begun to wish he hadn't given her privacy to take her call. Not when instinct urged him to march in and rip the phone out of her hand.

That, by itself, gave him pause.

He didn't interfere in the lives of others. He was never interested enough to do so. But, watching Marisa stand to attention beside the desk in his study, Damaso knew an inexplicable urge to break the habit of a lifetime.

What was the King saying? As far as he could see, she hadn't had the chance to say much. Yet her body spoke volumes. Her spine was ramrod-stiff and she paced with military precision, like a soldier on parade. Her mouth was a flat line and her shoulders inched high towards her ears.

She wore the figure-hugging white capri pants and yellow crop top from the beach. There she'd looked like a sexy embodiment of the summer sun—bright and vibrant. Now, with her pinched features, she seemed like another woman.

To hell with it. He strode towards the glass doors that separated them.

Then he stopped, for now Marisa was talking.

This close he heard her voice, though not the words. She spoke crisply, with definite emphasis. Her chin lifted and she looked every inch the pure-bred aristocrat: haughty and regal.

She paused, as if listening, then spoke sharply, her arm slicing the air in a violent sweep. She turned and marched across the room, her toned body taut and controlled, ripe with pride and determination.

Damaso stared, unable to believe the visceral stab of desire that hit him as he watched her lay down the law. A woman in control—that had never been his fantasy. Always he was the hunter, the master, the one who set the rules.

Was that what had made their night together so cataclysmically memorable? The sense of two matched people coming together as equals, neither in control?

If that was so, why this unfamiliar urge to protect her? It had to be because of the baby. Since he'd learned of her pregnancy she'd become the centre of his thoughts—a rival even to his business empire, which had given him purpose and identity all his adult life.

Damaso breathed hard, aware he was on unfamiliar ground.

It took him a few moments to realise she'd ended the call. Now she stood, shoulders slumped, hands braced wide on the desk. As he watched, her head bowed in a move that spoke of a bone-deep weariness.

Something stirred in Damaso's belly. That tickle of concern he'd first felt the morning he'd left her in the jungle. When, despite her anger and her hauteur, he'd sensed something out of kilter in her queenly dismissal of him.

'Marisa?' He was through the door before he had time to reconsider.

Instantly she straightened. If he hadn't been looking, he'd never have seen the strain etching her face before she smoothed it.

'Yes?'

Damaso stared, confronted by a cool, self-contained princess, the hint of a polite smile curving her soft lips.

Only the glitter of strong emotion in her eyes, now dark-ened to midnight sapphire, belied that regal poise.

'What did he want?'

Her delicate eyebrows arched high, as if surprised at his temerity in questioning her. That cut no ice with Damaso.

Silently he waited. Eventually her gaze skittered from his. She shrugged. 'King Cyrill wasn't pleased when his public relations advisors told him there were rumours I was pregnant.'

'They were quick off the mark!'

Her mouth tightened. 'They're always careful to keep tabs on me.' Did he imagine an emphasis on 'me'?

'And what did you say? Did you confirm the preg-nancy?' Damaso wished he knew more about the Bengar-ian monarchy. He'd had no interest in the small European kingdom till someone on the trek had pointed Marisa out as the infamous party princess he'd vaguely heard about. How close were she and the King? Obviously their con-versation had taxed Marisa's strength, despite her show of unconcern.

She half-turned and stroked a finger idly along the gleaming surface of his desk. 'It's none of his business.' Defiance edged her tone. 'But then I realised there was nothing to be gained by waiting. I'd have to face the flak sooner or later.'

'Flak? Because you're not married?' He knew next to nothing about royals—except that their lives seemed steeped in tradition.

She laughed, the sound so bitter he wondered if it hurt. 'Not married. Not in a relationship. Not seeing a man vet-ted and approved by the palace. Not doing what a Bengar-ian princess is supposed to do. Take your pick.'

Damaso stepped closer, drawn by the pain in her voice. 'What is it you're supposed to be doing?'

Marisa's head lifted, her chin angling, as if facing an opponent.

'Being respectably and sedately courted by a suitable prince, or at least a titled courtier. Keeping out of the press, except in carefully staged set pieces arranged by the palace. Not causing a scandal, particularly now.'

'Now? Why now?' Why hadn't he taken time to find out more about Marisa's European homeland?

Because his focus was and always had been on building his business. That was what he lived for. What made him who he was.

Marisa straightened, but once again refused to meet his gaze. 'I'd like to say it's because the country is still in mourning for Stefan. But it's because Cyrill doesn't want any scandal in the lead up to his coronation.'

At Damaso's enquiring look, she explained. 'Cyrill is my uncle, my father's younger brother. My father was king and after my father died Cyrill was Regent of Bengaria for eleven years, till Stefan came of age at twenty-one.' She sucked in a breath and for a moment he thought she'd finished speaking. 'Stefan was my twin brother and King of Bengaria. He died in a motorboat accident two months ago.'

Two months ago? Damaso frowned, searching her face. Her brother had been barely cold in his grave when Damaso had met Marisa. She hadn't acted like a woman grieving the loss of a loved one.

Yet what did he know of grief or loss? He'd never had so much as a best friend, let alone family.

'You don't like your uncle?'

Marisa turned startled eyes on him, then laughed again, the sound short and sharp. 'I can't stand him.' She paused. 'He was our guardian after our father died and to all intents and purposes King.' Her voice held a sour note that told far more about their relationship than her words. 'Even when Stefan was crowned, Cyrill was there in the background, trying to manipulate opinion whenever Stefan dared to instigate change.'

'But now you're free of him.'

   Marisa turned to stare out across the lawns to the sandy
crescent of Damaso's private beach. It looked so peaceful,
so perfect. But the sight did nothing to calm her. Not after
Cyrill's threats.

   The last day and a half, she'd been in a state of shock.
And now this… Once more her uncle threatened to turn
her life inside out.

   'It's not that simple.' Foolishly, she'd thought it was.
With Stefan gone, Marisa had no interest in Bengarian
politics. She just hadn't counted on the fact that Bengaria
wasn't ready to wash its hands of her. A fact her uncle had
been at pains to point out.

   'Marisa? What is it?' Damaso's voice deepened and she
forced herself to look up, only to find herself pinioned by
his questioning gaze. Between Damaso and her uncle, she
had no chance of peace! What she needed was time to sort
herself out, away from domineering men. Even if one of
them made her question her need for solitude.

   'Are you going to tell me or will I ring your uncle?'

   Shock warred with laughter at the idea of anyone calling Cyrill on the spur of the moment. Who would win? Her
uncle, with his smug self-importance and devious ways,
or Damaso with his my-way-or-the-highway approach?

   'He wouldn't talk to you.'

   'No one is that inaccessible, Marisa.' Damaso crossed
his arms, one slashing dark eyebrow lifting in enquiry.
He didn't bluster but there was such innate determination
in his stance, his expression, she had no doubt her uncle
would come off the worse in a contest of wills. 'Why aren't
you free of him?'

   With a sigh, she sank into a nearby armchair. 'Because
he holds the purse strings. As simple as that.' And, fool
that she was, she hadn't seen it coming. How could she not
have thought of it earlier?

   Because she'd been wiped out by grief, grimly battling
to face each new day after Stefan's death and not to wear

her pain publicly. She'd actually thought she could break her ties with the palace. How naïve, especially after experiencing her uncle's Machiavellian ways first-hand.

Every penny she had was now sequestered by royal command. How was she going to find herself a home and provide for her child when everything she owned no longer belonged to her? Marisa bit her cheek hard as she felt her mouth tremble.

She'd thought she was adrift and rudderless without Stefan, but now…

'He's threatened to stop your allowance?' Damaso's tone was casual.

'Yes, he's stopping my *allowance,* as you call it—the money invested for me by my parents.' She drew a deep breath. 'He's also threatening to freeze my assets, including my personal bank account.'

Fire kindled in Damaso's eyes. 'By what right?'

'By right of the sovereign. In Bengaria, that means everything. He has control over all members of his extended family if he chooses to use it.' She sank back in her seat, weary beyond reckoning. It was a power even her strict father wouldn't have invoked. 'It's legal. Just not ethical.'

That was Cyrill all over. Anything to get his own way.

Who'd have thought his plans would still include her after the breach between them? She shuddered, wondering if he really wanted her back in Bengaria, or whether this was an elaborate tactic to make her suffer for repudiating him.

Damaso sank down before her, his gaze capturing hers. 'You'll want for nothing now you're with me.'

He meant it. It was there in his steady stare.

'Except I'm not *with* you! I haven't agreed to marry you.' Her heart hammered high in her throat as she read his implacable expression.

He didn't say anything. He didn't need to. This was a

man used to giving orders and having them obeyed. Right now he wanted her.

Correction: *he wanted her baby.*

Chilled to the marrow, Marisa crossed her arms, shielding her child.

Damaso and Cyrill both wanted to control her for their own ends. Both wanted her child—Damaso for reasons she didn't fully understand, Cyrill because her baby had royal blood, making it a potential pawn in his elaborate schemes to extend the power of the crown.

'So, go out and get a job. Support yourself.' Impatience edged Damaso's tone. Marisa had heard it before from people who didn't know her but believed all they read in the press.

About to hide her feelings behind the usual show of casual disdain, something stopped her.

Damaso's good opinion shouldn't matter. He'd already shown how little he thought of her. Yet she paused. She was tired of being judged and found wanting.

'You think I haven't tried?' At the surprise in his eyes, she turned away, hunching her shoulder against his disbelief. 'Who'd take me seriously, especially when the press start hounding me, pestering my employer and other staff? Making bets on how long I'll stick it out?'

She shuddered, remembering how her naïve optimism had been shattered again and again. Failure had bred failure. Her reputation hung like an albatross around her neck: dilettante; party girl; frivolous, unable to stick to anything. How many times had she tried to do something worthwhile, only to have the opportunity snatched away?

Last time the press had camped outside the special school where she'd volunteered until both staff and children had become unsettled and nervous. Finally the director had asked her not to come any more.

'I've tried. Don't think I haven't.' Marisa heard the shaky echo of defeat in her voice. It scared her. All she had left was

her independence. She'd fought so long for that and she had
to be strong now.

Instantly she was on her feet, needing to move, to think.

But Damaso was before her, his large hand wrapping
around her wrist before she could take a step.

He looked down into her pale face, her wide eyes, shadowed now instead of bright, and felt the tiniest tremor ripple
under her skin. Slowly she lifted her chin as if distancing
herself from him. Was it an unconscious gesture, that superior set of the head, or a practised move designed to scare
off plebeians such as himself?

Yet, holding her slender wrist, it struck him that behind
the air of well-bred hauteur lurked a world of pain.

Damaso was an expert at reading people. It was a skill
he'd cultivated and exploited even as a child, gauging which
adults would respond to a skinny kid's wide-eyed hungry
look with an offer of food and which with a swift kick.
But in all his years his understanding had rarely turned
to empathy.

Yet, what other explanation could there be for this protectiveness? This need to wrap his arms around her and
hold her close?

There were violet smudges under her fine eyes and she
couldn't quite disguise the way her lips trembled. She did a
magnificent job of hiding it but once more he recognised a
vulnerability about Princess Marisa of Bengaria that went
far deeper than the mere loss of funds.

His hand gentled on her arm.

'Whatever he does, he can't touch you here.'

It was meant for reassurance, but he felt her stiffen.

'But I haven't said I'd stay.'

Sharp heat twisted in Damaso's belly. He refused to
countenance a future where his child grew up without him.
His child.

The words were like a beam of light, illuminating a hollow in the dark void of his soul he'd never known till now.

He'd never thought to belong to anyone. Yet he knew with deep gut instinct that he had to be part of his baby's life. His child would have a father, a family, such as he'd never known. His child would never be alone and frightened. It would never want for anything.

Damaso's hand tightened around Marisa's.

He wasn't the sort to step back from what he wanted. He'd never have survived the slums if he hadn't learned early to take life by the throat and hang on tight.

But there was more than one way to get what he wanted. He was fast learning Marisa wasn't the two-dimensional party girl the world thought she was. He'd seen hints of it from the first. Her revelations about her uncle and her distress when Damaso had snapped that she should get a job had shattered that image.

'Let me go, Damaso. You're hurting me.'

Yet she stood stock still, too proud to fight his hold. Unexpectedly, his chest squeezed at her defiant posture. Holding her as he did, he felt her tremble.

'Am I?' He slid his fingers down to wrap around hers and lifted her hand, inhaling the tang of her skin's scent. Slowly he lowered his head and pressed his lips to the inside of her wrist. Instantly her pulse flickered hard and fast. He kissed her again and heard her swift intake of breath.

'Damaso. Let go of me.' Her voice had a distinct wobble. It reminded him of her broken cry of ecstasy the first time she'd climaxed beneath him. Heat saturated his skin as his libido shifted gear, rousing in an instant.

'What if I don't want to?' Her fingers twitched in his hold as he kissed her again.

Damaso didn't look up. Instead he held her hand and laved the centre of her palm, feeling her tiny shudder of reaction and its echo in the tightening of his groin.

It was a warning that the seducer could also be the seduced. But Damaso had no doubt who was in control. He'd keep Marisa here by whatever means worked—by force, if necessary—but far better to convince her she wanted to remain exactly where she was.

'*I* want you to stay.'

'Really?'

He tugged her hand and she stumbled a half-step closer. Damaso took advantage of her momentum to wrap his other arm around her and draw her close. Slowly, with a thoroughness designed to break the strongest will, he pressed his lips to her wrist again, then higher, planting firm kisses along Marisa's forearm. When he got to her elbow she jerked in his hold, her breath a soft gasp.

Instantly the heat drenching his skin stabbed deep into his belly, igniting a fire that spread to his groin.

He wanted her.

Just like that, he wanted her again. Not only the baby—but Marisa, lithe and sexy, in his bed.

From her elbow he took his time tracing a path up her soft flesh till he reached her bare shoulder. He felt her choppy breathing flutter over his throat, the gentle softening of her body in his hold, and triumph filled him.

She'd stay, and on his terms.

Damaso nuzzled the pulse point at the base of her neck and she arched back, giving him unfettered access.

His groin was rock-hard as he gathered her in and kissed his way up her neck to the corner of her mouth.

Desperate hunger rose. Despite the carnal intimacies they'd shared, he'd yet to taste her lips. She'd always distracted him with her body, her caresses. He intended to remedy that.

He turned his head to take her mouth but she wrenched away. Taken by surprise, he wasn't quick enough to catch her back. She broke free and stood, breathing heavily, one palm pressed to her chest as if fearing her heart might catapult free.

Damaso was about to reach for her when his vision

cleared and he read her expression: confusion, desire and fear, all etched starkly on features drawn too tight.

An iron fist crushed his chest, forcing the air from his lungs.

She looked so weary. Yet she drew herself up, as if to repel a hostile takeover. Her chin angled proudly in that familiar tilt, but her face was flushed, and one hand twisted the edge of her top.

Damaso could seduce her. He'd felt her tremble on the brink of surrender. But at what cost?

For the first time in his life, Damaso pulled back from the edge of victory. Not because he didn't want her but because Marisa wasn't ready.

He breathed deep, stunned at the decision he'd made without thinking—putting her needs before his.

Somehow he managed a smile. He watched her eyes widen.

'I have a proposal, Marisa.'

Instantly she stiffened.

'Stay here while we get to know each other. Relax and recuperate till the morning sickness passes. Take the time to rest and don't worry about your uncle. He can't reach you here.' He swept an arm towards the windows. 'Swim, eat, sleep and take all the time you need. Then later we'll talk. In the meantime treat this as a private resort.'

'*Your* private resort.'

He nodded, barely stifling impatience. 'I'll be here. It's my home.' He neglected to mention his apartment in the city and the other residences scattered around the globe. He had no intention of leaving Marisa. How could he seduce her into staying permanently if he wasn't here?

Eyes bright as lasers sized him up and he had the unexpected sensation Marisa knew exactly what he intended. His hands clenched as she surveyed him. Patience wasn't his strong suit.

Finally, she spoke. 'I have one condition. There'll be no

coercion.' Her eyes flashed. 'As your guest, I expect you to respect my privacy. When I want to leave, you won't try to prevent me. I'm here of my own free will. I refuse to have my movements curtailed.'

Damaso inclined his head, wondering how long it would take to convince her it wasn't privacy she craved.

CHAPTER SIX

A SHADOW BLOTTED the sun and Marisa opened her eyes, squinting up from the sun lounger.

'You'll burn if you stay there any longer.' Damaso's voice turned the warning into a seductive samba of delicious sound. That deep, liquid, ultra-masculine voice, the lilt of his accent, sent her nerves into overdrive.

Immediately her drowsy comfort vanished as her heart took up a wild percussion rhythm. Even after weeks on his island she wasn't immune to the sheer sensual appeal of the man. And she'd tried. How she'd tried!

Her mouth dried as she saw he'd stripped off his shirt, his skin dark-gold in the afternoon sun. The board shorts he wore rode low over his hips, drawing the eye to the sculpted perfection of taut muscle.

A whorl of sensation twisted between her legs, making her shift uneasily.

'I put sunscreen on just a while ago.' Her voice sounded reedy, and no wonder. She'd never met a man as physically compelling as Damaso. Despite her efforts to blot their night together from her memory, she remembered exactly how it had felt, pressed up against that glorious body, embraced by those powerful arms.

She'd never thought she'd regret the end of her morning sickness, but after mere weeks it had waned and without its distraction Marisa found herself conscious of Damaso at a deep physical level that disturbed her.

'Here.' Damaso held up a tube of sunscreen, squirting some onto his palm. 'Let me protect you.'

'No!' Why did his words make her think of another sort of protection altogether? One that had already failed?

Heat scored Marisa's cheeks as she reached out and took the tube from him. 'Thanks, but I'll do it myself.' She did *not* need Damaso's hands on her.

Their time on his island had only escalated her awareness of him. He hadn't touched her, but the intensity in his dark eyes whenever they rested on her was proof he hadn't forgotten their night together either. And, despite the way her thoughts chased round in her head as she tried to plot a future for herself and her baby, Marisa found herself too drawn to this almost-stranger.

The last thing she needed was to give up her independence and allow another man power over her. She would rely only on herself now her baby was on its way. She was determined to protect her child from the negative influences she'd experienced, overbearing men included.

At least Damaso hadn't crowded her during these last weeks. Unlike her uncle, whose constant phone and email messages unsettled her.

Marisa slapped the cream on her arms, across her cleavage and down to her midriff and legs.

Still Damaso stood, unmoving. She felt him watching every slide of her palm and felt heat build deep inside. It was as if he was the one touching her flesh, making her nerves tingle in response to his heavy-lidded stare.

'What about your back?'

For answer, Marisa shrugged into a light linen turquoise shirt.

Was that a smile tugging his mouth at the corner?

'You're a very independent woman, Marisa.'

'What's wrong with that?' In her uncle's book, 'independent' had been synonymous with 'troublesome'.

'Absolutely nothing. I admire independence. It can make the difference between life and death.'

Marisa opened her mouth to ask what he meant when he dropped to his knees beside her, hemming her in. They hadn't been this close, close enough for his body to warm hers, for weeks.

Instantly, sexual awareness hummed through her body and effervesced in her bloodstream. The shocking intensity of it dried her automatic protest.

'You missed a bit,' he murmured, bending close.

Then he was touching her, but not in the long, sensuous strokes she'd expected. Instead his brow furrowed with concentration as he painted sun cream across her nose in gentle dabs, as if she were a child.

She didn't feel in the least childlike.

Damaso's eyelashes were long and lustrous, framing deep-set eyes dark as bitter chocolate. The late sun burnished his face and Marisa's breath hissed between her teeth at the force of the longing that pooled deep inside.

For she wanted him. She wanted his touch, his body, and above all his tenderness, with an urgency that appalled her.

Oh yes, he could be tender when it suited him. But she hadn't forgotten how he'd dismissed her after their night together, when she'd begun to wonder if she'd finally found someone who might value her.

Marisa sat back, jerking from his touch.

Never had she craved a man like this. Was it pregnancy hormones, playing havoc with her senses?

He surveyed her steadily, as if she wore her thoughts on her face. But surely he had no idea what she was thinking? She'd learned to hide her thoughts years ago.

Slowly Damaso lifted his hand but this time he swiped the remaining sun cream across his chest in a wide, glistening arc. Marisa swallowed and told herself to look away. But her fascination with his body hadn't abated. How could it, when in the late afternoon light he looked like some gilded deity, an embodiment of raw masculine potency?

'What's that scar?'

If he noticed the wobble in her voice, he didn't show it. Instead he looked down at the neat line that curved at the edge of his ribs.

'A nick from a knife.' His tone was matter-of-fact, just like his shrug.

Marisa tried not to cringe at the idea of a knife slicing that taut, golden flesh.

'And that one?' She'd noticed it the night they'd spent together: a puckered mark near his hip bone that had made her wince even though it was silvered with age.

'Why the curiosity?'

'Why not?' It was better than dwelling on how he made her feel. With him so close, she couldn't get up and move away, not without revealing how he unsettled her. It was a matter of pride that she kept that to herself.

The gleam in his eyes made her wonder if he knew she was looking for distraction. But he didn't look superior, or amused. Instead, he met her regard steadily.

'You want me to marry you but I don't know anything about you,' she prompted.

It was the first time marriage had been mentioned since she'd arrived, as if by common consent they'd agreed to avoid the matter. Marisa wondered if she'd opened a can of worms by mentioning it again.

Would he try to force her hand now she'd brought it up? That was her uncle's tactic—bulldozing through other people's wishes to get what he wanted.

Damaso crossed his arms over his chest, as if contemplating her question. The movement tautened each bunching muscle, highlighting the power in his torso.

Marisa kept her eyes on his face, refusing to be distracted.

'It was another knife.'

'Not the same one?' She frowned.

'No.'

So much for explanation. This was like drawing blood from a stone. 'You got yourself into trouble a lot when you were young?'

Damaso shook his head. 'I got myself *out* of it. There's a difference.'

At her puzzled look, he shrugged and Marisa swallowed quickly. Did he realise how tempted she was to reach out and explore the planes and curves of his naked torso?

Of course he knew. He watched her like a hawk, seeking signs of vulnerability.

'I'm a survivor, Marisa. That's why I'm still here— because I did what it took to look after myself. I never started a fight, but I ended plenty.'

There was no bravado in his words. They were plain, unadorned by vanity.

The realisation sent a trickle of horror down her spine. She'd had her troubles but none had involved fighting for survival against a knife attack.

'It sounds like life was tough.'

Something flickered in his eyes. Something she hadn't seen before. Then he inclined his head a fraction. 'You could say that.'

Abruptly he moved, rising in a single, powerful surge. He leaned down, reaching to help her up, but Marisa looked away, pretending she hadn't seen the gesture.

She'd never been a coward but inviting Damaso's touch was asking for trouble. She stood unaided then turned back to him, putting a pace between them as she did so. Nevertheless, her skin tingled from being so close.

'What about you? What's the scar at the back of your neck?'

Marisa's head jerked up. He couldn't see the scar now; it was covered by her single thick plait. Which meant he'd noted and remembered it from the night they'd spent together. Heat fizzed from her toes to her breasts as their gazes locked. Damaso had spent his time that night learning her body with a thoroughness that had undone her time and again.

'A fall off the beam.'

'The beam?' One eyebrow arched.

'In gymnastics we sometimes perform on a beam, elevated off the ground. This—' her hand went automatically to the spot on her nape just below her hairline '—was an accident when I was learning.'

'You're a gymnast?' He looked at her as if he'd never seen her before.

'Was. Not any more.' Bitterness welled on her tongue. 'I'm too old now to be a top-notch competitor.' But that wasn't why she was no longer involved in the sport she'd adored, why she wasn't even coaching it. She'd come to terms with that years before, so the sudden burst of regret took her by surprise.

Could pregnancy make you maudlin?

Despite her physical wellbeing after these weeks of rest and privacy from prying eyes, Marisa was unable to settle. Her emotions were too close to the surface. Perhaps all those years repressing them were finally catching up with her.

'I think I'll stretch my legs.' She turned and wasn't surprised when Damaso fell into step beside her, shortening his stride to fit hers.

In silence they walked along the soft sand of the beach. Surprisingly, despite the tug of awareness drawing her belly tight, Marisa felt almost comfortable in his company. If only she could forget about Damaso as a lover.

They'd reached the end of the beach when the thoughts she'd been bottling up demanded release.

'Why, Damaso?' She swung round to find him watching. 'Why do you want marriage?' Though he hadn't raised the idea recently, it still pressed down on her. 'Lots of parents don't marry.'

'Yours were married.'

'That's no recommendation.' She didn't bother to hide her bitterness.

'They weren't happy?'

She shrugged and bent to pick up a shell, pearly-pink and delicate on her palm.

'No, they weren't.' She paused, then sighed. Why not tell him? Then maybe he'd understand her reluctance to marry. 'It was an arranged marriage, made for dynastic reasons. My mother was beautiful, gentle, well-born—and rich, of course.' Her mouth twisted. Bengaria's royal family always looked for ways to shore up its wealth. 'My father wasn't a warm man.' She bit her lip. 'They weren't well-matched.' At least, not from what she remembered and the stories she'd heard. Her mother had died so long ago, she only had a few precious memories of her.

'That doesn't mean all marriages are doomed to failure.'

'So, were your parents happy together?' If he'd grown up in a close-knit, loving family, that might explain why he insisted on marriage.

Damaso watched her in silence so long, she felt tension knot between her shoulder blades.

'I doubt it.'

'You don't know?'

'I don't remember my parents.'

'You're an orphan?'

'No need to sound so shocked. I've had a long time to get used it.' His smile was perfunctory, not reaching his eyes.

'Then why marriage? Why not—?'

'Because I *will* be part of my son's life. Or my daughter's. I'm not interested in child support by proxy. My child will have *me* to support them.' His face was tight and implacable.

Marisa shivered. The way he spoke, all their child needed

was *him*. Where was she in his grand scheme? She intended to be there to protect her baby, come what may.

'You don't trust me to be a fit mother, is that it?' Pain bruised her chest as she thought of the scandal that dogged her. These past weeks had opened up emotional wounds she'd thought long buried. 'You're judging me on what you've read in the press.'

Sure, she'd done her share of partying, but the reality wasn't anything like the media's lurid reports. Her notoriety had gained a life of its own, with kiss-and-tell stories by men she'd never even met.

Damaso shook his head. 'I'm not judging you, Marisa. I'm simply saying I won't settle for a long-distance relationship with my own flesh and blood.' She heard the echo of something like yearning in his deep voice.

Was that it? Did he *want* their child, rather than just feel responsible for it? The idea held a powerful appeal. Already she knew she'd do whatever was needed to ensure her baby's well-being. Marisa blinked up at his stern face, looking for signs of softness.

If only she could read him. It was rare that she sensed the man behind his steely reserve. She saw only what he allowed.

How could she trust a man she didn't know?

'What sort of man would I be to walk away from our child and leave all the responsibility on your shoulders?'

He had no idea how much she wanted support now. But responsibility without caring was a dangerous combination. That was how Cyrill had been with her and Stefan and it had poisoned their lives. She had to protect her baby.

'Doesn't our child have a right to both parents?' His eyes searched hers. She felt the force of his stare right to her toes. 'Doesn't it deserve all the security we can give it?'

'Yes, but—'

'There are no buts, Marisa.' Suddenly his hands were on her shoulders, drawing her close enough to feel the ripple of energy radiating from him. 'I refuse to abandon my child to make its own way in the world. I want to keep it safe, nurture it, care for it and protect it from all danger. I want it never to feel alone. Is that a crime?'

Suddenly, it was as if the rigid blankness of a mask had been ripped aside, revealing a man who, far from being cold and remote, was racked by strong feeling. A man whose hands shook with the force of stark emotion she saw in eyes that glittered almost black.

Is that what had happened to him? Had there been no one to protect and care for him?

Marisa thought of the knife wounds. His previous iron-hard composure. His talk of independence as the difference between life and death.

Horror and pity welled. What had this man survived? How long had he been alone as a child?

But she knew better than to ask. Damaso Pires was many things but an open book wasn't one of them. He'd revealed what he had grudgingly, presumably to convince her to accept him.

'Of course it's not a crime.' Her voice held a husky edge as her see-sawing emotions overcame her diffidence. She lifted a hand and planted it on his chest—to comfort and reassure, she told herself. Yet the sharp thud of his heart beneath her palm told her it would take more than that to calm him. She tried not to react to the erotic pleasure of hot, male flesh and crisp chest hair against her palm.

'So you agree.' Triumph blazed in his face. 'Marriage is the only option.'

'I didn't say that.' Marisa backed away, or tried to. His hold on her shoulders stopped her. Those hard fingers flexed and drew her closer, till her hand on his bare torso was all that separated them. His heat encompassed her; the subtle tang of his skin invaded her nostrils, making her recall the salt taste of him the night they'd been lovers. She quivered as a blast of longing rocked her.

'I could persuade you.' His voice dropped to a deep timbre that brushed like raw silk across her skin. His hands softened, smoothing her shoulders and back in a caress that spoke of easy expertise. Marisa bit her lip as her body arched greedily under his touch.

He bent his head, his mouth brushing her hair, his breath hot on her forehead. 'You've kept your distance since we came here, and I've let you pretend, but we both feel the connection. You can't deny it. It's there every time you look at me, every time I look at you. It hasn't gone away.'

His marauding hands swept the curve of her spine and out to her hips. He dragged her close and her breath stopped when she felt his arousal hard against her belly.

She closed her eyes, willing her trembling body to move away. His hold was firm but not unbreakable. She could escape. If she wanted to.

Instead she pressed closer, rising on her toes, bringing them into more intimate contact.

Damaso's breath hissed and Marisa might have felt triumph if she hadn't been swamped by hunger.

He was right. She'd tried to ignore it but this was why she'd been restless. Not just her pregnancy and the quandary over her future. Those were problems for later, eclipsed by the immediacy of her desire for Damaso.

Seeing him daily but keeping her distance had been an exercise in futility. What control she'd clung to now shattered in response to his potent charisma.

Her neck bowed back as he dropped his head and kissed her throat.

'You'd like me to persuade you, wouldn't you? It will be a pleasure for us both. A pleasure we've denied too long.' His mouth, hot and sensual, moved up her neck, kisses becoming tiny, erotic nips that tightened her skin and puckered her nipples. Her hands slid across the planes of his chest, raking slick skin and coarse hair.

Then his hand slid round her hip, delving unerringly in

one quick, sure motion to her feminine core. His fingers pressed hard against the fabric of her bikini bottom, making a pulse thud hard and quick between her legs.

Her breath snagged again and a wisp of sanity invaded her clouded mind. It would be so easy to give in. But something about the knowing ease of his action evoked a memory: Andreas, with his practised seduction technique that she'd been too naïve to recognise. Andreas, who'd used her for his own ends.

Damaso's mouth dipped from her ear to the sensitive point at the corner of her jaw, sending every nerve into tingling ecstasy. Marisa felt him smile knowingly against her skin.

He knew precisely how to seduce her.

One desperate shove and a backward step and she was free, her chest heaving, her legs wobbling as if she'd run for her life. Shock hit her that she'd actually broken away. Her body screamed with loss now he wasn't touching her.

Marisa watched unguarded emotion flit across Damaso's features: shock, anger and desire. Determination.

Her heart sank. If he touched her again, she'd be lost; even knowing his every move was carefully orchestrated to make her putty in his hands.

It wasn't his seduction she fought but herself. Her face flamed.

He moved towards her and she shrank away.

Instantly he stopped.

In the silence all she heard was the thunder of blood in her ears and his ragged breathing.

'Don't.' Her voice was choked and thick. She swallowed hard. Her gaze dipped to the reddened streaks on his heaving chest. Her nails had scored him.

Marisa's scalp tightened as she saw that reminder of her unbridled response. It was one thing to give in to lust when they'd come together as equals. It was another to let herself be coaxed by a man ruthlessly assessing her weakness to achieve his own agenda.

'Please.' She gasped as the word slipped out, but her pride was already in tatters. Her vision glazed and she wanted to hide her face, ashamed at how easily she'd responded.

Forcing her eyes up, she met his slitted gaze. Marisa drew a shuddering breath. 'If you have any respect for me at all, if you want any possibility of a future together, don't *ever* do that again. Not unless you mean it.'

CHAPTER SEVEN

'DAMASO! IT'S BEEN an age.' The once familiar, sultry voice made him turn. It had been months since Adriana had shared his bed but, looking into her exquisite, model-perfect face, it felt like far longer.

Once he'd been eager to accept the invitation in her sherry-gold eyes. Now he looked and felt nothing, not even an echo of past satisfaction.

She was stunning, from her glossy fall of black hair to her ripe curves poured into a flame-coloured dress that looked like liquid fire in the mood lighting. Even the memory of her enthusiasm for pleasing him did nothing to ignite his interest.

'Adriana.' He inclined his head. 'How are you?'

'All the better for seeing you.' Her smile was a siren's, her hand on his jacket proprietorial.

Annoyance tracked a finger down his spine and he shifted, watching her frown as her hand dropped.

'You're not happy to see me?' Her lips were a seductive scarlet pout.

'It's always a pleasure.' Or it had been, until she'd started hinting about staying in his city penthouse and asking about his movements. Possessive women were guaranteed to dampen his libido.

'But not enough to call me.' Damaso opened his mouth to terminate the encounter but she spoke again, pressing close. 'Forgive me, Damaso. I didn't mean that.'

'There's nothing to forgive.' Yet he didn't respond to the blatant offer in her gaze or the way her body melted against his. He stood straighter. She was beautiful, but...

'I see you have a new friend.' Her voice dipped on the word. 'Aren't you going to introduce me?'

He turned to see Marisa threading her way through the throng. Her gold hair was piled elegantly high, adding inches to her small frame. Or maybe it was the way she held herself. The frothy skirt of her scant, sapphire-blue dress swung jauntily above her knees as she walked, drawing covetous glances.

She looked right at home among Brazil's elite as they celebrated. Marisa was chic, gorgeous and effervescent, thriving on the attention of so many besotted men.

She stopped to exchange a laughing comment with a debonair man in exquisitely tailored formal clothes. A man who obviously cared about looking good at Fashion Week's premier event. He might have been a model with that chiselled jaw shadowed with designer stubble.

The stranger reached out and touched Marisa lightly on the hand.

Damaso felt heat ignite deep inside, sparks shooting through his bloodstream. His fingers tightened on his glass as Marisa smiled at the man now blocking her path.

'Although it seems she's otherwise occupied.' Adriana's voice filtered through the fog of pulsing sound in his ears. 'Your princess appears to know a lot of people.'

Across the room she drew yet another slavering admirer into the conversation. She positively sparkled at the epi-centre of male attention.

Damaso slammed his glass onto a nearby table, his fingers flexing.

Marisa was *his*. She mightn't admit it yet but she soon would. He could have forced her to do so just days ago on the island. But that haunted look, her desperate dignity when she'd pleaded to be left alone, had stopped him.

Crazy, when he knew she wanted him.

Now the sight of another man, other *men*, fawning over her made him want to smash his fist into one of them. All because of a woman!

'Damaso? Are you okay?' Adriana touched his hand. 'You're burning up! Are you unwell?'

He wrenched his gaze away to focus on Adriana. She looked worried. Perhaps because it was the first time she or anyone had seen him lose his cool.

He'd brought Marisa to the city to keep her occupied while he worked through what had happened that day on the beach. The feelings Marisa provoked scared Damaso as nothing had since he'd been fifteen and he'd taken on the pair of knife-wielding thugs who'd ruled his squalid neighbourhood.

No other woman got to him the way she did.

His jaw tensed and seconds later he was looming over Marisa's admirers. Conversation faltered and they melted away.

'Damaso.' The husky way Marisa said his name, the way her eyes darkened as she looked up at him, made him want to hoist her over his shoulder and forget any pretensions at being civilised. 'I'm glad you're here.'

'Are you? You seemed to be enjoying yourself.' His jaw clenched.

She shrugged, her smile dying as she read his face. What did she see there? Anger? Possessiveness?

Marisa turned away but he wrapped his fingers around her chin, tipping it so he could read her expression. Long lashes veiled her eyes but her lips trembled. The animation bled from her face and he read weariness there, the hint of shadows beneath her make-up.

'Marisa?' Something swooped in his chest. 'What's wrong? I thought you were enjoying yourself.'

If anything was guaranteed to satisfy the party-girl princess, it was this, one of São Paolo's most chic, most exclu-

sive parties. The guest list was a who's who of beautiful
people and the music was an enticing pulse-beat of good
times.

'It's…nice. I'm just tired.'

'Tired?' The woman who thrived on celebrations? 'I
thought you loved this sort of thing.'

'Sometimes.' Marisa's smile was perfunctory. Damaso
stared at the taut line of her bare shoulders. Stunned, he
realised she was anything but happy.

She broke his hold and turned away, lifting an outrageously decorated cocktail to her lips.

His hand shot out, grasping her wrist. 'Alcohol isn't
good for the baby. Especially the potent cocktails they
serve here.'

Marisa's mouth flattened. The hairs at his nape rose as
her eyes narrowed to needle sharpness.

'You don't think much of me, do you? Here.' She shoved
the fruit-laden cocktail towards him so hard it sloshed over
the edges, dripping onto her wrist and down her dress. She
paid no heed. 'Go on, taste it.'

Dimly he was aware of the buzz of conversation, the
curious stares.

'Go on!' Her lips twisted derisively. 'Or are you afraid
it's too strong for you?'

Her eyes blazed as she pushed the neon-tinted straw to
his lips. Reluctantly he sucked and swallowed.

'Fruit juice!'

'Amazing, isn't it? Imagine me drinking anything but
alcohol, when all the world knows I only quaff champagne.'

Abruptly she let go of the glass and he grabbed it before it fell and shattered. Cold, sticky juice dribbled down
his hand.

'I didn't have so much as a sip of wine the whole time I
was on your precious island.' Her voice was an acerbic hiss
as she leaned close. 'Yet you assume I can't control myself
as soon as I hit a party.'

A smile curved Marisa's lips but her eyes were flat. 'I see my reputation precedes me.' She drew in a breath that pushed her breasts high and her shoulders back. 'What else did you think—that I'd be off having sex with some man in a dark corner while you chatted with your friends?' She paused, her eyes widening. 'Or, let me guess, with a couple of men? Is that why you looked like some Neanderthal, stomping over here?'

Damaso stared. The whispered vitriol was so at odds with the smile on her delicate features. Anyone watching would think she was playing up to him rather than tearing strips off him.

It hit him with the force of a bomb exploding that Marisa was an expert at projecting an image. Suddenly his certainties rocked on their foundations.

How real had her enjoyment been when she'd laughed with those guys? Had she been putting on a front?

'I came because I wanted to be with you.'

'I'm sure you did.' Her saccharine tone told him she didn't believe a word. 'You had to tear yourself away from your girlfriend. I assume she *is* a girlfriend?'

Damaso stiffened. 'This isn't the place.' He explained his private life to no one, especially to a woman who somehow managed to make him feel in the wrong. It wasn't a familiar sensation and he didn't like it.

'Of course she is.' Abruptly Marisa dropped her gaze. 'Well, far be it from me to play gooseberry. No doubt I'll see you tomorrow.' She turned away. 'Goodnight, Damaso.'

Her arm was supple and cool beneath his palm as he wrapped his hand around it.

Her eyebrows arched in a fine show of hauteur, as if he defiled her with his touch. She looked as she had the day in the jungle when she'd dismissed him so disdainfully. It irked now as it had then.

He didn't give a damn how superior she acted. He wasn't releasing her.

'Where do you think you're going?'

'Back to your city apartment. Where else?'

She looked like an ice maiden, ready to freeze any male foolish enough to approach.

As if that would stop him! She could pretend all she liked but he knew better.

'Good.' Damaso said. 'I'm ready to leave.'

He tucked her hand through his arm and strode out, oblivious to the curious crowd parting before them.

The short helicopter ride to his penthouse was completed in silence. Marisa sat with her face turned, as if admiring the diamond-bright net of city lights below, her profile calm and aristocratically elegant.

She ignored him, as if he was far beneath her attention. Anger sizzled. He wasn't the ragged kid he'd once been, looking in on society from the outside. He was Damaso Pires. Powerful, secure, in command of his world.

Yet he'd watched those men eat her up with their eyes and rage had consumed him. Rage and jealousy.

The realisation hit him with full force.

He didn't do jealousy.

Damaso shook his head.

He did now.

Is that why he'd been so tactless? He had a reputation for sophistication but tonight he'd felt out of control, trapped in a skin that didn't fit.

The chopper landed and soon they were alone in his apartment.

If he'd thought she'd shy from confrontation, he was wrong. Marisa swung around, hands on hips, before he'd done more than turn on a single lamp. In her glittering stilettos, with sapphires at her throat and her short, couture dress swinging around her delectable legs, she looked like any man's dream made flesh.

But it was her eyes that drew him. Despite their flash of fury, he saw shadows there.

He'd done that.

'I'm sorry.' He'd never said that to any woman. Even now he couldn't quite believe he'd spoken the words. 'I overreacted.'

'You can say that again.' Absurdly her combative attitude made him want to haul her close and comfort her. In the past, he'd have walked away from a woman who wasn't totally compliant. But Marisa hooked him in ways he didn't understand.

'I didn't think you'd been drinking or having sex.' Damaso paused. He could have phrased that better.

'And I'm supposed to be impressed by that?'

'No.' He ploughed a hand through his hair, frustrated that for the first time the words hadn't come out right. Usually persuading a woman was easy.

'I'm tired, Damaso. This can wait.' She turned away.

'No!' He lowered his voice. 'It can't. On the island, we got on well.'

'And?'

'And I want to understand you, Marisa.' It was true. For the first time in his life, he wanted to know a woman.

What did that mean?

'I want you to trust me.' That was better. Women loved talk of trust and emotions.

'Trust?' Her voice was harsh. 'Why should I trust you? We spent one night together. I don't recall *trust* being high on your agenda then.'

She clasped her hands, fingers twisting. The movement made her look young despite her expression of bored unconcern, making him recall his suspicion that she threw up defences to hide pain.

'Your eagerness to leave once you'd had your fill was downright insulting.' Her jaw angled high but didn't disguise the flush of colour across her cheekbones.

An answering rush of heat flooded his belly. Shame? He wasn't familiar with that emotion either.

Whenever he remembered that dawn confrontation, he focused on her disdain. It was easier to concentrate on that than the fact he'd bolted out of her bed, scared by the unaccustomed yearning that had filled him. It wasn't pressing business that had moved him, but the innate knowledge this woman was dangerous to his self-possession in ways he hadn't been ready to confront.

He hadn't stopped to think of her. Now he did.

'I shouldn't have left like that.'

A quick shrug told him it didn't matter to Marisa, but instinct told him she hid her feelings.

'I made a mistake.' Bright blue eyes locked with his and he read her shock, almost as strong as his own, that he'd admitted such a thing. 'But circumstances have changed. It's in both our interests to understand each other better.'

'Like you did at the party when you thought I was boozing and—'

'I was wrong.' His voice grew loud in frustration and he hefted in a deep breath, willing himself to be calm. This was unfamiliar territory but he was determined to see it through. Whatever it took to secure his child.

'I know you hide behind that smile of yours.' As he said it, Damaso realised it was true. How often on the trek had he seen her dazzling her audience with a smile? Yet when she was alone there was an air of sadness about her.

'You're an expert on me now, are you?' Her tone was accusatory but Damaso didn't take the bait. He had her measure, realising instinctively she'd try to alienate him rather than let him close.

But he wanted to be close. How else could he get what he wanted?

'No,' he said slowly, feeling his way. 'But I know the woman the press talks about isn't the real you. I know that far from being shallow you have unplumbed depths.'

It had taken him too long to realise that. His thinking had been muddled by emotion—something new and unfamiliar. Now the inconsistencies that had puzzled him coalesced into a fascinating whole.

How would a woman who was nothing but a shallow socialite have the patience for painstaking photography? He'd seen it engross her in the rainforest and again on his private estate.

Why would such a woman be upset at not being able to work if all she wanted was to party?

Above all, why hadn't she jumped at the chance to marry a billionaire who could buy and sell her quaint little kingdom several times over?

He should have wondered about that when she'd had two full days in the city to shop and had come back to the apartment with just one purchase: the dress she wore tonight.

'I don't claim to know who you are, Marisa.' His voice was raspy with self-disgust at his slowness. 'But I want to.'

'You have a strange way of showing it.' Her clipped words bit into what passed for his conscience. 'You left me as soon as we got to the party.'

It was true. He'd thought it wise to give her space. He'd kept his distance, more or less, these last weeks because crowding her would be counterproductive. Look what happened that afternoon on the beach.

'You were nervous?' He frowned. Marisa was so confident, used to being at the centre of a throng.

'Not nervous. But it would have been nice...' She shrugged, her gaze sliding away. 'Forget it.'

'No.' He paced closer. 'Tell me.'

Her head swung up, her stare impaling him. 'Let's just say fielding pointed questions about our relationship and the pregnancy isn't the best way to relax among strangers.'

'Someone had the gall to ask you about that?' He'd been so caught up in his strategy of giving her the illusion of space he hadn't considered that. He'd believed her status as his guest would protect her.

Guilt squirmed anew in his belly.

What was wrong with him? Usually he was ahead of the game, not six steps behind.

'Not directly.' Her mouth and nose pinched tight. 'But indirectly...' She shrugged, stress plain in her taut frame. 'It wasn't the most comfortable evening.'

'I shouldn't have left you.'

One pale brow arched as if she didn't believe him, then she looked away. 'The fact you took me there, then ostentatiously left me to fend for myself, sent a very particular signal.' Her tone was bitter.

Damaso scowled. '*Who* dared to insult you?'

Her head jerked round and he caught a flicker of surprise in her stare.

'There was no insult,' she said, her voice clipped and her chin high. 'But some of the men—'

'I can imagine.' Damn it. He could imagine all too well.

He swiped a hand round the back of his neck, massaging knotted muscles. If he'd been thinking instead of trying to find the best way forward with Marisa he'd have realised: he'd inadvertently signalled she was fair game for any man on the prowl for a quick fling with a gorgeous woman.

And she was gorgeous. He couldn't drag his eyes from her.

But she wasn't available.

She was *his*.

'I'm sorry.' Ineffectual as they were, he couldn't stop the words rising again to his lips. 'I should have been with you.'

He wasn't used to taking responsibility for anyone but himself. Now he cursed his failure. This woman made him re-evaluate so much he'd taken for granted. It was discomfiting.

Marisa walked to the window, her straight back and

shoulders telling their own story. 'I'm used to fighting my own battles. Tonight was no different.'

But it was—because he'd put her in that situation.

He'd never known guilt or regret before Marisa.

He'd never felt half the things he felt around her.

The laugh would be on him if she knew. She thought his embrace on the beach had been a tactic to seduce her into marrying him.

The truth was he'd wanted Marisa since the day they'd met. He wanted her with a sharp, stabbing hunger that grew daily.

He wanted her body. But he wanted her company too. Her smile. Her attention.

He wanted to keep her safe.

He wanted...

'I'm not used to apologising.' His voice came from just behind her and she shivered as its dark richness slid through her, making a mockery of her defences. 'But, for what it's worth, I really am sorry. For *everything*.'

If she wasn't careful, Damaso would overwhelm her. Over the past weeks she'd seen glimpses in him of a man she could come to care for. Marisa fought desperately to keep her distance but part of her wanted to surrender, give up the fight and be persuaded to trust him.

His hand on her shoulder was firm but gentle and she found herself turning at his insistence. In the soft lighting his eyes were unreadable yet the intensity of his stare made something in her chest tumble over.

'I should never have put you in that situation.' His lips twisted in a grimace. 'I thought to give you a treat.'

'A treat?' Marisa breathed deep. 'I'm not a child.'

But that was how he viewed her. Not surprising, given her reputation. She'd been maligned and vilified and she hadn't exactly led the life of a nun. There'd been a time when living up to her reputation of partying every night had been her life. But she'd bored of it quickly.

'Believe me, Marisa.' His accent thickened deliciously as he stepped squarely into her personal space. 'I know you're not a child.'

Lightning jagged through her at the rough, seductive timbre of his voice. At the feel of his hand warm on her shoulder. He seduced her so easily. Desperation rose. How could she resist him when she wanted so badly to give in?

'I'm not an easy lay, either.' The words shot out as she fought the sizzle of excitement in her blood. If he'd had a fight with his girlfriend, he needn't think he could turn to Marisa to warm his bed.

'I know, *querida*.'

'You're just saying that. At the party—'

'At the party I couldn't see straight for jealousy.'

'Jealousy?' The word stunned her, stealing her voice.

To be jealous, he'd have to care about her. She'd done her homework via the Internet and knew Damaso had a notoriously short attention span when it came to lovers. He thrived on pursuit. He certainly didn't stick around long enough for possessiveness. Yet the idea of him caring, just a little, cracked open a frozen part of her heart. 'You don't have a jealous bone in your body.'

'Don't I?' His mouth turned down in a tight grimace as he loomed close, hemming her in.

'What about this one? It's held you close.' Damaso picked up her hand and placed it on his forearm. She felt his heat through his clothes.

'Or this one.' He slid her hand up his arm and across to his collarbone. Her palm tingled at the contact and tiny ripples of delight fluttered up her arm. 'You slept there, do you remember? Your head on me, your leg over my belly.'

Damaso's voice was hypnotic, drawing her into a place where nothing existed beyond the pair of them and the haze of desire clouding her mind. No, not just desire. A longing for the warmth and…contentment she'd found so briefly with him. She swallowed hard, feeling herself weaken.

'Don't, Damaso.' She yanked but he wouldn't release her hand. Her heart hammered high in her throat as she fought panic.

'Why don't you go to your girlfriend?' Marisa hated the tell-tale way her voice wobbled. It revealed how much she cared.

'She's not my girlfriend.' His ebony gaze captured hers and her breath stalled. 'She stopped being that before I met you. Besides, I have no desire for any other woman.' The way he said it, as if the truth throbbed in his husky tones, made Marisa's knees turn to water.

'Stop it! Don't play these games.' She hated that he could make her feel so vulnerable, so hurt. So needy.

His other hand cupped her jaw, his touch gentle.

'I never play games, Marisa. Ever. Ask anyone—it's not my way.'

'Of course you do.' Her voice was half an octave too high. Was it his touch that did that? Or the fixed way he stared at her mouth? Or the searing tide of need rising inside? She jutted her chin.

'You tried to seduce me just days ago so I'd agree—'

His hand slid over her lips. She breathed in the fresh, salt scent of him, tasted it on her tongue when she swallowed. Why did it affect her so?

'And you told me not to touch you unless I meant it.'

Finally he dragged his hand away but, instead of releasing her, he spread long fingers over her throat, down to her collarbone, where her pulse hammered unevenly.

'I want you, Marisa.' He leaned in so the words caressed her face. 'You have no idea how much.'

She planted both hands on his wide chest and pushed. Nothing happened except her palms moulded to the solid shape of his torso.

'Don't lie. You only want me because I'm carrying your baby.' She'd never found a man she could trust. They were all out for something. And now it wasn't just her wellbeing at stake, but her unborn baby's. She had to keep a clear head for its sake and make the right decisions for its future. 'You want to secure me, that's all—trap me into marriage.'

Something dark and untamed glimmered in his eyes and Marisa's heart leapt against her ribs. Slowly, infinitesimally slowly, his lips curved into a smile that turned her insides to liquid fire. His hands slipped to her shoulders and, despite her caution, his touch on her bare skin melted another layer of her defences.

'It's true that I find the fact you're carrying my child unbelievably erotic.' His voice was husky and inviting. She'd never heard anything so mesmerising.

Damaso moved, one thigh wedging hers apart and pushing up against her. She gasped as she came in contact with his erection. Her inner muscles clenched needily, making a lie of her resistance.

His Adam's apple rose and fell as if he was nervous. Yet she was the one whose nerves were stretched to breaking.

'I mean it this time, Marisa. I want you. I've wanted you from the moment I saw you.' His chest rose as he drew in a shuddering breath. 'This is about more than the baby, or what the world thinks. This is about me and you. Right now, all I care about is how you make me feel, and how I make you feel.'

Despite everything, she wanted to believe him. How she wanted to!

He plucked one of her hands from his chest and planted a kiss at the centre of her palm. Her knees buckled as he sucked at her flesh, sending waves of weakness through her.

'Can't we forget tonight and start again?' His voice was dark, liquid temptation.

'Why?' Marisa clung to his shoulder for support, trying to shore up the distrust that would keep her and her child safe. 'What is it you want?'

'I want us to be just Damaso and Marisa. Simply that.'

Did he have any idea how perfect that sounded? How *real* and uncomplicated? How tempting?

Damaso's head swooped low and, with a sigh, Marisa gave up the battle she'd been losing for so long.

CHAPTER EIGHT

THIS TIME WHEN Damaso bent to kiss her, Marisa lifted her mouth to him, desire filling her. For the first time she didn't turn aside so his lips brushed her face, her throat or the sensitive point behind her ear.

The sensation of his mouth on hers, sure and hard, demanding the response she could no longer stop, blasted her into another world.

Wave upon wave of pleasure crashed through her. She clung to broad shoulders as his marauding mouth demanded more, ever more. Her surrender elicited a growl of satisfaction from Damaso that she felt right through her core as he gathered her close.

She needed this, him, filling her senses, as she couldn't remember needing anything in her life.

Even the night they'd shared—giving in to instinct and reaching out to Damaso in the hope he was different from the rest—Marisa had shied from this particular intimacy. She'd shared her body but kissing on the mouth had been a step too far. It was a boundary she hadn't crossed since Andreas had seduced and betrayed her. In her mind, it had become a symbol of gullibility and defeat.

Yet now she revelled in Damaso's hot, delving kiss, the tangle of tongues and hot breath, the flagrant openness and hunger.

There was no trace of bitterness, only the spicy, addic-

tive taste of Damaso spinning her senses out of control
and a thrill almost of triumph in her effervescent blood.

There was something else she couldn't name, something
strong and pure, that filled her with elation and wonder.

This felt *right*. More than right.

She gave up trying to put a name to it as her mind
fogged.

Marisa clamped her hands to the back of Damaso's head,
revelling in the tangle of his thick, soft hair between her
fingers. She angled her head to give him better access as
he devoured her. His big hands held her close, his body
anchoring her.

If this was defeat, it was glorious.

This kiss wasn't like Andreas's practised moves. Nor
was it like Damaso's earlier attempt to seduce her into
compliance. It was potent, hungry, untamed and it affected
them both equally.

She felt the shudders rake Damaso's big frame as she
moved against him; heard the raw delight in his gasp as
she licked into his mouth; registered the convulsive tightening of his hands at her waist as she pressed even closer,
trying to meld herself with him.

The air sizzled with the charge they generated.

Marisa wasn't surprised when a flash of light flickered
across her closed eyes and a boom that could only be thunder ripped open the night. It was as if the elements had been
triggered by the force of passion unleashed when Damaso
set his mouth on hers.

Something cool and hard hit her bare shoulders; Damaso held her pinioned against the reinforced glass wall
that gave such a spectacular view of the city. The cool glass
made her even more aware of the intense heat of Damaso's
aroused body. He was like a furnace.

Greedily, she wanted that heat for herself.

She dropped her hands to his shoulders and pushed his
jacket back. He growled again, low in his throat, as if an-

noyed at the interruption, but let her go long enough to shake free of the jacket.

When he reached for her an instant later his hands moulded her breasts and she choked on a sigh of satisfaction.

'Yes! That!' Her head arched back against the glass, her breasts thrusting up into his palms as he caressed her, gently at first, then demandingly.

A guttural murmur broke from Damaso's throat. She didn't understand the Portuguese but her body responded to the urgency in his voice.

Her fingers fumbled at his collar, yanking at buttons till her hands met hard flesh. She wanted to bury her face there and taste the salty tang that rose sharp in her nostrils. She was wrestling with another button when Damaso's hands dropped away and she had to bite down hard to stop the mew of disappointment that rose on her lips.

She needed his touch on her body.

She wanted...

With one tremendous heave of shoulders and arms, Damaso ripped his shirt wide, buttons spattering to the floor. In the semi-dark Marisa watched the play of heavy muscles, the ripple of movement all the way down his dark, gold torso as he fought to tear the sleeves away.

Then he was bare-chested, snatching her hands in his and planting them high on his solid pectorals. Her palms tingled as hot flesh and the brush of body hair tickled.

'You're stunning,' she murmured. 'How did you get to look so good?'

He shook his head, his features taut as if fired in metal. 'It's you who's stunning, *querida*. I've never known a more perfect woman.'

'I'm not—'

Damaso's index finger closed her lips and it was a sign of her need that her tongue streaked out to taste him. His eyelids drooped as she licked him and the flesh beneath her hands rippled in spasm.

She did that to him so easily?

'You're perfect for *me*, Marisa.' His voice, thick with that sexy accent, brooked no argument. 'You're exactly what I want.'

Why that statement stilled her soul, Marisa didn't know.

Surely this was about lust? But when Damaso watched her like that, spoke of wanting her and only her, her heart gave a strange little leap. That look, those words, spoke to a part of her she'd kept hidden most of her life—the part that craved love.

'Stop thinking,' he growled, but his touch was gentle as he raised his hands and pulled the pins from her hair so it fell around her bare shoulders, a sensual caress that made her shiver. 'This is just you and me—Marisa and Damaso. Yes?'

His breath warmed her face; his hands dropped to her shoulders then down to the exquisitely tender upper slopes of her breasts. His fingertips traced the sweetheart neckline of her strapless dress, centimetre by slow centimetre, till she could take no more and clapped her hands over his, dragging them down to cup her breasts as she leaned close.

'Say yes, Marisa.'

She licked dry lips and through slitted eyes saw his gaze flicker.

'Yes, Damaso.'

It didn't matter whether she was saying yes to his statement that he wanted her, or his demand to stop thinking. Or whether she was simply urging him not to end the magic shimmering like stormy heat between them.

Whatever this was, she needed it, treasured it. For the first time in her life she felt not just passably pretty but beautiful, inside and out. No one had ever made her feel like this.

She blinked, her mouth hitching up in a tremulous smile

as a glow filled her that had nothing to do with the warmth of Damaso's body or the sultry night.

'Marisa.' His lips touched hers. Outside another crash of thunder shook the air, but it was the tenderness in Damaso's bass voice that made her quake. She leaned into him, her face upturned, her mouth clinging to his. He plunged one hand into her hair, holding her to him as he slowly, thoroughly, savoured the taste of her.

How could a kiss make her weak at the knees? She wobbled in her high heels, clutching Damaso for support.

She half-expected to see a satisfied smile at her reaction when he drew back. Instead she read nothing but taut control that made his features severe.

Then he was gone, dropping silently to his knees before her, hands knotting in the spangled froth of her skirt. She shivered as his hands slid up her bare legs, pushing the fabric up and up. Ripples of excitement shivered along her thighs. She pressed them together as she felt a rush of liquid desire.

Damaso lifted her shirt higher, then higher still, pausing when he saw the little silk bikini panties in aqua that she'd chosen to go with her new dress.

The sight of his dark head close enough for his breath to heat her skin like a phantom touch made excitement twist inside.

He pushed the fabric right up to her breasts, baring her to his gaze.

Marisa's breath laboured. There was something indescribably erotic about the way Damaso knelt at her feet, studying her so intently.

One large hand spread across her stomach, gently stroking till the tide of pleasure rose even higher.

'You're carrying our child in there.' He looked up, midnight eyes transfixing her. Before Marisa could think of anything to say, he leaned in and pressed a kiss to her flesh, then another and another. And all the while his eyes held hers.

She felt…treasured, vulnerable, different. The look on his face, the tenderness of his touch, the raw curl of arousal in her belly, created a moment of rapt awareness. She was a goddess come to life, the embodiment of femininity: creator, mother and seductress combined.

In that moment she felt awe at the miracle happening inside her and an unexpected sliver of hope. Damaso's reaction was genuine. Could this pregnancy really help them forge a relationship?

Damaso's mouth curved up in a smile. His eyes glittered in the soft light as he slid his hand down to the delicate silk of her panties, then with one swift tug dragged them down.

Over the sound of her gasp Marisa heard the whisper of tearing silk. Soft fabric fluttered down her legs.

'They were new!' Could he tell that was a gasp of anticipation, not outrage?

Damaso's smile widened. 'They were in the way.'

Before she could think of a retort, he dipped his head and her body convulsed as he pressed his lips to the centre point of every nerve. One stroke of his tongue and the trembling in her legs became a quaking shudder.

'Damaso!' Her fingers knotted in his hair, holding on, torn between wanting to pull him away and wanting him never to stop. For the storm was inside her now, the blasts of white-hot light jagging right through her again and again until, with a sob of shock, she shattered.

Marisa was tumbling, falling through a darkened sky lit by flashes of brilliant sparks. But she didn't fall. She was cushioned, wrapped close, gentled as she shuddered again and again, her body strung out on ecstasy.

A hand brushed her face and, dazed, she felt wetness. Marisa gulped in air and realised there were tears trickling down her cheeks.

She felt like she'd never recover from the surge of energy that had wracked her. More than delight, this was euphoria.

'I've never...' Her throat closed. How could she explain the depth of what she'd felt—the combination of sensual pleasure and emotional crisis that had created a perfect storm?

'Shh, *minha querida*. It's all right. I have you safe.'

And he did. Even in her bemused state she knew he protected her. Damaso's warmth and strength encompassed her, cocooning her. She burrowed closer, hands clinging.

She sank into soft cushions and Damaso eased away.

'No!' She clutched at him, hands sliding on his solid shoulders. 'Don't leave me.'

'I don't want to crush you.'

Marisa tried and failed to find the energy to lift her eyelids. 'I need you.'

Had she really said that?

For a moment there was no response. Then her limp body was picked up again and she found herself draped across Damaso. He was long and hard and spectacularly aroused.

'Sorry.' Her leg brushed his erection through his trousers and he tensed.

'It's okay. Just relax.'

That was new in her experience of men, she realised foggily. He really *was* putting her first.

She snuggled closer and he tensed, his hands clamping tight as if to stop her moving. Her head was pressed to his chest and she inhaled the delicious scent of his skin. She pressed a kiss there and felt a quiver ripple through him.

Marisa's exhaustion ebbed. She opened her eyes to a close-up view of Damaso's shoulder and taut biceps as he cradled her. She touched the tip of her tongue to his skin, tasting that curious combination of potent male and sea spice.

'Don't!'

'Why not?' She slipped her hand down to cover the heavy bulge in his trousers. His guttural response was part protest, part approval as he jerked hard beneath her.

'Because you're not ready.'

Marisa looked down to see his hand hovering over hers, as if he wanted to pull her away but couldn't quite manage it. She rubbed her hand up his length and saw his fingers clench. Beneath her ear, Damaso's heartbeat quickened.

She smiled. Now the power was hers. 'Let me be the judge of that.'

Deliberately she leaned over and licked his nipple, drawing it into her mouth.

Seconds later she was flat on her back on the sofa, pressed into the cushions by Damaso's big frame. Between them his hand scrabbled at his belt and zip. His other hand caught one of hers above her head.

His mouth closed with hers and this kiss was hunger and heat. It was utterly carnal, Damaso's tongue thrusting and demanding as he pushed her down into the soft upholstery. Wild elation rose as Marisa met each demand and added her own.

She needed Damaso to make her whole. Despite her shattering climax, there was an emptiness at her core only he could fill.

She was gasping when he surged back, rising to strip the last of his clothes and kick his shoes away.

Deep within, every muscle tightened as she surveyed Damaso, bronzed and powerful. Then he moved, shoving her legs wide, settling between them; his arms braced beside her, his breath warm on her lips, his eyes glittering as they ate her up.

He lay still so long she wondered if he'd changed his mind. Or was he waiting to see if she had?

Marisa reached down and took him in her hand, hot silk over rigid strength, and he shuddered.

In one fluid movement he dragged her hand away and

thrust slowly to the place she needed him. Her breath expelled in a sigh.

He moved again, sure and unhurried, as if savouring every sensation.

Next time he withdrew, Marisa tilted her hips, but instead of pressing deeper or harder Damaso took his time, centimetre by slow centimetre.

He was killing her. From complete satiation just minutes ago, remarkably now Marisa trembled with the need for more. She opened her mouth to urge him on then shut it as she registered his knotted brow, hazed in perspiration, the tendons tight to snapping point in his neck and arms, his gritted teeth.

This was killing him too!

'I won't break,' she gasped as he eased away and stroked gently back, teasing her unbearably with the need for more.

His eyes snapped open and she wondered if he saw her clearly. His gaze looked blind.

She planted her hands on his buttocks, feeling the twitch and bunch of muscle as she tried to draw him close, yet he resisted.

His eyes focused and her heart thudded at the look he gave her. Slowly he shook his head. 'The baby.'

He was afraid for the baby?

Marisa blinked. Emotions surged, engulfing her in a pool of warmth. At first she'd told herself she wasn't ready to have a child. More, she was scared about the responsibility of motherhood. But now she knew a certainty as deep as primitive instinct—that she wanted this child and would do anything to protect it.

And so would Damaso. This was connection at a visceral level, more profound than anything she'd ever expected.

He genuinely cared. He'd opened his heart to their unborn baby.

Could he open his heart to her too?

Something fluttered in her chest, her heart throbbing

too fast. A wave of emotion swept her, tumbling her into depths where the only anchor point was Damaso.

Hers. A voice in the deep murmured he was hers.

'The baby will be fine,' she whispered, wondering at the enormity of what she felt.

'How do you know?'

From instinct as old as time.

Marisa guessed he wouldn't be convinced by that. She focused on something more tangible. 'The doctor told me.'

Damaso breathed deep, his body sinking into hers. 'Still...' He shook his head, moving so slowly it was exquisite torture.

He was so obstinate, yet how could she protest when he thought to protect something so precious?

Marisa slipped her hands to his shoulders and hauled herself higher, nuzzling his jaw, kissing his ear, feeling the friction of his chest against her tender breasts. His breathing drew ragged

'I want you now,' she whispered, and bit down hard at the curve between his tanned neck and shoulder.

Damaso juddered, surging hard and high.

'Yes, like that.'

'Marisa.' It was a warning that became a groan as she wrapped her legs tight around him. For an instant he held strong, then his control broke and he surged into her, driving them hard and fast in a compulsive rhythm.

Marisa hugged him tight, filled with a feeling of openness, of protectiveness, as the big, powerful man who'd taken over her world let go and gave himself up to the force of passion.

Sex with Damaso had been spectacular.

Making love with him was indescribably better.

Marisa cradled him, overwhelmed by the belief they had shared something profound. Then, as their rhythm spun out of control, he bent to suckle her breast and both shattered in a climax that tumbled them into a new world.

CHAPTER NINE

THE STORM HAD PASSED, and the steady drum of rain should have lulled Damaso to sleep, yet it eluded him.

Staying with Marisa was too distracting. The rumpled disarray of the guest bedroom, the first one he'd staggered to with her in his arms, proved that.

He'd promised himself he wouldn't touch her after that cataclysmic coming together in the sitting room. He'd assured himself he could hold back from the need to imprint himself on her, taste and hold her. But his willpower had snapped when she'd turned to him again.

He hoped she and the doctor were right. Logic told him sex wouldn't harm the baby, yet he'd felt a profound fear of doing the wrong thing until Marisa had touched him.

He flung up an arm over his head, staring at the dark ceiling. His resolve had been renowned, and unbreakable, until her.

How had she done it? How had she overridden his determination to be gentle?

This wasn't what he'd planned. Granted, he'd wanted her in his bed. What better way to bind her to him than with sex? He'd use any tactic he could to convince her marriage was best.

But now he had her where he wanted her, Damaso realised things weren't so simple.

Tonight hadn't felt like any sex he'd had before.

It hadn't felt like he was in control.

On the contrary, his loss of control had been spectacular.

Then there was the way he'd *felt*. When he'd realised he'd hurt Marisa with his easy assumptions. When he'd knelt and kissed the woman who carried his baby. When she'd come apart so completely, her vulnerability had unravelled something inside, something he couldn't mend.

Each time he'd climaxed, it seemed he'd lost a little of himself in her.

He shifted. That was nonsense.

'Damaso?' Her drowsy voice was like rich, dark honey, sweet and enticing, making his mouth water.

He remembered being twenty-two, a kid from the slums who'd dragged himself into the commercial world with a mix of relentless determination, hard work and luck. He'd put his past behind him and thought he knew it all: how to turn a quick deal, where to find profits, how to satisfy a woman, how to protect himself on streets so much safer and more respectable than the ones he'd known.

He'd been in a breakfast meeting at a hotel. Damaso had followed the other man's lead, eating as they talked so as not to look too eager. He'd taken a bite of bread slathered in honey and had been instantly addicted.

Such a simple thing that most people took for granted. Yet just a taste had the power to drag him straight back to his past, deprived and wanting. To a time when honey had been a luxury he'd only heard of.

'Damaso?' Her hand touched his chest. 'What's wrong?'

He mentally shook himself out of abstraction. 'Nothing.' He paused, realising how abrupt he sounded. 'You must be tired. You should sleep.'

Her hand shifted, fluttering over his ribs, and he sucked in a breath as arousal stirred.

'Would you hold me?' She sounded tentative, unlike the feisty woman who'd faced him down time and again.

Did the past haunt her too?

How little he knew of her.

Silently he reached out and dragged her close, hoisting her leg over his and pushing her head onto his chest. Then he pulled the sheet over them both.

Holding her in his arms felt surprisingly satisfying. She was soft and serene and fitted snugly against him, as if designed for this. His breathing evened to a slow, relaxed rhythm.

'I should never have left you alone at the party.' Naked against him, he realised how tiny she was. She might have energy to burn, and an attitude the size of São Paolo, but that didn't mean she could take on the world alone.

'You've already said that.' Her mouth moved against his chest.

He had, hadn't he? It wasn't like him to dwell on mistakes. Yet he couldn't shake the guilt that he'd made her a target for unwanted attention.

'Nevertheless, I'm sorry. You—'

'Forget it, Damaso. I handled it.'

Damaso firmed his mouth rather than blurt that she shouldn't have needed to handle it.

'I'm sorry I lost my temper with you in public.' She puffed out a breath that warmed his skin. 'That will just fuel public interest.'

An apology from Marisa, too? Perhaps they *were* making progress. Damaso stroked a hand along her spine, enjoying its sensuous curve and the way she arched ever so slightly in response.

'Don't apologise. I should have known better.'

'What? Known I wasn't busy seducing other men and generally behaving badly?' Marisa's voice was a whisper yet he heard the tinge of bitterness she couldn't conceal. 'How could you? That's what everyone expects. It's in all the gossip magazines.'

She lay taut in his arms, that delicious lassitude replaced by tension. Damaso wished now he'd never raised the subject. But he owed her.

'The magazines are wrong.'

'I'd rather not discuss it.' She shifted as if to pull away and he wrapped both arms around her, holding her gently but firmly.

'I *know* they're wrong.'

Marisa stilled. 'You can't know that.'

'But I do.'

'Don't!' She twisted in his hold and he saw her pale face look up at him in the darkness. 'You don't need to pretend.' Her voice was scratchy and over-loud and it made something inside him ache.

'I don't know the details, Marisa. Only you do. But I do know you're not the woman the media paints you.' He paused, wondering how much he should admit. Then he registered the tiny shivers running through her taut frame and went on. 'I believed it at first but the more time I spent with you the more I came to realise you're someone quite different.' He ventured a caress along her bare shoulder. 'Someone I want to know.'

It was true. Marisa intrigued him. More than that, he'd discovered he *liked* her, even when she was prickly and refused to give in to his wishes.

'Why don't you tell me about it?' he murmured.

'Why would I do that?' No mistaking the wariness in her voice.

'Because you're hurting, and talking about it might make you feel better.'

His words surprised even himself. Not that he didn't mean them. It was how much he meant them, how much he wanted to help, that made him frown.

Since when had he been there for anyone? He was a loner. He'd never been in a long-term relationship. He didn't dwell on feelings. Yet here he was, offering a sympathetic ear as if he was the go-to guy for emotional support.

Yet he was sincere.

Another first.

If he wasn't careful this woman would change his life. Already she had him re-thinking so much he'd taken for granted.

'Why? Because you're such a good listener?' Marisa forced lightness into her tone but it didn't quite mask her pain. Her restless fingers moved over his rib cage until he clamped his hand over hers, spreading it wide against his chest. He liked her touch on him.

'I have no idea.' He didn't bother to add he'd never been anyone's confidant. 'Why don't you try me?'

He said no more but waited, slowly stroking the luxurious softness of her hair from her head down her back.

Marisa's words, when they came, surprised him.

'I was fifteen when the press came after me the first time.' Her voice was firm but a little breathless, as if she couldn't fill her lungs. Damaso forced himself to keep up the rhythm of his long strokes.

'There'd been press attention before then, of course. It was inevitable, with us orphaned when we were only ten. Every time we appeared in public they went into a frenzy— the poor little orphan royals.' Bitterness laced her words. 'Not that anyone cared enough to check we were all right.'

Damaso digested that in silence. He knew Marisa's relationship with her uncle, the current king and former regent, was poor, but better not to interrupt her with questions.

She drew a slow breath. 'Things eased a little over the years. Stefan and I got used to the media presence. Then at fifteen I was trying out for the national gymnastics team and suddenly I was in the spotlight again, initially because of the novelty of me competing with "ordinary" girls, and then...'

Damaso waited.

'Someone with an axe to grind fed them a story that I was a slut, partying all night with one guy after another, then playing the privileged prima donna among the rest of the competitors by day.'

'Who was it?'

'Who was what?'

'The person who invented the story.'

She lifted her head and even in the darkness he knew she searched his face. 'You believe me?'

'Of course.' It hadn't occurred to him she might lie. Everything about her, from her repressed emotion to her obvious tension, proclaimed the truth. 'Besides, I doubt you'd have the energy for bed hopping during the competition. Plus, you're anything but a prima donna, despite your pedigree.'

He'd watched her play the icy aristocrat when it suited, but he'd also seen how open and accessible she was to everyone on their tour. In his home she treated his staff with courtesy and genuine friendliness.

Marisa fisted one hand on his chest and propped her chin on it, staring.

'What?' He couldn't read her expression, but felt her gaze like the rasp of sharp metal on his flesh.

'You're the first person apart from Stefan and my coach to believe me.' Her voice had a curious, flat tone that he knew hid more than it revealed. He wondered how it had felt being vilified so publicly at such an age.

At least she'd had her brother.

'Surely your uncle's PR people would have helped?'

Marisa turned, lying again on her side, her face obscured. 'You'd have thought so, wouldn't you?'

Damaso waited, curious.

'They were spectacularly ineffective. But my uncle had never approved of my passion for gymnastics. He thought it unladylike and definitely not suitable for a royal. He disapproved of me being seen in leotards, getting sweaty and dishevelled in public, and especially on live TV. And as for competing with commoners!'

'He ordered his staff not to support you?' Damaso frowned. He knew how hard elite athletes worked. One

of his few peers to succeed and, like him, make a life outside the slum where they'd grown up had gone on to represent Brazil at football. He'd seen how much dedication
and hard work that took.

Marisa shrugged, her shoulder moving against his chest.
'I never found out. Eventually the gymnastics committee
decided it was too counter-productive having me on the
team. The press attention was affecting everyone. A week
after I turned sixteen, I was dropped from the squad.'

Damaso fought the urge to wrap his arms tight around
her. The fact that her voice was devoid of emotion told its
own story. His chest tightened.

'Mighty convenient for your uncle.' Had he used the
negative press stories to push his own ends?

'That's what Stefan said.' Bitterness coloured Marisa's
words. 'But we could never prove anything, no matter what
we suspected.'

Damaso stared into the darkness, putting two and two
together. He recalled her hatred of the current king, the
way even talking with him on the phone had sapped her
energy. He remembered her comment about no one bothering to check she and her brother had been well-cared-for
once Cyrill had become their guardian. That level of re-
sentment must have deep roots. Was it possible her uncle
had actually fostered the press stories?

'It's too late to worry about that now.' She did a good
job of sounding matter-of-fact but he heard the undercurrent in her voice.

'Because the damage is done?'

'Sometimes it doesn't matter if a reputation is deserved.
It takes on a life of its own.' She shifted against him. 'You'd
be amazed how much difference a provocative caption can
make to an innocent photo. Anything that didn't fit was
seen as me or the palace trying to put a good face on things.'

'So you couldn't win.'

Abruptly Marisa tugged her hand free of his grip and

sat up, her back to him. She anchored the sheet beneath her arms and took her time pushing her hair back from her face.

'I survived.' Her tone was light. 'In fact, being known as a party girl made it easier to flout convention when the fancy took me, which it did. Eventually I learned to enjoy the benefits of notoriety, so it's not all bad. I always get invited to the most *interesting* parties.'

Damaso propped himself on one elbow, trying to read her profile in the darkness. He guessed her physical withdrawal meant he was getting too close for comfort.

Instinct told him Marisa wasn't used to sharing confidences either. She was strong and self-reliant in a way he recognised in himself, despite their dissimilar backgrounds.

Which meant it was time to back off. She didn't want him probing further.

Fat chance. He wanted to know all there was to know about her.

Besides, despite her tone of unconcern he sensed a fragility that intrigued him.

'Except you wanted something more. You said the other day you'd wanted to work but the press exposure stopped you.'

Had she stiffened or did he imagine it?

Her shoulders rose and fell in what passed for a shrug. 'It wouldn't have worked out anyway. I don't have any qualifications or useful skills.' Her chin lifted, reminding him of that morning in the jungle resort when she'd turned from beddable siren to haughty empress in the blink of an eye. Now, he'd swear it was a self-protection mechanism. Had it been that, then, too?

Marisa spoke, distracting him. 'I'm not academically minded. I barely made it through high school. Unless an employer wants someone who can make a perfect curtsey, or chat aimlessly with doddering aristocrats and bland-faced diplomats, my skills aren't exactly in demand.'

'Putting yourself down before someone else does it for you?'

That drew a reaction. She whipped round to face him, her hair flaring wide around her shoulders.

'Just facing facts, Damaso. I'm a realist.'

'Me too.' And what he saw was a woman who'd been badly hurt time and again but conditioned herself not to show it.

He should be grateful she didn't cry on his shoulder.

But he wasn't. Something wild and dark inside clawed with fury at the way she'd been treated. The way she'd been judged and dismissed.

He wanted to grab her uncle and the media piranhas by their collective throats and choke some apologies out of them.

He wanted to crush Marisa in his arms and hold her till the pain went away. She'd probably shove him aside for his trouble. Besides, what did he know of offering comfort?

'Let's end this conversation, Damaso. I've had enough.'

Yet he couldn't leave this.

'So you played up to your reputation. Who wouldn't in the circumstances? But we've already established you're not as promiscuous as the world thinks.'

'Don't forget the drug-taking and high-stakes gambling.' Even in the gloom he saw her chin jut higher.

Damaso tilted his head. Why was she raising those rumours? It was as if she'd changed her mind about sharing herself with him and took refuge instead in her reputation for licence.

'And did you? Snort coke and lose a fortune gambling?'

'I lost my driver's licence just two and a half months ago doing twice the speed limit on the hairpin bends above the palace.'

Two and a half months ago. 'After your brother died?'

'Leave Stefan out of this.' Marisa swung her legs out

of bed but Damaso's hand on her arm shackled her so she couldn't move.

'Let me go. I told you I'd had enough.' Her voice was clipped and condescending and a frisson of long-forgotten shame feathered his spine—as if he was still a ragged slum kid who'd dared to touch a princess with his dirty paw.

His hand gentled.

'You're too fit to be a regular drug user, Marisa. I've seen too many of them to be fooled. And as for gambling... You've had ample opportunity since you arrived but you've shown no interest.' He paused. 'That leaves your reputation with men.'

'I'm hardly a virgin, Damaso.'

For which he was grateful. Sex with Marisa was one of life's high points.

'So how many have there been, Marisa?'

She tugged at his arm but he held firm.

'You can't seriously be asking that.'

'I seriously am.'

For four pulse beats, five, six, she stared him down. Then she leaned towards him, her free hand sliding from his thigh to his groin, closing around his already quickening shaft.

'Enough.' Her voice was a throaty murmur that turned his bones molten.

'Convince me.'

For a flicker of a moment she hesitated. Then she shoved him back on the pillow and bent her head. Long tresses of silk caressed his skin. Her lips were hot and soft, wickedly arousing on his burgeoning flesh.

But something was wrong. Damaso felt the tension in her frame, as if her nerves had been stretched to breaking point.

With a groan of disbelief at what he was about to do, Damaso pushed her away, rolling her onto her back and imprisoning her with the weight of his body.

They lay so close he saw the over-bright glitter of her fine eyes and the uneven twist of her lips.

'Don't *ever* do that unless you want it too.' The idea of her servicing him rather than acting out of shared arousal left a bitter taste on his tongue. For that was what she'd been doing, he was sure of it—trying to distract him.

Slowly, tenderly, he leaned down and planted a kiss at the corner of her mouth, another near her nose, then across her cheek to follow a leisurely trail down her neck. By the time he reached the base of her throat, her pulse was frantic. He kissed her there, ridiculously reassured by this proof of her response.

Marisa wanted him. Had wanted him all along. It was just that she'd tried to side-track him to avoid answering questions.

His hand slipped between her legs as he moved lower to kiss her nipple. With a sigh she tilted her hips and he pressed harder, rewarding her responsiveness.

'How many men, Marisa?'

She stiffened, her indrawn breath a hiss in the darkness.

Damaso feathered teasing kisses across her breast, his fingers delving into her most sensitive place. Marisa's hands threaded through his hair, holding him close.

When she was soft again beneath him he stopped.

'How many?'

'You're a devil, Damaso Pires.'

'So I've been told.' He nipped gently at her breast and watched her arch high. 'How many?' Deliberately he lifted his hand away. Still Marisa didn't admit defeat.

It took ten minutes of delicious pleasure before she finally gave in, by which time Damaso was close to losing the last of his own control.

'Two,' she gasped, her body writhing beneath his.

'Two?' Damaso couldn't believe his ears. Only two men before him?

'Well…one and a half.' She drew him down till he sank between her thighs.

'How can there be a half?' He groaned when he found his voice. She was slowly killing him.

Marisa's eyes opened and for a moment he could have sworn he read pain in her eyes, though it should have been impossible in the darkness.

'The first one seduced me so he could brag about it to his friends. After that…' She looked away. 'After that I found it hard to trust, so the second one didn't get as far as he expected.'

Damaso braced himself high and joined them with one easy move that took him home. 'Not this far?'

'No.'

'But you don't mind…with me?'

Slowly she smiled and the tightness banding his chest fell away.

'I don't mind.' She gasped when he moved and clutched his upper arms. 'I could even…come to quite enjoy it.'

Quite enjoy it!

There was a challenge if ever he'd heard one.

Damaso made absolutely sure she'd more than 'quite enjoyed' herself before he was finished.

Finally she lay limp against him, curled up with her head tucked beneath his chin, her knee between his and her hand flung across him where it had fallen when he'd rolled onto his back.

Her breathing was deep and steady, and he told himself if she dreamed it was of something pleasant, not the disappointments and pain of her past.

Damaso was sure he had only half the story. But that was enough. Duped and betrayed by her first lover, hung out to dry by the uncle who should have protected her, scorned by the world's press… Who'd been on her side?

Her twin, Stefan, who'd died just months ago.

Damaso had assumed the passion he'd shared with

Marisa that first night was the product of two healthy libidos and a wildfire of mutual attraction. Yet he recalled the blind look on Marisa's face as she'd tackled that notorious climb on the trek. She'd been lost in her own world and the blankness of her stare had scared him. Had that been grief driving her?

Had grief pushed her into his arms?

He swallowed and turned his gaze to the first grey fingers of dawn spreading across the sprawling city.

She'd had only one real lover before him.

One!

Damaso would love to think it was his sheer magnetism that had made her walk into his arms. But did that ring true with a woman who'd guarded her lack of sexual experience under the eyes of the gloating world press? Who, even when she partied all night, kept herself apart from casual sexual encounters?

There'd been a wealth of pain in Marisa's voice as she'd spoke of the man who'd betrayed her. It made Damaso want to commit violence.

What had it done to her?

He'd thought Marisa sexy and alluring with a feisty, 'don't give a damn what society thinks' attitude that matched his.

Instead he'd discovered she was a woman who needed careful handling. She had so much front it was hard to tell where the public persona ended and the real woman began. One thing he knew for sure—behind her masks of hauteur and unconcern was a woman who felt, and hurt, deeply.

His fingers twitched as she shifted, her breath hazing his skin. He wanted her again with a hunger he found almost impossible to conquer.

If she'd been the woman he'd first thought, he'd have had no qualms about waking her.

Instead Marisa was a unique mix of fragility and

strength. A woman who, instinct told him, needed the sort of man he didn't know how to be.

For the first time in years, he felt inadequate. Tension made his jaw ache as he contemplated the tangle that was their relationship.

Damaso wasn't equipped to deal with the nuances of emotional pain. He'd experienced and witnessed so much trauma as a kid he'd all but excised feelings from his life until he'd met Marisa.

He didn't know how to give Marisa what she needed.

Her vulnerability made him feel like a clumsy lout who'd blundered in and smashed what was left of her fragile peace by getting her pregnant.

A better man would regret that.

A better man would support her yet let her go.

Damaso had never been anything like a good man. He was too used to getting his own way. He'd been driven solely by the need to survive, then thrive.

He couldn't bring himself to wish Marisa's pregnancy away. He was too selfish for that.

He wanted his child.

He wanted Marisa.

His hand tightened on her hip and he smiled grimly when she snuggled closer, as if this was where she wanted to be.

Who was he kidding? He'd seduced her, taking advantage of her vulnerability after the stress of the party. He'd used his superior sexual experience to make her open up to him, physically and emotionally.

And he'd continued to push his way into her life, inveigling her to become part of his.

A better man...

No, he'd never be a better man. He was hard, bent on winning at all costs.

His one concession would be that from now on, knowing what he did of Marisa's story, he'd treat her gently, give her space and time to adjust to her new life with him.

He'd learn what he needed to protect her and keep her with him till she wanted to stay by choice.

Even if it meant keeping his distance till she did.

CHAPTER TEN

'But you can't have considered, Your Highness!'

Marisa leaned back in her cushioned seat and raised one eyebrow, knowing her silence would be like a red rag to a bull. She seethed at the superior attitude taken by the Bengarian ambassador. He was her uncle's crony, and no doubt Cyrill's belief that he could command and she'd obey had rubbed off.

'Think of the publicity,' he urged. 'Think of the gossip. You *have* to be there for the King's coronation.'

'I don't recall anything about that in the constitution.' She should know; she'd been force-fed the document as a child, reminded again and again of her royal obligations and all the ways she didn't measure up.

Languidly she crossed one leg over the other. The ambassador's gaze dropped to her bright sandals, then up past her linen trousers to the gauzy top in tropical shades of lime-green and vivid yellow that she'd picked up just last week in the markets.

No wonder he pursed his lips and frowned. She looked good, she reminded herself. In fact, she looked blooming. Obviously the early stages of pregnancy agreed with her now the sickness had passed. But, though she was dressed with casual chic, she'd refused to don the staid, formal clothes expected of a Bengarian princess.

She wasn't in Bengaria and had no intention of returning.

'If I may say, princess...' he paused long enough for

her to feel bile rise at that unctuous tone '…you have an obligation not only to your country but to your uncle, who sacrificed so much for you. Remember that he raised you.'

'And I'm the woman I am today because of him.' Let him chew on that for a while. When the ambassador simply frowned, she added, 'We've never been close. He'll hardly miss me in the throng.'

No doubt Cyrill would be surrounded by sycophants, people who had feathered their nests from the royal coffers.

'If I may say, Your Highness, that's a very…' He read her expression and paused. 'Unhelpful attitude.'

If he expected that to convince her, he had a lot to learn.

'I wasn't aware anyone expected me to be helpful.' She leaned forward a fraction. 'In fact, I seem to recall being advised months ago that it would be to the country's benefit if I left as quickly and quietly as possible.'

He had the grace to blush.

'Now.' She rose to her feet. 'Thank you for your visit. As always, it's a delight to be brought up to date with the news from Bengaria. But I'm afraid I've another appointment.'

'But you can't just—' She watched him swallow, his Adam's apple bobbing in that scrawny throat. She'd feel sorry for him if she didn't know him for one of Cyrill's yes-men who'd made Stefan's life and her own a nightmare obstacle course of deliberate disruption and sabotage. 'I mean.' He fiddled with his tie as if it were too tight. 'The baby.'

'Baby?' Marisa surveyed him with a glacial stare that would have done Cyrill himself proud.

'Your baby.'

Marisa said nothing. She had no intention of discussing her pregnancy with her uncle's envoy.

'King Cyrill had hoped… That is to say, he's already making arrangements…'

Arrangements to do what? Adopt out her child? Force her to have an abortion? Marisa's flesh crawled.

In the innermost recesses of her heart lurked a fear she might not have what it took to be a good mother. That she might let her child down. But despite her doubts Marisa would face down the King of Bengaria and the whole of his parliament before she let him lay a hand on her child.

'As ever, I'm fascinated by my uncle's plans.' She forced the words beyond the knot of fear in her constricting throat. 'Do tell.'

The ambassador shifted and cleared his throat.

Finally he spoke. 'The King has graciously decided to negotiate a royal match that will give your child legitimacy and save your reputation. He's been in discussion with the Prince of—'

Marisa flung up a hand and the ambassador lapsed into silence. Her stomach heaved as his words penetrated like arrows. This time it took almost a minute before she could speak.

'With someone who is willing to overlook the little matter of another man's child,' she murmured. 'In return for my uncle's help in shoring up his social position.' Her mouth twisted. 'Or is it his wealth? No, don't tell me, I really don't want to know.'

Cyrill must be desperate to contain any possible damage to the royal family's reputation. Or, just as likely, to have some positive media to counteract the negativity his harsh rule was attracting. There was nothing like a royal wedding and a royal baby to turn the tide of public opinion.

But not *her* baby!

Marisa would do anything to ensure her child wasn't a royal pawn. It would grow up as far from palace machinations as possible.

She was determined her child would have what she hadn't: love and a nurturing environment. She'd even begun to wonder if perhaps marriage to Damaso might provide that. He didn't love *her* but she had no doubt he cared for their baby.

Marisa drew a slow breath and dredged the depths of her strength. She felt ridiculously shaky but determined not to show it.

'You can thank my uncle for his concern but I'll be making my own arrangements from now on. Good day.'

Without a second glance, she turned and swept out of the room, the ambassador's protests a vague background babble over the sound of her rough breathing and the blood pulsing in her ears. If she didn't get to the bathroom soon...

'Madam, are you all right?'

It was Ernesto, Damaso's butler-come-bodyguard, assigned to accompany her whenever she went out. For the first time, she was truly thankful for his enormous height and sheer bulk.

'Please make sure the ambassador is escorted from the apartment.' She swallowed convulsively, feeling her insides churn uncomfortably, and pressed her hand to her mouth.

Ernesto hesitated only a split second, concern in his shrewd, dark eyes, then swung away.

'And make sure he doesn't return,' Marisa gasped.

'You'll never see him again, madam.' The bass rumble was ridiculously reassuring as she stumbled to the bathroom.

When she emerged Ernesto appeared with a laden tray.

'Thanks, but I'm not hungry.'

'If you've been unwell you need to replace your fluids. The mint tea will make you feel better.'

At Marisa's stare, he shrugged and put the tray on the coffee table. 'So Beatriz says.'

Great; he and the housekeeper were discussing her health now.

Yet the knowledge soothed rather than annoyed her. Ernesto and Beatriz, like Damaso's staff on the island, were unlike any servants she'd known. They genuinely cared about their employer and, by extension, her.

She wasn't used to being cared for. Stefan and she had shared a bond nothing could sever, but each had had their own pursuits and, once he'd become King, Stefan shouldered new responsibilities.

As for Damaso, Marisa was sure he cared. Look at the way he personally escorted her now to restaurants, dance clubs and parties, never leaving her side. Every night his tender seduction drew her more and more under his spell.

Damaso cared, all right. But whether for her or her baby, she wasn't sure.

She'd spilled her secrets to him, revealing details she'd never shared, and he'd held her and made love to her in such a way, she'd swear he understood.

And yet...

Marisa chewed her lip, confronting the doubts that had racked her since that memorable night when she'd given herself to him again. She'd opened up to Damaso in ways she never had with any man. The catharsis of reliving her past, and giving herself so completely, had left her limp and drained, yet more whole than she'd felt in years. Even the devastating loss of her twin seemed more bearable.

The next morning she'd woken with scratchy eyes and heavy limbs but to a sense of renewed hope. Until she'd found Damaso had left her to sleep late while he went to work.

What had she expected? That he'd stay with her, sharing his own secrets as she'd done hers?

She wasn't so naïve. Yet she'd hoped for *something*. Some breaking down of the barriers between them. At a physical level, the barriers had shattered, but emotionally? It felt like Damaso had retreated even further. She was no closer to knowing him than she'd been a month ago.

Oh, he was tender in bed, and solicitous when they went out. Her mouth twisted as she remembered how he'd staked his claim over her just last night at another exclusive party. Marisa wanted to believe it was because he felt something for her. But more likely he was doing what was necessary to get what he wanted—access to their baby.

The trouble was she longed to trust him as he urged, not just with her body but with her future and her child's. Even with her heart.

She sucked in a sharp, shocked breath.

How could she think like that? She'd loved two people in her life, her mother and her brother, and their deaths had all but shattered her. Loving was far too dangerous.

'Madam?'

Ernesto held out a steaming porcelain cup in his massive hand.

Dragged from her circling thoughts, Marisa accepted the cup. She was too wired to sit and eat the pastries Beatriz had prepared, but she'd learned to appreciate Brazilian mint tea. She lowered her head and inhaled, feeling a modicum of calm ease her tense body.

'I'll go out when I've had this.' She was too restless to stay indoors.

Ernesto nodded. 'By helicopter or car?'

It was on the tip of Marisa's tongue to say she wanted to walk, blocks and blocks through the teeming city. Anything to numb the pain and the trickle of fear the ambassador's words had stirred. Anything to blot out the fear that she was in danger of swapping one gilded cage for another.

She was safe from her uncle's machinations—he couldn't force her into an arranged marriage—but the fact remained she'd let weeks race by without coming up with a plan for her future and the baby's. She needed to decide where they'd live, not drift aimlessly.

A vision of Damaso's private island swam in her brain and her lips curved as she imagined splashing in the shallows with an ebony-haired toddler.

Marisa blinked and sipped her tea. Maybe it would soothe her need for action.

'Where is Damaso today?'

Stupid that her thoughts turned to him so often. He'd never pretended to care for her as anything more than the woman carrying his child. But this last week, despite logic, she'd imagined a deeper connection between them.

How could that be when he left her to her own devices all day? She told herself she was glad he found it so easy to push aside the intimacy of their nights together. Better than having him on hand, reminding her of his demand that they marry.

'He's out in the city.'

'In his office?' Damaso had pointed out the building to Marisa one night on their way to an exclusive club.

'No, madam.'

Ernesto's less than helpful answer made her prick up her ears. Or maybe it was because she sought distraction from her fears.

'I'd like to see him.' She watched over the top of the delicate cup as Ernesto's eyes widened a fraction.

'I'm not sure that's a good idea.'

'Why not?' What was Damaso doing that he wanted to keep from her? He was as close as a clam about his life.

Ernesto hesitated a moment. 'He's in one of the *favelas*.'

'*Favelas*?' Marisa was sure she'd heard the word before.

'Poor neighbourhoods. Where the houses aren't—' He shrugged, his English apparently failing him. 'A slum,' he said finally.

Marisa frowned. That was the last thing she'd expected. She put down her cup and saucer, relieved to have something to divert her from Cyrill's schemes. 'You can take me there.'

'Truly, madam, this isn't a good idea.'

Marisa smiled her sympathy at Ernesto as they negotiated a rutted dirt road, but refused to turn back. Not till she found Damaso and what had brought him here.

On either side of the track rose haphazard buildings,

some solid-looking and painted in bright colours, others looking like they'd been cobbled together with whatever materials could be salvaged. The scent of fires, spicy food and something much less savoury lingered in the air. Marisa plodded on. It wasn't the first place she'd visited that didn't have a reliable sewage system.

They approached a long building painted saffron-yellow and the bodyguards Ernesto had brought fanned out. Ernesto gestured for her to accompany him inside.

The first face she saw was Damaso's. He sat at a battered metal table with a group of men, all sipping coffee out of tiny cups, engrossed in conversation. His proud features were intent as he listened to an older man speak and he leaned back, as if fading into the background. Yet even in casual jeans and shirt he stood out from the rest.

Marisa's breath caught as she drank in the sight of him.

He didn't see her and she stopped just inside the open door, letting her senses adjust.

The building was cavernous. Over behind the men was an indoor basketball court where a bunch of gangly teens played, encouraged by catcalls and cheers.

From a door to the left came the clanging of pots and a delicious savoury scent that could only mean someone was cooking. Over on the far left, she heard music and voices, and straight ahead on a battered wall was tacked a collection of photos.

Instinctively she moved towards the photos, telling herself she hadn't lost her nerve about seeing Damaso. He was busy, and not with some dusky beauty as she'd half-feared.

Marisa wrestled with self-directed anger. Why had it been so imperative she see him? She could deal with her uncle's schemes without running to Damaso for support.

The photos ranged from ordinary snapshots to one or two that made her pulse trip a beat. That one of the skinny teenager, his eyes far too old for his face, his expression weary yet his stance all pugnacious machismo, as if he dared the world to mess with him. The wistful look on the old woman's crinkled face as she watched a young couple in bright colours dance on a cracked concrete floor, their bodies lithe and sinuous, the embodiment of sexual energy.

'What are you doing here, Marisa?'

'Admiring the art.' She didn't turn, preferring not to respond to Damaso's dark tone. 'Some of these are remarkable.'

'You shouldn't have come.' She heard him drag in a breath. 'Ernesto should have known better.'

'Don't blame Ernesto.' She turned and met his shadowed glare, wondering exactly what she'd interrupted. Damaso's tension was palpable. She'd never seen him so edgy. 'He didn't want to bring me here but his orders are to keep me safe, not a prisoner.'

Damaso's nostrils flared as he breathed deep, apparently searching for calm. He couldn't have missed the challenge in her tone. She'd agreed to stay with him, but on condition there was no coercion. Restricting her movements would violate that.

Marisa watched his hands bunch then flex, as if he resisted the urge to pick her up and cart her away. For a moment she was tempted to provoke him, break the invisible barrier that kept him so aloof while she felt impossibly needy.

Hurt and anger warred with pride. This wasn't the place.

'You think this place is safe?' Warning filled his voice.

'I have guards. Besides, you're here.' She didn't add that at least some of the locals had seemed friendly. She hadn't missed the wary looks of others and the way a few figures had skulked away into the shadows as they'd passed.

'That's different.'

Marisa tilted her head to one side, taking in his clenched jaw and the tight line of white around his mouth.

'I can see it is.' She wasn't a fool. 'But I was curious.'

'Now you've seen it, you can leave.'

That didn't even deserve a response. 'What is this place?'

Damaso shoved his hands into his pockets. 'A local gathering place. A community centre, if you like.'

'I'm sorry I interrupted your meeting.' She nodded to the group of seated men watching them.

'We'd finished. Now.' He reached out and took her arm, his hold implacable. 'It's time we left.'

'What are you hiding, Damaso?'

His head jerked back as if she'd slapped him and his gaze slid away. Marisa stared, stunned that her instinct had been right. He was concealing something.

Damaso's lips moved as if he were about to speak but he said nothing. His face took on that spare, hewn look that she'd come to suspect meant he repressed strong feeling.

Instinctively she covered his hand with her own.

'Now I'm here, won't you show me around?' She met his stare openly. 'It's important to you,' she said slowly, 'or you wouldn't be here.' For clearly this wasn't some high-powered finance meeting that would reap more profits for his ever-expanding empire. 'Please?'

His exhalation of breath was a warm gust on her face. 'You're not leaving till I do, are you?'

Marisa shook her head and felt the rock-solid muscle of his arm ease a little against hers.

'Very well.'

Damaso intended the tour to take a brief ten minutes but he'd reckoned without the inevitable interest Marisa aroused. People came out of the woodwork to see the gorgeous blonde Damaso Pires had brought into their midst.

As the clustering numbers grew, tension ratcheted up again. He couldn't believe she was in any danger with him. Yet he couldn't be comfortable with Marisa in these surroundings. It just wasn't right.

To her credit, Marisa wasn't fazed. She was interested in everything, not pushing herself forward, but not afraid to initiate conversation in her halting Portuguese that Damaso for one found endearing and sexy.

They loved her, drawn by her bright energy and enthusiasm. By the way she didn't shy from shaking hands and sharing a joke. By her interest, especially in the kids. Some girls had been having a dance class and showed what they'd learnt. When one, a little over-eager, stumbled when she attempted a cartwheel, Marisa showed her how to place her hands, shucking off her shoes and demonstrating, then helping the little one get the move right.

Damaso smothered a smile. It was the first time he'd seen his security staff lost for words. As for the kids, they regarded her with a mix of awe and acceptance that made him proud and infuriated at the same time.

'This is marvellous.' Marisa smiled up at the woman who'd served her at the large communal table and dipped her spoon back into the bowl that had been set before her. 'Tell me what it's called?'

'Feijoada—black bean stew.' Even now, with the budget to live on champagne and lobster, it was Damaso's favourite dish. In the days when he'd first eaten it, of course, there'd been very little meat to flavour the rich dish, and much more of the rice and beans.

'Do you think Beatriz would make it for us?'

He nodded. Beatriz, like he, had grown up with it.

One of the little girls sidled closer to Marisa on the long bench seat, her eyes wide. At a comment from Marisa in hesitant Portuguese, she grinned and began talking.

Damaso watched them communicate easily with so few words and felt something tighten and twist deep in his belly. He should have known Marisa would take a visit to a poor neighbourhood in her stride. As a princess, she was no doubt used to playing Lady Bountiful, bringing out that practised smile to charm the adoring crowds.

But this was something else. This wasn't stage-managed. He felt the warmth of her personality reach out and encompass him as it enthralled the little girl.

Yet some dark thing inside him rebelled at Marisa being here. It coiled through his gut, clawed through his veins and made him itch to drag her away to the world where she belonged. A world of luxury and ease, where he could take care of her while she nurtured the baby they'd created.

That was it. The baby.

She had to think of the baby's wellbeing, not salve her social conscience visiting the poor.

'It's time we left.'

He rose and held out his hand. Even to his own ears the words were abrupt and he saw startled looks directed his way.

The little girl shrank away as if he'd shouted at her and he felt heat score his cheeks as shame flared. But it couldn't counteract the terrible urgency gnawing at his innards. He had to get Marisa away from here. Now!

It took a lifetime for Marisa to move. His pulse galloped as he watched her turn and say something to the girl that made her grin shyly. Then Marisa rose from her wooden seat with all the grace of an empress. An empress who ignored his outstretched hand with a disdain that knifed right to his chest. Her gaze slid across his face before she turned and thanked first one person and then another for their hospitality.

They clustered around, responding to her warmth and sincerity, and absurdly Damaso felt locked out, as if he were alone in the darkness, cut off from a happiness he hadn't even known he'd grown accustomed to.

Absurd!

He was successful. Sought-after. He had it all, everything he'd ever dreamed of and more.

Yet when Marisa finally made a move to leave, turning not to him but to Ernesto, something fractured inside.

In two strides Damaso was at her side, tugging her arm through his. She stiffened and her smile grew fixed but she didn't pull away.

Good! He'd run out of patience.

CHAPTER ELEVEN

NEITHER SPOKE ON the journey. He was reminded of the night of the party when he'd been jealous and suspicious, when she'd stood up to him and they'd come together in such a conflagration it had melted his self-control.

But this was different. This was… He shook his head, unable to put a name to the vast, nameless void that had taken up residence in this chest the moment he'd seen Marisa in the squalor that had been the only world he'd known.

Nevertheless, he held himself in check as they entered the apartment and Marisa headed to the bedroom they shared.

Did he expect her to pack her things? Was that the source of the tension knotting his belly?

But she merely dropped her bag on the bed and headed for the bathroom. His hand on the door stopped it closing behind her.

'I'd like some privacy while I take a bath.' Her eyes fixed on his left ear and turbulent anger rose in a coiling wave. He would *not* be dismissed.

'Since when have you needed privacy for that?' Deliberately he let his gaze rove her body, lingering on the swift rise and fall of her lush, pert breasts, the narrow waist that always seemed impossibly tiny beneath his hands and the delicious curve of her hips.

'Since now, Damaso.' She turned away, unclasping her

chunky silver bracelet and putting it on a tray beneath the
mirror. 'I'm not in the mood for dealing with you.'

'*Dealing* with me?'

His gaze collided with hers in the mirror and he realised
when she flinched that he'd shouted.

Her chin inched up as she took a silver and turquoise
stud from her ear and let it clatter onto the tray.

'Your disapproval.' Her throat worked and something
dragged at his belly, like a plough raking deep and drawing blood. 'You couldn't have made it any clearer that you
don't want me meeting your friends. And don't try to tell
me those people aren't important to you. Anyone could see
they mean more than the social set you party with.'

Her hands worked at the other stud yet she couldn't
seem to drag it free.

'But if you think you can just dismiss me as not good
enough because I don't have a vocation or a career, because
I haven't yet made anything of my life, then you can think
again.' Her voice wobbled and the raw furrow in his belly
gaped wider, sucking his breath out as pain stabbed.

'I don't—'

'I don't want to hear it, Damaso. Not now.' Finally she
loosened the earring and it clattered onto the tray then
bounced to the floor. Marisa didn't notice. 'Not while I'm
trying to decide whether to leave.'

Her gaze dropped to her watch as she fumbled with
the band.

Damaso didn't realise he'd moved till he saw his hand
reach out and brush her fingers aside.

He swallowed down a toxic brew of self-disgust and
anger as he unclasped her watch and placed it on the crystal tray with her jewellery.

'I don't want you to leave.' For a miracle, the words
emerged steadily. He told himself Marisa was grieving and
insecure. She'd misunderstood his actions. There was no
danger of her leaving. He'd stop her, one way or another.

She shook her head and tendrils of spun gold feathered her cheeks. 'It's too late for that.' She put a hand to his chest and shoved.

As if that would move him. For all her energy, she was tiny. He captured her hand in his, pressing it hard against his chest.

'Marisa, you've got it wrong.' Damaso searched his brain for an explanation. That was it: the child. 'You have to be careful of the baby. In an area like that—'

'Stop it! I don't want to hear any more.' The way her voice suddenly rose silenced him. He'd never heard Marisa so...desperate.

She drew a shuddering breath. 'I know the baby is ultimately all you care about, Damaso, but don't try to dress up what happened today.' Her eyes met his, boring right into his soul. 'You disapproved of me being there because you disapprove of me. It was plain as the nose on your face.'

He saw the bright sheen of her eyes and knew he was on the verge of losing her.

'Disapprove of you?' His laugh was harsh. 'You have no idea.' He crowded her back against the vanity unit, his hands running over her as if learning her body's shape all over again, or ensuring she was whole and unscarred by today's outing.

'Don't try to seduce me, Damaso. It won't work. Not this time.'

He shook his head as he searched for the right words.

'I didn't want you there. It's not safe. It's not...' The words dried as his throat constricted. How could he explain that awful blank fear that had consumed him, seeing her there? His hands balled into straining fists. 'You shouldn't be in such a place.'

'I might have been born a princess, Damaso, but I don't live in an ivory tower.'

'You don't understand.' He hefted a deep breath that didn't fill his lungs. 'It's too dangerous.'

'For the baby. So you say.'

He gripped her shoulders and her startled eyes met his. 'Not just the baby. You too.' He ground the words out past a clenched jaw. 'You have no idea what can happen in a place like that. I needed to protect you, get you away from there.'

His breath sawed loud and fast, competing with the drumming blood in his ears. He knew he held her too tight but he couldn't get his hands to relax.

'What can happen, Damaso?' Her quiet voice penetrated the thunder of his pulse. Her eyes held his and for the first time he had her full attention. Maybe she'd listen now.

Her hand touched his cheek and the delicacy of it against his unshaven jaw reminded him of all the differences between them. Differences he'd ignored until today, when their two worlds had collided with shattering impact.

The palace and the slum.

'Too much.' His voice was hoarse as he ran his hands up and down her back, reassuring himself she really was all right. 'Disease, danger, violence.'

'Those people live there every day.'

'Because they have to. You don't. You're safe here. With me.' He planted a possessive palm over her breast, feeling its warm weight, satisfaction rising at the gasp of delight she couldn't stop.

She was his and he'd protect her.

He pressed closer, his thighs surrounding her, one arm wrapping around her, drawing her to him, while the other slipped under her top and flicked her bra undone.

'Damaso!' Her voice wasn't strident this time. She wasn't fighting him any more, *graças a Deus*. But something in her tone stopped him. Her gaze was steady and serious.

'How do you know so much about the *favelas*?'

He felt his lips hitch up in a mirthless smile. No point

denying it; she'd find out sooner or later, even if it wasn't public knowledge. 'Because it's where I'm from.'

Damaso waited for the shock to show in her eyes. The disgust.

Her hand brushed his cheek again then tunnelled through his hair, pulling his head down till his forehead touched hers.

'The place where we were today?'

Slowly he shook his head and drew another breath into cramped lungs that burned as they expanded. 'Somewhere much worse. It's long gone, bulldozed and redeveloped.'

She said nothing and with each second's silence he waited for her to pull away. Now she knew what he really was.

The opinion of others had never mattered. He'd been too busy clawing his way out of poverty to care about anything but climbing each successive step to success. But Marisa's reaction mattered.

His fingers flexed against her satiny skin, his hands big and rough against her delicate, refined body.

When she did move it took a moment to realise what she was doing. She pulled back but only to haul off her top and bra. Her summer-bright eyes held his as her clothes, a tangle of bright silk, fell to the floor.

'I'm sorry I worried you.' Her voice was high and breathless, but not as oxygen-starved as he was, watching her small hands anchor his much larger ones over her delectable breasts. The warmth of her soft body melted a little of the ice in his veins. Her nipples, firm and peaked, tickled his palms, making his breath ease out on a sigh.

His brain struggled to compute what she was doing. How had they gone from his life in poverty to this?

'You could just have told me.' Her gaze meshed with his as her hand went to the zip of his jeans.

Damaso swallowed hard, giving thanks for the strange yet wonderful impulses of his reckless princess.

* * *

Damaso drowsed at her breast, his hold encompassing her even in sleep. For the first time he hadn't demurred when she'd told him to stay where he was in the languid aftermath of love-making. Instead of rolling aside, he lay spread across her, as if melding himself with her.

For that was how their loving had felt. Slow and deliberate and possessive in a way that made Marisa's throat catch and her heart drum when she remembered it.

Yet there'd been desperation too, in his eyes and in the barely contained power of his body bringing her to ecstasy again and again.

Marisa smiled against his warm skin. She was making up for all those years of sexual abstinence. Just one of the benefits of having a lover like Damaso.

Her smile faded.

What would he be like as a husband?

For the first time she allowed herself to consider the possibility dispassionately, pushing aside her anxiety at the idea of tying herself to any man. Would Damaso be any more controlling than the unknown aristocrat her uncle wanted her to marry?

Damaso was dominant, bossy, used to getting his own way. But he'd never bullied her like her uncle, and no one could accuse him of being cold like her father. The more she knew him, the more she wondered how she'd ever thought him cold. Damaso was hot-blooded and passionate. Not just in bed; when he talked of their baby the glow in his eyes revealed a depth of feeling that had at first scared her and now... Marisa blinked. It soothed her, she realised.

She *liked* him caring so strongly for their baby. It was reassuring to know that if something happened to her Damaso would be there to look after their child.

He made her feel less alone. In the past she'd had Stefan and losing him had devastated her. That tearing hurt had made her even more determined not to open herself up to anyone. But slowly Damaso had been breaking down her barriers. Now he was *there*, firmly planted in her life, pushing the yawning chasm of darkness back till she no longer felt on a precipice of pain.

He tried to protect her too. Damaso was always at her side now at any society event.

Then there was his reaction to her visit today.

Marisa's brow puckered, remembering his stark expression when he'd spoken of the danger. She remembered the scars on his body and how he'd got them. Yet instinct told her this was about more than some physical threat.

Clearly Damaso had reacted on a visceral level. Perhaps, if she understood him, she might trust him enough to accept what he offered.

Shame bit. She'd been focused on her independence and on grappling with the changes this pregnancy would bring. She'd been self-absorbed, every bit as selfish as the press painted her.

Oh, she'd been curious about Damaso, always fascinated by the man who'd slowly begun to reveal himself to her. But she'd never pushed to delve deeper. True, he was taciturn about his past, always focusing on the here and now or the future. But she could have tried harder. He'd been genuinely sympathetic when she'd told him about herself. What had she given in return?

Damaso was inextricably part of her life now. As her child's father and more, much more.

Marisa swept her hands over his broad shoulders, marvelling at the closeness she felt, the bond that wasn't just to do with the baby but with them as a couple. She hugged him tight.

A couple. It was a new concept.

Maybe for the first time she had, after all, found a man she could trust.

* * *

Her second trip to the *favela* tested his temper but not in
the way she'd expected.

'I thought we'd agreed it was too risky for you to spend
time there.' He stood, tie wrenched undone at his throat,
shirt sleeves rolled up to reveal strong, sinewy arms and
fists buried in his pockets. His brow was like a thunder-
cloud as he watched her from the door to the private roof-
garden.

He looked vital and sexy, and something clenched hard
in Marisa's stomach as she met his scowl. Kneeling as she
was, she had to crane her neck to survey his long, powerful body but it was worth it. She had to scotch the impulse
to go to him and let him kiss her. If she did there was a
danger she might cave in rather than stand her ground. He
was that persuasive.

'I listened to what you said, Damaso, which is why I
agreed when Ernesto insisted on taking other guards.' Pri-
vately she thought the security precautions overkill but
she'd fight one battle at a time.

'He should never have allowed you—'

'We've been over that.' She lifted one wet hand and
pushed her hair off her face with the back of her wrist.
'Don't you dare bully Ernesto. He was just doing his job. If
he'd tried to stop me I'd have gone without him.' It wouldn't
be the first time she'd evaded professional minders.

'I was safe. And I was welcome.' The generous welcome
she'd received had been heart-warming. 'I helped a little
with one of the classes and talked to the co-ordinator about
reviving the photography project.'

Marisa wasn't qualified to teach but knew a little about
that. Enough to foster the efforts of the few youngsters
who'd taken part in an earlier program to develop photography skills. The co-ordinator had talked enthusiastically
about career-building. For Marisa, though, it was about

helping others find the peace and satisfaction she herself felt looking at the world through the lens of a camera.

'That would mean going there regularly!'

Marisa didn't bother answering. She'd known Damaso would be angry but she was determined to proceed. For herself, because selfishly she clung to the idea she could be useful, and for the kids.

Was it preposterous to think she also did this for Damaso? For the orphan he'd been, struggling to survive in a tough environment? Who had helped him? Ever since he'd let her glimpse the pain of his past, she'd found herself imagining him on streets like those she'd walked today. Was it hardship that had honed him into the man he was—ruthless and single-minded, guarding his heart so closely?

She groped for the soap that had fallen into the basin of warm water, feeling it slippery on her palm.

'And it doesn't explain what you're doing with *that*.' Damaso's voice dropped to resonant disapproval.

Marisa surveyed the skinny dog she held by the scruff of the neck. It trembled as it stood in the big basin of tepid water but made no move to escape.

'He needed a home.'

'Not this home.' Damaso stalked across to stand over them, his long shadow falling on the pup.

'If it's a problem, I'll take him elsewhere.' She paused, more nervous than she'd expected now it came to it. She was sure of her ground, wasn't she? Yet if he called her bluff... No, that wouldn't happen. 'I'm sure I'll have no trouble finding somewhere to stay where dogs are welcome.'

The silence was so loud it reverberated in her ears.

'Is this you making a point, Marisa?'

She looked up to see him watching her through narrowed eyes.

'No one ever accused me of subtlety. But, no, it's not.

The poor thing was in need of a home, that's all. And I...'
She shrugged and lathered the dog's fur. 'It seemed right.'

She could have said more—about how she'd always
wanted a pet, about her growing desire to care for something after being so alone. But in truth she'd looked into
those hopeful, canine eyes and felt a twang of fellow feeling. Here was another outcast, someone who didn't fit and
didn't expect to be wanted.

Damaso moved closer and the dog shivered. Marisa put
out a soothing hand to gentle it.

'I can find a good home for it. It doesn't belong here.'
His offer surprised her and she jerked her gaze back up.

'Thank you.' His expression told her he didn't want anything to do with the dog. 'I appreciate it. But I want to look
after him myself.'

If she could do a good job of looking after a dog, perhaps
she could work her way up to caring for a baby. Besides,
he trusted her; she couldn't let him down now.

Damaso's gaze shifted to the dog and Marisa sucked
in her breath at the antipathy in that stare. No wonder the
poor thing was shaking.

'You can't be serious. Look at it! It's a mongrel. If you
must have a dog, at least let me get one for you from a
breeder.'

'A pure-bred, you mean?' Her hand slowed and she put
the soap down.

'Why not? Surely that's more fitting?'

'For a princess?'

'It's what you are, Marisa. There's no point pretending
otherwise.'

'Is that what you think I'm doing? Pretending to be
someone I'm not?' Hurt scored her voice. Is that what he
thought she'd been doing on her visit today?

'Of course not.' He strode away then spun on his foot.
'Just look at it. No matter what you do, it will always be a
slum-bred mongrel.'

The words echoed in her head. Marisa read Damaso's taut features, the rigidity of his big frame. She'd only seen him like this once before, when he'd been so adamant she stay away from the *favela*.

Because he was ashamed of where and how he'd grown up?

It didn't seem possible. She'd never met a man more grounded and self-assured than Damaso.

Yet he harped so often about her royal lineage, as if that mattered a scrap compared with character.

'It's probably carrying disease too.'

Marisa shook her head and reached for a bucket of rinse water. 'I've taken Max to the vet and he's had the all clear.'

'Max?'

Marisa tipped the water gently over the dog and reached for another bucket.

'He reminds me of my great-uncle, Prince Maximilian.' Despite the tension in the air, she smiled. 'Same long nose, same big brown eyes.'

Great-Uncle Max had been a scholar, happier with his books than playing politics, but he'd always had time for Marisa, even hiding her when she'd played hooky from history classes. But then Uncle Max had had a way of bringing the past alive in a way her teachers didn't.

She blinked hard, surprised to feel her eyes prickle at the memory of those brief snatches of childhood happiness.

Damaso watched her intently from beneath lowered brows, his gaze shifting from her to the dog.

'You really do care about the animal.' There was a thread of shock in Damaso's voice.

Admittedly Max, drenched and bony, wasn't the most handsome dog around, but he had character.

Marisa shrugged and finished rinsing off the soap suds. Even she was surprised at how quickly she and Max had bonded. She couldn't send him back to the streets, not now. Despite what Damaso thought, this wasn't some deliberate

test of his forbearance. It had been an impulsive decision
that she'd known instinctively was right.

'Very well, it can stay, but I don't want to see it inside.'

Damaso turned back into the apartment before Marisa
could thank him, but a tiny glow of heat flared inside and
spread. 'Hear that, Max?' She reached for the towel Beatriz had provided and began to dry him. 'You can stay.'

They'd both found sanctuary with Damaso. His reasons
weren't purely altruistic, since he was angling to convince
her to stay long-term. But Marisa had experienced enough
duplicity to know actions did count louder than words.

She wondered if Damaso had any idea how much his
generosity meant.

CHAPTER TWELVE

'THE CITY LOOKS wonderful at this time of night.'

Damaso watched across the table as Marisa leaned back in her seat, sipping from a goblet of sparkling water as she surveyed the panorama. The view from his private roof garden had always been spectacular but he'd never found time to appreciate it until Marisa had moved in with him.

There were a lot of things he hadn't fully appreciated.

His gaze roved her golden hair, loose over her shoulders, the dreamy expression in her eyes and the ripe lushness of her breasts beneath the filmy, sea-green top.

He'd known many beautiful women but none of them had made the breath seize in his lungs or his chest contract.

'I love this city.' Her smile widened.

'You do?' He raised his beer glass to his lips rather than reveal how pleased he was by her announcement. 'Why?'

She shrugged. 'It's vibrant, so different from Bengaria. There's so much happening, and the Paulistanos have such energy.' She looked at the table between them and the remains of the meal Beatriz had served. Her hand slipped to her stomach. 'Plus, I love the food. If I'm not careful, I'll be fat as butter by the time the baby's born.'

Damaso shook his head. Only a lover would know she'd put on a mere couple of pounds during her pregnancy. As that had only made her pert breasts fuller, he wasn't complaining.

He tried to imagine her swollen with his child and a stab of possessiveness seared through him.

Just as well she enjoyed the life here. He wasn't letting her go, even if she had yet to come to terms with the fact.

'My uncle has invited me to his coronation.'

Damaso stilled, fingers tightening on his glass. 'You're not going? You hate Cyrill.'

'I don't know,' she said slowly. 'At first I didn't intend to, but I'm wondering. I don't want to see *him*, but sometimes it feels like I'm hiding here, afraid to go home and face the music.' Her jaw angled higher in that determined way she had. 'I don't like that.'

He frowned. 'I thought you told me Bengaria wasn't home.'

She shrugged. 'I wasn't happy there but it's in my blood.'

'So what are you thinking? That you owe it to your uncle to hold his hand through the coronation? You want to play happy families with him?'

Marisa's mouth turned down. 'Not that. I just wondered if it wasn't better to face them all.'

'Why?' He leaned close. 'So they can lecture you about your irresponsible behaviour in getting pregnant?'

Damaso silently cursed his straight talking when she winced and looked away. Yet everything in him rose up in protest at the idea of her leaving, even for a short visit.

If she went to Bengaria, what was to stop her staying? Certainly not love for him. They had great sex, and she seemed as content as he to spend time together, but nothing she'd done or said indicated she'd fallen for him.

His pulse quickened. Was that what he wanted—Marisa head over heels in love with him?

That would solve all his problems. Marisa in love would be a Marisa committed to staying. It would hardly matter that he didn't know the first thing about love or relationships. She had enough warmth for the pair of them, the three of them.

In his bleaker moments he wondered if he had it in him to learn how to love.

'You think going back would be a mistake?'

Damaso paused, conscious that this was the first time Marisa had asked his advice.

Was it wishful thinking, or was this a turning point?

Stifling a triumphant smile, he tempered his words, cautious not to sound dictatorial like her uncle. Marisa could be persuaded, not ordered. He'd learned that quickly. Better if she thought staying was her decision.

'I think you need to consider how your uncle will try to use your presence to his advantage. Do you want to be his dupe?'

The tightening of her lips told him he'd struck a chord. Marisa was proud. She wouldn't want to play into the hands of a man she despised.

'Why don't you decide later?' Damaso knew better than to push his advantage. 'Tell me about your day,' he urged. 'I haven't seen you for hours.'

There was another first. He looked forward to their evenings together, discussing the day's events. It was something he'd never experienced with anyone else.

'I took the kids to the gallery.' She leaned forward, her eyes shining, and he congratulated himself on hitting on something to take her mind off Cyrill. 'You should have seen how excited they were. Silvio spent a couple of hours with them and they drank it all in.'

'I'm sure they did.' He remembered the first time he'd left the neighbourhood where he'd grown up. The excitement and fear. The children Marisa had taken under her wing with her photography classes would never have dreamed of anything as plush as Silvio's gallery. As the most successful photographer in South America, and probably beyond, he could name his own price for his work.

'I have to thank you for introducing me to him.' Marisa's hand found his and he threaded his fingers through hers, marvelling again at how something so delicate and soft could be so strong. 'I've admired his work for years, but...'

'No need to thank me.' They'd been over that weeks ago, when Damaso had taken her to Silvio's gallery. She'd been in seventh heaven, so rapt in Silvio's artwork that the photographer had taken an immediate shine to her. They'd been thick as thieves ever since.

Damaso might have been jealous of the way Marisa spoke so often of Silvio, except it was his work she was interested in, and her responsiveness to Damaso was unabated.

Anything that strengthened Marisa's ties to Brazil, such as her friendship with Silvio, was something Damaso encouraged. Besides, watching her enthusiasm as she talked about how her young photographers had blossomed at this rare opportunity was like watching a flower open to the sun.

Something stirred and eddied in his chest as a smile lit her face.

She was so happy.

It was only now, seeing her excitement, hearing her enthusiasm, that he realised how she'd changed. She'd always seemed vibrantly alive. But now Damaso knew her well enough to recognise that in the past some of her vivacity had been a persona, like clothing worn to project an image.

Damaso knew about that. In the early days he'd acted the part of successful businessman even when he'd had barely enough money to feed himself. He'd poured everything into becoming the man he was determined to be. Convincing others to trust him had been part of that.

Seeing Marisa glow from within, he realised the woman he'd met in the jungle had been going through the motions, despite her bright, engaging smile. Grief had muted her.

The real Marisa was stunning, almost incandescent. The sort of woman to draw men, like moths to flame.

He'd never felt as lucky as he did now, despite the niggle

of doubt, because she hadn't yet agreed to marry him. His hand tightened on his beer and he took another swallow.

'Silvio offered to meet them again and look at their work. Isn't that fantastic?'

'Fantastic,' he murmured. 'But they're already learning a lot from you.'

Marisa's sessions with the kids had been a huge success. He'd heard from a number of sources how enthusiastically not only the teens but their parents too had responded, plus he'd seen the results.

Marisa shook her head. 'I'm an amateur.'

'A talented amateur.'

'Flatterer.' Her eyes danced and again Damaso felt familiar heat in his belly.

It still unsettled him, knowing Marisa was going to the *favela*. He wanted to lock her away so she couldn't be hurt. But seeing her now, he knew he was right to hold back.

Movement at the end of the table caught his eye as the mongrel dog sidled up to her chair. With a fond glance, Marisa reached down and stroked its head, then tickled it under the chin. The dog closed its eyes in ecstasy and leaned closer.

Damaso's mouth thinned. What did she see in it? Watching her delicate fingers ruffle its fur just seemed wrong. He could give her a dog bred specifically to be a perfect companion. Instead she settled for a ragged mongrel that looked like it belonged on the streets, no matter how much she bathed and brushed it.

Marisa caught the direction of his stare.

'Why don't you like him?' Marisa's head tilted to one side in that characteristic look of enquiry.

Damaso shrugged. 'I don't have time for pets.'

Her silence told him she didn't buy that.

'But it's not just any pet, is it? You offered to get me another dog to replace him.' She paused, studying him carefully. 'It's something about Max.'

Damaso said nothing. He'd agreed to let the animal stay. What more could she want?

'It's because of where he comes from, isn't it?' She leaned across the table. 'Is that why you can't bear to look at him?'

Marisa sank back in her chair, her fingers burrowing deep into Max's fur as understanding hit out of the blue.

She'd been in Damaso's island home, and here in his city penthouse, and only now realised that, while he didn't display his wealth with crass ostentation, everything was of the highest quality materials and craftsmanship.

Nor had she seen anything with the patina of age— no antiques, nothing second-hand. Everything was pristine, as if it had been made yesterday. Many of the pieces had been created by world-renowned artisans, from the artwork to the furniture, and of course the architectural design of the buildings.

The same applied to his luxury hotel in the Andes. Only the best, nothing ordinary or even old.

Terrible foreboding tingled down Marisa's backbone and she straightened, putting down her glass. She put both hands on the table, as if to draw strength from the polished metal.

'What is it?' No fool, Damaso had picked up her sudden mood change, from curiosity to stomach-curdling distress.

'Everything you own is top of the range, isn't it? Only the absolute best.' Even the kitchen where Beatriz presided would do a Michelin-starred restaurant proud.

'What of it? I can afford it and I appreciate quality.'

'Quality.' The word tasted bitter. It had been a favourite of her uncle's, especially when he berated her for mixing with the 'wrong' sort of people.

Marisa swallowed hard, telling herself she was mistaken. Yet nothing could dispel the suspicion now it had surfaced.

'Marisa? What is it?' Damaso's brows drew down in a

ANNIE WEST155

frown that, instead of marring his features, emphasised their adamantine charisma. 'There's nothing wrong with owning beautiful things.'

'It depends why you want them.'

For long seconds she fought the sickening idea, but it was no good. Finally the words poured out. 'Is that why you're so insistent marriage is our only option?'

His eyes widened. 'What are you talking about? I don't see the connection.'

'I come with a pedigree. Having a royal title means I'm *quality*.' She dragged in a breath that didn't fill her lungs and stared into his expressionless features, looking for some sign she was wrong.

'You think I'm hung up on a royal title?'

Marisa pressed her palms harder into the cool metal of the table.

'I know you want my baby.' How stark the words sounded, crashing through the truce they'd built so painstakingly. Yet she couldn't shy away from the truth. 'But maybe there's more to it.'

Inside a voice cried that she was wrong. That Damaso was different. But how could she trust her judgement on this? She'd been wrong before.

'What do you mean?' He sat so still she knew he exercised steely control.

'Your reaction to me visiting the *favela* is out of proportion to the danger, especially given the bodyguards you insist on.' Something flashed in his eyes and her heart dived. 'I think the reason you don't like Max is because he comes from a slum.'

Marisa paused and waited but Damaso said nothing. The only animation was the tic of a pulse in his clenched jaw.

'Tell me the truth, Damaso.' She sucked in an unsteady breath. 'Do you want me as a trophy to add to your collection? After all, a princess comes pretty close to the top of the heap if you care for titles and *quality*.' Try as she might, she couldn't stop herself gagging on the word.

She'd thought she knew Damaso, that they shared something fragile and precious, something that made her happier than she could ever remember being. She'd begun to trust him, to hope.

'If you want to hide from your past and pretend it never happened, saddling yourself with me isn't the way to do it. Remember, most people don't think of me as a quality item. I'm sullied goods.'

'Don't talk like that!' He lunged across the table, his hand slamming down on hers, holding her captive. His dark eyes sparked, as if she'd tapped into a live volcano. 'Don't ever say such things about yourself.'

Marisa tried to look down her nose at him. She'd learned the trick from her haughty uncle and it had proven invaluable when she'd wanted to hide private hurt. But it didn't work now. Somehow she'd lost the knack—or Damaso had burrowed too far beneath her defences.

Desperation added an edge to her voice. 'Why not? It's what everyone thinks, even if they don't say it to my face. You might consider me the royal icing on the cake of your success, something special to add to your collection.' She swept a glance beyond the exquisite hand-forged table and chairs to the sculptures scattered through his private garden that would have done any national gallery proud. She gulped, her throat raw. 'But I'm flawed, remember? That detracts from my value.'

He moved so fast, her head spun. Large hands cupped her cheeks, turning her head up to where he towered above her.

'Don't ever say that again.' He bit the words out, his face drawn as if in pain, his eyes furious. Oddly, though, his hands felt gentle against her chilled flesh. 'I won't have it, do you hear? You're so wrong.'

Damaso looked down into her wide, drenched eyes and

had never felt so furious or helpless. Why couldn't she see what he saw? A woman worthy of admiration and respect. A woman unlike any he'd known.

Marisa blinked, refusing to let the glittering tears fall. It was typical that even now she put on a show of pride.

Yet the reminder of her vulnerability tore through him. Damaso dropped to his knees beside her seat, only vaguely aware of the dog darting out of the way.

He felt as if something had broken inside him when he saw her hurting so badly.

Leaning close, he drew in the familiar scent of green apples and sweet woman. Every instinct clamoured for him to haul her to him and make love to her till he blotted all doubt from her mind. But she needed to hear the words.

He swallowed hard. 'You've begun to believe your uncle's lies.' He saw her eyes widen. 'He's always put you down, tried to restrict you and mould you, but you didn't let him. You were too strong for that. Don't let him win now by undermining your confidence.'

Damaso paused, letting her digest that.

'For the record, any man would be proud to have you as his wife. And not because of your royal blood. You're bright and caring, not to mention beautiful. You're intelligent, fun and good company. You must have noticed how everyone wants to be with you.'

It was painful to watch the doubt still clouding her eyes. 'You know how much I want you, Marisa.' He grabbed one of her hands and planted it on his chest so she could feel the way his heart sprinted.

'You want my baby,' she said slowly. 'But do you want me or the cachet of marrying into royalty? If social status is important, that would be some achievement for a boy from the slums.'

'I want us to be a family.' The words rumbled up from some place deep inside. *Family.* The strength of his need for Marisa and their child undid him. 'I want to be with

our child and I want to be with *you*. You know that. You
felt the chemistry between us from the first.'

'You mean the sex?' She breathed deep and he had the
impression she had to force the words out. 'People don't
marry for that. What other reason could you have?'

Damaso looked into those brilliant, guarded eyes and
realisation slammed into him. He'd seen that yearning look
before, years ago, when he'd broken off with a lover who'd
begun to want too much.

Perhaps Marisa didn't know it, but it was emotion she
craved from him. Shunned by her family and her country,
Marisa needed love.

A lead weight plummeted through his gut.

Marisa wanted the one thing he didn't know how to give.

For a moment he thought of lying, trotting out the trite
words that would salve her pain. But Damaso couldn't do
it. She'd see straight through the lie and convince herself
it was for the worst possible reason.

Panic rocked him. He'd do so much for her. Anything
except let her go.

He had nothing to give her except the truth.

Damaso reached for her hand and closed his fingers
around it. Her other hand was still plastered against his
chest. Did she notice how his heart raced?

'You think I surround myself with beautiful things to
escape my past?' He drew a harsh breath and forced himself to go on, ignoring a lifetime's instinct for privacy. He
had to share what he'd hidden from the world or risk losing Marisa.

'You could be right,' he said eventually and heard her
hiss of indrawn breath. Her hands twitched in his and he
tightened his hold implacably, refusing to let her pull away.
He stroked his thumb over hers where it rested on his chest.

'I started with nothing but the clothes on my back.' He
grimaced. 'I was determined to shake off the dust of what
passed for my home as soon as I could. By sheer hard work

and some very lucky breaks I succeeded and, believe me, I never once looked back with regret. As soon as I could, I surrounded myself with the trappings of success. Sharp clothes, swanky office, beautiful women.'

At Marisa's expression he smiled, buoyed a little at what he hoped might be jealousy. 'Why wouldn't I? I'm only human.'

'I'm not judging.'

He shrugged. 'I'm not ashamed of enjoying success. My priority was always to plough back profits into the business and have enough capital to optimise any opportunity. That's how I moved from running errands to being a tourist guide and then owner of a tour company. We became known for delivering the best vacation experiences, taking people to places others couldn't or wouldn't.

'As the profits grew, my interests spread across a range of ventures. I'd always had a taste for clean clothes and comfortable housing and saw no reason not to indulge myself.'

He watched Marisa digest that. 'Along the way I developed an interest in modern art, possibly from visiting so many galleries. When I got money, I bought pieces I liked. Just as I bought cars and houses that appealed.'

Damaso paused, remembering her accusation. 'I'd never considered it before but you're right. I prefer to own beautiful things. I feel no need for external reminders of where and how I grew up. I'm surrounded by others who share similar memories, even if we don't speak of them.'

Marisa was silent for a moment. 'Ernesto?'

Damaso nodded. 'And Beatriz. All my personal staff. I didn't know them when I was a kid, but they come from similar places.'

'No wonder they think the world of you. You've given them the chance they needed.'

He shrugged. It was easy to lend a hand when you had

his advantages. Marisa made it sound like he was some
sort of saviour of the slums.

He thought of her dog, rescued from a similar place,
and winced. Marisa had hit the nail on the head. Whenever
he looked at her petting that mutt, it highlighted the gulf
between her and him: the refined princess and the rough-
and-ready slum kid.

'Damaso? What is it? You're holding me so tight.'

Instantly he eased his grip. But he didn't let her go.
Anxiety clutched his belly. He'd never spoken about his
childhood. But if he wanted to keep Marisa…

'You think I can't bear to be reminded of where I came
from, but I carry it in my bones.'

He wanted to leave it at that but Marisa needed more. At
the same time, he realised this wasn't just about easing her
fears. She'd cared enough to wonder about his past, not just
now, but before this. How many had done that?

Pleasure and horror surged.

'Tell me.'

He let her hands go and stood, turning towards the city
vista.

'I barely remember my mother and I have no idea who
my father was. I didn't have a real home. I lived…' He swallowed and forced himself to go on. 'You've seen photos of
ragged kids scavenging on garbage heaps? That was me.'

Suddenly he was there again, the odours pungent in the
rain, the ground slippery mud and worse beneath his feet,
his saturated clothes sticking to his skinny body.

Damaso felt movement and realised she'd come to stand
beside him.

'Later there were charity hand-outs, but my main memory is the pain of an empty belly. All day, every night.' He
blinked and the images before his eyes resolved into the
downtown cityscape.

Marisa's hand slipped into his and his fingers closed
around it. Strange how good that touch felt.

'You think I overestimate the danger for you. Maybe I do.' The admission cost him. Every instinct urged him to keep Marisa and their child away from there. 'But where I grew up...' He lifted tight shoulders. 'I saw too much violence to take safety for granted.'

'Those knife scars,' she said, her voice soft.

Damaso nodded. He refused to tell her the details of gang rivalries, drug dealing and more. 'I saw death up close too often. I was lucky to get out when I did. A lot of kids didn't. The neighbourhood you visit is much safer than mine, but something inside me screams out every time you go there.'

'I'm sorry.' She leaned against him, her weight warming his side.

'But you still want to help those children.' His mouth twisted. He hated her being there but how could he be anything but proud and moved that she wanted to help?

'You think I'm being selfish?' Her face turned up to his and he read her doubt.

'I think you're a wonderful, warm-hearted woman and I want you in my life.' He turned and put his arms around her, pulling her close.

'Really?'

'Absolutely. Your social status and bloodline never mattered to me. I take people as I find them— rich, poor or in between.' He lifted her face so she looked into his eyes. 'I want you for purely personal reasons and I don't give a damn what anyone else thinks. Understood?'

For long seconds she watched him silently then she stood on tiptoe and whispered against his mouth. 'Understood.'

The look in her eyes made his heart swell.

CHAPTER THIRTEEN

'YOU LOOK STUNNING.' Damaso surveyed her appreciatively. From the top of her golden head to her jewelled stilettos, she was perfection.

Covertly he searched for some evidence of her pregnancy but even after several months she still appeared trim and taut. He looked forward to the day when it would be obvious she was pregnant.

Possessiveness raked familiar talons through his insides. He didn't want to share Marisa. He wanted to keep her with him, away from the men who slavered after her wherever she went.

'Why, thank you.' She twirled, her multi-coloured dress flaring high, revealing toned legs, lightly tanned and delectable. His groin tightened as he thought of some of the things he'd prefer to do with the evening.

But this was her night.

'I have something for you.' His voice was gruff. He told himself that just because she'd refused to accept anything but hospitality from him didn't mean she'd refuse this. He reached for the slim leather case on the bedside table. She was so stubbornly independent, who knew how she'd react?

Damaso forced a smile, feeling tense muscles stretch. What was wrong with him? He'd given women gifts before, casually lavish presents that had meant little.

But this wasn't casual. This he'd chosen personally, had had it designed specifically for Marisa.

He watched her eyebrows arch as she recognised the distinctive logo of one of the world's top jewellery designers.

'There was no need.' She made no move to reach for it and a cold feeling invaded the pit of his stomach.

'I know.' He held her eyes but for the first time in weeks had no idea what she was thinking. Had the closeness between them been a mirage?

'You admire so many Brazilian designers, I thought this would appeal. When I saw it I thought of you.' It was true. No need to reveal his long consultation with the designer about Marisa and her style.

He proffered the box and after a moment she took it. Heat swirled through him in a ribbon of satisfaction.

She didn't open the gift immediately but smoothed her hand over the embossed emblem. Finally she lifted the lid and he heard the snatch of her indrawn breath.

For long seconds she said nothing, eyes fixed on the contents, lush lips slightly parted. Then her throat worked.

Had he miscalculated? Got it wrong?

Eyes as brilliant as the summer sky met his. The way she looked at him made him feel ten feet tall.

'They're absolutely gorgeous.' The catch in her voice tugged at something inside and Damaso wanted to reach out and gather her close. He told himself to wait. 'I've never seen anything like them.'

That was exactly what he'd wanted, because he'd never met a woman like her. 'You like them?'

'*Like* them?' She shook her head, her expression bordering on dazed. 'They're fabulous. How could anyone not like them?'

'Good, then you can wear them tonight.'

Was it his imagination or did she retreat a fraction?

'Why, Damaso? Why the expensive gift?'

He stared down, willing her to accept. 'You deserve to celebrate your first public exhibition. The cost is immaterial; you know I can afford it.'

'Not *my* exhibition.' Despite the doubt in her eyes, her lips curved slightly. 'Tonight is about the kids' photography.'

'Not according to Silvio. From the way he talks, he has big plans for you.' Damaso watched as delicate colour washed her cheeks. 'As well as for your class.'

'So it's a congratulatory gift, because you think I should celebrate?'

Damaso hesitated, reading her anticipation. She wanted more but what could he say? That seeing her contentment and purpose had made him happier than he could ever remember ?

That he wanted to keep that and keep *her*?

That he wanted to put his ring on her finger and bind her to him?

He'd had enough of waiting and battled not to behave like an unreconstructed male chauvinist, forcing her to stay despite her doubts.

'You've worked hard and achieved so much,' he said at last. 'You're making a difference to those kids, giving them skills and confidence and using your connections to open up a new world to them.'

'Really?' It didn't seem possible but Marisa's eyes shone brighter.

He nodded, his throat closing as he saw how much his words meant. Marisa was so active and energetic, sometimes it was easy to forget the burden of doubt she struggled with.

'As an up and coming photographer, you need to look glamorous at your premiere.'

'Looking the part, then?' Her eyes dropped and Damaso reached out and tilted her chin up. Her soft skin made his fingers slide wide, caressing her.

'Far more than that, Marisa. I…'

She leaned towards him and he had the sudden overwhelming conviction she was waiting for him to say something deep, something about how he felt.

Damaso swallowed, knowing he was on dangerous ground.

She'd become a vital part of his future, her and the baby. They brightened his world in a way he'd never thought possible. Yet if he blurted that out her beautiful mouth would thin and she'd turn away.

'I'm proud of you, Marisa. You're a special woman and I'd be honoured if you'd wear my gift tonight.'

Something that might have been disappointment flickered in her eyes then she nodded, but her lips curved in a smile. Damaso assured himself he'd misread her.

'Thank you. I'd like that,' she said huskily.

He reached into the open box and took out the necklace, letting the fall of brilliant burnt-orange gems spill across his palm.

'They remind me of you,' he murmured, watching the light catch them. 'Light and colour and exuberance, but with innate integrity.' He looked up to find her wide gaze fixed not on the strands of gems but on him.

'Really?'

He nodded and moved behind her, drawing the ends carefully together around her throat. 'Absolutely.' Quickly he fastened the clasp and drew her across to a full-length mirror. 'They're pure summer, just like you.'

'What are the stones?' She sounded awed, as well she might. A frisson ran through him at how perfect they looked on her—how perfect she looked, wearing his gift.

'Imperial topaz, mined here in Brazil.'

Marisa lifted a hand to her throat then let it drop, her eyes wide as she stared at the necklace. From its wide topaz-and-diamond collar, separate strands of faceted topaz fell in an asymmetrical cluster to just above her cleavage. It was modern, sexy and ultra-feminine. Just like Marisa.

'You're the most beautiful woman I've ever seen.' At least he could admit that truthfully.

Predictably she opened her mouth as if to protest, but Damaso reached around her and pressed a finger to her siren's mouth.

'Put the earrings on.'

Silently she complied.

'And the bracelet.' A moment later diamonds and topaz encircled her slim arm and Damaso wrapped his arms around her and drew her back against his chest, watching their reflections in the long mirror.

'You like them? You're happy?'

Marisa nodded silently, but her eyes glowed.

He told himself that was enough for tonight. He'd been right to hold the ring back instead of proposing. But time was running out. He refused to wait much longer to claim her.

Marisa's cheeks ached from smiling. Ever since she and Damaso had stepped off the red carpet and into Silvio's soaring studio, she'd been accepting congratulations for her work and for the youngsters she'd been mentoring.

Silvio had been brilliant with the kids, letting them bask in the positive reception their work received without letting them be overwhelmed. One success, he'd warned them, didn't build a career. But hard work and application would.

Now, for the first time in what seemed hours, she found herself alone with Damaso amidst the buzzing, sophisticated crowd. His hand closed on hers and her heart took up a familiar, sultry beat as she looked into his gleaming eyes.

She was hyper-aware of the weight of his jewellery at her throat and wrist, a tangible proclamation of his ownership. That was one of the reasons she'd resisted accepting his gifts. He was a man who'd take a mile when offered an inch. She'd clung to her independence with the tenacity of a drowning man grabbing at flotsam as he went under for the last time.

Yet what was the point in pretending? It wasn't the jewellery that branded her as Damaso's but her feelings.

When he'd presented her with the exquisite pieces she'd been on tenterhooks, waiting for him to announce they were a symbol of what he felt for her. She'd hoped his feelings for her had matured miraculously through sexual attraction, admiration, liking and caring to...

A shiver rippled across her skin.

'Come on,' she urged before he could guess her thoughts. 'There's one piece you haven't seen, at least not blown up to this size.' Threading her fingers through his, she tugged him towards an inner room.

Damaso lowered his head, his mouth hovering near her ear, his breath warm on her skin. 'The portrait of me?'

Marisa nodded and kept walking, the jittery, excited feeling in her stomach telling her she was in danger of revealing too much to this perceptive man.

They stopped on the threshold of the room and, as luck would have it, the spectators parted so they had an unhindered view.

The tingling began somewhere in her chest and spread out in ever-widening ripples just as it did every time she saw it. The photographer in her saw composition and light, focus and angle. The woman saw Damaso.

Not the Damaso the world was used to—the fiercely focused businessman—but a man she'd only just discovered. The slanting light traced his features lovingly in the black and white shot, revealing the broad brow, strong nose, the angle of cheekbone and jaw and the tiny lines at the corner of his eyes. But it did more. It captured him in a rare, unguarded moment, hunkering down with a dark-haired little boy, bent over a battered toy truck.

The man in the photo leant protectively close to the tot, as if to shield him from the football game that was a blur

of action on the uneven dirt behind them. His eyes were
on the boy and his expression...

Marisa swallowed. How had she ever wondered if Damaso would make a good father? It was all there in his
face: the intense focus on the child; the protectiveness;
the pleasure lurking at the corners of his firm mouth as he
solemnly helped the boy fill the back of the truck with dirt
scooped from the earth at their feet.

Damaso would make a wonderful father; she knew it
in her bones. Since being with him her doubts about her
ability to be a good mother had receded too. His praise and
his trust did so much for her. His steady presence had even
helped her to find a purpose.

'Thank you for agreeing to let me hang this one.' Her
voice was husky and she had to work to counter the urge
to press her palm to the tiny swell where her belly shel-
tered their child.

Beside her, Damaso shrugged. 'You and Silvio were so
adamant it had to be included. How could I refuse?'

'I—'

'How fortunate to find you here, princess.'

Marisa's head jerked around at the interruption, her
hackles rising at the deliberate emphasis on her title. Her
stomach dropped as she recognised the country's most notorious art critic, an older woman renowned for her venom
rather than her eye for talent. They'd met at a high-profile
event where they'd had opposing views on the merit of a
young sculptor.

The woman's cold, hazel eyes told Marisa she hadn't
forgotten, or forgiven.

'Damaso.' She turned. 'Have you met—?'

'I have indeed. How are you, Senhora Avila?'

'Senhor Pires.' The woman's toothy smile made Marisa
shiver. 'You're admiring the princess's work?' Again that
emphasis on her title. 'I hear Silvio is quite taken with his
protégée.' Her gimlet gaze and arch tone said she couldn't

see why. 'That he's even considering taking her on as an assistant!'

Fed up with being spoken about as if she wasn't there, Marisa simply pasted a smile on her face. If this vulture wanted details, let her pump Silvio. Knowing how Silvio despised the woman, she wouldn't get far.

When the silence lengthened the woman's face tightened. 'Of course, there are some who'd say social status is no replacement for real talent. But these days so much of the art scene is about crass commercialisation rather than true excellence. Anything novel sells.'

Her dismissive attitude scored at something dark inside Marisa. The belief that beneath her determined bravado her uncle had been right. That she had nothing of value to offer.

Dimly she was aware of Damaso squeezing her fingers.

She caught herself up. She'd let doubts undermine her too long. No more. She opened her mouth to respond but Damaso was quicker.

'Personally I think anyone with real discernment only has to see these works to recognise an amazing talent.' His tone was rich, dark chocolate coating a lethal blade. 'As for milking social status, I don't see any reference in the studio or the catalogue to the princess's royal status.'

Beside her he loomed somehow taller, though she hadn't seen him move. 'I suspect those who gripe about social status are only hung up on it because they're not happy with their own.'

Marisa bit back a gasp. It was the sort of thing she'd often longed to say but had never felt free to express.

'Well!' Senhora Avila stiffened as if she'd been slapped. Her eyes narrowed as she took in Damaso's challenging stance. Finally she looked away, her gaze sliding to the photo.

'I must say, Senhor Pires, this piece paints you in a new light. You look quite at home in that slum.' Her eyes darted back to him, glittering with malice. 'Could it be true, after all? The whisper that that's where you came from? No one seems to know for sure.'

Marisa stepped forward, instinctively moving to block the woman's venom. She knew how raw and real Damaso's past was to him, even now. His hand pulled her back to his side and she leaned into him as his arm circled her shoulders.

'I don't see why my birthplace is noteworthy to someone whose interest *purports* to be in art.' His tone lowered the temperature by several degrees. 'It's true I grew up in a *favela*. What of it? It wasn't an auspicious start but it taught me a lot.'

He leaned towards the woman and Marisa saw her eyes widen. 'I'm proud of what I've done with my life, Senhora Avila. What about you? Can you name something constructive you've done with yours?'

The critic mouthed something inarticulate and spun on her heel, scuttling away into the crowd beyond.

'You shouldn't have done that,' Marisa murmured. 'She'll blab to the whole world what she's learned.'

'Let her. I'm not ashamed of who I am.' He turned her towards him, his gaze piercing, as if the glamorous throng around them didn't exist. 'Are you all right?'

'Of course.' Marisa stood straighter, still shaken by the force of anger that had welled when the woman had turned on Damaso.

Because Marisa loved him.

There, she'd admitted it, if only silently. She'd fought so hard against the truth, acknowledging it was a relief. Marisa hugged the knowledge to herself, excitement fizzing through her veins.

She felt as if she could take on the world.

'You should have let me answer for myself. I'm not some dumb bimbo, you know.'

His mouth curled up at one corner. That smile should be outlawed for the way it made her insides melt.

'You? A bimbo?' He laughed and she had to fight the urge to lean closer. 'As if.' His expression sobered. 'But you can't ask me to stand by while that viper makes snide comments about the woman I intend to marry.'

Was it her imagination or did the crowd around her ripple in response to that low-voiced announcement?

'Not here, Damaso!' Suddenly she wanted more than anything to be alone with him. She longed for the privacy of his city penthouse or, even better, his island hideaway. 'Let's talk at home.'

The promise in his sultry stare sent her heart fluttering against her ribs. He looked like he wanted to devour her on the spot. Even his public assertion that he intended to marry her, something that would once have raised her ire, sent a thrill of excitement through her.

Yet it was another hour before they could leave, an hour of accolades that should have meant everything to her. Instead, Marisa was on edge, her mind reeling as she finally confronted her true feelings for Damaso. She wanted him...permanently.

The one thing she didn't know was what he felt for her. He'd publicly revealed his past to deflect that critic's spite. A past he'd once guarded jealously.

At last they were in the limo. Marisa couldn't sit still. Adrenalin streamed through her body, making it impossible to relax. She wanted to blurt out her feelings but what would that achieve? He famously didn't do relationships. Just marriage for the sake of his child.

But surely the way he'd stood up to that harpy meant something?

Something as impossible as him loving her?

The idea shimmered like a beacon in the distance, filling her heart with hope.

Even if he didn't love her, Marisa couldn't resist any

longer. She'd marry him anyway. She'd never meet a better man than Damaso, or a man she cared about more.

She wanted to spend her life with him.

A weight slid off her shoulders as doubt was banished. She wanted love, she'd fight to get it, but she'd start small if she had to. Surely she could make him love her in time?

She was so engrossed in her thoughts she barely noticed him talking on his phone until he spoke to her.

'It's bad news, Marisa. A fire in the new Caribbean eco-resort.'

'Is anyone hurt?'

'They're checking now. It's too early to say. But I need to go there tonight.'

Marisa reached out and wrapped her hands around his tight fist. She knew how much worker safety meant to him and this new complex, due to open in weeks, had been the focus of his attention for so long.

'Of course you should go. You've invested too much time and effort not to.'

'I'll be gone a week, probably more like two. You can come with me. I don't like leaving you alone.'

'I'll hardly be alone.' She shook her head. 'You'd get more done without me and I have lots of work to do too, remember? Silvio and the kids are relying on me.'

Besides, it struck her that she had other unfinished business.

She'd used Damaso's opposition as an excuse to stay away from her homeland. Yet increasingly she'd known she had to face her past just as Damaso had faced his.

Her past took the form of her uncle and the Bengarian court and press. Staying in Brazil, pretending the coronation wasn't happening, felt too much like hiding, as if she was ashamed of who she was and what she'd done.

If she didn't stand up to them, how could she hold her head high?

Marisa was determined to become the woman she wanted

so badly to be—not just for herself but for Damaso and their child. For Stefan too. She'd make them proud.

She wanted to be strong the way Damaso was. The past was part of her, but she had to prove to herself she wasn't cowed by it.

Besides, she had to be stronger now than ever before. Enough to take the chance and stay with a man who had never said he loved her and who might never say it.

Marisa swallowed hard, trying to ignore the fear crawling down her spine.

She'd go to the coronation, face her past and reconcile the two parts of her life. Maybe then she'd be the sort of woman Damaso could love.

'Marisa? What is it? You have the strangest expression.'

She turned, her emotions welling unstoppably. 'Don't worry about me,' she urged. 'Just go. I'll be fine while you're away. I'll be busy.'

She needed to do this alone.

CHAPTER FOURTEEN

His two weeks in the Caribbean had felt like two months. More.

Damaso jabbed the button for the penthouse and shoved his hand through his hair. He needed a haircut. He rubbed his chin, feeling the rasp of stubble, and knew he should have shaved on the plane. But he'd still been working frantically, trying to get everything organised so he could come back a couple of days early.

He'd shave when he got to the apartment.

Except he knew once he saw Marisa his good intentions of sparing her delicate skin would fly out of the window. There would be no holding back.

He needed her *now*.

He needed her in ways he'd never needed a woman. His arms felt empty without her. He missed her smile, her sassy challenges, the sly way she teased him, the fearless way she stood up to him. He missed having her nearby, sharing the small stuff from their days he'd never thought important before he met her.

The doors opened and he strode into the apartment.

'Marisa?'

Long strides took him past the vast sitting room to their bedroom suite. She wasn't there. He headed back down the corridor.

'Marisa?'

'Senhor Pires.' It was Beatriz, wiping her hands on an apron. 'I didn't expect you back yet.'

'I changed my plans.' He looked past her for Marisa. Surely she'd heard him by now. 'Where is the princess?'

Beatriz stilled, her brows lifting. 'She's gone, Senhor.' Damaso felt his blood turn sluggish, as if his heart had slowed. 'Back to Bengaria for the coronation.'

Damaso rocked on his feet, absorbing the smack of shock. He'd spoken to Marisa daily and she'd said nothing about leaving.

Because she feared he'd stop her?

It was the only explanation.

That last night at the exhibition he'd mentioned marriage and she'd tried to hustle him away. Because she'd decided to leave him?

'Senhor? Are you all right?'

Damaso shook his head, trying to stop the sick feeling surging through him. He reached out and splayed a hand against the wall, grateful for its solidity.

'Can I get you—?'

'Nothing,' he croaked. 'I don't need anything.'

Except Marisa. Hell! It felt like the world crumbled beneath his feet.

Heedless of Beatriz's concerned gaze, he stumbled back to the bedroom.

Fifteen minutes later Damaso slumped on the bed. He'd tried her phone but it was switched off. He'd checked his email—nothing. He'd even accessed her personal email, something he'd never before stooped to doing, and found nothing relevant.

There was no note, no message. Nothing except, in the drawer of her bedside table, a crumpled letter from her uncle. A letter demanding her presence for the coronation. A letter that spelled out the importance of Marisa returning to meet the man her uncle intended her to marry.

Bile rose in Damaso's throat as his gut knotted.

She'd left him and gone to her uncle, the man she abhorred.

Because she'd rather marry some blue-blooded aristocrat than Damaso, a man without a family tree to his name? A man whose only pretensions to respectability had been bought with his phenomenal success. A man who still bore scars from his slum background.

He'd have sworn that didn't matter to Marisa. But, if not that, then what?

Unless, like him, Marisa had doubts about his ability to be a father. To provide love.

How could you give what you've never known?

Fear gouged his belly, scraping at his deepest, most hidden self-doubt.

Something nudged his knee and he slanted his gaze down. That ragged mutt of Marisa's leaned against him, its chin resting on his leg, its eyes soulful in its ugly face.

The dog's coat felt surprisingly soft under his fingers. Its huge eyes narrowed to slits of pleasure as Damaso stroked one torn ear.

'You miss her too, don't you, Max?'

Strangely, it seemed completely natural to talk to the dog. It leaned close, its weight warm and comforting.

Surely she'd have taken the mutt if she'd intended leaving for good?

That shard of hope gave him strength.

'Don't fret.' Damaso straightened his spine. 'I'm going to get her back, whatever it takes.' He refused to dwell on whether he spoke to reassure the dog or himself.

The cathedral was huge and impressive. Damaso barely gave it a glance as he stalked up the red carpet, ignoring the usher frantically trying to catch his attention.

The atmosphere was expectant and the air smelt of massed blooms, expensive scent and incense. Baroque organ music swelled, lending pomp to the occasion.

Damaso slowed, surveying the crowd. He saw uniforms and dark suits on the packed seats, clerical robes and women in designer dresses. But the hats the women wore obscured profiles and made it impossible to identify the wearers till they turned and stared.

'Princess Marisa,' he barked to the usher. 'Where is she?'

'The princess?' The man's gaze flicked nervously up the centre aisle to the front seats. Instantly Damaso strode away, leaving the goggling man behind.

Heads whipped around as he passed but he looked neither right nor left as he scanned the front rows. Pale blue, lemon, ivory, that light shade of brown women insisted on giving names like 'beige' or 'taupe'. His stare rested on each woman then moved on, dismissing them in turn. White, pink, more pink, light grey. They were dressed expensively but sedately. Obviously there was a book of etiquette on what to wear for a coronation: expensive but subdued.

Damaso shifted his gaze to the other side of the aisle. Grey, black, and…deep sapphire-blue swirled with an orange so vivid it reminded him of the sun blazing on his island beach at sunset. He faltered, his heart pounding.

He'd found her.

Instead of a suit she wore a dress that left the golden skin of her arms bare. She looked like a ray of light amidst the sedate pastels. She moved her head and the jaunty concoction of orange on her golden hair caught the light. It looked saucy even from behind.

His pace lengthened till he stood at the end of the row and he caught the full impact of her outfit. Elegant, but subtly sexy in the way the fabric hugged her curves. At her throat she wore the magnificent topaz necklace and for a moment Damaso could only stare, wondering what it meant that she'd chosen to wear *his* gift to an event that would be televised to millions.

The murmurs became a ripple of sound around him. The usher had caught up and was whispering urgently about the correct seating.

Still Marisa didn't turn. Her attention was on the man sitting on her far side. A man with a chiselled jaw, wide brow and face so picture-book handsome he didn't look real. Or maybe that was because of the uniform he wore. His jacket was white with gold epaulets, a double row of golden buttons down the front, and he sported a broad sash of indigo that perfectly matched his eyes.

Damaso's fists curled. Was *this* the man she was supposed to marry?

Far from spurning him, she was in deep conversation with the guy. He said something and she leaned closer, her hand on his sleeve.

Something tore wide open inside Damaso. Cold rage drenched him as his fists tightened.

'Sir, really, if you come with me I'll just—'

'Not now.' His voice was low, almost inaudible, but it had the quality of an animal growl. The usher jumped back and heads whipped round.

'Damaso?' Marisa's eyes were wide and wondering.

She'd forgotten to remove her hand from Prince Charming's sleeve and Damaso felt a wave of roiling fury rise up inside him.

Marisa stared up at the man blocking the aisle. Despite his formal clothes, his perfectly cut hair and clean-shaven face, there was something untamed about him.

Emotion leapt. A thrill of excitement, of pure delight that Damaso was here.

'How did you get here?' Cyril wouldn't have invited the father of her unborn child.

'Does it matter?' Damaso shrugged off a couple of ushers who were trying to lead him away. He looked broad and bold and impossibly dangerous, like a big jungle cat caged with a bunch of tabbies.

Silently she shook her head. No, it didn't matter. All she cared about was the fact he was here. Her heart tilted and beat faster.

He held out his arm, palm up. 'Come on.'

Marisa stared. 'But the coronation! It's due to begin in a couple of minutes.'

'I'm not here for the coronation. I'm here for you.'

Her pulse fluttered high in her throat at the command and possessiveness in his voice. She prized her independence but his proprietorial attitude spoke to a primitive yearning within.

Behind her, women leaned close, fanning themselves.

'Marisa?' Alex spoke beside her. 'Do you want me to deal with this?'

Before she could answer, Damaso stepped close, shoving aside an empty chair into the path of a uniformed man who'd reached to restrain him.

'Marisa can speak for herself. She doesn't need *you*.' She'd never heard Damaso sound so threatening. His eyes flashed pure heat and there was violence in his expression.

'Damaso. Please.'

'Please what? Go away?' Those hot eyes turned to her, scorching her skin and sending delicious chills rippling through her tummy. 'Not a chance, *querida*. You don't get rid of me so easily.'

'It's not a matter of getting rid—'

'We need to talk, Marisa, *now*.'

'After the ceremony.' She gestured to the fallen chair. 'I'm sure we could arrange for you...'

Damaso's eyes cut to Alex and his look was downright ugly. 'If you think I'm leaving you with him...' He shook his head. 'I know you don't want to be here, Marisa. Don't let them force you.'

Marisa frowned, trying to make sense of his attitude.

Then Alex surged to his feet and so did Marisa, arm out to separate him from Damaso.

'Stop this now,' she hissed. 'You're making a scene, both of you. Everyone's watching.' Yet part of her revelled in Damaso's single-mindedness.

'Are you coming with me?' His accent was thicker, enticing, like rich coffee laced with rum. It slid along her senses, beckoning.

'Damaso, I don't know what this is about but I—'

A swoop of movement caught the rest of the sentence in her throat. Next thing Marisa knew, she was in Damaso's arms, held high against his chest. On her peripheral vision, she saw a television camera turn to focus on them. A babble of sound erupted.

'Marisa.' Low, urgent, Alex's voice reached her. She turned her head and saw him just inches away, scowling, as if about to tackle Damaso. He had no idea she'd rather be in Damaso's arms than anywhere. She groped for Alex's hand, squeezing it quickly.

'It's okay, really,' she whispered. 'I'm fine.' And then his hand slipped from hers as Damaso swung round, stalking through the protesting crowd to turn back up the long aisle.

Perhaps the tabloids were right—she was lost to all propriety. Rather than being outraged by Damaso's scandalous behaviour, Marisa found herself thrilled at his masculine display of ownership. Hope rose.

He *must* care for her.

No man would behave so outrageously unless he cared. She was sure that was jealousy she'd seen glinting in the basilisk stare he'd given Alex.

'You could just have phoned,' she murmured, snuggling closer to his solid chest.

His firm stride faltered and he looked down at her. 'Your phone was off.' A ferocious scowl marred his brow and beneath it his eyes were shadowed by something that looked like doubt. 'You didn't tell me you were coming.'

Marisa frowned and lifted her hand to his face. His skin was tight and hot.

'I thought you'd follow me if I told you.'

His nostrils flared and his jaw set as he looked away and started moving again, shouldering his way through the clustering crowd. 'You wanted to be alone to meet the man your uncle has arranged for you to marry.'

'You know about that?' To her amazement, she still had the capacity to feel shock.

'Isn't that why you came? To get engaged to some pretty-boy aristocrat who doesn't give a damn who you really are? Who doesn't even care you're carrying another man's baby?'

Marisa heard the gasps around them but only had eyes for Damaso. What she read in his face outweighed any annoyance she might have felt for his careless words. She read *pain*. The sort of pain that tore at the heart and shredded pride.

She should know. She'd seen the symptoms in her own face when she'd faced a future loving a man who cared only for their baby.

How it hurt to see Damaso suffering too.

His big body hummed with tension. His jaw was set so hard she wondered how he'd ever unclench it.

'I won't let you do it. He's not the man for you, Marisa.'

'I know.' Her voice was so soft she thought at first he hadn't heard. Then he juddered to a halt, his head jerking round. The intensity of that midnight gaze transfixed her.

'You know?' His voice was muted roar. She'd never seen a man so close to the edge. Her heart clenched. Could it be true? Could the miracle she'd hoped for have happened?

'I'm not here to choose a fiancé.' She planted her palm on Damaso's chest, feeling the racing rhythm of his heart. 'I'm here because I'm a princess of Bengaria. I have a right to be at the coronation, as well as a duty. This is my country, even if I don't plan to live here full-time.'

'Where do you plan to live?' His low voice was barely audible, yet the echo of it rolled across her flesh, raising shivery goose bumps.

'Brazil looks nice.'

Marisa felt the jolt of shock hit him. His hands tightened as his head lowered to hers.

Dimly she was aware of a distant camera flash.

'You're not trying to leaving me then?'

She shook her head, her throat closing, as for the first time she saw right to his soul. Longing, pain and determination were there, plain for her to see.

'You'll marry me.' It was a statement, not a question, but Marisa nodded.

'Why?'

The question floored her. From the first, he'd been the one demanding marriage. Had he changed his mind? Her stomach swooped. 'I could ask you the same thing,' she whispered.

'Why do I want to marry you?'

She nodded again, aware that this wasn't the best place for this conversation. But nothing, not protocol or natural disaster, would have stopped her now. She had to know.

A slow movement started at the corner of his mouth, pulling it up in a crooked smile that grew till it carved a dimple down one cheek and broadened into a grin. It transformed Damaso's face from hard and determined to charismatically sexy. Marisa's heart missed a beat.

'Because I want to spend the rest of my days with you.' He lifted her in his arms till his words were an invisible caress on her parted lips. His dark gaze locked with hers, promising a gift far more precious than any regal entitlement. 'Because I love you.'

She blinked but still couldn't take it in. 'Say that again.'

This time Damaso lifted his head and when he spoke his words rang through the crowded cathedral for all to hear. 'I love you, Marisa, with all my heart and soul. I want to be your husband, because there's no woman in the world more perfect for me than you.'

He loved her?

Marisa felt the hot glaze of tears film her eyes as emotion welled from deep within. A sob rose, turning into a hiccup of desperate happiness. Never in her life had she felt like this.

'Now, *meu anjo,* tell my why you want to marry me.' His gaze dropped to her belly and she knew he was thinking of their child.

She shook her head. That wasn't the reason.

'Because I love you too, Damaso. I love you from the bottom of my heart and I couldn't bear to be with anyone else.'

Beyond them the sophisticated crowd went wild.

'I've been in love with you so long,' she whispered, drawing him closer, her words for his ears only. 'It feels like I've only come alive since I've been with you.'

Finally Damaso spoke, his voice uneven, his eyes glittering. 'Do you really want to stay for the ceremony, since you came all this way?'

'I'd rather be with you, Senhor Pires. Take me home.'

Marisa had thought his last smile potent but this one was enough to stop clocks. Two ladies-in-waiting swooned as Damaso tucked her against his heart and strode down the aisle.

'And they accuse *me* of being scandalous! Your behaviour was outrageous.'

Damaso smiled at the lush, lovely woman sitting in the jet's private lounge, sipping sparkling water.

Marisa was his. Incontrovertibly, absolutely *his*.

Something smacked him hard in the chest. Relief? Triumph? Joy? He didn't give a damn what name it went by. It was the best feeling in the world. He felt like he might burst with happiness.

'Your uncle will get over it,' he murmured, sitting down beside her, one hand on her thigh. The whisper-thin silk of her dress was warm from her flesh, inviting further exploration.

'I doubt it. The look on Cyrill's face when you told him I couldn't stay for the ceremony because I had another engagement! I thought he was going to have a seizure.' She shook her head. 'Upstaging him at his own coronation! Such lack of decorum.'

Marisa looked down as his hand slipped higher up her leg but did nothing to stop him. 'At least that will have dashed any plans he had to marry me off.'

'You wouldn't have been happy with that pretty-boy aristocrat.' Only he could give her what she needed, for he was the one she loved. He'd never known love. It took some getting used to.

'Of course not.' She leaned forward and he was momentarily distracted by a glimpse of delicious cleavage.

'He didn't even have the gumption to stop me.' Satisfied, he ran his fingers lightly up to her hip, feeling her shiver under his touch.

His.

'You mean Alex?' Her brow puckered. 'He's not the man Cyrill wanted me to marry. He's a friend.'

'I thought you didn't have any friends in Bengaria.' Despite everything, jealousy stirred. Just how close a friend was this Alex?

She shrugged. 'Okay, more Stefan's friend than mine. I haven't seen him for years. He's been away. And, no.' She paused, studying his face. 'He's not the man for me.'

'But I am.' He intended to make sure she remembered it, and rejoiced in it, every day for the rest of her life.

'You definitely are.' She lifted her hand to his cheek and an incredible peace descended as she feathered a touch across his skin. 'I'm a better person with you, Damaso. I feel...proud of what I've done and what I'm doing. Confident about the future. You gave me the strength to face what I'd been running from.'

'You were strong before you met me, Marisa.' He'd never known a woman more feisty and independent.

She shook her head. 'It was only when I saw how you'd faced your past and got on with your life that I realised I'd been a coward, letting Cyrill and the press drive me from my home. That's why I had to go back. To prove to them, and to myself, that I'm happy with who I am. I mightn't fit their mould but that doesn't matter.'

'You're perfect just the way you are.' His hand strayed to her abdomen and the baby bulge that had popped out in the two weeks since he'd seen her. His palm closed protectively over it. His woman. His child.

Marisa shifted, her eyes skimming away from his. She took a swift sip from her glass.

'What is it?' Instantly he sensed her discomfort. 'What's wrong?'

She lifted one shoulder. 'Nothing. Everything's perfect.'

Yet her smile wasn't quite as radiant as it had been. Damaso tilted her head around till she had no choice but to meet his scrutiny. 'Something's bothering you. Tell me.'

One slim shoulder lifted. 'No, really, I—'

'Don't, Marisa. You've never lied before. Your honesty is one of the qualities I admire most. Tell me the truth. If there's anything wrong, we need to work it out together.'

Eyes of bright azure locked with his, her regard so searching it was as if she looked deep into him.

Damaso looked right back. He had no secrets from Marisa.

'I *like* that you're so eager to be a father.' She paused, giving him time to process the doubt in her voice.

'But...?'

A flush coloured her cheeks. 'But...' She bit her lip, reminding him of the early days on his island estate when she'd refused his offer of marriage. She hadn't thought a child sufficient reason to marry.

'But you're afraid it's our baby I want,' he murmured. 'Rather than you.'

She opened her mouth to answer but his finger on her lips forestalled her.

'I love our child already, *meu anjo,* and I'll work hard to learn to be a good father.' He swallowed hard, knowing that would be a bigger challenge than any corporate dealings. 'But, even if there was no child, even if there could never *be* a child, I would love you with my whole heart.'

Marisa's eyes shone brilliantly as she looked up at him. He took the glass from her hand and set it down, then gathered both her hands in his. They trembled. Or perhaps it was he who shook.

'You are my sun and stars and moon, Marisa. You've taught me how to care about more than a balance sheet. That it's not my corporate empire that defines who I am. It's who I love.'

He raised her hand and kissed it, revelling in the fresh apple and sunshine scent of her skin, knowing it would always be his favourite perfume.

'I didn't know I *could* love till until you came into my life.'

Her eyes glittered with tears but her smile was the most wonderful thing he'd ever seen.

Damaso dropped to his knees in front of her. 'Will you be mine? We don't need to marry if you—'

This time it was Marisa's finger on his mouth.

'I'll marry you, Damaso. I want everyone to know you're mine.' Her smile was incandescent. Damaso felt its warmth in every cell of her body. 'Besides, for a scandalous princess, I have a hankering for respectability, so long as it's with you.'

'Ah.' Damaso rose and lifted her into his arms, turning towards the luxuriously appointed bedroom. 'That's a shame. I was rather hoping for a little scandalous behaviour now and then.'

Marisa reached out and with one quick tug undid his bow tie and tossed it over her shoulder. Her smile was pure seduction. 'I'm sure that could be arranged, Senhor Pires.'

* * * * *

HER SECRET, HIS DUTY

CARLA CASSIDY

Carla Cassidy is an award-winning author who has written more than one hundred novels. In 1995 she won Best Silhouette Romance from RT Book Reviews for Anything for Danny. In 1998 she also won a Career Achievement Award for Best Innovative Series from RT Book Reviews.

Carla believes the only thing better than curling up with a good book to read is sitting down at the computer with a good story to write. She's looking forward to writing many more books and bringing hours of pleasure to readers.

Chapter 1

"Impossible." The single word escaped Debra Prentice's lips in disbelieving horror as she stared at the three separate pregnancy tests lined up like little soldiers on her bathroom vanity.

Not one, not two, but three tests and each showing a positive sign. Undeniable results that her brain tried to absorb.

Pregnant. There was no question now that she was pregnant. She'd wondered about it when she was late with her period, but had written it off as stress. She'd been late in the past.

Pregnant. How was it possible? Even as the question formed in her mind, memories of a single night six weeks ago gave her the answer.

An unexpected encounter, too many drinks and a mad dash to a nearby hotel room where she'd found complete abandon with a man she had no business being with at all.

Her cheeks burned as she remembered the awkward morning after. Gazes not meeting as they both hurriedly dressed and then the humiliating ride in a cab from the hotel to her front door. And now this, the icing on a cake that should have never been baked in the first place. Pregnant.

A glance at the small clock in the bathroom forced a gasp from her. If she didn't hurry she'd be late to work, and in all the years that Debra had worked as personal secretary and assistant to Kate Adair Winston, she had never been late to work.

She got up and tossed the tests into the trash, then gave herself a quick glance in the bathroom mirror. The slim black pencil skirt she wore didn't display a hint of her current condition but the red tailored button-up blouse only emphasized the paleness of her face, a paleness that the results of the tests had surely created.

Her light brown hair was already attempting to escape the twisted bun she'd trapped it in earlier, but she didn't have time to fix it now.

She left the bathroom, deciding that she couldn't, she wouldn't think about her pregnancy right now. She had a little time to figure things out, but right now she had to get her brain in work mode.

She pulled on a black winter coat and grabbed her purse, then left her two-story townhouse and headed for her car parked at the curb. There was parking behind the townhouse, but she rarely used it, preferring the convenience of curbside parking instead.

The January air was bracing, hovering right around

the freezing mark. Thankfully the sky was bright blue and she didn't have to worry about snow or sleet.

The townhouse was located just off Glenwood Avenue in the uptown district of Raleigh, North Carolina. It was Debra's pride and joy, bought two years ago after years of renting. She loved the area, loved the fact that she could paint walls and hang pictures without getting a landlord's approval. It was cozy and filled with all the colors and textiles she loved.

Once inside the car she checked the clock. It was just after seven, but she still had to maneuver morning traffic to get to North Raleigh where the Winston Estate was located.

Every morning in the capital city of North Carolina the morning rush traffic was bad, but on this Wednesday morning it seemed particularly heavy.

Or, maybe it was the racing of her thoughts that made the ride feel longer and more difficult than usual. Even though it was unplanned and unexpected there was no doubt in her mind that she would keep the baby. For her, that decision was a no-brainer.

She would just need to keep the father's identity to herself for the rest of her life. She would let the people close to her assume that the baby was Barry's, the snake-in-the-grass boyfriend who had broken up with her on the night she'd been in that restaurant bar, the same night she'd done something completely out of character.

But, there was no question in her mind who the father was because she hadn't been pregnant when she and Barry had broken up and she was pregnant now. There had only been that single night of utter madness to account for her current condition.

She steered her thoughts away from the pregnancy as she approached her workplace. The impressive Winston Estate was located on two acres of lush, meticulously manicured grounds.

Built in 1975, the six-bedroom, nine-bath white-and-red brick house also boasted a beautiful swimming pool, a backyard area around the pool big enough for entertaining and a small guest house where Kate's security, a Secret Service detail, worked from.

The front entrance boasted a large black iron gate that was opened only when security and Kate allowed. The entire estate was fenced in except for a side entrance through which staff and service vehicles came and went.

Debra turned into the access entrance and waved to Jeff Benton, part of the security team that kept Kate and her family safe when the former vice president was in the house.

Debra pulled into a parking spot specifically for staff and hurriedly got out of the car. She entered the house through a side door that led into a large, empty mudroom and then into the huge kitchen where at the moment fresh coffee and cinnamon were the predominant scents.

None of the help was in the large, airy room that had the latest cooking equipment, but Sam Winston, Kate's thirty-three-year-old middle son, sat at a small table next to a window with a cup of coffee before him.

"Good morning, Sam," she said tentatively. Since Sam's return from overseas where he'd served in Army Special Forces, he'd been distant, at times downright unpleasant, and she never knew exactly what to expect from him when they happened to run into each other.

He looked up from his coffee, his blue eyes dark and unreadable. "Morning," he replied and then shifted his gaze back into the depths of his cup, obviously not encouraging any further conversation.

Debra passed through the kitchen and entered the main foyer. As always, her breath was half stolen from her by the beauty of the black-and-white marble floors and the exquisite winding wooden staircase that led up to the second level.

Beyond the foyer were Kate's official office and a doorway right next to it that led to Debra's much smaller office. She knew that Kate didn't usually go into her office to begin her day until sometime after eight, but that didn't mean Debra didn't have things to do before Kate made her official appearance.

Debra's office was small but efficient with a desk that held a computer, a multifunctional printer and memo pads. A wooden five-drawer file cabinet sat nearby on the right wall. The other wall was a white dry-erase area that took up the left side of the room, where she kept track of Kate's ever-busy, ever-changing social calendar with dry-erase markers in a variety of colors.

She closed the door, took off her coat and hung it in the tiny closet that stored extra paper and printer supplies and then sat at the desk and powered up her computer.

There was only one personal item in the whole room. It was a framed picture that hung on the wall, a photo of Debra with a Parisian street vendor who sold hot croissants and coffee from a colorful cart just down the block from the U.S. Embassy in Paris.

Debra had lived in Paris for the two years that Kate had served as U.S. ambassador to France. It had been an amazing experience for Debra. She'd learned some of the language, wandered the streets on her time off and breathed in the local ambiance.

When Kate's time in that position had ended and it was time to return to the states, Debra hadn't wanted the usual souvenirs of a picture or a miniature statue of the famous Eiffel Tower.

She'd wanted a photo of herself and Pierre, the charming Frenchman who had begun her mornings with a bright smile, a hot croissant and a cup of steaming café au lait. A fellow staffer had taken the photo and Debra had brought it into a local craft store to have it enlarged and framed.

The time in France had been wonderful, but that was then and this was now. Pregnant. She was pregnant. She couldn't quite wrap her mind around it yet, but she knew one thing for sure, once the baby was born her life would be irrevocably changed.

She shoved the thought away and instead focused on her morning work. It took twenty minutes to go through her emails, deleting spam that had managed to get through the filter, marking messages to forward to Kate and answering those that didn't require her boss's attention.

Once the email was finished, she moved to the file folder on her desk that held a stack of invitations for Kate. As a former U.S. ambassador and vice president, Kate was invited to hundreds of events each week.

As Debra looked at each one, she made a list of who, what and where for each event that required a response in the next week or so. The social calendar Debra kept on the wall was an ever-morphing, color-coded animal that required constant attention.

There were rumors that Kate was being groomed to run for president in the next election and she was already being courted by special-interest groups and powerful party movers and shakers.

So far she hadn't mentioned her plans to anyone, but Debra suspected the idea of becoming the first female president of the United States was definitely appealing. Kate had a reputation as a loving mother, a family-oriented person, but Debra knew she was also a woman of great convictions about how the country should move forward in the coming years.

It was just after eight when a familiar soft knock sounded on Debra's door. She grabbed her memo pad and left her desk. It was their routine; Kate knocked to let Debra know she was now in her office and it was time for a morning update.

At fifty-eight years old, Kathleen Adair Winston was an attractive woman with short, stylish light brown hair and blue eyes that radiated honesty, kindness and intelligence. Debra had worked for her long enough to know that she also possessed a will of steel, a slight streak of stubbornness and a love of her family that was enviable.

This morning she was dressed in a pair of tailored navy slacks and a pale blue blouse that emphasized the bright hue of her eyes. Her jewelry was tasteful, a wedding ring despite the fact that she was a widow and a silver necklace with matching earrings.

"Good morning, Debra." Her smile was warm, and adoration for the woman who had been her boss since she'd been a college graduate swelled up inside Debra.

"Good morning to you, Kate," she replied and took the chair opposite the large ornate desk where Kate sat. "Did you sleep well?"

"I always sleep well," Kate replied. "It seems the days are too long and the nights are far too short for my taste."

Debra nodded and smiled and then got down to business. "I have several pressing things we need to discuss this morning," she said.

It took nearly forty-five minutes for Debra to update Kate and get confirmation or regrets on the invitations that required answers.

When they had finished that particular task, Kate leaned back in her chair and sipped the coffee she must have carried with her into the office. "You look tired," she said. "Did you not sleep well last night?"

Debra stared at her in surprise. Did it already show somehow on her face? Did newly discovered pregnancy make a woman look tired the day she realized she was pregnant?

"Nothing to worry about," Debra said, pleased that her voice sounded normal. "I did do a lot of tossing and turning last night. I think it was indigestion, but I'm sure I'll sleep fine tonight."

"Anything in particular on your mind?"

Debra smiled with a forced brightness. "Yes, I'm wondering along with the rest of the world if my boss intends to make a run for the presidency."

Deflect, she thought. She had always been good about making the conversation about other people rather than about herself.

"Your boss still hasn't made up her mind," Kate replied ruefully. She turned in her chair and stared at the wall that held an array of family photos. Most of them were of Kate with her three handsome sons.

"Although I know I need to come to a decision in

the next couple of weeks. It's a long, arduous process to begin a campaign, but the men who have already thrown their hats in the ring are not what the country needs right now. I do believe I'd do a better job than any of them, but I also realize the price I'd be asking my family to pay if I decide to become an official candidate," she said as she turned back to look at Debra.

"You'll make the right decision," Debra said confidently. "You always do. Either way, you'll do what's best for both your family and the country."

Kate flashed her the bright smile that had been her trademark both when she'd served her four years as vice president and as a beloved ambassador to France. "You're the special secret in my pocket, Debra. There are days that your efficiency and loyalty are responsible for my very sanity. Thank goodness you possess the organizational skills that keep me on track."

"I have a feeling you'd be just fine without me, but I love what I do, and now I'd better get back to my office and take care of the RSVPs on these invitations." Debra stood. "You'll let me know if there's anything else I can do for you. You have nothing on your calendar for the day so hopefully you can give yourself a break and just relax a bit."

"Maybe." Kate stood and carried her coffee to the window that looked out on a lovely garden.

Debra left the room aware that Kate didn't know how to relax—until she made up her mind about the next presidential election, she would worry and stew, weigh pros and cons, until she made a final decision about what her future would hold.

Debra didn't even want to think about her own future. She knew that the first thing she needed to do was see a doctor. She'd try to schedule an appointment with her gynecologist for the weekend to confirm what she already knew.

In the meantime, day by day—that's how she would have to take things right now. She'd scarcely had time to process the reality of her condition.

Eventually her pregnancy would show and she'd have some explaining to do, but until that day came she had to focus on her work.

She remained at her desk until just after eleven when Kate used the intercom to call her back into her office. Debra grabbed her notepad and reentered Kate's office, only to stop short at the sight of the ridiculously handsome man seated in the chair she had vacated earlier.

Trey Winston was not only incredibly handsome with his rich dark brown hair and striking blue eyes, he was also the CEO of Adair Enterprises, the family business, a rich and powerful man who was well liked by his employees and friends. He was also the father of the baby Debra carried.

"Here we are," Kate said as Debra entered the room. She gestured her assistant to the chair next to Trey's. Trey offered Debra a faint, rather uncomfortable smile.

Uncomfortable. That's the way things had been for him whenever he saw Debra after the crazy one night they'd spent together—a night that should never have happened.

He'd been at the popular bar/restaurant celebrating the close of a big business deal and she'd been there commiserating a breakup with her boyfriend. The two of them had somehow hooked up, shared too many drinks and then had continued to make the mistake of heading to a nearby hotel and having hot, passionate sex.

He hadn't been too drunk to know what he was doing and neither had she, but he should never have allowed it to happen at all.

He'd spent the past six weeks putting it out of his mind, trying to pretend that it had never happened. Unfortunately, trying to forget had been difficult.

His mother would kill him if she found out. Kate would give him a motherly smackdown to end all smackdowns if she believed he had taken advantage of her assistant, a young woman he knew his mother loved and trusted.

"Trey has just informed me that I'm not the only political beast in the family," Kate said once Debra was seated next to Trey. "He's thinking about running for the Senate."

Debra looked at him in surprise and then quickly averted her gaze back to Kate. "I'm sure he'd make a fine senator."

"You know that and I know that, but what we need to do is see how much support he would be able to get behind him," Kate replied.

Trey could see the wheels turning in his mother's head. Of all the people in his life, Trey trusted his mother more than anyone. He'd been flirting with the idea of entering politics for some time and finally felt the time was right now.

"What do you have in mind?" Debra asked.

Her voice was sweet and soft, but Trey had memories of husky moans and sighs of pleasure. He also couldn't help but notice and remember the fresh, clean scent of her, so unlike the cloying perfumes most of the women in his social circle wore.

"A fund-raiser dinner party." Kate's words snapped Trey back to the matter at hand. "And we'd need to get it scheduled and on the calendar in the next two weeks."

"Two weeks?" Debra sounded horrified as she stared at Kate. "But that's impossible."

"Nonsense. Nothing is impossible," Kate replied confidently, "especially if you're in charge. You've set up these kinds of things a thousand times for me in the past, Debra."

"But not in less than a month," she protested.

Trey watched the interplay between Debra and his mother, knowing no matter how the conversation went the dinner would get done in two weeks' time. Kate usually got her way and Debra was one of the most efficient women Trey had ever known.

"I'll have Haley step in and do most of the work you normally do for me," Kate said, mentioning one of her senior interns. "That will free you up to work closely with Trey to get this done. I recommend you both go into the sitting room right now and figure out a specific date and a venue. Let's get this thing rolling."

Trey could tell that this was probably the last thing on earth that Debra wanted to do. He could see her reluctance as she slowly stood from her chair, in the small crease that darted across her forehead.

He wasn't exactly thrilled by the idea of working closely with his one-night stand, either. But, he also knew that if anyone could pull this event off on time and with flair, it was Debra Prentice.

They could work together, he told himself as he followed her slender frame into the informal sitting area at the back of the house. All they had to do was continue doing what they had been doing for the past six weeks: pretend that crazy night they had shared hadn't happened.

"I didn't realize she was going to pull you into this," he said as she sat in one of the plush, comfortable beige chairs and he sank down on the sofa opposite her.

The family sitting room was large, with floor to ceiling windows on one side and comfortable, yet attractive furnishings. A bar was located at the back of the room and doors led out to the patio and pool area.

It was in this room that the family had often come together to discuss problems or simply to enjoy each other's company and catch up on busy lives.

"My job is to do whatever Kate needs done and since this is important to you, it's important to her." She stared down at her notepad. "The first thing we need to do is find a venue. With less than a month lead time that might be a problem. Do you have any place specific in mind?" Her vivid green eyes finally made contact with him.

"I was thinking maybe the Raleigh Regent or the Capital Hotel," he suggested. "Both places are popular for such events."

"That's the problem." That tiny crease deepened again across her forehead. "I'm fairly sure that the Capital Hotel ballroom will be impossible to get at this late date. I'll check with the Regent and see what's available. Last I heard the ballroom was undergoing some renovations and I'm not certain if they are complete or not. I'm still not sure I'm going to be able to make this happen so soon. I'm assuming you want a Saturday night?"

"Or a Friday night would be fine," he replied. He

watched as she made several notes on the pad. Debra Prentice wasn't a knockout kind of woman, but she also didn't play up her pretty features. She wore little makeup and her hair always looked as if it had been tortured into a position at the back of her head that it couldn't possibly hold.

Still, he knew that her light brown hair was incredibly silky and that she had a cute, perfectly proportioned figure that had fit perfectly in his arms. He knew how her eyes sparkled while in the throes of passion and exactly how her lips tasted.

"Trey?" Her eyes held a touch of impatience, making him realize she must have tried to get his attention while he'd been lost in thought.

"Sorry. What was the question?"

"How many people are you expecting to invite?"

"Two hundred or maybe two hundred and fifty," he replied.

"Pick a number," she said with a light edge to her voice. "I need a specific number to tell the event planner when we settle where this is going take place."

"Two hundred and fifty," he said firmly.

She nodded. "I'll need the guest list from you as soon as possible. Invitations will have to go out in the next couple of days or so. Thank goodness it's January and there isn't much else going on around town." She wrote a couple more notes on her pad and then met his gaze again. "I think that's all I need from you to get started. By the end of the day I'll have a list of dates and places for you to consider."

She stood as if dismissing him, her body instantly poised to run back to her little office.

"Then tomorrow let's make arrangements to see

some of the venues together," he said as he also stood. "And I'll want to be with you when you speak to the event planner. We'll need to pick the menu and make decisions on a number of other things."

It was obvious he'd surprised her. She'd probably just assumed everything would be left up to her. But Trey freely admitted that he was something of a control freak. He couldn't run Adair Enterprises and be as successful as he'd been without being detail oriented and on top of every element in his life.

"I just assumed…" Her voice trailed off.

"This is important to me, Debra. Assume that I'll be at your side every step of the way until this dinner party is over."

Her eyes widened slightly and then she gave him a curt, professional nod. "Then I'll call you later this evening and we'll make arrangements for tomorrow."

She left the sitting room and Trey sank back into the chair, his thoughts a riot inside his head. He'd taken over the running of the family business when his grandfather had died. Walt Winston had mentored Trey and instilled in him the need to be the best that he could be.

It was Walt who'd wanted to see Trey in politics. The old man had even made a list of women he thought would be an asset in his quest for public office. At thirty-five years old, Trey knew it was time for him to marry. He also knew he'd make a more attractive candidate if he had a wife by his side.

With that thought in mind he'd dated dozens of women over the past year and finally eight months ago he'd begun to see Cecily McKenna exclusively.

Although he wasn't madly in love with Cecily, he knew she'd make the perfect wife for him. She was a thirty-three-year-old heiress. Articulate, charming and beautiful, Cecily also possessed a fierce ambition not just for herself, but for him, as well.

He knew there were rumors swirling of an imminent engagement between him and Cecily, rumors he suspected Cecily had started herself. He smiled inwardly. He wouldn't put it past her.

He looked up as Sam came into the room. "So, word has it that you're joining the ranks of the sex-scandal-ridden, fake and crooked politicians of the world." Sam threw himself into the chair that Debra had vacated.

It was obvious his brother was in one of his foul moods. "Actually, I'm hoping to do something good for the people of North Carolina."

"That's my big brother, the overachieving perfect son."

Trey drew a steadying breath. He knew the man seated before him with the scowl on his handsome face wasn't the brother, wasn't the man who had left here to serve his country.

"Sam, why don't you talk to me?" he asked softly. Sam had spent three months imprisoned overseas and months in a hospital recovering from the severe torture he'd endured while a prisoner. He had since been deemed unfit to return to duty and had been mad at the world ever since.

"I don't need to talk to anyone," Sam growled and got up from the chair. "I'm fine just the way I am."

Trey watched helplessly, troubled for his brother as Sam left the room. Sam was a powder keg, but he refused to speak about his time in prison or what had been done to him. The scars he carried were deep and dark and Trey wished he'd share some of the horror with somebody…anybody who could help him heal.

Unfortunately, Sam wouldn't be fixed until Sam wanted to be fixed and at the moment he appeared to be perfectly satisfied being angry.

Trey checked his watch and stood. It was time for him to get back to his own office. Now that he'd pretty much made up his mind to run for Senator, he didn't want to just run, he wanted to win.

He also needed to call Cecily. He hadn't even told her yet that he'd made up his mind to begin the process of gaining support and throwing his hat in the ring. She would be beyond thrilled. She'd been telling him for months that he was what the state needed, that he could do great things.

As he left the house he found himself wondering what Debra thought of his decision to run. Did she believe he was capable of doing great things?

Who cares what she thinks? he asked himself. All he needed from her was her skills at pulling together an event that would provide him a solid foundation on which to begin to build his campaign.

Chapter 2

Debra had suffered a crush on Trey Winston from the very first time she'd met him years ago. She'd always known he was out of her league, but her crush had never really diminished over the years.

She couldn't help the fact that her heart always leapt a bit at the sight of him, that she often grew tongue-tied and clumsy in his presence. Even sharing the single night that they'd had together hadn't changed her attraction to him; instead it had only deepened her feelings for Trey.

But, it didn't matter what she felt about him because she knew that she was the last woman on earth he would ever want to have a public relationship with. He had his future neatly planned out with Cecily McKenna by his side.

As she drove to the Regent Hotel to meet both him

and the hotel manager to discuss the event, she couldn't halt the tingling nerves that fluttered through her veins at the thought of working with him so closely.

She knew he'd probably marry Cecily, a gorgeous heiress who had the social savvy and political chops to be an asset to him.

Debra also knew that she would be a definite liability to Trey. She'd been born out of wedlock. Her father, who had been a married CEO of a Fortune 500 company at the time, had never acknowledged her existence personally. In fact, Debra had been raised by her mother to never mention her father's name, to never expect anything but a monthly support check in the mail from him.

When her mother died right after Debra's graduation from college, she had met with her father for the first and the last time. She had requested one thing from him—she wanted him to use his influence to get her a job in the political arena, specifically with Kathleen Adair Winston. As one of Kate's top contributors to her political campaign when she'd run for vice president, he had been instrumental in her attaining her position with Kate.

That's the only thing Debra had ever asked from the man who had never been anything but a name on a check, but he hadn't even managed to follow through on that. In recent years, there had been whispers of scandals within his company and talk of her father having some shady dealings.

Debra could crush on Trey all she wanted, but she knew she would only be an embarrassing one-night stand and right now a valuable tool to use to achieve his dreams. She would work her butt off to help him in his bid for a seat in the Senate. She wanted him to have his dream and she'd also do the best she could because Kate had asked her to.

She parked in front of the prestigious thirty-story hotel and looked at her watch. She was twenty minutes early for their ten-o'clock appointment so she remained in the car with the engine running and warm air blowing from the heater vents.

She'd been surprised when she'd called the hotel and discovered that the ballroom was available on a Friday night two weeks from now. Two weeks. Jeez, Kate must think she was some kind of magician.

But there had to be some magic at work for the ballroom not to already be booked, Debra thought.

Her hand fell to her stomach, caressing the place where she knew eventually there would be a baby bump, a bump that could potentially destroy Trey's future plans.

Politics thrived on scandals and any of Trey's adversaries would turn a simple night between two consenting adults into something ugly to use against him. Everyone knew he'd been seeing Cecily so that one-night stand would be a testimony to a lack of morals on both their parts. He would be painted with the same brush that had darkened his father's Senate term.

Debra knew that neither of them lacked a moral compass. The night had simply gotten away from them, both of them making mistakes in judgment.

He would never know about the baby, although it broke her heart that she felt like she was somehow repeating a history she'd never wanted for any child of her own.

She loved the baby, despite the circumstances of the conception. She would be the best mother she could and maybe eventually she'd meet a man who wanted her and her child enough to form a family unit.

She checked her watch once again and then cut the car engine. She grabbed her purse with her electronic notepad inside and then got out of the car. She'd power dressed today in a stylish dark brown skirt and suit jacket with a beige blouse. Brown pumps adorned her feet and tiny gold hoop earrings were her only jewelry.

Drawing in several deep breaths as she walked to the hotel entrance, she shoved all thoughts from her mind except what needed to be here to do her job well.

She still couldn't believe how lucky they had been that the Regent's ballroom was available on a Friday night two weeks from now. Two weeks was the mere blink of an eye in planning the kind of event they intended to have.

Whenever possible, Debra used the hotel's event planner, but the Regent had a new woman working in that position, somebody Debra had never worked with before. It wouldn't take long for Debra to discern if the woman was adequately prepared to do the job they needed and if she wasn't then Debra would bring in an event planner of her own.

Debra knew she had a reputation as being sweet and accommodating, but she could be a vicious shark when it was necessary to get what was best for the Winston family.

She went to the reservation desk and asked for Donald Rasworth, the hotel manager. She smelled Trey before she saw him, the expensive scent of a slightly spicy cologne that had clung intimately to her skin the morning after their wild, impetuous encounter.

She turned and nearly bumped into him. "Oh. You're here," she said.

He smiled. "Aren't I supposed to be here?"

"Yes, but I just didn't know that you were here… That you'd actually arrived…"

Thankfully she was rescued from her inane ramble by a tall slender man who approached them with a hand extended and a wide smile of welcome on his face.

"Mr. Winston," he said as he grabbed Trey's hand in a shake. "It's a pleasure to meet you, sir. We're hoping here at the Raleigh Regent that we can meet all your needs for whatever event you want to plan."

Trey turned to Debra and introduced her. "This is the person you need to please," Trey said. "She's our special weapon when it comes to planning these things."

"I understand you have a new event planner. Will she be joining us?" Debra asked.

"Stacy Boone and yes, she should be joining us at any moment." He looked around the lobby, as if expecting the woman to be hiding behind a potted plant or an elegant column. "While we wait for her why don't I go ahead and take you to our main ballroom and let you have a look around."

One demerit for the late Stacy Boone, Debra thought as she followed behind the two men. Trey was clad in a navy suit with a matching shirt, and she couldn't help but notice that he looked as good from the back as he did from the front.

Broad shoulders, slim waist and long legs, the man was definitely eye candy even without his confident stride and the aura of power that radiated from him.

A vision of his naked body flashed in her brain, causing her to stumble over a bump in the carpet that didn't exist. Trey turned in time to put a hand on her shoulder to steady her. "Okay?" he asked with concern.

"I'm fine," she assured him quickly. It was a relief when he dropped his hand from her. He was a warm and friendly man, a toucher by nature, but she didn't want him touching her in any way. It evoked too many memories she definitely needed to forget.

They had just reached the ballroom's double doors when a young blonde in a pink dress and high heels to heaven came rushing in. She carried a messy pile of paperwork and a smile of apology. "Sorry I'm late." Her gaze landed on Trey and admiration filled her eyes. "I'm so sorry I'm late."

Donald introduced the woman as Stacy, not only his new event planner but his favorite niece, as well. *Uh-oh,* Debra thought. She didn't have any real problem with the nepotism, but Stacy looked very young and definitely had the aura of an airhead about her.

Even Trey looked slightly troubled as he said hello and then exchanged a quick glance with Debra. Debra returned a reassuring smile to him. She'd know within an hour if Stacy was up to the job or not and if she wasn't then she'd be out and Debra would be working with somebody she knew could help her get this job done right.

Stacy led them into the ballroom and set her papers on a nearby table. "You're lucky you called when you did. Most people don't know yet that we just recently finished the renovation of the ballroom. New lighting, carpeting and wall covering. We also have the ability to remove the carpeting, which is actually big squares, in order to lay down a fantastic dance floor."

"I like that," Trey said with enthusiasm. "Dinner and dancing."

"That means we'll have to hire a small orchestra," Debra said as she stifled an inward groan. She'd been so flustered yesterday when she'd initially met with Trey they hadn't talked about the budget for this affair.

"Then we'll hire an orchestra," he replied breezily. "I want people leaving that night feeling good about their evening and me. Dancing after dinner definitely has to happen," he replied.

"Then we'll make it happen." Debra pulled her tablet out of her purse and made notes to add to the computer file she'd started for Trey's dinner party.

Stacy pulled a paper form from her stack and gestured for the three of them to sit at the single table just inside the room. Debra took off her coat and flung it across the back of her chair while Trey took off his overcoat and did the same.

As they began talking about the basic logistics, the date and time and how many would be attending, Stacy took notes and Trey leaned back in his chair and looked around the room, making Debra wonder what thoughts were tumbling around in his head.

Was he thinking about the dinner and maybe writing, in his head, the speech he'd give that night? Or perhaps he was mulling over how difficult the Senate race would be. The incumbent Senator William DeCrow was seeking another term and he was known to be a down and dirty fighter.

Thankfully, Trey had no dirt from his past or present that could be thrown on him, as long as nobody ever knew about their night together, as long as nobody ever knew about the baby she carried he should be fine.

Stacy might have flown in like an airhead, but when it got right down to business, she appeared to be savvy and eager to please, a perfect combination for getting things done properly.

"I can email you a variety of menus first thing tomorrow," she said to Debra after they'd both signed a contract to rent the ballroom for the date. "And are we doing a cash or an open bar?"

"We'll serve wine with dinner, but set up a cash bar," Debra replied. Trey leaned forward and opened his mouth as if to protest, but Debra didn't allow him.

"Cash bar," she said firmly. "This night is supposed to be about you beginning to build a support base, not about a bunch of drunks who won't remember what you said in your speech the next morning."

"And people never drink as much when they have to pay for it out of their own pockets," Stacy added.

"Okay, then I guess I'm outvoted on this topic," he replied and once again leaned back in the chair.

"Let's talk about room setup," Stacy said.

Debra and Stacy began to discuss placement of tables and the dance floor that Trey wanted. As the two women spoke, Debra was acutely aware of the scent of Trey's cologne, the warmth of his body far too close to hers.

Somehow, someway, she needed to get over the silly, schoolgirl crush or whatever it was she had where he was concerned.

Even though the night they'd shared was burned indelibly into her brain, she doubted that it had crossed his mind after he'd put her in the cab to take her home the next morning.

Trey Winston was off-limits, always had been and always would be. He had no interest in her other than using her as an effective weapon to achieve his ambitious desire of becoming the next senator of North Carolina.

She'd told herself she would do whatever she could to help him because of her devotion to Kate, but the truth of the matter was she'd do it because she cared about him enough to want to see him get everything he wanted in life.

Trey tried to keep his gaze off Debra and Stacy as they went over the initial planning stages. The two women were polar opposites. Stacy looked like a fashion doll with her bleached blond hair and black-fringed blue eyes. Her pink dress hugged her body in all the right places and she would instantly draw the gaze of any man who was breathing.

Debra, on the other hand, flew just under the radar in her brown suit and with her hair pulled back into a messy knot at the back of her head.

And yet it was Debra who kept drawing his gaze. She had the loveliest eyes he'd ever seen, so big and so green. Her slightly heart-shaped face expressed each and every emotion she felt.

As the two women talked, Debra displayed both earnestness and an underlying will of steel. She listened to Stacy's ideas, tossing some while accepting others.

He knew Debra was his mother's go-to woman, practically Kate's right hand, moving behind the scenes to keep his mother's life in order and running as smoothly as possible six days a week.

He also knew that the night they had met up in the bar, Debra had been upset about a breakup with some guy named Gary or Larry, or something like that.

Initially, he'd just wanted to console her, but he was in such good spirits about his own business deal, it wasn't long before he had Debra laughing and the surprising sparks had flown between them.

Debra was a constant at the Winston Estate, but he suddenly realized he knew virtually nothing about her personal life or who she was when she wasn't Kate Winston's assistant.

Did she like to dance? What was her favorite kind of music? Did she have any hobbies? How did she spend her evenings and Sundays?

He frowned and stared up at an elaborate crystal chandelier. He shouldn't be wondering about Debra's personal life. It... *She* was none of his business. Just because they'd hooked up for one night didn't mean anything at all.

He knew without doubt that it was a secret neither of them would speak of to anyone else. He trusted Debra. Her loyalty and love had always been with the family.

Still, she had stunned him with her passion, delighted him with her abandon that night. Granted, they'd both been buzzed on champagne, but neither of them could claim inebriation to the point of a lack of consent.

He knew he shouldn't even be thinking about that night. It had been a foolish misstep on both their parts. Instead he should be thinking about Cecily and her excitement when he'd called her the night before and told her about the dinner party and his decision to enter the race.

"Then I guess we're done here for now." Stacy's perky voice brought him back to the present. "I'll email you the various menus and a couple of tentative table and floor plans first thing in the morning."

Debra nodded and stood. "And I'll get back to you on exactly what we want for a speaker's podium and maybe a head table."

"Sounds like a plan," Stacy replied and also got to her feet. Trey followed suit, rising and taking Debra's coat from the back of her chair to help her into it.

Even her coat smelled of that fresh scent that had dizzied his senses when he'd held her in his arms. She quickly slid her arms in and stepped away from him with a murmured thanks.

Trey pulled his coat on and at the ballroom doorway they both said goodbye to Stacy, who scurried off in one direction while Trey and Debra headed back to the lobby and the front door.

They stepped outside into the bracing air. "It's after eleven. Do you want to go someplace for a quick lunch before you head back to the office?" he asked.

He could tell that he'd surprised her by the look on her face. "Oh, no, thanks. I really need to get back to work. All I need from you is a guest list as quickly as possible so that we can get the invitations out."

"I'll work on it this afternoon and how about I drop it by your place this evening? That way you'll have it first thing in the morning to start working on. I've got business meetings tomorrow that will keep me at Adair Enterprises for most of the day. You'll be home this evening?"

"Yes, I'll be home by six-thirty or so."

He shoved his hands into his coat pockets, noting how the brisk breeze whipped a pretty pink into her cheeks. "How are things with Larry?" It was the first time either of them had made any mention of what had transpired six weeks ago.

"It's Barry, and things are fine. He's gone and I'm happy. He was nothing but a creep."

"You seemed pretty upset about the breakup," Trey replied.

The pink in her cheeks was definitely brighter now and he had a feeling it had nothing to do with the weather. "I was mostly upset because I intended to break up with him that night and he beat me to the punch and broke up with me first." She looked toward her car and shifted from one foot to the other, as if wishing for an immediate escape route.

"Okay then, I guess I'll see you later this evening. Shall we say around seven?" he asked.

She nodded. "That would be fine." With a murmured goodbye she made her escape, hurrying away from him as if unable to get out of his presence fast enough.

He frowned as he headed for his own car. He found it impossible to discern what Debra thought of him. In all the years he'd known her, he'd never been able to figure out if she actually liked him or not. The night of sharing a bed and hot sex hadn't changed the fact that he didn't know what to think about her or what she might think about him.

And it irritated him that he cared. He got into his car and tried to push thoughts of Debra Prentice away. He had so many other things to focus on, like how he intended to continue to run the successful Adair Enterprises at the same time he launched a campaign.

Grandfather Walt would be proud of him. The old man was probably dancing with the angels at Trey's decision to enter the world of politics. Running the family business and politics had been what the old man had wanted for him.

Trey knew he had a good chance of winning. He didn't lean too far left or too far to the right. His politics were middle-of-the-road. He'd already proven his business acumen in the success of Adair Enterprises and he knew he'd made a reputation for himself as a hard worker and decent man who was willing to compromise when it was necessary.

In the course of doing business, he'd made enemies, but he knew that his opponents would have a hard time slinging mud at him.

He'd always been the good son, the firstborn who had excelled in college, had taken the family business into a new level of success and had never done drugs or slept with married women. He'd never taken pictures of his body parts and put them online.

In fact, he'd worked hard to keep his nose clean for just this time. Walt had wanted this for him since Trey was old enough to understand the world of politics and now Trey wanted it for himself.

He knew Cecily would put more pressure on him now for the announcement of their engagement. She would reason that an engaged or newly married candidate only made a man more appealing to the masses. It suggested stability and commitment, considered good character traits by voters.

She was right, but he wasn't ready yet to pop the

question to her. Maybe he'd ask her to marry him once the dinner party was finished. The event would be his first real step in declaring himself ready to be a serious contender and at the moment he needed all his energy and attention focused on that.

The main office of Adair Enterprises was located in downtown Raleigh, but they also had offices in Seattle and factories in Durham and Iowa.

The company had been started by his mother's grandfather in the 1930s as a shipping company for tobacco and local farmers to get their products across the country.

When Walt had taken over, the business had evolved into shipping containers and then to plastics and Trey had transformed it once again into a company also known for computer systems.

One of the strengths of the business was in its ability to be ever-changing with the times, and Trey prided himself on not only being a visionary, but also smart enough to hire equally driven and bright people to work with him.

As he walked through the glass doors of the building he was instantly greeted by security guard Jason Ridgeway. "Good morning, Mr. Winston."

"Morning, Jason. How are Stella and the kids doing?"

"Great, everyone is great."

"Billy's broken arm healing all right?"

Jason nodded. "The cast is due to come off sometime next week. I swear that kid is going to age me before my time."

Trey laughed. "Just keep him out of trees," he said and then with a wave headed to the bank of elevators that would take him to the top floor of the building and his personal office.

The elevator opened into a spacious airy reception area and Rhonda Wilson sat behind the large, modern reception desk. Rhonda was part beauty, part bulldog, the perfect final gatekeeper to Trey.

In her mid-fifties, Rhonda was tall and broad shouldered. She could be exceedingly pleasant and was fiercely devoted to Trey, but she also could tear a new one in any reporter or the like who tried to breach Trey's privacy.

"Good morning, boss," she greeted him with a pleasant smile.

"It's almost twelve," he replied. "Hopefully you're going to tell me I have nothing on my calendar for the rest of the afternoon?"

"You have nothing on your calendar for the rest of the afternoon," she repeated dutifully. "Although you do have a ton of phone messages on your desk."

"As usual," he replied as he took off his coat. "Could you order a roast-beef sub for me and keep everyone out of my hair for the next couple of hours?"

"No problem." She picked up the phone to call the nearby restaurant Trey often ordered his lunch from as Trey went into the inner sanctum that often felt more like home than his huge new mansion just outside the Raleigh beltline.

His personal office was the size of a large apartment. Not only did it boast a desk the size of a small boat, but also a sitting area complete with sofa and chairs, a minibar and a bathroom that had both a shower and sauna, and a large walk-in closet.

There had been many nights when working on an

intricate deal that Trey had slept on the sofa and then awakened the next morning to shower and dress for another day of mergers or hiccups that needed to be solved.

He tossed his coat on the back of the sleek leather sofa and then took his place at his desk and powered up the state-of-the-art computer system that allowed him to monitor every area of the business, video chat with managers in other parts of the country and stay on top of each and every problem that might arise.

Today he did a cursory check of emails to make sure there were no major issues at any of the plants or offices. He quickly flew through the phone messages, setting aside the ones he intended to return later and then pulled up his list of contacts and began to work on an invitation list for the dinner.

He wanted his friends and business associates there, but he knew it was even more important that invitations went to labor-union leaders, local and state government officials, and political backers who could bring both clout and campaign contributions.

He started his list but found himself distracted by the anticipation of going to Debra's place later that evening. He'd never been to the townhouse she'd bought, but he remembered her excitement over no longer having to rent and being a real homeowner.

He knew the silkiness of her skin, the smooth slide of her body against his own. He knew the contours of her body intimately, but he couldn't imagine how her home would be decorated.

What definitely confounded him was the fact that even though it wasn't quite noon yet, he couldn't wait for seven o'clock to come.

* * *

Kate Winston stood at her office window. It was just after six and Debra had left to go home. Business was officially ended for the day, but it would still be twenty minutes or so before dinner was served.

A softness filled her as she thought of Debra. In many ways Debra had taken the place of the daughter nobody knew she'd had, the baby girl who had died at birth. Kate had only been seventeen when she'd given birth and after learning the baby did not survive, she had fallen into a deep depression that she'd believed would last forever.

She'd been sent away to school, where she pretended that she was just like all the other debutantes with nothing to trouble her except which dress to wear to what event, but she'd never quite gotten over the heartache of the loss of the baby girl.

It was only when Buchanan Winston had entered her life that Kate discovered a new reason for living. She had fallen head over heels in love with Buck. She'd not only given him three healthy sons, but had also supported him in his political aspirations that began on a local level and eventually ended in the Senate.

It was during the Senate election that she'd found out that Buck had been having affairs for most of their marriage. Her heart had been broken and she'd threatened to leave him, but he'd told her if she left he'd declare her an unfit mother and seek to gain full custody of their children.

Afraid of his power and influence, Kate had stayed and played the role of supportive wife, and then, like a bad cliché, Buck had died in one of his mistress's arms.

He'd had one year left in his term as senator and Kate had stepped in to fill his shoes.

She'd discovered she loved politics and had run for a term of her own the next year. After that had come a four-year stint as the first female vice president of the United States. Her party had lost the next election and now she had people whispering in her ear about running for president when election time rolled around again.

She wanted it. But her decision about running for the most prestigious and powerful position in the world was tempered by other elements besides her own desire.

She'd made many friends in her years of public service, but she'd also made enemies and she didn't have just herself to worry about when the election got dirty, and elections always got dirty.

Moving away from the window, she thought of her sons and how the decision to run for president might affect each of them. Trey would be all right. He was a strong man and already preparing himself for the battle arena of politics.

She worried about Sam. He'd come home so damaged and unwilling to seek help from either family members or professionals. He was a loose cannon at the moment and she was concerned how the bright spotlight of a national campaign might affect him.

Then there was Thad. Her youngest, Thaddeus had turned his back on the family business and had made a modest life for himself in Garner, North Carolina. He worked for the Raleigh Police Department as a crime-scene investigator.

He led a quiet life alone and would hate having any role in the world she loved. Maybe she should just flip a coin to come to a final decision, she thought ruefully.

She only knew two things for sure. She believed with all her heart that she was the right person for the job, that she would be far better for the country than the front-runners who had already begun the political dance of becoming elected.

The second thing she knew with certainty was that some of the enemies she'd made over the years were utterly ruthless and would do everything in their power to destroy her and anyone she loved, not only politically, but personally, as well.

Chapter 3

Debra arrived home, hung her coat in the hall closet and then raced around like a mad woman to make sure her living room/dining area and the kitchen were spotlessly clean.

She was by nature a neat and tidy woman, so there was little to do, but with the thought that Trey would be seeing her home for the very first time she wanted everything perfect.

She fluffed the red-and-yellow throw pillows on the black sofa twice and dithered over lighting several of the scented candles she normally lit in the evenings. She finally decided against it, not wanting him to believe that she was in any way attempting to create an intimate, romantic setting.

At six forty-five she sat down on the edge of the sofa and told herself she was acting completely ridiculous.

Trey probably wouldn't even take a step into the small, gleaming hardwood-floor foyer. He'd meet her at the door, hand her the list of names he'd prepared and then leave with his mission accomplished.

The last thing Trey Winston cared about was sitting around and chatting with his mother's assistant. Debra had eaten on the way home from the estate and had put on coffee, which now filled the air with its freshly brewed scent.

The coffee wasn't for him. She always made coffee or hot tea when she got home from work, especially at this time of year when outside the cold knocked on every window and attempted to seep into every crack.

She was thankful that the townhouse seemed well insulated and she loved to keep the thermostat low and build a nice fire in the stone see-through fireplace that was between the living room and kitchen.

There were no flames in the fireplace now. Again, she didn't want Trey to get any ideas that she had any thought about another encounter with him. The last thing she wanted was to come off as some pathetic one-night stand who didn't understand exactly what she'd been.

She'd changed out of her suit and into a pair of comfortable jeans and a mint-green fleece sweatshirt. She hadn't even bothered to check herself in a mirror as she'd left her upstairs bedroom to come down here to wait for Trey's appearance.

She jumped when the doorbell rang, nerves jangling discordantly through her as she got up from the sofa and hurried to answer.

Her breath caught slightly in her throat as she opened the door and he smiled at her. Trey Winston definitely had a killèr smile, all white straight teeth and warmth. "Hi," he said.

"Hi," she replied.

His smile widened, crinkling the corners of his eyes. "Are you going to invite me in?"

"Oh, of course…if you want to come in… I mean you don't have to if you don't want to."

"Thanks, I'd love to come in." He swept past her, trailing the bold scent of his cologne as she quickly closed the front door and followed him into her living room.

He shrugged out of his coat and slung it across the back of one of the two chairs that faced the sofa as if he'd done it a hundred times before. He'd changed clothes, too. Instead of his usual suit, he was dressed in a pair of casual black slacks and a white polo shirt that hugged his shoulders and chest as if specifically tailored for him.

"Is that fresh coffee I smell?" he asked.

"Yes, it is. Would you like a cup?" To say that she was shocked to have him not only actually in her townhouse, but also asking for a cup of coffee was an understatement.

"I'd love a cup," he replied.

She motioned him to the sofa. "Just make yourself comfortable and I'll bring it in here."

"I don't mind sitting in the kitchen," he said as he followed at her heels. His gaze seemed to take in every nook and corner of the room. "Nice place."

"Thanks, I like it." She was grateful when he sank down at the round wooden table with its centerpiece of a crystal bowl with red and yellow flowers.

The kitchen was her favorite place to spend time.

Located at the back of the townhouse, the windows looked out on a lush flower garden she'd planted last spring, although now there was nothing to see but dormant plants and the redbrick tiers of the flowerbeds.

Above the butcher-block center island hung a rack with gleaming copper-bottomed pots and pans. The counters not only held the coffeepot but a variety of small appliances she used on a regular basis on the weekends.

"You like to cook," he said as he looked around with obvious interest.

"On the weekends," she replied as she reached with slightly nervous fingers to get two of her nicest black mugs down from the cabinet. She swallowed hard as she nearly dropped one. *Get a grip,* she commanded herself.

She poured the coffee and managed to deliver both cups to the table without incident. "Sugar? Cream?"

"Black is fine," he replied.

She sank down onto the chair opposite him, wondering how it was possible that his mere presence diminished the size of her kitchen and sucked up the energy, making her feel slightly lightheaded, as if she was suffering from a lack of oxygen.

"What kind of food do you like to cook?" he asked, his big hands cradling the coffee mug.

"Anything…everything, whatever sounds good. I try to do a new recipe every weekend on Sunday. Last week it was chicken *malai* curry, an Indian dish. The week before that was spicy cherry pork stir fry."

"Sounds delicious and adventurous," he replied, his head cocked slightly to one side and his gaze intent on her as if trying to see inside her head.

She forced a dry laugh. "*Adventurous* isn't exactly

an adjective that is normally used when describing me."
She mentally begged him not to mention the night they'd
spent together, a night that had been out of character
for both of them. She'd definitely been adventurous
and bold then.

"Efficient and driven. Sweet but with a touch of barracuda," he replied. He took a sip of his coffee and then
set the mug back down. "That's how I would describe
you. I was impressed with how you handled the negotiations today with Stacy."

"Thanks. We'll see how well I did when I get the
menus and floor plans from her in the morning," she
replied, beginning to relax. "And we never discussed
what your budget was for the event."

"Whatever it takes to do it right," he replied.

"Everything needs a budget, Trey," she admonished.
"If you can't stick to a budget, then how can the voters
trust you with their tax dollars?"

"Okay." He named an amount that was adequate and
yet not too extravagant. "We'll use that figure as our
budget. What do you think about my decision to run
for senator?"

She looked at him, surprised he would care one way
or the other what she thought about it. She took a sip
of her coffee, unwilling to give him a quick, flippant
answer.

"You've always been successful at whatever en-
deavor you've undertaken," she said thoughtfully. "You
have all the qualities to be a great senator, but have you
considered how you're going to juggle the running of
Adair Enterprises with the responsibilities of being a
state senator? Not only does the job take a lot of hours

and work, but campaigning will be a huge commitment of both time and energy."

"I know, but I'm lucky that I have good people working with me at Adair Enterprises and they will step up to cover whenever I can't be at the business." He took another drink. "Has Mom given you any hint as to whether she's going to take up the challenge and run for president?"

Debra smiled. "Your mother shares a lot with me, but this is one decision she's keeping pretty close to her chest. I know there is pressure on her from a variety of places to run, but I have no idea what she's going to decide."

"She should go for it. She'd be great for the country. Not only is she strong and intelligent, but she's more than paid her dues and she's smarter than any of the other schmucks who are making noise about running."

"You're preaching to the choir," Debra replied with a smile. "She'd have my vote in a minute."

He returned her smile and suddenly the nerves jumped through her veins once again. "This is nice," he said as his gaze swept the room and lingered on the fireplace. "I'll bet it's quite cozy in here when the fire is lit and you have something exotic cooking in the oven or on the stove."

"It is nice," she agreed. "Buying this place was the best decision I've ever made."

He finished his coffee and when he set the mug down on the table and looked at her, something in the depths of his eyes caused her to tense warily.

"Debra, about that night…"

"What night?" she said quickly. "I have no idea what you're talking about." She pled with her eyes for him to take it no further. She didn't want to have a discussion about a night that shouldn't have happened. A hand automatically fell to her lap, as if in an attempt to hide the secret she carried.

"I'm your mother's assistant and I'll do everything I can to help you reach your goal of becoming a North Carolina state senator," she said softly. "And that's really all we have to discuss."

He held her gaze for a long moment and then gave a curt nod of his head and stood. "Thanks for the coffee, Debra, and all your hard work."

"No problem. One more thing, did you bring me the list of names of people you want to invite?" She got up from the table.

He snapped his finger and grinned at her. "I knew there was a reason I stopped by here. The list is in my coat pocket."

Together they left the kitchen and went back into the living room where he grabbed his coat from the back of the chair and put it on. He reached into one of the pockets and pulled out the printed list.

"Thanks," she said as she took it from him. "I'll get the invitations ordered tomorrow and have them addressed and mailed by the end of the next day. Do you want to look at the invitations before they go out? I was thinking something simple and elegant."

"I trust your judgment."

"You can trust me in everything," she said pointedly, hoping her words were enough to put him at ease about that damned night they'd spent together.

He'd probably wanted to mention it to her to assure himself that she had no plans to take it public. She could probably make a little extra money selling the story to the tabloids.

She could only imagine the salacious headlines if the information got out that he'd slept with a member of his mother's staff while practically engaged to a wealthy socialite. But he had nothing to worry about where she was concerned.

"You have absolutely nothing to be worried about," she said to reiterate to him that the secret of their unexpected tryst would remain just that—a secret.

"Then I guess I'll leave you to the rest of your evening," he said, and they walked together toward the front door.

"I'll get in touch with you sometime tomorrow, as soon as I get the things emailed over from Stacy," she replied, grateful that they'd broached the subject of their night together without really talking about it.

"This dinner party is an important first step and together we're going to make it amazing," he said. He gave her one last devastating smile and then stepped out the front door and disappeared into the gloom of a cloudy twilight.

Debra locked the door behind him and leaned against the door. Curse that man. She could still smell the heady scent of his cologne, feel a lingering vibrating energy in the air despite his absence.

She shoved herself off the door with a muttered curse and carried the list of names he'd given her into the small chamber just off the living room that served as her home office.

She placed the list on her desk next to her computer and then left the room and returned to the kitchen. She placed Trey's coffee mug in the dishwasher and silently cursed him for even making her think about that night.

Her body flushed with heat as she thought of how he'd slowly caressed each and every inch of her skin. His kisses had driven her half out of her mind with desire and she knew making love with Trey Winston was an experience she'd never, ever forget.

What bothered her more than anything was the knowledge that even knowing it was wrong, even with the unexpected result that had occurred, she'd do it again in a hot minute.

Trey wasn't sure what he had hoped to accomplish by bringing up the night he'd spent with Debra after all this time. Over six weeks had passed and they'd spoken numerous times since then without ever mentioning what had transpired between them.

So, what had he wanted to say to her tonight? What had he wanted her to say to him? That she'd liked being with him? That he'd been a pleasing lover?

He mentally scoffed at his own thoughts. As terrible as it sounded, he probably just wanted to double-check that she didn't intend to go public with their misdeed, but even thinking that did a disservice to the woman he knew that Debra was. He knew how devoted she was to the family. She would never do anything to hurt any of them in any way.

Instead of heading home to his mansion, he decided to drop in and visit with his grandmother in the nursing home. As he drove his thoughts continued to be filled with Debra.

She'd looked cute as a bug in her jeans and green sweatshirt. He'd never seen her in casual clothes before and the jeans had hugged her long legs, shapely legs that he remembered wrapped around him.

He tightened his grip on the steering wheel, realizing the skies were spitting a bit of ice. January in Raleigh could be surprisingly unpredictable. It might be cold with a bit of snow or ice, or it could be surprisingly mild. Occasionally they got a killer ice storm, but thankfully nothing like that so far this year.

The weather forecast that morning had mentioned the threat of a little frozen precipitation, but nothing for travelers to worry about. Slowing his speed a bit, his thoughts went back to Debra.

Her townhome had surprised him. He'd expected the furnishings to be utilitarian and rather cold, but stepping into her living room had been like being welcomed into a place where he'd wanted to stay and linger awhile.

The living space had been warm and inviting, as had the kitchen, as well. He thought of the stark formal furnishings in his own mansion and for a moment entertained the idea of hiring Debra to do a bit of decorating transformation.

It was a silly thought. If he worked his plan to achieve his ultimate goal, then Cecily would be moving into the mansion and she'd want to put her own personal stamp in place there, although he doubted that Cecily would have the taste for warm and inviting. She'd want formal and expensive. She'd want to create a showcase rather than a home.

He punched the button on his steering wheel that would connect him to phone services. He gave the command to call Cecily on her cell and then waited for her to answer.

"Darling," her voice chirped through the interior of the car. "I was wondering if I was going to hear from you today."

"Between work at the office and planning this dinner party, I've been swamped." He could hear from the background noise on her phone that she wasn't at home. "Where are you now?"

"At a Women's League meeting. I'm already not-so-subtly campaigning for you, Trey."

He smiled, certain that she was doing just that. "You know I appreciate it."

"You'd better," she replied with a laugh. "Rumor has it your mother is seriously considering running for president. We'll let her have that position for two terms and then *we'll* be ready to move into the White House."

Trey laughed. "One step at a time, Cecily. This dinner party will let me know if I can get some of the big hitters in town behind me in order to achieve the first step in the process."

"You can take it one step at a time, but I'm already envisioning what the White House Christmas tree will look like," she replied with a laugh. "Oh, gotta go. I'll talk to you tomorrow."

She ended the call and Trey shook his head. Cecily McKenna was like a force of nature, unstoppable and powerful and completely in his corner. She would make a perfect ally and support as a wife.

He pulled into the parking lot of the Brookside Nursing Home, an upscale establishment where his grandmother, Eunice, had resided since Walt's death.

When she'd lost her husband she had spiraled into a depression so deep nobody seemed to be able to pull her out. Trey knew one of the most difficult decisions his mother had made was to move her own mother here instead of keeping her living at the estate. But Eunice needed more than what Kate and the family could provide.

After several months of residency Eunice had appeared to rally from her depression. She seemed quite content where she was, in a small apartmentlike set of rooms with an aid who stayed with her twenty-four hours a day.

He nodded to the security guard on duty outside the front door and entered into a small lobby with a couple of elegant chairs and a front desk.

"Good evening, Mr. Winston," Amy Fedder, a middle-aged woman behind the reception desk greeted him. He was a frequent visitor and knew most of the people on staff.

"Hi, Amy." He walked to the desk where there was a sign-in sheet and quickly signed his name and the time he'd arrived. "Have you heard how she's doing today?"

"I know she had dinner in the dining room and earlier in the day she joined a group of women playing bingo."

"Then it sounds like it's been a good day for her," he replied, a happiness filling him. He adored his grandmother. "Thanks Amy, I'll see you on my way out." He left the front desk and headed for the elevator, which would take him to the second floor where his grandmother's little apartment was located. It amused him that her place was in what the nursing home called the west wing.

There were only forty residents at any given time in Brookside and almost as many staff members. The nursing home catered to the wealthy and powerful who wanted their loved ones in an upscale environment with exceptional care and security. Every member of the staff had undergone intense background and security checks before being hired and there was a front door and a back door, both with an armed security guard on duty at all times.

He got off the elevator and walked down a long hallway, passing several closed doors before he arrived at apartment 211.

He knocked and the door was answered by Serena Sue Sana, a tall beautiful African-American woman who went by the nickname of Sassy. She was of an indeterminable age, but Trey guessed her to be somewhere in her mid-sixties.

"Mr. Trey," she greeted him, her white teeth flashing in a bright smile. "Come in." She opened the door wider. "Ms. Eunice will be so happy to see you." She leaned closer to him. "She's had a good day but seems a bit agitated this evening," she whispered.

He nodded and walked into the nice-size living room with a small kitchenette area and doors that led to the bathroom and two bedrooms, one large and one smaller.

His eighty-six-year-old grandmother was where she usually was at this time of the evening, her small frame nearly swallowed up by the comfortable light blue chair surrounding her.

Her silvery-white hair was pulled up neatly into a bun atop her head and her blue eyes lit up and a smile curved her lips at the sight of him. "I know you," she said, her affection for him thick in her voice.

"And I know you," Trey replied as he walked over to her and planted a kiss on her forehead.

"I'll just go on into my room so you two can have a nice private chat," Sassy said.

"Before you go, would you make this television be quiet?" Eunice held out the remote control to Sassy.

"I'll take care of it," Trey replied. He sat in the chair next to Eunice and took the remote control and hit the mute button as Sassy disappeared into the small bedroom and closed the door behind her.

"I love Sassy to death, but she likes to watch the silliest television shows," Eunice said. "And sometimes I just like to sit and visit with my favorite grandson."

"I'll bet you say that to all your grandsons," Trey said teasingly.

She giggled like a young girl. "You might be right about that." Her blue eyes, so like Trey's mother's, sparkled merrily.

"I heard you played bingo this afternoon," Trey said.

Her smile instantly transformed into a frown. "Did I…? Yes, yes I did, although I didn't win. I never win." She leaned closer to him. "That woman from downstairs in 108 always wins. I think the fix is in."

Trey laughed and leaned over and covered her frail hand with his. "You don't have to win all the time."

Her eyes flashed and her chin jutted forward with a show of stubbornness. "Adairs always win," she said, her voice strident as she pulled her hand back from his and instead worried the edge of the fringed shawl that was around her shoulders.

"That's what we do," she muttered more to herself than to him. "We win."

"Speaking of winning, have you talked to Mom lately?"

She frowned again in thought. "She called yesterday…or maybe it was the day before." She shook her head with obvious agitation. "I can't remember. Sometimes I can't remember what happened when, except I have lots of memories of when you boys were young. You three were such a handful. But sometimes my brain just gets a bit scrambled."

"It's okay," Trey said gently. "I was just wondering if she told you that I'm considering a run for the Senate."

Eunice's eyes widened. "No, she didn't tell me." Her fingers threaded through the shawl fringe at a quicker pace. "She never mentioned that to me before."

"Then I guess she didn't tell you that we think she's also considering a run for the White House," Trey said.

Eunice appeared to freeze in place, the only movement being her gaze darting frantically around the room as if seeking something she'd misplaced and desperately needed to find.

"Grandma, what is it?" Trey asked.

She stood from her chair and began to pace in front of him, her back slightly bent from the osteoporosis that plagued her. "No. No. No." The word snapped out of her louder and more frantic with each shuffled step of her feet.

Trey stood in an attempt to reach out and draw her back into her chair, but she slapped his hands away and continued to pace.

"This is bad news…. It's terrible, terrible news." She stopped her movement and stared at him, her eyes wide with fear. "You shouldn't do this. She shouldn't do this. Pandora's box, that's all it will be."

"What are you talking about? Grandma, what are you afraid of?"

Her eyes filled with tears as she looked at him in horror. "Secrets and lies," she said in a bare whisper.

Chapter 4

It has to be here, Debra thought frantically as she searched the area on top of her desk. The early morning sun drifted through the office window, letting her know it was getting later and later.

She moved file folders and papers helter-skelter, her heart pounding in her ears as she looked for the missing paperwork. It had to be here, it just had to be.

She distinctly remembered putting the guest list that Trey had given her next to her computer the night before, but it wasn't there now.

She was already dressed to go to work and had come into the office to grab the list before leaving her place. In a panic she now fell to her hands and knees in the plush carpeting, searching on the floor, hoping that it had somehow drifted off the desk, but it wasn't there, either.

She checked the wastebasket to make sure it hadn't fallen into it somehow during the night. Nothing. No list magically appeared.

Half-breathless from her anxious search, she sank down at her desk chair. *Think,* she commanded herself. After she'd placed it on the desk the night before had she come back in here for any reason and mindlessly placed it elsewhere?

No, she was certain she hadn't reentered the office again last night. After Trey had left she'd watched a little television and then had gone upstairs to bed. She had not come back into the office.

Was it possible she had sleepwalked and moved the list?

She couldn't imagine such a thing. As far as she knew she'd never sleepwalked in her life. Besides, she would have had to maneuver herself not just out of her bed, but also down the stairs and into the office all the while being unconscious in sleep.

Impossible. Utterly ridiculous to even entertain such an idea, but the darned list didn't get up and walk away on its own.

Granted, she'd been unsettled after Trey had left. Maybe she had wandered in here and taken the list someplace else in the house before she'd gone to bed.

With this thought in mind, she jumped out of the chair and raced through the lower level of the house. Her heart pounded in an unsteady rhythm as she checked the kitchen counters, the living-room coffee table and any reasonable place she might have put the list, but it was nowhere to be found.

The thought of calling Trey and asking him for another copy horrified her. She was organized and efficient. She didn't lose things. So how had she lost such an important piece of paper?

After a run-through of the entire house yielded no results, she finally returned to the kitchen, defeated and knowing she needed to get on the road or she'd definitely be late to work.

She hurried to the refrigerator and opened the freezer to take out a small package of chicken breasts to thaw for dinner and stared at the piece of paper that was slid between them and a frozen pizza.

She grabbed the paper, saw that it was the missing list and hugged it tight to her chest in relief. Hurriedly yanking out the chicken breasts, she set them in the fridge and then raced for the front door, grabbing her purse and coat on the way out.

As she waited for her car to warm up, she folded the guest list and tucked it into her purse, then pulled her coat around her shoulders. She tried to ignore the rapid beating of her heart that still continued, the frantic beat that had begun the moment she'd realized the list was missing.

Heading toward the Winston Estate, she wondered if somehow between last night and this morning her brain had slipped a cog. Had she been so flustered by Trey's visit that she'd mindlessly placed the list in the freezer?

It was crazy. It was insane, but she couldn't ignore the fact that she was the only person in the house who could have put the list in the freezer.

Maybe it had something to do with hormones. She had called her doctor to make an appointment for the weekend. Was it possible that pregnancy hormones made you lose your mind? She'd be sure and ask her doctor.

As if to make the day worse, Jerry Cahill was on guard duty as she pulled into the side entrance. The tall, sandy-haired Secret Service man gave her the creeps. He seemed to have some sort of a weird crush on her and had asked her out twice. Both times she'd politely declined but one time last month she'd thought she'd seen him standing on the sidewalk in front of her place and staring at her townhouse.

He stopped her car before she could pull into her usual parking space and motioned for her to roll down her window. "Hey, doll, running a little late this morning, aren't you?" He leaned too far into her window, invading her personal space.

"Maybe just a few minutes," she replied.

Jerry had hazel eyes that should have been warm in hue, but instead reminded her of an untamed jungle animal that could spring at a vulnerable throat at any moment.

His breath smelled of peppermint and the fact that he was close enough to smell his breath freaked her out just a little bit.

He held her gaze for a long moment and then stepped back and tapped the top of her car. "Well, I just wanted to tell you to have a good day."

She rolled up her window and parked her car, feeling revulsion just from the brief encounter. Jerry Cahill might be a Secret Service agent, but that didn't make him any less of a creep.

She hurried into the house to find Maddie Fitzgerald, head housekeeper, and Myra Henry, head cook, seated at the small table enjoying a cup of coffee together.

"Good morning, Ms. Debra," Maddie said. Her plump cheeks danced upward with her smile. With red hair cut in a no-nonsense style and her perpetual optimism, Maddie had been around long before Debra. She'd not only been the first person Kate had hired, but she'd helped Kate raise the boys and was intensely devoted to the Winston family, as they all were to her.

"Good morning, ladies," Debra said. She smiled at Myra and drew in a deep breath. "Is that your famous cinnamon rolls I smell?"

"It is. If you want to get settled into your office I'll bring you a couple with a nice cup of coffee," Myra said.

"That sounds heavenly," Debra replied. "Thanks, Myra."

She kept her smile pasted on her lips until she reached her office where she hung up her coat and then sank down at her desk. She opened her purse and retrieved the list that Trey had given her.

She'd just set it next to her computer when Myra arrived with a steaming cup of coffee and two large iced cinnamon rolls on an oversize saucer.

"Those look too sinful to eat," Debra exclaimed as she eyed the goodies.

Myra grinned at her. "I make them special, no calories so there's no guilt."

"Yeah, right," Debra replied with a laugh.

"Enjoy," Myra said and left the office.

Debra took a sip of the coffee and then got to work typing up the list of names Trey had given her so she'd have a hard copy on her computer. Once it was in the computer she wouldn't have to worry about losing it again.

She was still troubled twenty minutes later when she had the copy made and leaned back in her chair and drew a deep breath.

"Crisis averted," she muttered aloud to herself. She picked up one of the cinnamon rolls and took a bite, but her stomach was still in knots because of the morning trauma.

Or was it morning sickness?

She couldn't think about being pregnant now. She'd think about it after she saw her doctor. Right now she had work to do, not only did she have to pick invitations to be printed and addressed and mailed, there was also the matter of finding a good orchestra to hire for the night of the dinner. Once she got information from Stacy she'd need to meet with Trey to make some final decisions.

It would be easy for her to feel overwhelmed, but Debra knew the way to get things done was focus on one item at a time and not look too far ahead.

Kate's morning knock came at eight-thirty and Debra instantly got up to join her boss in her office.

"Good morning, Kate," Debra said as she sat in the chair opposite the desk.

"And a good morning to you," Kate said with a fond smile. "I've already given Haley the things that needed to be taken care of for me this morning. One thing I love about interns is that they're so eager to please. What I want from you is an update on you and Trey's visit to the Regent yesterday."

For the next half an hour Debra filled Kate in on what had transpired at the hotel and where they were in the planning stages.

"I know you're pulling everything together quickly," Kate said. "If you need more help, let me know and I'll assign an assistant for you."

"Actually, I think Stacy, the hotel event planner is

going to be all I need. She seemed to understand exactly what we want, what we need for a successful evening for Trey. I'm expecting her to get me a floor plan and some menu options sometime this morning. That will tell me how good she is at her job."

"Do you think he's ready for this?" Kate asked.

"I think he's more ready than anyone could be," Debra replied. "I know he's saying that this dinner party is just to dip his toes in the water to see what kind of support he might have if he decides to run, but I believe he's already made up his mind. His head is definitely already in the game."

Kate nodded. "That's what I believe, too, and Trey never does anything halfway."

"He'll make a wonderful senator," Debra said, unable to keep the passion of her belief out of her voice. "He'll bring new life and new hope to the people of North Carolina."

Kate nodded. "I know my son. Even if he decided to be a garbage man he'd be the best in the business. He always does everything well."

"He's a chip off the old block," Debra replied with a smile.

Kate laughed. "Get out of here and get to work on helping my son. I won't need anything from you today. I know the time constraints you have to get the details of this dinner party under control are incredibly tight, so get to it."

By the time she got back to her office she'd received a number of emails from Stacy. The young event planner had sent several different seating plans and three menus with prices. Even though she'd had to pull teeth in order for Trey to come up with a budget, Debra intended to negotiate hard to keep costs low and quality high.

She was an old pro at this, having set up dozens of such events in the past for Kate. Despite what Trey had said, budgets always mattered, and it would reflect poorly on his business acumen to not bring the dinner party in as reasonably as possible.

If you wanted the taxpayers to back you, then you had to show a willingness to work within budgets, she thought.

Gathering the emails all together, she knew what she needed now was for she and Trey to have another meeting and make more decisions. She picked up the phone to call him at Adair Enterprises.

The receptionist connected her to him immediately.

"Good morning, Debra." His deep smooth voice was like a physical caress through the line.

She returned the greeting, although what she wanted to do was tell him about her frantic search for his list that morning, the ridiculousness of finally finding it in the freezer and that Myra's cinnamon rolls had made her slightly queasy.

Trey told her he intended to come to the house around two and they would meet then to hammer out any decisions that needed to be made. Then they disconnected.

Debra leaned back in her chair and for the first time in years wished she had a best friend. Her entire adult life had been built surrounded by the Winston family. There hadn't been time for friends outside of the intimacy of the family members.

Certainly her childhood hadn't been conducive to making friends. She'd never invited anyone to her home, afraid that her classmates might see her mother drunk or hungover. Once she started working for Kate, the work and the family had taken precedence over anything and everyone else.

That had been part of her problem with dating Barry. There had been little time to really grow any meaningful relationship. Although ultimately he'd broken up with her because he told her he wasn't getting what he needed from her, she'd already intended to break up with him because she'd figured out he was getting what he needed from his married secretary. The jerk.

Maybe it was best that she didn't have a best friend, she thought as her hand fell to her lap and she caressed her lower belly.

Perhaps she would be tempted to share too much with a best friend, and a secret wasn't a secret if two people knew about it. And Debra knew better than anyone that she had a secret that had the potential to destroy a career before it began.

Trey had been disturbed since he'd left the nursing home the night before. His grandmother had become quite agitated before he'd left, frantic as she continued to whisper about secrets and lies.

Sassy had finally come out of her room to deal with the older woman. She'd given Eunice a mild sedative and by the time Trey had left, Eunice had fallen asleep in her chair.

Sassy had assured him that she'd be fine, but as Trey drove to the Winston Estate, he couldn't help the worry that had been with him since the visit the night before.

He'd always been close to his Adair grandparents and had mourned deeply when Walt had died. Now he was both concerned and confused about his grandmother and after meeting with Debra he intended to speak to his mother about the issue.

The front door of the estate was opened by house-keeper Maddie, who always greeted him as if it had been months since she'd seen him. "And aren't you look-ing just fine today," she said as she took his coat from him. "You know I've always liked you in a nice blue suit, it makes those eyes of yours downright beautiful."

Trey laughed. "You've been charming me since I was a baby, Maddie, and the years haven't changed anything a bit. I'm assuming Debra is in?"

"Holed up in that little office of hers as usual."

"Would you tell her that I'm here and that I'll meet her in the sitting room?"

"I'd be happy to. Tea or coffee? Maybe a plate of cookies?" she asked, knowing his weakness for sweets.

"Coffee and what kind of cookies?" he asked.

She smiled at him slyly. "Does it really matter?"

He laughed. "No, it doesn't, not as long as Myra baked them. Okay, a couple of cookies would be good." He was still smiling as he entered the informal sitting room where the afternoon sun flooded through the floor to ceiling windows at one end.

The weather system that had brought the little bit of icing the night before had moved on, leaving behind blue skies and sunshine.

Trey sank into one of two beige easy chairs in front of the windows, enjoying the warmth of the sun on his back. Within seconds Myra entered the room, carrying with her a tray that held a small coffeepot, two cups and a plate of oatmeal-raisin cookies he knew would be soft and gooey, just the way he liked them.

"Thanks, Myra," he told the cook, who nodded and then left him alone in the room.

He poured the coffee into the two cups and thought about having coffee in Debra's townhome the night before. She was bright and sweet and easy to be around. Last night as he'd sat in her kitchen he'd felt more relaxed than he had in months and he thought it had not been just the cozy surroundings, but also her company.

She didn't seem to have one high-maintenance bone in her body. He found her blushes charming and the fact that she cooked something special and new just to please herself each Sunday intriguing.

He had nearly destroyed the nice interaction between them by attempting to bring up the night they had spent together, but she'd made it clear that she didn't want to discuss it and was more than a bit embarrassed by the whole affair.

He should feel embarrassed about it, too. Still, he couldn't help but admit that he was looking forward to seeing her again. He tried to tell himself that it had nothing to do with any feelings he might have for her. Granted, he'd more than enjoyed his one night with her, but he knew where his duty, where his future lay and it definitely wasn't with Debra.

The subject of his thoughts entered the room. Clad in a pair of tailored black slacks and a white blouse, she looked all business as she offered him a curt smile.

"I had Myra bring in some cookies and coffee," he said as she sat in the chair next to him. "It's been my experience that every important decision should be made over a good cookie."

She smiled and set a handful of papers on the coffee table next to the silver tray of refreshments. "No cookies for me, and no coffee. I've been trying to cut down on my caffeine."

As always whenever she was around he was aware of the scent of her, that fresh, clean fragrance that stirred something deep inside him. What kind of perfume did Cecily wear? For the life of him he couldn't seem to bring it to his mind whenever Debra was close to him.

"So, what have we got?" he asked, slightly irritated with himself and the crazy tug of attraction he felt for a woman who had no place in his future plans.

She leaned forward and grabbed the small stack of papers. "Stacy sent me these this morning. The first three are various floor plans, including an area for an orchestra and dance floor and the table arrangements." She handed them to him.

He tried to focus on the papers in his hands and not on how the brilliant sunshine streaming through the window made her light brown hair sparkle as if lit by a thousand fireflies.

She got up from her chair and moved to the back of his where she could lean over to see which plan he was looking at. "Do you want to hear my thoughts about each one?" she asked hesitantly.

"Absolutely. You're the expert at these kinds of things."

She leaned closer, so close that if he turned his head he'd be able to place his lips on the long length of her graceful neck. He narrowed his eyes and stared at the piece of paper on top.

"I don't like this one because she's got the orchestra and dance floor both on the same side, which makes the room look uneven and off-balance," she explained.

He cast her a quick sideways glance and noted the

long length of her sable eyelashes, the skin that looked bare and beautiful and like smooth porcelain. His fingers tingled as he remembered stroking that skin.

"This is the plan I think works much better," she said, leaning farther over him to take the papers from his hand and shuffle them around.

He stared back down again, wondering what in the hell was wrong with him. Tonight he had a date with Cecily, the woman who was the front-runner to be by his side for the rest of his life and yet all he could think about at the moment was the soft press of Debra's breasts against his back as she leaned over him, the sweet fresh scent that eddied in the air whenever she was near.

"See how the orchestra is on the left side, but the dance floor is in the center, right in front of the head table? The tables all seat eight and that means with a head table of eight and two hundred and fifty guests we'll need thirty-one tables."

"This looks fine to me," he replied and released a small sigh of relief as she straightened up, returned to her chair and gave him a little breathing room from her.

"I figured you, Cecily, your mother, your brother Sam, the governor and his wife, Thad and his guest would comprise the people at the head table," she said.

"Thad won't come." Trey thought of his youngest brother. "There's no point in even inviting him. He has his own life and has no interest in this." He fought back a touch of hurt as he thought of the distance between himself and Thad that had grown bigger and deeper with each year that passed.

"Then we'll put the mayor and his wife at the head

table," Debra replied. "They probably should be there anyway."

Trey nodded, still attempting to regain control of the swift desire that had momentarily taken ahold of him with her nearness.

"This is the invitation I thought would be nice." She handed him a black-and-white invitation, bold and slightly masculine. "If you approve it I've got the printers standing by and I can have them in the mail by to-morrow morning."

He looked at her in surprise. "Hand addressed?"

"Absolutely." The brilliant green of her eyes was filled with quiet confidence.

"But won't that take you half the night?"

She shrugged. "It takes however long it takes. They should have gone out a month ago. They definitely have to go out tomorrow."

He handed her back the invitation. "It's perfect. You can start the printers."

"And now we move on to the menu issue."

It took them almost an hour to go through the variety of menus Stacy had presented, along with the suggested price per plate.

"Don't pay any attention to the prices," Debra said. "There's no way we'll pay what the hotel is asking." This time there was a gleam of challenge in her eyes that he found very hot.

They spoke for another half an hour about food, finally settling on what he'd like to see served. He was almost disappointed when she told him that was all she had to discuss with him today and that she'd be back in touch with him the first of next week to talk about decor and silverware and dish choice.

They left the sitting room and as she disappeared into her office and closed the door, he poked his head into his mother's office, but she wasn't there.

Instead, her head intern, Haley, was filing folders in the file cabinet. "Hi, Trey," she said, a bright smile on her youthful face.

"Hey, where's the boss?" he asked.

"She mentioned a bit of a headache and went up to her room a little while ago. Is there something I can help you with?" Haley asked with the overeagerness of a young woman wanting to prove her worth.

"No, thanks, I think I'll just head up to check on her." With a wave of his hand he headed for the wooden spiral staircase in the entry that would take him to the bedrooms located on the second floor. He could have used the small elevator located just beneath the stairs, but he preferred the exercise of walking up.

When he reached the top of the stairs he continued down the long hallway, passing bedrooms and baths on either side and finally reaching his mother's doorway at the end of the hall. He knocked and heard her say, "Come in."

When he opened the door she was seated in one of the two plush white chairs that formed a sitting area complete with fireplace and French doors that led to an upper-deck patio. At the far end of the room her white-canopied bed was visible through double doors that could be closed at night.

She smiled in surprise. "I didn't expect it to be you. I thought it might be Myra—she's bringing me up some hot tea. Would you like me to ring her to bring you a cup, too?"

"No, thanks, I just had coffee with Debra." He sank

into the chair next to hers. "Are you doing okay? Haley said you had a headache."

She waved a hand as if to dismiss the idea. "Just a little one. I decided to escape the office and come up here to do a little thinking away from everyone else and any distractions."

"Have you come to a decision?"

She shook her head. "No, and I think that's what's giving me my headache. How did things go with you and Debra? Weren't you two getting together to talk about menus and such?"

"I just finished up with her. She'd definitely on top of things. We've now settled on the floor plan and a tentative menu for the evening." He paused a moment and then continued. "She's going to get the invitations out tomorrow and find an orchestra, but I really didn't come up here to talk about all that. I stopped last night and had a visit with Grandma."

Kate sat up a little taller in her chair. "How was she doing? I'm planning on visiting her this Sunday."

Trey frowned. "To be honest, I'm a little worried about her."

"Worried how?" Kate leaned forward and rubbed the center of her forehead as if he'd definitely made her head ache a little more.

"Maybe now isn't a good time to talk about it," Trey said sympathetically.

At that moment a knock sounded at the door and Myra entered with a tray holding a cup of tea and sugar and lemon wedges. She placed it on the dainty table between the two chairs. "Is there anything else you need?" she asked Kate first and then looked at Trey who shook his head.

"We're fine, Myra, thank you." She waited until Myra had left the room and then stirred a spoonful of sugar into the cup of green tea. She squeezed a lemon slice and placed the wedge on the side of the saucer. "Now, where were we?"

"I was saying that if you have a headache, then maybe we should have this conversation another time."

"We'll have it now," Kate replied and lifted her cup to her lips.

"Okay, she seemed fine when I first arrived. She'd eaten dinner in the dining room and had played bingo during the day, but Sassy told me when I arrived that she'd been a bit anxious throughout the evening. Initially the visit went fine, but when I mentioned to her my plans for the Senate and your possible plans to run for president, she went crazy."

Kate lowered her cup with a frown. "What do you mean by that? Went crazy how?"

"She starting pacing and screaming no and muttering about secrets and lies. I mean, she was so upset Sassy had to give her a sedative. I'm not even sure she knew who I was when she was having her tirade." Trey paused to draw a breath, to get the strength to tell his mother what really worried him. "I think maybe she's getting dementia."

Kate's forehead creased with pain, but Trey had a feeling the pain was less physical and more emotional. "She is eighty-six years old, Trey. Maybe her mind is starting to slip a bit."

"Yeah, but all that stuff about secrets and lies? What could she possibly be talking about?"

Kate took another sip of her tea and when she placed the cup back on the saucer she released a deep sigh.

"Trey, I know how fond you were of my father, but to be honest, he wasn't a very good husband and he definitely wasn't the greatest of fathers."

"What do you mean?" Trey couldn't imagine the man who had mentored him as being anything but a wonderful man. Walt had shown Trey infinite patience, had spent hours talking to him, leading him in learning the family business and encouraging Trey's natural competiveness and ambition.

"You probably don't know that my mother miscarried three sons before she finally had me. My father never let her forget that she had been unable to give him what he wanted most—a son. He was verbally abusive both to my mother and to me. The one thing that seemed to transform him was your birth. He saw you as the son he'd never had. I imagine some details of my mother's tumultuous relationship with my father are coming to play in her mind."

Trey studied his mother, thinking about what she'd just said. Was it possible that Eunice's breakdown had merely been her replaying portions of her own past in her mind? She'd told him she remembered the days of old but had trouble remembering what had happened the day before.

"And you're sure there's nothing more to it?" he asked.

Kate averted her gaze from his and rubbed her forehead once again, as if attempting to ease a much bigger headache than she'd professed to have suffered earlier. "I'm sure I don't want to talk about it anymore. My mother is old and who knows what goes on in her mind anymore."

"Then I'll leave you to drink your tea in peace and

quiet," he replied. He got up from his chair and left her room.

If he'd been troubled before about how his grandmother had reacted to the news that he was running for senator and his mother might be seeking the presidency, the conversation with his mother certainly hadn't eased his concerns.

Was Eunice really suffering from the onset of dementia or working through issues she'd had with her husband? Or were there secrets and lies someplace in the family history that might be dangerous to both his own and his mother's political future?

Chapter 5

The ring of the phone awakened Debra. She jerked up, scattering envelopes not just across the kitchen table but also to the floor.

A quick glance at the kitchen clock let her know it was after eleven. The phone rang again and she jumped up from the table and frowned as she saw that the caller ID indicated a private number.

She grabbed the cordless phone from its base. "Hello?"

Nobody spoke, but Debra was certain somebody was on the line. "Hello?" she repeated. "Are you there?"

Silence, although the line remained open and the faint sound of somebody breathing sent a chill up her spine. "Is this some sort of juvenile prank phone call?" Debra asked and was rewarded by a click.

She hung up the phone, unsettled by the call but

grateful that the ring had awakened her. She still had envelopes to finish up addressing and apparently had accidentally fallen asleep in the middle of the process.

The hot cocoa she'd fixed earlier was now cold in the pot. She poured herself a cup and set it in the microwave to warm and then returned to the kitchen table where she'd been working.

As she sat back down at the table she remembered the dream she'd been having while she slept. It was more than a dream, it had been a memory of a conversation she'd had with her mother when Debra had been about ten years old.

Debra had wanted to know why she didn't have a daddy who lived with them. Why she was never, ever allowed to talk to her father or see him.

Debra's mother, Glenda, had tried to explain to Debra that her father was an important man and that he had another family he lived with and Debra would be a bad girl if she ever tried to contact her father because she would destroy his life.

As she grew older Debra had recognized that the truth of the matter was that her mother had been far more enchanted with the generous support checks that came every month than she had probably ever been with the wealthy married man she'd slept with that had resulted in Debra.

The support checks had allowed Glenda to not have to work, to continue to have a party-girl lifestyle that had ultimately killed her in a drunk driving accident the summer after Debra had graduated from college. Those support checks had stolen Debra's childhood as she'd tried to take care of a mother who was drunk most of the time.

The dream had created ancient memories of rejection, the wistful hopes of a little girl who had just wanted her daddy to want her back. The pang of wistfulness the dream had evoked still lingered in the depths of her heart.

And she was about to place a child of her own in the very same position.

No, it won't be the same at all, she told herself as she dropped down to her knees to retrieve the envelopes that had fallen to the floor when she'd jumped up to answer the phone.

She gathered the envelopes and then sat back down at the table and took a drink of her cocoa. Glenda hadn't been much of a mother, preferring her booze and men to spending much time with her lonely daughter.

Debra would be better than that. She would make sure her child knew the depth of her love. She'd love her son or daughter so madly, so deeply, that he or she wouldn't feel the absence of a father figure.

Besides, there was a chance that eventually Debra would meet a man and marry and then the baby would have a stepfather. She could still create a family unit.

The phone rang again. Debra frowned and once again got up from the table. And again the caller ID displayed a private number. "Hello," she snapped into the receiver.

Silence. Just like the call before.

"Stop calling, you jerk," Debra said and slammed down the phone. She unplugged it from the wall. If anyone important needed to get ahold of her, they'd use her cell phone. Her landline seldom rang and usually it was only sales calls. Anyone who knew her always called her on her cell.

Once again she sat at the table and rubbed her eyes wearily and then took another drink of her cocoa. She hadn't meant to fall asleep. She needed to get the last of the invitations stuffed and addressed before morning.

She knew that most people in Kate and Trey's positions hired professional calligraphers to do the hand writing, but early in her employment with Kate, Debra had taken classes so that she could develop the skills so that nobody would have to be hired. It was just one effort a young new employee had done to try to make herself as indispensable as possible.

It was well after midnight when she finally finished. Exhaustion weighed heavily upon her as she climbed the stairs to her bedroom.

The townhouse had a guest bedroom and bath and a master suite upstairs with its own large bathroom. Debra stumbled into the bathroom and quickly shucked her clothes.

It had been a ridiculously long day. After her meeting with Trey she'd contacted the printers who were standing by to get the invitations done. They'd been delivered to her at the estate right before she'd left to go home for the day.

She'd also made a doctor's appointment for the next day, deciding to get that off her mind instead of putting it off.

Too tired to think about a shower or bath, she pulled on her nightgown and headed for her king-size bed.

The last thing she did before tumbling into bed was unplug the cordless beside her, not wanting her sleep disrupted by any further obvious prank phone calls.

Despite the late night her alarm went off at six and although her desire was to linger beneath the sheets and the navy-and-peach-colored spread, she got up without hitting the snooze button.

After a long hot shower and getting dressed, she plodded down the stairs, feeling almost as exhausted as she'd been when she'd finally gone to bed.

She plugged her phone back in, rechecked the caller ID and was surprised to see that the blocked calls she'd received the night before didn't show up there. Neither did any other calls show up in the history.

Odd, she thought as she leaned against the counter and waited for her teakettle of water to boil. Maybe her machine was on its way to answering machine heaven. It was certainly old enough to die a natural death.

She'd decided to skip the coffee this morning, knowing that she should have as little caffeine as possible in her condition, and instead stick to a nice hot cup of tea and maybe a couple of crackers. Although she didn't feel nauseous yet, she remembered the uneasy roll of her stomach the day before when she'd thought about food first thing in the morning.

The neatly addressed invitations were ready to go in a large tote bag on the table. They would be picked up by a special mail carrier at ten that morning from Debra's office.

She went to the cabinet that held her favorite mug, a pink Support the Cause mug that was her go-to vessel for either hot tea or cocoa.

The mug wasn't in its usual place. She frowned at the conspicuous empty spot in the cabinet. Where was her mug? She felt a déjà vu from the morning before when she'd had the frantic hunt for Trey's guest list.

Although she hadn't used the mug for a couple of days, she walked over to the dishwasher that was full of clean dishes and checked for it there. There was no sign of it.

As the teakettle whistled, she moved it off the burner and then grabbed a teabag and another mug to make her tea.

Still, the mystery of the missing mug bothered her. On impulse before sitting down, she walked over to the refrigerator and checked the freezer, grateful that she didn't see the familiar pink cup nestled uncomfortably next to the frozen pizza.

She sat at the table and drank the hot tea and nibbled on a couple of saltines, wondering if she was slowly losing her mind. First the list yesterday and now the mug today. Maybe she hadn't even really gotten those phone calls last night. Maybe she'd only imagined them and that's why they didn't register on the telephone caller identification.

Despite the fact that it was Saturday, she had a doctor's appointment that afternoon at two. Maybe she'd ask her doctor if pregnancy could make a woman go stark raving mad.

She left her house by seven, deciding to go in a little early since her plans were to leave early for her appointment. She still felt tired. Thankfully tomorrow was Sunday and if she felt like it she could sleep until noon.

When she'd initially taken the job with Kate, she'd known it was a six-day-a-week job, that the hours were often unpredictable and could include evenings, but she hadn't cared. As far as she was concerned, working for Kate wasn't just a job, it was her passion.

As she pulled up to the side entrance of the gate she was relieved to see Secret Service Agent Jeff Benton on duty. He waved her on through with a cheerful smile.

At least this morning she didn't have to start her day with another creepy encounter with Jerry Cahill. She got out of her car and noticed that several of the agents stood in front of the carriage house. Even from the distance she recognized Robert D'Angelis, Daniel Henderson and Jerry Cahill. She figured it was a morning meeting of assignments and knew that on most Saturdays the senior Secret Service man, Robert, gave Kate a security update.

Myra was pulling a tray of golden biscuits out of the oven as Debra came into the house. "Mmm, those look yummy," she said as she greeted the cook.

"Ms. Cecily is joining Ms. Kate for brunch this morning," Myra explained.

"Oh, that's nice." Debra was surprised by the tiny flair of jealousy that winged through her. Of course Cecily and Kate would be growing close, fostering the beginning of a relationship that would probably be a lifelong one. By the time the election happened, Cecily would be Kate's daughter-in-law. Trey was smart enough to know that being married would make him a more enticing candidate.

"I've got biscuits done and I'm about to make that cheesy egg casserole that Ms. Kate loves. I've also prepared little fruit cups."

"Sounds delicious, I'm sure they'll enjoy it."

"Would you like a little plate of your own?" Myra asked.

"Thanks for the offer, but no, thank you. I already had some breakfast this morning," Debra replied.

As Myra busied herself cracking eggs into a large bowl, Debra carried her purse and the large tote of envelopes to her office. Once there she took off her coat and then sat at her desk, fighting against the unexpected jealousy that had momentarily filled her as she thought of Cecily McKenna.

She had no right to feel jealous. She had no right to wish things could be different, because it was just a waste of energy.

Instead of examining the unusual emotion, she shoved it aside and turned her computer on, knowing that she needed to get all her work done early this morning in order to head out around one for the doctor's appointment. She was lucky that her doctor saw patients on Saturday.

What she needed to get together for the morning were table dressings that were available for the dinner party that would now take place in just a little under two weeks' time. She wanted to have a list of tablecloth colors and dinnerware options for Trey on Monday. They also needed to discuss how the head table would be dressed and what kind of centerpieces he wanted for each of the tables.

Details, details. A successful event was always in the minutia of the details and Debra wanted this particular dinner party to be perfect, not just because she was in charge of it, but because it was for Trey.

The special mail courier arrived and Debra was grateful to hand him the tote of invitations, knowing that they would go out today and probably be received by invited guests by Monday or Tuesday at the latest. The RSVPs were due the following week. Debra was expecting very few regrets.

She and Stacy had exchanged half a dozen emails when a knock fell on her door and Cecily poked her head in. Cecily McKenna was a beautiful woman. Her hair was raven-black, cut short and chic, and her eyes were doe-brown. Her features were classically elegant, and when she smiled it gave her face a warmth that was instantly inviting.

"Hi, Debra. I just wanted to stop in before meeting with Kate and let you know how much I appreciate everything you're doing to help Trey."

"No problem, we're all working toward a common goal," Debra replied, hoping her smile hid her unease at the unusual visit.

"I wanted to give you my personal thank-you," Cecily replied. "This isn't just important to the family and staff and me, but I think it's important for all of the people of North Carolina. Trey is the right man for this job and the dinner party is the first step in assuring that he's considered a legitimate contender."

Cecily released a tinkling burst of laughter. "Listen to me babbling on. You know that about Trey already."

"He's definitely got my vote," Debra replied. As she saw the stylish black slacks, gold blouse and tasteful necklace and earrings that Cecily wore Debra felt downright dowdy with her hair in a messy knot at the back of her head and the olive-green skirt and blouse she'd bought two seasons before off a clearance rack.

At that moment Kate called to Cecily. "Oh, gotta go. It was nice seeing you again, Debra. I'm sure we'll be seeing a lot of each other in the future." With another one of her warm smiles, Cecily stepped back and closed Debra's door.

Debra released a deep sigh. Everything would be so much easier for her if she hated Cecily, if Cecily was snarky and egotistical instead of nice. Things would be so much easier if Debra truly believed that the beautiful woman was all wrong for Trey.

But Debra knew Cecily was the right woman to be at Trey's side. She was bright and articulate, she came from a stable wealthy family and had influential friends and she appeared to genuinely love people, just like Trey.

Yes, they would make a perfect power couple. It would only be so much easier if in the past three minutes Debra hadn't realized that she wasn't just crushing on Trey Winston...but that she was in love with him.

Trey got a phone call from Debra at noon. "We need to get together on Monday to finalize the rest of the details for the dinner party," she said. "Is that doable for you?"

"Actually, Monday isn't good for me," he replied. "I'm going to be tied up in meetings all day long. What about tomorrow? What's on your Sunday menu?"

He knew he'd surprised her by the long silence that followed the question. Hell, he'd surprised himself with the question. What was he thinking?

"Actually I was going to try a recipe for bourbon barbecue pork chops," she said tentatively.

"Sounds delicious. Could I maybe wrangle an invite from you and we could talk about the business end of things over dinner?" Somewhere in the back of his mind he wondered what in the hell he was doing. It was obvious he wasn't thinking rationally at all.

He already had dinner plans with Cecily for this evening, there was no reason for him to eat dinner with Debra tomorrow night to discuss work issues. And yet he didn't take back his words. He was surprised to realize he didn't want to.

"Around six?" she asked hesitantly.

"Works for me," he agreed.

When he hung up his phone he didn't want to consider what he looked forward to more: an elegant fine dining experience with the beautiful Cecily or a smoky bourbon barbeque dinner with his mother's personal secretary/assistant?

Maybe the pressure of having made up his mind to run for senator already had him cracking up. Maybe he was already seeking some form of escape from the crazy world he was about to enter, and somehow, someway, Debra felt like an escape.

The minute he hung up the phone Rhonda buzzed him to let him know that Chad Brothers, an experienced campaign manager, had arrived.

Dismissing thoughts of Debra, he rose as Chad walked into the office, extending his hand to the man who looked more like a professional wrestler than a savvy political expert.

"I hope you called this meeting for the reason I want it to be," Chad said after he shook Trey's hand and took a seat in the chair in front of his desk. He leaned forward, his bald head gleaming in the sunshine flowing in through the windows.

"You know I've been kicking around the idea of running for the Senate—" Trey began.

"I'd be happy to," Chad replied before Trey had gotten his entire sentence out of his mouth. "And you know I'm the man who can help get you where you want to go, but if we agree to work together, then we need to get busy right away."

"I've already set up a dinner party that's taking place a week from next Friday night." Trey shared the details of the dinner and dance event with the man he trusted to run a fair and honest campaign.

Chad was not only fair and honest, he was also tenacious and brilliant when it came to putting in place a political machine. He was also an old friend that had shown his loyalty to the Winston family for years.

The two men chatted for a little over two hours, talking about plans and tossing out ideas back and forth. Trey found the meeting invigorating and he was in a great mood when he left the office at six for dinner with Cecily at La Palace, a French restaurant where the food was excellent, but equally important was that most of the mover and shakers of Raleigh could be found there on a Friday or Saturday night.

He was meeting Cecily at the restaurant as she was coming from a charity event she'd attended that afternoon for an anti-domestic abuse initiative.

He was eager to tell her about his meeting with Chad. She'd be ecstatic to hear that he'd be working with a man who had the reputation of running an election both effortlessly and with winning results.

Trey had only been inside the restaurant a few minutes when Cecily arrived. As always when she entered a room, men's heads turned in her direction. Tonight she looked particularly beautiful in a red dress that was just tight enough to showcase her dynamite figure, but not so tight as to be tasteless.

"Darling," she said as she air-kissed near his cheek. "I hope you haven't been waiting for me long."

"Not long at all," he replied. "And our table is ready," he said as the host nodded at him.

Trey placed a hand in the small of her back as they were led to a table by the front windows of the restaurant. They were coveted tables in the world of power, places to sit and eat where you could see and be seen.

The host took their coats and the minute he departed a waitress appeared with menus and the wine listing. Trey ordered them each a glass of white wine and ordered their meals. As they waited for their food to arrive Trey told her about his meeting with Chad.

"So, it's really going to happen," she said, her brown eyes sparkling with not just excitement but that shine of an ambition that resonated deep inside him.

"It's really going to happen," he agreed. "The dinner-dance party will be the official kickoff of my campaign. I've got to write a rousing speech and then I'll officially declare my bid for Senate and hope that the money and the support follow."

"You know it will." Cecily clapped her hands together and then reached across the table and grasped one of his hands with hers. "I'm so excited for you, so excited for us." She released his hand and picked up her wineglass.

"You know it's going to be a crazy ride," he warned her. "It isn't just about parties and fun. It's going to be long days and longer nights, nasty rumors and traveling from city to city, never knowing when or where we'll see each other again."

He saw the flash of disappointment in her eyes, there only a moment and then gone. He knew she'd probably expected a proposal, but he just wasn't ready to take that step right now. He intended to marry only once in his life and he wanted to be absolutely certain when he proposed.

"You know I'm in this for the long run, Trey," she said softly.

"I know," he replied somberly. "I just need to get things moving, get plans together in my head. Once we get beyond the dinner party and a press conference to announce my official declaration, we'll see where things shake out."

"Of course. I understand," Cecily replied smoothly as if that quick look of disappointment that he'd seen in her eyes had only been a figment of his imagination. "And whenever you're not with me, I'll be working to help achieve our goals."

Their food was served and for the remainder of the meal Cecily talked about the charity auction she'd attended that afternoon and her plans to immediately begin to form a Women for Winston coalition.

As she talked and they ate, Trey's mind drifted, first to all the things that would need to be done to achieve his ultimate goals, and secondly to the dinner he would be having the next night at Debra's.

A business dinner, he reminded himself, a dinner that he'd invited himself to. He should be focused on the beautiful woman across from him, a woman who would add her ambition to his own to see that he reached his goals, followed his duties as his grandfather had wanted for him in public service.

Trey had always been so clear on where he was going and who would be at his side when he arrived there… until that night almost seven weeks ago. That night had somehow thrown him off his personal game, awakened yearnings inside him he hadn't known he possessed.

He mentally shook himself and focused on Cecily,

the woman who was right for him, a woman his grandfather and his mother would have handpicked to be at his side as he traversed through the murky waters of politics.

Chapter 6

That morning the pink mug had been front and center in the cabinet where Debra would have sworn it hadn't been the morning before. The mystery of the mug's reappearance had set a discordant tone for the beginning of the day.

Yesterday afternoon Dr. Gina Finnegan had confirmed what Debra already knew, that she was about six and a half weeks pregnant. After Dr. Finnegan had done the blood work and physical, discussed vitamins and handed Debra a pamphlet about pregnancy, Debra had asked about forgetfulness being a part of the condition.

"We've coined a term for it here in the clinic," Dr. Finnegan had said with a laugh. "Pregnesia...the condition of absentmindedness that comes with all the hormonal changes due to pregnancy. Don't worry, most of my patients tell me it goes away by the second trimester along with any morning sickness you might be suffering."

Dr. Finnegan had set her due date around the third week of August. A summer baby, Debra had thought. It would probably be a long, uncomfortable July but it would be worth it. By summer's end she'd have a precious bundle of joy to love.

As she sliced potatoes for a cheesy scalloped dish to go with the pork chops, she tried not to think about the evening ahead, an evening where she'd be sharing dinner, sharing private time and conversation with Trey.

It was a cold gray blustery day and she'd built a fire in the fireplace despite her concern that it might look too romantic. There was nothing she liked better than a roaring fire on a wintry day while she worked in the kitchen and she'd decided she didn't care what he thought, it was just a good day for a fire.

It was just before five and both the potatoes and the pork chops would take about an hour to cook. The table was already set for two with her good black-and-red dinnerware and she had a salad made and in the refrigerator.

The smoky bourbon barbecue sauce smelled like heaven and half of it was in a saucepan ready to be reheated and poured over the chops when they were finished cooking. The other half of the sauce was marinating the meat.

All she had to do was put the two baking dishes into the oven and then take a shower and dress for Trey's arrival at six. She had all the paperwork ready for him to look at to make the final decisions on the setup of the ballroom and that's what the meeting was all about.

It had been *his* idea to do it over dinner. *It was strictly*

a business dinner, she reminded herself over and over
again throughout the day.

Once they went over those last final details there
would be no reason for her to meet with him again until
possibly the night before the event.

She would be there the night of the dinner, not as a
guest, but she'd arrive at the hotel at least an hour or
so before things got started to make certain that everything had been handled properly, that the evening was
set perfectly for Trey's special night.

Fifteen minutes later she stood beneath a warm spray
of water, far too eager for the night to come. It was
wrong of her to want to see Trey, to see him seated at
her table across from her. It was wrong of her to want
to hear his deep, smooth voice talking just to her. More
than anything it was wrong on every level for her to
want him again.

He belonged to Cecily. They were so right together.
Debra might carry his baby, but nobody would ever
know that. She would never screw up his dreams by
telling him about her condition because she knew he
was the kind of man who would have to do something
about it and that something would destroy all of the
goals he had for himself.

He was a Winston, bred for business and politics.
He deserved to have winners surrounding him. He deserved to have a winner as a wife and that woman was
Cecily. He definitely didn't need a mousy, efficient
woman like Debra in his life.

By the time she dressed in a pair of jeans and a long-
sleeved navy fleece shirt, she felt as if she had all of her
emotions under control. They would enjoy a good meal,
discuss business and then he would leave.

Once the dinner party at the Regent was finished, she would see him only rarely when he came to visit his mother. Even then it was possible they wouldn't run into each other often at all.

Her emotions remained cool and calm until six o'clock when her doorbell rang. She answered and with a slightly nervous smile invited him in. She took his coat and hung it in her foyer closet, noting that he had dressed casual, as well.

Trey Winston wore a suit like he'd been born in one, but he looked equally as hot in a pair of slightly worn, tight blue jeans and a navy-and-white-striped sweater that emphasized the broadness of his shoulders.

"Something smells delicious," he said as he followed her into the kitchen where she gestured him to a chair at the table.

"Let's hope it tastes as good as it smells," she replied. As with the last time he'd been sitting in her kitchen, she felt as if the walls closed in and got smaller with his very presence in the room. He emanated such energy, commanded all the space around him.

She was grateful she'd done most of the work ahead of time because she suddenly felt clumsy.

"Let me help," he said, and jumped out of his chair as she opened the oven door to take the baking dishes out of the oven.

"Okay, knock yourself out," she replied and handed him two pot holders. She'd nearly tripped just carrying the salad from the refrigerator to the table. "You can just set the pork and potatoes on top of the hot pads here." She pointed to the two awaiting pads on the counter.

She stepped back and watched as he maneuvered the two large dishes onto the counter next to the oven. He smelled so good and as he moved his sweater pulled tightly across his broad shoulders. She averted her gaze, not wanting to care about the way he looked or remember that scent that he'd worn when they'd hooked up on that fateful night.

He pulled the tin foil off the dishes and sighed in obvious delight. "This all looks amazing."

"Wait for it," she said as she pulled the saucepan of bubbling sauce from the stovetop and poured the last of it over the pork chops. "There's enough bourbon in here I'm not sure we'll need before-dinner drinks," she said jokingly. "We'll be half-snookered by the time we finish eating the sauce." She flushed as she remembered that half-snookered was what had put her in the condition she was in.

"Why don't we just bring our plates over here and dig in straight from the baking pans?" he suggested. "No need to be formal on my account."

"Okay," she agreed, grateful that she didn't have to attempt to take the two hot dishes to the center of the table. That was just a disaster waiting to happen.

"Other than cooking, did you have a busy day or were you able to rest up a little on your day off?" he asked as he grabbed the two red-and-black-patterned plates from the table and rejoined her by the stove.

"Actually, I managed to sleep a little later than usual and then I cleaned a bit. I even managed to work in a little reading so it was a fairly restful day."

She waited for him to snag one of the thick pork chops along with a large serving of the cheesy potatoes. "What about you? Busy day?" she asked.

"Not too bad at all. I feel like today was the calm

before the storm. Chad is already busy working to fill every minute of my schedule."

She smiled. "But everyone in town knows he turns out winners." Chad was a household name in the city of Raleigh among the political crowd.

Trey carried his plate back to the table while she served herself, eternally grateful that she didn't drop a chop on the floor or dribble cheese potatoes down the front of her.

Once they were both seated and Debra took out the salad and dinner rolls, they both dug in. "These pork chops are to die for," he exclaimed after his first bite.

She smiled with pleasure. "Thanks, I was hoping they would come out tasty."

"Do you generally invite people over to share in your Sunday culinary delights?"

"Barry used to occasionally join me but since we broke up, never. I cook for myself because I enjoy it and it's the one hobby I have time for one day a week."

"Between your work for my mom and now for me, we've been keeping you too busy."

"Not at all," she protested. "I love my work. I adore your mother and I can't imagine doing anything else. I'm doing what I always wanted to do." *Except for being a mom,* she thought. That would soon be added to the things she loved.

With the thought of motherhood, the sight of Trey so masculine and handsome across from her and with a flash of sudden visions of their hot and wild night together all swirling around in her mind, she attempted to grab a roll from the center of the table and bring it to her plate, but nearly dropped it to the floor.

"That was a close one," he said with a grin.

She flushed. "Lately I seem to be suffering episodes of extreme clumsiness. So if I happen to flip a chunk of lettuce or a cherry tomato across the table at you or drop a roll in your lap, please don't take it personally."

"Will do," he said with a cheerful smile.

"So, are you all geared up to work with Chad? I've heard he's a rough taskmaster."

He laughed and shook his head ruefully. "I'm ready for whatever Chad brings. He has some great ideas and I'm excited to have him on my team."

All that was important to Debra was that she keep her secret. What was important was that Trey maintain his pristine reputation because for him the sky was the limit.

She had to keep her pregnancy as far away from Trey and his campaign as possible. She knew what his adversaries would do to him if they knew he'd slept with his mother's assistant and now that assistant was pregnant.

They would massacre him.

Dinner conversation remained light and pleasant and the meal was better than any Trey had ever enjoyed in a five-star restaurant.

Afterward he helped her clear the table and she suggested they drink her special mint hot cocoa in the living room where she had all the paperwork ready for him to make some final decisions about the ballroom decor.

As they sat side by side on the sofa with the paperwork on the coffee table in front of them, he realized he wasn't ready yet to talk business. What he wanted to talk about was her.

"You know, you've worked for my mother for years and yet I realized the other day that I know so little about you and about how you came to work for Mom. Did you grow up here? Are your parents still alive? I've never heard you mention anything about family."

She leaned back against the black sofa, the dark background making her hair look lighter and her large eyes more green than ever. "Yes, I was born and raised right here in Raleigh. My father is alive, although I've only spoken to him once in my entire life." Her eyes darkened slightly.

He leaned toward her, sensing pain trapped someplace deep inside her. "And why is that?"

Her beautiful eyes darkened even more and a crease danced across her brow. "My father is a highly successful businessman who is married and has two children who are just a couple of years older than me. My mother was his mistress for about six months before she got pregnant. He tried to pay her off to have an abortion, but I think my mother thought that I'd be worth more if I was alive, so she had me and she and my father came to an understanding."

"An understanding?" Trey fought his desire to move closer to her, to take one of her hands in his and offer her some sort of support. While her story was not completely uncommon, especially in the world of politics and successful, egomaniacal businessmen, that didn't make it any less ugly.

She gave a curt nod. "My father would financially support us as long as my mother and I never mentioned his name, never went public and ruined not only his image, but also his happy marriage. For me, my father was a once-a-month check in the mail that kept a roof over our heads and food on the table."

"That stinks," he said softly.

Her lush lips curved up slightly in a wry smile. "Yeah, it did. But what's equally as bad is that the support money allowed my mother the freedom to continue her party-girl lifestyle."

She paused to take a drink of her cocoa and eyed him somberly over the rim of the cup. "Having an alcoholic mother made me grow up pretty fast. She died the year I graduated from college in a drunk-driving accident. She was the drunk driver." She set her cup back down and Trey couldn't stand it any longer, he reached out and took one of her hands in his.

Cold and small, he thought as he held tight in an attempt to warm it. "I'm sorry, Debra. I'm sorry that's the life you were dealt."

She squeezed his hand and then pulled hers away. "They say what doesn't kill you makes you stronger, and in this case maybe it was true. I realized early on that I would not be following in my mother's footsteps. I studied hard and during my free time I watched on television whenever Congress was in session. That's when I first saw your mother, when she was serving out the last of your father's term. I fell in love with her politics, with her style and strength. I researched everything I could about her and when I was ready I went to my father and told him all I'd ever ask of him was for him to somehow arrange for an interview for me to intern for your mother."

She paused and drew a deep breath. It was the longest monologue Trey had ever heard from her. "And so he got you an interview with Mom," he said.

"No, he said he'd do what he could do, but I knew by his dismissive attitude that he wasn't going to do anything. So, I began a writing campaign to Kate. I wrote to her once a week, telling her why I'd be perfect working for her, what I would bring to the table as a valuable employee. I quoted bits and pieces of her speeches and told her why they had resonated with me." She smiled. "I think she finally decided to interview me to cut down on her mail. Anyway, she took me on and I've never looked back since then. I don't have any family but I feel like after all these years your mother has become my family."

Trey had a feeling there was a lot of ugliness in her early life that she'd left out of her story. Having an absent father and being raised by an alcoholic mother had to have been more than just a little difficult.

"So, the truth of my past is that I'm just the illegitimate daughter of an immoral businessman, who, rumor has it, is doing some shady business, and an alcoholic mother who wound up killing herself in an accident of her own doing," she finished. There was no bitterness in her voice. It was just a simple statement of facts.

"Those are just the circumstances of your birth and early life, but that doesn't begin to describe who you are now," Trey said, unable to hide his admiration for her. "I was lucky, I had a great role model in my mother, but my dad certainly tarnished the family name with his many affairs."

"The pitfalls of public service," she replied. "Sometimes I think most of the men in Washington have women on the side. A lot of them eventually get caught with their pants down, but a lot of them never get caught."

"I won't," he said firmly. "I mean I shouldn't have with you. I'm a one-woman man and when it comes time for me to marry, I won't cheat. I saw what my mother went through when the scandal about my father broke. I saw how his lies and cheating broke her heart. Besides, despite what happened between us, I believe in monogamy—one man, one woman and a family."

"Your mother rode out that scandal like the strong lady she is and went on to become vice president," Debra replied. She eyed him soberly. "And I believe you're cut from the same moral cloth as she is and that's why you'll be a great senator, a man who others will admire."

For several long seconds their gazes remained locked. Trey had never wanted a woman as badly as he did Debra at this moment and he was certain he saw a spark of desire in the depths of her eyes, as well.

She was the one who broke the gaze with an uncomfortable laugh. "We'd better get focused on the work. After all, that's why you're here, to pin down all the final details on your dinner event."

"Of course," he replied, still fighting the intense desire she had stirred inside him without even trying. Why didn't he feel this mind-numbing desire to touch, to taste, to make love to Cecily whenever he was with her? What was it about Debra that shot such heat through his veins and made his mouth hunger for hers?

He focused on the papers Debra shoved at him, papers showing tablecloths and dishes, silverware and glassware, but they were all a blur as he heard the snap and crackle of the fire in the fireplace, smelled that dizzying scent of Debra and imagined making love to her on the bright red throw rug in front of the warmth of the fire.

"Trey?"

He turned and stared at her and snapped out of his

momentary vision of her naked and gasping beneath him. "Yeah, I think we definitely want classic white tablecloths." He placed the paper with tablecloth colors to the side and stared at the dishware.

She leaned toward him, only making his concentration more difficult. The plates all seemed to blur together on the page, making it impossible for him to form a coherent decision.

"I think maybe the white plates with the black rims might be nice," she offered after a moment of silence from him. "They look bold and masculine. It wouldn't be a choice I'd usually make, but since this night is all about you, I think they'd be perfect."

"Done," he replied and moved on to the silverware page. What should have been easy decisions had become difficult with her seated so close and muddying his thoughts.

"These," he pointed to a set of plain silverware with tapered ends and moved on to the last page. "And these glasses." He set the paperwork down and reached for his cup, hoping a jolt of cocoa would wash all the inappropriate thoughts of her out of his mind.

"Good," she said with a wide smile as she gathered the paperwork together and set it on the end table next to her side of the sofa. "Now all we have left to talk about are the centerpieces and whether you want an official podium or not."

"Not," he replied immediately. "I figure my speech is only going to be about fifteen minutes long and I'll deliver it from my place at the head table."

"Okay, then I'll make sure we have a cordless microphone ready for you to use," she replied. "And the centerpieces?"

"I'll leave that to you, maybe something in black and white and crystal, but I don't want anything big and ornate. It's irritating to sit at a table and try to talk to somebody across some big plant or fancy centerpiece that is three feet high."

She laughed and again a burst of desire washed over him. She had a beautiful laugh, rich and full-bodied. He picked up his cup again, needing to keep his hands busy so they wouldn't reach out for her.

Other than that single moment when he thought he'd seen a spark of want in her eyes, she'd given him absolutely no indication that she'd be open to having anything to do with him other than on a business level.

He knew that he was here now only because he'd invited himself. Knowing her history with her mother, he was sure the last thing she'd want for herself was to become another quick hit for him on his way to his future.

And he didn't want that, either. She deserved better than that and it was completely out of character for him to even think of such a thing. It didn't fit with his vision for his future, it didn't speak to the kind of man he thought himself to be, the man he wanted to be.

It was bad enough that they'd already made a mistake, sleeping with her again would only compound the error. He turned his attention to the dancing flames in the fireplace.

"I've got five fireplaces in my house and have never burned a fire in any of them," he said.

"It's one of my guilty pleasures," she replied. "I order a cord of wood in the fall so that I can enjoy a fire whenever I want to through the winter, although I rarely burn one during the week. How's Cecily doing?" she asked, as if reading his thoughts and needing to mention the name of the woman he was certain to marry.

He turned his attention from the fire to her. "Cecily is fine. She's excited about what she jokingly calls my coming-out party. She knows I'm going to declare my intentions to run for the Senate on the night of the dinner and then hold a press conference to follow up. Which reminds me, I have one more guest to add to the list for that night."

Debra frowned. "It better be somebody important because I've almost finished a draft of the seating arrangements."

"It is somebody important. It's you. I want you to be there."

"Oh, don't worry, I'll be there well ahead of time to make sure that everything is in place for a successful night for everyone," she replied.

"That's not what I meant," he protested. "I mean I want you there as an invited guest."

"Oh, Trey, I don't think—"

"It's what I think that is important here," he interrupted her. "I want you there as my guest, Debra. It's important to me. You've done all the work, it's only right that you enjoy the fruits of your labor."

"I've enjoyed working on this project," she said, as if that was enough.

"That's nice, but it doesn't change the fact that I want you there in attendance through the entire thing. If you don't have anyone to bring as a guest, then we'll seat you next to Chad Brothers at one of the tables. He's already told me he's coming alone and you'll find him an entertaining companion who will regale you with stories of titillating political scandals and missteps that will make for fun entertainment."

He saw the hesitance in her eyes but pressed on. "Please, Debra. For me. Put on a fancy dress and your dancing shoes. I'll feel better giving my speech if I can look out and see your friendly face in the crowd."

"Okay, fine. I'll come." She said the words as if he'd placed a great burden on her, but her eyes glittered as if secretly pleased.

"Great. It's going to be a terrific night thanks to all your help. I know you got roped into this because of Mom, but I want to let you know how much I appreciate everything you've done to assure the success of the evening."

"It's been my pleasure," she replied, her cheeks dusting with a faint blush.

"And I imagine that once this night is done you'll just have time to barely catch your breath and Mom will announce."

One of Debra's light eyebrows shot upward. "Has she told you she's definitely going to run?"

"Not specifically, but she did mention that she's been invited to speak at a chamber of commerce Valentine's Day ball and I have a feeling that's when she'll make her big announcement."

"It's all so exciting," Debra said.

He nodded. "Exciting days for the Winston family. And now I should probably get out of your hair and let you enjoy what's left of your night off." He stood, oddly reluctant to go, and picked up his cup.

"Just leave that," she replied. "I'll take care of it."

He put his cup down and walked with her to the foyer where she pulled his coat from the closet. He shrugged it on. "Just think, in about two weeks' time you'll be the belle of the ball."

She laughed, that low and husky sound that stirred every sense he owned and surged desire through his veins. "I certainly doubt that, but I will enjoy being there."

"I think you underestimate yourself, Debra," he replied. She opened the door and he took one step out and then turned back to her, unable to halt the impulse he knew he'd later regret.

She gasped in surprise as he drew her into his arms and took possession of her mouth. She stiffened for just an instant and then melted against him, her mouth opening wider to invite him in.

She tasted just as he remembered, sweet and hot as their tongues met, moving together in an erotic dance of pleasure.

He wanted more from her, much more. He wasn't sure where his desire came from, but it burned through him like a white-hot fire. It was she who broke the kiss, stumbling back from him with wide eyes. She raised a hand and touched her lips and then dropped her hand to her side.

"You shouldn't have done that, Trey," she said, her voice trembling slightly and holding a faint touch of censure.

"Yeah, I know." Without saying another word, he pulled his coat collar up more tightly around his neck and stepped out into the cold night.

Chapter 7

It had been a bad week.

Actually, it had been one of the worst weeks of Debra's life.

She felt as if for the past seven days she'd existed in the Twilight Zone. Not only had she had problems forgetting the unexpected kiss that Trey had planted on her the week before, but for the past week she'd felt as if some mysterious imp had entered her life to create utter havoc.

And the worst part about it was that she knew that she was the imp and felt as if she were slowly losing her mind.

As she pulled up Monday morning at the Winston Estate and saw that Jerry Cahill was on duty, she didn't see how things could get any worse.

She stifled a deep sigh as he stopped her car and gestured for her to roll down her window and as usual he leaned into the car and smiled. "Hey, Debra. Did you have a good day off yesterday?" He smelled of a cloying cologne and the ever-present peppermint. The mixed scents twisted a faint nausea in the pit of her stomach.

"It was nice and quiet, just the way I like it." In truth she had slept most of the day away and hadn't even bothered with cooking anything except the frozen pizza that had been in her freezer for months.

"I have just one question to ask you on this fine morning," he said.

"And what's that?" Dread added to the slight nausea rolling around in her stomach. She wondered what he would do if she just hit the button to raise her window while his head was still stuck inside her car.

She nearly giggled as a vision of her driving around town with him hanging off her car like an additional rearview mirror filled her head.

"Why won't you go out with me?" he asked, a twinge of impatience in his tone.

"It's nothing personal, Jerry," she fibbed. "I'm just too busy to date."

He frowned. "You were dating that other guy a few months ago."

"His name is Barry and he's gone because I didn't have time to date." There was no way Debra wanted to tell him that she'd never go out with him because something about him set her teeth on edge and made her feel icky inside.

"You know I could show you a good time," Jerry said.

"I'm sure you could," she agreed. "But I'm not dating right now. I'm completely focused on my professional life. And now I've got work to do, so if you'd excuse me..."

He jerked away from the car as she pulled forward. She wondered if she should say something to Kate about his forwardness, but then dismissed the idea. Kate was already busy working on her speech for the Valentine's Day night celebration and she had enough on her mind without handling a Secret Service man who was more than a little annoying, but certainly hadn't been particularly out of line.

He just wanted to date her and she didn't want to date him. End of story and no need to make a big drama out of it.

She parked her car and took a moment before getting out. She'd only been up for an hour and a half and already she was exhausted.

Of course, it didn't help that three nights in the past week her sleep had been interrupted by hang-up phone calls in the middle of the night. It didn't help that items kept disappearing and reappearing in her home, making her not able to trust her own sanity.

She'd read everything available on the internet about pregnancy. She understood her exhaustion and the bouts of nausea when food was the last thing she wanted in the morning. She understood a little bit of absentmindedness was normal, but surely nothing to the extent of what she had been experiencing.

Pregnesia, indeed. What scared her more than anything was the possibility that for some reason she was having a nervous breakdown.

Maybe she was working too hard. Maybe she'd reached her limits in trying to pull off the party for Trey and process her pregnancy, and now her mind was playing tricks on her because of exhaustion and stress.

She hoped that wasn't the case because if Kate followed through on deciding to run for president, Debra's workload would triple. Hard work had never stressed her before. She loved what she did, so what was the problem?

She grabbed her purse from the seat next to her and shot a glance out of her rearview mirror to see Jerry still staring at her with a frown. Ignoring him, she left the car, grateful that nobody was in the kitchen when she stepped inside.

She didn't feel like interacting with anyone at the moment. She just wanted to get to her office and close the door. Once she was behind her desk she leaned back in her chair and closed her eyes, playing over the disturbing events of the past week.

Absentmindedness was forgetting to return a phone call or that you'd put a load of clothing in the washing machine. It was not remembering to pull something out of the freezer to defrost for dinner.

It wasn't a crystal paperweight that disappeared from the top of your desk and then reappeared where it belonged two days later. It wasn't the dry cleaner's calling to tell you that the suit you'd brought in for cleaning was ready for pickup when you had no memory of taking anything to the dry cleaner's.

She was beginning to wonder if she was not only growing a baby in her belly, but maybe some sort of terrible brain tumor in her head, as well. She was starting to question her own sanity and the timing couldn't be worse for her to be going crazy.

Unexpected tears burned at her eyes and she swiped

at them, feeling foolish and overemotional. Darned hormones. Maybe she needed to start some sort of a diary or journal detailing the things that were happening to her, the things that made her feel as if she were slowly losing her mind.

She could take the journal in to her doctor when she had her next appointment in three weeks and maybe Dr. Finnegan could make sense of the things that Debra seemed incapable of figuring out at the moment.

At least she had something to look forward to tonight. After work she was going shopping for a gown to wear to Trey's party. Because her place was normally behind the scenes, she didn't have an adequate gown to wear as a guest and she was actually looking forward to shopping, which she rarely did.

She checked in with Kate and then worked until just after noon when she heard a knock on her door. The door opened and Trey filled the space. "Can I come in for a minute?" he asked.

"Sure," she replied and fought the sudden rapid beat of her heart. She hadn't seen him since the night he'd had dinner at her place, the night he'd kissed her like he meant it. That darned kiss, this darned man, had haunted her for the entire week.

He plopped down in the chair across from her small desk. "I just thought I'd check in and make sure everything was on schedule for Friday night."

"Everything is in place. Stacy has been like a bulldog getting things done." Debra shuffled several papers on top of her desk and pulled out one that displayed the centerpieces she and Stacy had agreed upon.

Short crystal vases that would hold an array of white and red flowers with silver and black sticks of onyx and

crystal poking upward, the centerpieces were sophisticated, chic and short enough not to impede conversation across the table.

"Looks good," he replied and handed her back the
paper. He frowned. "But you don't look so well."

"Gee, thanks, you sure know how to flatter a girl,"
Debra replied dryly. Self-consciously she tucked an er-
rant strand of hair, that had escaped the knot at the nape
of her neck, behind her ear.

"No, I'm serious. You look tired. You have dark circles under your eyes and your features looked strained
with exhaustion." The worry in his eyes made the threat
of tears rise up the back of her throat and burn at her
eyes.

She swallowed hard to staunch her emotion. *Darned
hormones anyway,* she thought. "I'm fine. I just haven't
been sleeping very well, that's all. I'll catch up this
weekend, once the dinner party is over and done."

"This has been too much on you, dealing with both
my party and mom's work," he said with a guilty tone.
"I should have taken a bigger role in putting together
the dinner party or I should have seen that I was over-
working you and gotten you an assistant."

"Don't be silly," she replied. "Haley has been a big
help with Kate's work. I'll be fine and you did take on
a big role in this process. I just need to grab a couple
of hours of extra sleep this week."

His obvious concern touched her and she told herself
that she'd better either get more rest or start wearing
more makeup. She suspected it was the pregnancy and
the worry about her mental state that was draining her
energy, not the work she'd put in on the party.

"Is there anything else I can do to help?" he asked,

his tone gentle and filled with a caring that wasn't appropriate between them.

"I promise I'm fine," she said firmly. "You need to focus on your own health. You're about to enter months of a marathon race to get yourself elected. You'll be traveling all over the state and beyond, getting out your vision of what you want to see for the state of North Carolina in the future."

She wanted to tell him to go worry about the woman he was going to marry, not about a woman who had spent one night with him when they'd both been a little bit drunk and a lot stupid.

"I'm not your concern, Trey. You have bigger and more important things to focus on," she said.

His eyes turned a deep midnight-blue as he held her gaze.

Suddenly she was afraid he might say something, might do something that both of them would regret. "Go on, get out of here," she said, the words coming out more harshly than she intended. "I have lots of work to do and you are holding me up."

She held his gaze, as if daring him to do anything other than get out of her office. He finally sighed, raked a hand through his thick brown hair and stood. "Then I guess the next time I see you will be on Friday night at the party."

She nodded and stared down at her desk, as if already distracted. "See you then," she replied airily.

When he'd left, she once again leaned back in her chair and drew a deep steadying breath. She knew he felt something for her. Passion definitely, a caring certainly, but they were unacceptable emotions from a man who had far bigger fish to fry.

Her love for him was equally unacceptable and would remain unrequited. She had no illusions. She wasn't a dreamer. Trey would do what was expected of him, as he always had done in the past.

He'd choose a wife that would help him accomplish his ambitions and once his campaign kicked into full gear it would be Cecily at his side.

He wouldn't be around the Winston Estate much after that, and that was fine with Debra. Even though she carried his baby, she had to forget him. She had to emotionally separate herself from him.

Somehow, someway, she had to figure out how to stop loving Trey Winston.

Trey felt ridiculously nervous as he pulled up in front of Cecily's house to pick her up for the night's event. His tuxedo felt too tight, although he knew that it fit him exactly right. The evening air seemed too hot as he got out of his car, but in truth it was in the low forties.

Tonight was what he'd waited for. Tonight was his night to shine. Out of the two hundred and fifty invitations they'd sent out they'd only received eight regrets. It would be a full house and he was nervous as hell now that his moment had finally arrived.

Cecily's butler, John, met him at the door. "Good evening, Mr. Winston. Ms. Cecily will be down momentarily," he said.

In all the months that Trey had been seeing Cecily, she'd never been ready when he arrived to pick her up for any occasion. He stood patiently, knowing they had plenty of time as he'd made sure to build in waiting-on-Cecily time when he'd made the arrangements to pick her up.

At that moment Cecily appeared at the top of the staircase. She stood for just a moment, as if allowing him to appreciate how beautiful she looked in her silver formfitting gown and with her short dark hair coiffed to perfection.

"You look nervous," she said as she started down the stairs.

He grinned at her. "Does it show that badly?"

"Only to somebody who knows you as well as I do." Her ruby lips smiled as she reached him.

Up close she was utter perfection. Diamond earrings adorned her ears, sparkling as brightly as her brown eyes, and her makeup appeared effortless and yet enhanced her elegant beauty. She reached up and straightened his black bow tie. "Don't be nervous. You're going to be dynamite."

John held out her wrap for the evening, a silver cape that matched her dress. Yes, Cecily was perfection in heels. She would spend the evening at his side saying all the right things to all the right people.

It would be a good night for a proposal, he thought as he ushered her out to his car in the driveway. Yes, he knew Cecily was ready for the ring, but he hadn't bought a ring yet, and he had a feeling she'd much rather have a proposal be all about her instead of at the tail end of a party that had been all about him.

On second thought, it was a bad night for a proposal. Cecily would expect roses and him on bended knee, at least a five-carat ring and a band playing their song. Did they have a song? He frowned and tried to think of what it might be.

Proposing to her was going to be a lot of work, but he couldn't think about that now. He had a party to throw, people to persuade and a speech to give that would hopefully make campaign donations fall into his hands.

Tonight was the beginning of a long process and he knew with certainty that he was up for the battle. His nerves calmed the minute they were in the car and headed to the Raleigh Regent Hotel.

He knew his speech by heart, he knew that Debra and Stacy would have everything on point. The night was going to be a huge success, in large part due to Debra.

He didn't want to think about her right now, either. Thoughts of Debra confused the hell out of him and he needed to be clearheaded. Besides, the woman he intended to marry sat just beside him.

"You're very quiet," Cecily said.

"Just going over everything in my head," he replied.

"It's all going to be fine. Debra and Stacy have done a great job putting things all together and you always perform well. You'll charm everyone in the room."

"From your lips…"

She laughed. "Trey, honestly, for a man who has accomplished everything that you've done, you manage to have a humble streak in you that is quite charming." She paused a moment. "Is Sam planning on attending?"

"No. He told me he'd rather eat dirt than go anywhere tonight." Trey frowned. "I just wish we could get him to talk to somebody, to help him process everything he's been through."

"What about Thaddeus?" she asked.

"He sent his regrets also, as I figured he would."

She was silent for another long moment. "Will either of them become a liability to you as you move forward?"

"Not as far as I'm concerned. Sam is a war hero and

Thad is a respected crime-scene investigator. The fact that neither of them are particularly enthralled with politics shouldn't be an issue for anyone to use against me."

He frowned as he thought of his grandmother. Secrets and lies. What had she meant? Did she know something that could destroy them all?

Each time in the past week he'd tried to talk about his concerns with his mother, she'd insisted he needed to forget about his conversation with his grandmother and get on with his business of winning an election.

"I can't believe I haven't heard your speech yet," Cecily said.

He flashed her a quick smile. "Nobody has heard it. I wanted it to be all mine, with no input from anyone. If I can't write a fifteen-minute speech without help to excite people to get behind me, then I have no business being in politics at all."

"You're definitely bullheaded enough to be in politics," she replied teasingly. "Is your mother giving any kind of a speech?"

"No, just me. She's showing her support by being at my side, but we don't want to confuse what tonight is about, and it's about the state Senate race, not the next presidential race."

"You're a wise man not to let her steal any of your thunder," Cecily said.

For some reason her words irritated him. The last thing his mother would ever do was attempt to overshadow him or "steal his thunder," and the fact that Cecily's brain worked that way showed the cold, calculating streak he knew she possessed, but didn't show often.

Of course, it was that calculating, unemotional streak that would make her such a good wife. He would be able to depend on her to remove any emotion from any issue he might have to address if he became the next senator.

The Raleigh Regent Hotel was at the top of a fairly steep hill and Trey was thankful the weather was cooperating, not making it difficult for people to attend this special night.

By the time they reached the entrance of the hotel, any irritation he felt toward his beautiful passenger had passed and he couldn't wait to get inside and see the final results of all of his and Debra's preparations.

They were half an hour early, as Debra had requested them to be and as he handed his keys to the valet, his heart thrummed with restrained excitement.

As they walked into the lobby, there was an air of anticipation that he breathed in eagerly as he led Cecily toward the ballroom.

The doors were closed and an attendant stood at attention, obviously there to keep people out before the appropriate time for the festivities to begin.

He greeted Trey with a respectful nod of his head. "Mr. Winston, Ms. Prentice said to let you in as soon as you arrived." He opened the door and Trey and Cecily stepped inside.

"Oh, Trey," Cecily said and grabbed his hand. "It's all so perfect."

Members of the orchestra were already there, pulling instruments from bags and setting up on a raised stage on one side of the room. Black-and-white-uniformed waitresses and waiters scurried around the room, checking tables that already looked beautiful.

The dance floor gleamed with polish and the centerpieces with their pop of red were perfect foils against the white tablecloths and with the black-and-white dishes.

The head table was also on a dais and Debra had made the decision for it to be a table of nine, placing him in the center with four people on his left and four on his right. His mother and Cecily would sit directly on either side of him. The two most important women in his life, he thought.

Stacy came up to greet them. Clad in a plain black dress, with little makeup on her face, it was obvious she was here to keep things running smoothly with the staff and work behind the scenes.

"Everything looks great," Trey said after he'd made the introductions between the event planner and Cecily.

"It does look nice, doesn't it?" Stacy replied with obvious pride. "Of course, you can thank your assistant, Debra, for bringing things together. She's a tough taskmaster and a killer at negotiations."

"Is she here yet?" Trey asked.

"She's been here for about a half an hour. She checked everything out and then went to the office to sign off on some paperwork. She should be back here any moment now."

Trey nodded, hating himself for wanting to see her when he had the beautiful Cecily right by his side.

Stacy checked her watch. "We have about twenty minutes before people will begin to arrive. Debra wanted the two of you to stand at the doors and personally receive each guest as they arrive. We'll have hosts that will then see people to their assigned tables and on the tables are nameplates to indicate where they are to sit."

She flashed them a bright smile. "It should go relatively smoothly as long as you keep the initial greetings at the door to just a handshake and a welcome."

"Got it," Trey replied, his heart once again thundering in anticipation for the evening to come.

In just a little while he would take the place that his grandfather had groomed him for, he would begin to fulfill dreams long ago destined for him.

This was just the beginning and the excitement, the energy that flowed through him was one of challenge and there was nothing Trey loved more than a good challenge.

At five minutes before the doors were to open, the orchestra began playing soft dinner music and Cecily grabbed him by the arm, her eyes lit with a calm determination. She would perform brilliantly tonight, charming friends and adversaries alike.

His mother entered through the doors. Clad in a blue gown that emphasized the bright color of her eyes, she looked beautiful.

"Good luck tonight," she said as she pulled him to her for a hug. "And Cecily, you look wonderful on my son's arm."

"Thank you, Kate. We're all here for the same reason and it's going to be a wonderfully successful night for Trey."

At that moment the door opened once again and Debra walked in. Trey felt as if he'd been sucker punched in the gut as he took in her dazzling appearance.

The emerald-green dress she wore skimmed her body in silk from her shoulders to the tips of her silver high-heeled shoes. The neckline dipped just low enough to show a flirty hint of the tops of her breasts.

It was the first time since that crazy night they'd shared that he'd seen her with her hair down, rather than in one of her usual messy buns. It fell in soft waves to her shoulders, looking shiny and touchable.

Mascara darkened her eyelashes and a coppery pink lipstick colored her lips. Her cheeks grew pink and he realized he was staring at her as if she were the only woman in the entire room.

He also realized that this had been part of the anticipation he'd felt upon arriving at the hotel, the desire to see her all dressed up. He knew she'd look great, but he hadn't expected such beauty.

Everyone said hello to everyone else and then it was time for Trey and Cecily to stand at the door and greet the guests who had begun to arrive.

As Debra faded back near a large potted plant in the corner of the room, Trey swore that before the night was over he'd hold her in his arms. It was only right that he dance with all the women who had arrived without male companions. He told himself it was the gentlemanly thing to do, but deep in his soul he knew it was a simple decision of desire that he didn't want to try to justify or analyze.

He just wanted to hold Debra.

Chapter 8

The night was going magnificently well. Trey had begun the festive evening with a short but rousing speech about his desire to make a difference in the state of North Carolina. He'd spoken with passion and enthusiasm that had resulted in the crowd being on their feet clapping and cheering when he'd finished.

Cecily and his mother had beamed and Debra felt the same pride and joy that she knew they must be feeling for him. Once the speech was given, dinner was served.

The servers moved like silent, efficient ghosts, filling glasses, placing plates with filet mignon and salmon without interrupting conversations.

Debra found Chad Brothers to be exactly the way Trey had described him, an entertaining dinner companion who had a big, bold laugh that escaped him often.

By the second course he'd declared himself madly

in love with her and wanted to hire her away from Kate to work for him. "Sorry, Chad," she said with a laugh. "No matter how many times you declare your undying love for me, my loyalty is with the Winston family."

"You cut me to my very soul," he declared with a mock look of dismay. "But I suppose I'll forgive you if you cut the rug with me when the dancing begins."

"I would be most delighted," Debra replied. "Though I have to warn you that I don't dance very well at all."

"Not a problem, I've got two left feet so we should be just fine together," he assured her with a charming smile.

Tonight she wasn't thinking about the fact that within another few weeks or so her pregnancy might be impossible to hide. She refused to dwell on the troubling events that had her believing herself half-crazy.

Tonight she wasn't anyone's assistant, she was simply a guest at a dinner party in a waterfall of green silk that made her feel sexy and carefree.

She'd refused wine at dinner, but felt intoxicated by the surroundings, the soft music and the fact that each time she glanced in Trey's direction she caught his gaze on her and her heart would beat a little bit faster.

He probably found it hard to believe that she could actually clean up so nicely, she thought. Still, she felt heady with knowing she had actually managed to turn a few male heads, that the event she'd worked so hard to put into place was going off without a single hiccup.

When the last dish had been removed from all the tables the band began to play a little louder and Trey and Cecily took to the dance floor.

"They make a nice couple, don't they?" Chad said.

Debra watched the couple gliding smoothly as if born

to dance together and couldn't help the wistful yearning that filled her. "Yes, they do," she replied.

"She'll make a perfect political wife," Chad continued. "She's bright and beautiful, but more importantly, she probably wants this more than Trey does. She knows the ins and outs of the game and she plays well with others when she needs to."

Cecily plays well with others and I run with scissors, Debra thought dryly. Chad couldn't know that with each compliment he gave Cecily, every time he mentioned what a perfect couple she and Trey made, he broke Debra's heart just a little bit.

Even though she knew that everything Chad said was right, that didn't mean that Debra couldn't wish that things could somehow be different.

But she knew her future, and there was no Trey in it anywhere. She would be a single parent raising a child alone unless she eventually met a good man she wanted to invite into her life, into her child's life.

Even without a man she would be fine and at the moment her love for Trey made it impossible for her to think of having any other man in her life.

There were moments when she ached with her love for Trey, but it was a love that would destroy him, destroy every plan he had for his future. It was a love she would have to lock deep in her heart forever.

By ten o'clock the cash bar was active and the dance floor was filled with couples enjoying the music. Small groups of people dotted various areas of the room, talking and laughing among themselves.

She saw Trey on the dance floor with his mother while Cecily danced with the mayor. Debra danced once with Chad and then gracefully declined two other men who approached her.

She was growing tired, and by eleven she'd found a spot at the edge of the room where a chair sat beneath a potted tree. She was content to hide out and just watch the rest of the evening unfold.

Another hour and it would all be over. The laughter, the music and the spirit of community that permeated the room would be finished and the tables would be broken down, chairs stored away to await the next big event.

After tonight there would be no more meetings with Trey. She wouldn't be surprised if this evening was followed fairly quickly by a public announcement of his and Cecily's engagement.

"Hiding out?"

The familiar deep voice shot a fire of warmth in the pit of her stomach. She turned to see Trey standing next to her. "Just watching the fun," she replied, and tried to ignore the slight flutter of her heartbeat.

"You look much too lovely tonight to be hiding out beneath a potted plant," he replied and held out a hand to her. "Come dance with me. I think they're playing our song." His eyes twinkled brightly.

"We don't have a song," she replied. The orchestra was playing a slow song and the last thing she wanted was to be held in his arms. The last thing she needed was to dance with him. Even as these thoughts flew through her head, she found her hand in his as he pulled her up from her chair.

She felt extremely self-conscious as he pulled her to the dance floor and into his arms. It was only then that she leaned closer to him. "I have two left feet, I can't dance," she whispered.

He smiled down at her. "You can dance with me." His words held such confidence that he made her believe if she was in his arms she could float across water.

His hand on her back was strong and masterful as they took off across the dance floor. "You look amazing tonight," he said and thankfully didn't mention that at that moment she stepped squarely on his toes.

"Thank you," she replied, hoping he couldn't hear the loud thunder of her heartbeat. She wanted to dip her head into the hollow of his throat, feel his body scandalously close against hers. "Your speech was pretty amazing, too. You had everyone in the room eating right out of the palm of your hand."

He laughed. "We'll see about that by the campaign donations that appear in the next few weeks. If nothing else it seems that everyone has had a wonderful time tonight. My only regret is that I haven't had a chance to dance with you before now."

She raised her head to gaze up at him and in his blue eyes she saw what she felt, desire and want and everything that shouldn't be in those blue depths.

She broke the eye contact and gazed over his shoulder. "I'm just glad it's finally over and I can get back to my regular work."

He stiffened slightly, as if perhaps hurt by her words. "I've enjoyed working with you," he finally said.

"And I've enjoyed working with you, too," she replied with forced lightness. "But now it's over and it's time for us each to get back to our own work, back to our own worlds."

Thankfully the music ended and she immediately dropped her hands from him and stepped away. "I'll just tell you good-night now," she said. "You'll be busy later telling your guests goodbye."

She turned and hurried away, leaving him on the dance floor as she returned to the chair beneath the potted plant. For just a moment as he'd held her in his arms and glided her across the floor, she'd felt as graceful as a ballerina, as beautiful as a fairy-tale princess.

It was a single moment in time that she would cherish for a very long time to come. By the time she was seated once again, Cecily was back at Trey's side, smiling up to him with a possessive confidence that Debra could only envy.

At midnight the orchestra stopped playing, indicating that the festivities were over. As people began to straggle out, Debra went in search of Stacy and found her in a small office just off the industrial kitchen.

The two women remained there, chatting about the evening and what a success it had been until everyone had left. "Come on, I'll walk you out," Stacy said.

As they reentered the ballroom Debra looked around. There was something almost sad about a ballroom with no people, an orchestra pit without music and a silky green dress going home all alone.

"You'll keep me and the hotel in mind for anything that comes up in the future?" Stacy asked as they reached the lobby.

"Absolutely," Debra replied without hesitation. "We worked very well together and I look forward to doing it again."

"Great." The two women said goodbye and Debra walked out into the cold night air.

She got into her car and waited for her heater to begin to blow hot air. Her exhaustion hit her like a ton of bricks. It had been a long night. It had been a long couple of weeks and now the letdown of it all being over made her realize just how tired she was.

Maybe she was crazy because she could have sworn Trey's gaze had been on her far too often throughout the night. And she must be crazy because she thought she'd seen desire in those beautiful blue eyes of his.

But that couldn't be right. She had to be misreading him. His life was mapped out before him by duty and responsibilities. He had a path to follow that didn't include her, but she couldn't get that spark in his eyes when he'd looked at her out of her head.

With the interior of her car finally warmed, she pulled out of the now-quiet parking lot and onto the outer road that would take her to the highway. Thankfully the weather had cooperated tonight, with a big full moon overhead and no clouds. A snow or ice storm would have been a potential disaster.

Eager to get home, she picked up speed as she went downhill, just wanting the comfort of her bed now. It had been a magical evening but she definitely felt as if she'd been turned into a pumpkin.

When she saw the red light gleaming in the night at the intersection coming up, she stepped on her brakes and the pedal slammed right to the floor.

With a sharp spike in her adrenaline that drove all tiredness from her body, she tried to pump the pedal, but there was no pump in it. It remained depressed to the floor as her car continued down the hill, picking up speed as it traveled.

The red light turned green just as she zoomed through

the intersection, now frantic as she realized she had no brakes at all and she was a long way from the bottom of the hill.

If she turned off the engine, then she would lose her ability to steer.

Frantic terror poured through her. She was going almost seventy miles an hour as she continued downward and there was no way to slow down. Several stoplights were between her and the bottom of the hill and although traffic was light, it wasn't nonexistent.

Panic crawled up the back of her throat and in desperation she yanked up the emergency brake, but nothing happened. In that instant, with another red light approaching, she realized the possibility that she might die. She was in a speeding bullet with no way to avoid some sort of impact.

As the red light came closer and her car careened down the hill, she gripped the wheel tightly and fought the impulse to close her eyes.

With the red light and the intersection imminent, she took one of her hands and laid on the horn, hoping to warn anyone else that might be coming that she was out of control. The horn blared, echoing inside her brain.

A hill was just ahead. If she could just make it to the hill then hopefully the car would slow down enough that she could maneuver it off the side of the road safely.

She was halfway through the intersection when she saw a car coming from the left. She turned her head, blinded by its headlights and braced. There was a squeal of brakes and then she felt the slam to the back left side of her car.

Instantly she went into a spin. The car swung around and around, dizzying her as she tried to control it, but the steering wheel careened wildly and with a gasp of resignation, she followed her impulse and squeezed her eyes closed.

The car came to an abrupt halt, crashing into something. As the airbag deployed, everything went black around her.

"The night couldn't have gone any better for us," Cecily said as Trey pulled into her driveway.

"It was a great time," he agreed. He parked his car in front of her door but didn't turn off the engine.

"You aren't coming in?" Cecily arched a perfect dark brow and looked at him with disappointment.

"I'm exhausted, Cecily. I think I'm going to head on home," he replied. It had been weeks since he'd had any intimacy with Cecily. In fact, he hadn't slept with her since he'd been with Debra. How could he make love to Cecily when he couldn't get the feel of Debra in his arms, the scent of her, out of his head?

"It's been weeks," Cecily said softly. "Are we okay?"

He forced a tired smile. "We're fine. I've just been so tied up with business and putting together tonight, I'm afraid my sexual drive has taken a temporary vacation."

She leaned over and placed a hand on his shoulder, her gaze soft with understanding. "Okay, I'll give you a pass for now. I know how hard you've been working to get things lined up between Adair Enterprises and starting the campaign. I just want to remind you that sex is a great stress reliever," she added flirtatiously.

He laughed, but wasn't a bit tempted. "I'll keep that in mind." He sobered as he looked at her. "I think what I need most from you right now is a little patience."

"I can give you that," she replied. "Just don't shut me out, Trey."

"That won't happen." He opened his door to get out and usher her to the front entrance, but she stopped him.

"Don't bother." She opened her car door and then leaned over to give him a kiss on his cheek. "No point in both of us getting out. You'll call me tomorrow?"

"You've got it," he replied.

He watched as she got out of the car and then headed to her front steps. Only when she was safely inside did he pull out of her circular driveway.

What was wrong with him? His sex drive had never taken any kind of a vacation before.

As he thought over the night he could think of two high points—the applause and hoots and hollers that had followed his speech and dancing with Debra.

Debra.

Why couldn't he get her out of his head? He'd hardly been able to take his eyes off her all night long. Surely it was just because it had been the first time he'd seen her in evening wear.

Dancing with Cecily was like dancing with a professional. She moved smoothly and gracefully, accustomed to partnering with him. Dancing with Cecily was effortless.

That hadn't been the case with Debra. She'd been stiff in his arms, difficult to guide in a natural rhythm and had stepped on his toes more than once, and yet he'd enjoyed that dance more than any one he'd had throughout the entire night.

His duty dictated that he chose a wife that would be best suited for his future plans and that woman was Cecily. But there was no question that Debra had somehow managed to crawl into his brain where she didn't belong.

But at the end of the dance they'd shared, she'd reminded him that their work together was over and it was time for both of them to get back to their separate lives.

Of course she was right. She was his mother's personal assistant and he hoped to become the next state senator. It was time to put her firmly out of his mind. He'd probably be far too busy in the next weeks and months to even think about her.

By the time he got home the adrenaline of the night had left him and he couldn't wait to get out of his tux and hit the hay. Tomorrow he would know how well he had been received tonight. Hoots and hollers were great, but donations to his campaign, endorsements from unions and fellow politicians would tell the true tale.

Included in the guest list had been several reporters to ensure that he got a little press time, all of them friends of Cecily's.

He knew Chad would already be busy filling his schedule with speaking engagements and burning up the phone lines to solicit support. Thankfully his right-hand man at Adair Enterprises was ready to step up when Trey wasn't there. He'd done everything humanly possible to prepare for what was ahead.

He'd just gotten his clothes off and was looking longingly at the king-size bed in his massive master suite when his cell phone rang.

Who would possibly be calling him so early in the morning? He grabbed his cell phone and saw his mother's number on the display.

"Are you calling to tell me how terrific I was tonight?" he asked teasingly upon answering.

"Actually, I'm calling to tell you there's been an accident," Kate's voice was brisk and filled with a concern that dropped Trey's stomach.

"Is it Grandma?" he asked.

"No, it's Debra. She had a car accident on the way home from the hotel and has been rushed by ambulance to Duke University Hospital."

Trey's heart hammered. "Is...is she badly hurt?" The words came out tortured by his tightening of the back of his throat.

"I don't have any details. Apparently Debra had me written down as her emergency contact. I got a call from the hospital but that's all they would tell me. I'm on my way there now."

"I'll meet you there," Trey replied. He hung up the phone and grabbed a pair of jeans and a shirt from his closet. His heart threatened to erupt from his chest with its frantic beating.

He was out the door and back in his car within ten minutes. An accident. She'd been in a car accident where an ambulance had carried her away. That meant it hadn't been a simple fender bender. It had been something far worse. How badly was she hurt? *Please, don't let her be hurt badly*, his heart pled.

At just a little after two o'clock in the morning he had little traffic to fight to get to the hospital. Had she fallen asleep at the wheel? He knew she'd appeared more tired than usual lately, but tonight she'd appeared well rested and glowing with good health.

He was relatively certain alcohol wasn't involved. He'd noticed that she'd only had club soda all night long and hadn't even drunk the wine that had been served with dinner.

So what could have happened and how badly was she hurt? By the time he entered the hospital parking area he had whipped himself into a near frenzy.

He followed the bright red signs that pointed him to the emergency area and found his mother already seated in one of the chairs. She rose at the sight of him, her features taut and radiating her own worry.

"I've let them know I'm here, but so far nobody has told me anything about her condition," Kate said. She had changed out of her evening gown and into a pair of black slacks and a blue-and-black-print blouse.

She looked tired and afraid, and seeing his mother's fear only increased Trey's. "How long have you been here?"

"Just a few minutes. They assured me that a doctor would be out as soon as possible to let me know what's going on and how she's doing."

Trey leaned back and released a deep sigh. Patience wasn't one of his strong suits. He wanted to rush through the double doors that separated him from wherever she was and demand immediate answers.

He needed to know that she wasn't clinging to life by a mere thread. But he also understood that he had to be patient and let the doctors perform whatever miracles needed to be accomplished to help Debra.

A police officer appeared just inside the door. He walked over to the receptionist station and then was allowed back through the doors to the emergency rooms.

Was he here about Debra? Had he been at the scene of the accident? Had anyone else been hurt? He felt as if he was going to explode with all the questions and frantic worry whirling around in his head.

It felt as if they'd been sitting there for hours when a

doctor finally came out to greet them. "Kate Winston?" he asked as Kate stood and nodded.

"I'm Dr. Abel Morsi and I've been tending to Debra."

"How is she?" Trey asked, unable to hide the worry in his voice.

"At the moment she's just starting to become conscious. From what I understand from the police who were at the scene, she blew through a red light, got hit on the rear end by another vehicle, spun out and hit a traffic pole head-on going at an excessive speed. Thankfully nobody else was hurt."

"And her injuries?" Kate asked, her voice trembling slightly.

Trey held his breath, his head pounding along with his heart in anxiety.

"She's a very lucky young woman," Dr. Morsi replied. "The worst of her injuries appears to be a concussion. She also has enough bumps and bruises that she isn't going to feel very well for the next few days. We're moving her to a regular room now. We'll keep her overnight for observation but she should be able to be released sometime tomorrow if all goes well and there are no complications."

Trey released the breath he'd been holding. "Can we see her?"

The doctor hesitated a moment and then nodded. "She's going to room two twenty-five. They should be getting her settled in there right now. My suggestion is that you peek in and let her know you're here and that she's in good hands, but don't stay too long."

Trey grabbed his mother's arm and pulled her toward the elevator bank, his mind tumbling inside out as he thought of what he'd just learned.

"She hit a pole at a high speed?" He looked at his mother with disbelief as they stepped into the elevator. "Debra isn't the type to speed or run a red light."

"Maybe she was so tired she didn't notice her speed," Kate replied. "Only she can tell us exactly what happened." They exited the elevator and followed the signs that would take them to her room.

They found it and entered, but stopped just inside as a tall nurse with long dark auburn hair was taking her vitals. She looked up at them, her eyes green like Debra's. She gave them a soft, caring smile. Her name-tag identified her as Lucy Sinclair.

Debra lay on the bed with her eyes closed, a bruise already forming on her forehead and another on her cheek. She looked so pale, so lifeless. Trey could only imagine how many other bruises would appear over the next couple of days.

Lucy was just about to move away from her bedside when Debra's eyes snapped open and she gasped in obvious terror. Her hands rose out of the sheet and clawed the air.

Trey took a step forward, but his mother held him back as Lucy grabbed one of Debra's hands and leaned over her. "Debra, you need to relax. You're fine." Lucy's voice was soft and soothing.

"You're in the hospital," Lucy continued. "You've been in a car accident."

Debra's arms dropped and her hands covered her stomach. "A car accident? Oh, God, my baby," she whispered in what sounded like frantic desperation. "Is my baby okay?"

Baby? Trey felt as if all air had suddenly been sucked

out of the room, as if all the sound had completely disappeared. Debra was pregnant?

It was at that moment that Debra turned her head and saw him and his mother standing just inside the door. Her eyes widened and she began to weep.

Chapter 9

Debra sat on the edge of the hospital bed, waiting to sign release forms and for one of Kate's staff members to come and pick her up. The midafternoon sun shone through the nearby window, but there was a chill inside her that had refused to go away since the moment she'd opened her eyes that morning.

A policeman had been her first visitor of the day, needing details from her of what had happened to file a report. She'd told him about her brakes not working, but when he heard where she had been right before the accident, she had a feeling he believed she might have been drunk. The blood work the doctors had arranged would clear her on alcohol being a contributing factor in the accident.

But what had happened? Why had her brakes failed? She got her car maintenance done regularly. In fact, it had only been about two months since she'd brought her car in to have the oil changed and hoses checked. So what had happened?

The chill intensified as she remembered the speeding of her car, the knowledge that she was going to crash and the frantic blare of her horn to warn anyone in her path.

The horn blare still resounded deep inside her brain, along with the terror that had accompanied the sound.

She'd been assured that the baby was fine, but there wasn't a single part of her body that didn't hurt. She felt as if somebody had taken the traffic pole she'd hit and beaten her with it over and over again.

Kate had called at ten that morning to tell her that arrangements had been made for Debra to spend the next couple of days in a guest room at the Winston Estate. There had been no arguing with Kate and Debra had to admit that the idea of being pampered and waited on for a day or two held more than a little appeal.

What she didn't want to think about was that moment the night before when she'd asked the nurse Lucy Sinclair about the welfare of her baby and then had realized that Trey and Kate had also been in the room.

They'd heard what she'd asked. They both now knew she was pregnant. The thought added to the echoing blare of the car horn from the night before, intensifying the headache that had been with her since she'd awakened.

Trey's face had radiated such a stunned expression and then Debra had burst into tears and the nurse had chased both Trey and his mother out of her room.

The cat was definitely out of the bag, Debra thought as she plucked a thread from the sweater that Haley had brought to her an hour before. Kate had sent Haley to Debra's townhouse to gather up not only clothing for her to wear while leaving the hospital, but also items for the next couple of days of recuperation.

Although Debra knew Kate and several of her staff had a spare key to her townhouse, she assumed Haley had used the key that had been in her purse since her purse was now missing and the morning nurse on duty had told her somebody from the Winston family had come to retrieve it.

"Here we are." RN Tracy Ferrell swept into the room with a handful of papers in her hands. "Dismissal papers for your John Hancock, and your driver has arrived to take you home."

She was somehow unsurprised to see Trey step into the room, followed by another nurse with a wheelchair. Debra's hand trembled slightly as she signed the dismissal papers, knowing that she had some lying to do in a very short time.

"How are you feeling?" Trey asked once the papers had been signed.

"Like I've been beaten up by the biggest thug on the streets," she replied. She winced as she transferred herself from the bed into the wheelchair.

They spoke no more as they got on the elevator and then she and the nurse waited at the hospital's front entrance while Trey went outside to bring the car to the curb.

Aside from the aches and pains that seemed to exist in every area of her body, she now had to face Trey and lie to him about the baby she carried.

As she slid into the passenger seat she saw the fatigue that lined his face; she could only guess the stress and

concern that had probably kept him tossing and turning all night long.

"I was so worried about you," he said as he waited
for her to pull the seat belt around her. "When we got
the call that you'd been in an accident, I was scared to
death."

"It isn't yours," she said, wanting to put him out of
his misery as soon as possible. "I was already pregnant
on the night we slept together."

His features showed nothing as he pulled away from
the curb. "You're sure about that?"

"Positive," she replied with all the conviction of a
woman telling the truth.

"So the baby is Barry's?"

"The baby is mine," she replied firmly.

He shot her a quick glance and then focused back on
the road. "I'm assuming it wasn't an immaculate conception," he replied dryly.

"As far as I'm concerned that's exactly what it was,"
she replied. "Barry definitely isn't father material. I
have no intention of telling him or ever talking to him
again. The baby is mine and I'll… We'll be just fine."

He was silent for a long moment. "I'd want to know.
If a woman was pregnant with my child I'd definitely
want to know."

His words were like arrows through her heart, but
she couldn't allow her own personal wants and desires
to screw up his whole future, and that's exactly what
this baby would do to him. She couldn't tell him the
truth. She had to maintain her lie because despite what
he'd just said to her the consequences to him were just
too high.

He'd want to know, but he also wanted to be a senator and there was no way that she could see that the two could fit together.

"Barry wouldn't care," she finally replied. "A woman having his baby wouldn't change the kind of man he is, and he's not a good candidate for fatherhood. I'd rather raise my baby alone."

They drove for a few minutes in silence and she was sure that she'd convinced him the baby wasn't any of his concern. "So what happened last night?" He broke the slightly uncomfortable silence. "The report we got was that you were speeding and blew through a red light."

An arctic breeze blew through her as she thought of the night before and the certainty that she was going to die. "I was speeding and blew through a couple of red lights because my brakes didn't work."

"What do you mean?"

She shrugged and winced as every muscle in her back and shoulders protested the movement. "I braked and the pedal hit the floor, but nothing happened. I even pulled up the emergency brake, but the car still didn't slow."

A shudder went through her. "I was going down that big hill in front of the hotel and I picked up speed, but I couldn't stop. I couldn't even slow down. I kept thinking if I could just make it to the bottom and then start going uphill the car would slow enough that I could maneuver it off the road, but I never got the chance. I think the police officer who spoke to me this morning thought I left the party drunk last night and that's what caused the accident, but I didn't have a drop of alcohol last night."

"We'll get it all sorted out," he said. "Right now I'm just glad you survived. I was scared about your wellbeing, Debra." His voice was smooth as a caress and she wondered if he charmed all the women he came into contact with. It was possible he wasn't even aware of how deeply he affected her when he spoke to her, when he gazed at her with those beautiful blue eyes of his.

She settled deeper into the seat, exhausted both by her thoughts and the emotions that were far too close to the surface.

Thankfully the rest of the ride was accomplished in silence and by the time he pulled up at the front door of the Winston Estate, she was ready for a pain pill and bed.

Maddie met her at the front door and took her directly to the elevator that would carry her upstairs to the bedrooms. "You poor dear," Maddie said as she wrapped a gentle arm around Debra's shoulder. "We'll just get you into bed and take good care of you until you're feeling better."

Emotion rushed up inside her and tears burned at her eyes. Debra had never had anyone in her life who had taken care of her and right now she was more than grateful to Kate for insisting that she come here for a couple of days.

"Ms. Kate thought you might feel better with a nice new nightgown. It's hanging in the bathroom, if you'd like to change and go back to bed for a nap."

"That sounds perfect," Debra replied wearily. From a small sack she'd been sent home with she took out the bottle of pain pills she'd had filled at the hospital pharmacy and slowly walked to the adjoining bathroom. She'd been assured by the doctor that the pills were a low dosage that could cause no harm to her baby. Besides, she only intended to take one or two and then she'd be fine without them.

The nightgown was long white cotton with green trim and had a matching robe. Debra was grateful it wasn't silk. She was a cotton girl when it came to her favorite sleepwear.

A glance in the mirror showed her what her earlier reflection had shown her in the hospital bathroom. She had no idea how she'd gotten the bruise across her forehead, but since the accident it had turned a violent purple. *Lovely,* she thought and turned away.

The rest of her injuries were bruised knees, a friction burn on her shoulder from the seat belt and just the overall soreness of muscles. With a moan, she got out of the clothes she'd worn home and pulled on the nightgown that Kate had provided for her. The soft cotton fell around her like a comforting cloud.

She used a crystal glass next to the sink to wash down two pain pills and then carried the glass and the pills back into the bedroom where Maddie awaited her.

"You need to rest now," Maddie said as she took both the pill bottle and the glass from her and set them on the nightstand. She then tucked the sheets around Debra like a mother hen securing her chick for the night. "Myra is making her famous chicken soup for you to have later."

"She shouldn't go to any trouble," Debra replied, already feeling a deep drowsiness sweeping through her. The trip home from the hospital and the conversation with Trey had exhausted her.

"Don't you worry about it. Don't you worry about anything. You just relax and if you need anything, Birdie is working up here today and she'll be checking in on you regularly. You call for her and she'll come running." With a final sympathetic smile, Maddie left the room.

"Birdie" was actually Roberta Vitter, a fifty-year-old woman who worked as one of the maids in the house. Her domain was the upstairs, dusting and cleaning the bedrooms and baths so they were always ready for any guest who might arrive.

Debra had been placed in the bedroom they all referred to as the blue room. The walls were a faint blue and the bedspread was a rich royal-blue. The lamp next to the bed had a blue-and-white flower pattern and the furniture was all dark cherry.

It was a beautiful room, but as Debra waited for sleep to take her all she could think about was that the blue of the room reflected the blue of Trey's eyes and the blueness of her emotions.

She'd done it. She'd managed to make Trey believe the baby wasn't his. She should be feeling enormous relief, as if a big weight had been lifted from her heart.

Instead her heart felt as if somehow in the past half an hour it had irrevocably broken.

Trey had left the Winston Estate the moment he'd delivered Debra there, knowing she would be in good hands between his mother and the staff. He'd driven to Adair Enterprises and holed up in his office.

A deep weariness made the sofa look inviting, but he knew a quick power nap wouldn't solve the problems. At the moment he wasn't even sure what the problems were, he only knew he was troubled on a number of levels.

He should be feeling triumphant. The morning paper

had carried a photo of him and Cecily with the headline of North Carolina's New Power Couple, and had gone on to quote part of his speech from the night before and his aspirations to serve as senator for the beautiful state that was his home.

However, the trauma of Debra's accident and then the bombshell news that she was pregnant had kept him awake most of the night. He'd alternated between praying that she would be okay and wondering if the baby she carried was his, and if it was, what he intended to do about it.

He hadn't come to any concrete conclusions other than he would support Debra and be an active participant in his baby's life. He wanted children and while he hadn't thought about a pregnancy being the consequence of the night he'd shared with Debra, he realized he wasn't so upset to believe that he might be the father of her baby.

He'd been oddly disappointed this morning when she'd told him the baby wasn't his and that small twinge of disappointment had only managed to confuse him. He wasn't sure he absolutely believed that the baby was Barry's and not his. Unfortunately there was nothing he could do about it as she'd told him so.

She'd created a confusion in his life since the night they'd spent together. Since that night he had desired her to the point of distraction, but he had to be stronger than his desire for her.

Duty. It had been pounded into his head by Walt and his mother since he was a child, duty to the family business and to a place in politics. As the eldest of the Winston children, his mother had encouraged him to be a good example to his younger brothers and Walt had told Trey his destiny was to do great things both for Adair Enterprises and for the country.

And duty required difficult decisions, personal choices that were smart. And Debra definitely wasn't a smart decision, especially now if she was in fact carrying another man's child.

What concerned him the most at the moment was her telling him that the car accident had been caused because her brakes had failed. It took him a single phone call to find out that her car had been towed to an impound lot.

The next call he made was to his brother Thad. Thad answered his cell phone on the second ring. "Winston."

"Thad, it's Trey."

"Ah, half of the new power couple in town," Thad said dryly. "I saw your photo in the paper. Calling to try to get my vote?"

"Actually, I'm calling you because I need a crime-scene investigator. Would you have some time this afternoon to stop by my office so we can have a discussion about something that has come up?"

"You've definitely captured my attention, brother," Thad replied. "Anything else you can tell me?"

"I'd rather we talk in person," Trey said.

"How about four o'clock?"

"Whatever works for you."

"Then let's make it four o'clock at your office. And if I'm not out of there by five you buy dinner from that bistro or whatever it is where you normally order those killer sandwiches."

Trey smiled. "It's a deal."

The two men hung up and Trey's smile fell. He leaned

back in his chair and steepled his fingers in thoughtful contemplation.

There was no way he believed that the car accident had happened in any way other than what Debra had told him. She had no reason to lie about the brakes not working and it was something that could easily be checked.

He didn't have the resources to fully investigate what had happened in Debra's car, but Thad did. And what good was it to have a law-enforcement official in the family if you didn't occasionally take advantage of the fact?

With the meeting set for four, Trey got to work on Adair Enterprises business. Saturdays were always the time he checked in with their satellite operations and with the end of the month approaching he had the usual financial busywork to do.

The afternoon flew by both with work and thoughts of Debra. He had been so frightened last night when he'd heard she'd been in a car accident and rushed to the hospital. She had appeared so fragile, so vulnerable this morning when he'd arrived to pick her up.

The bruise on her forehead told only part of the story of her injuries. He could tell with each movement of her feet, with every small action of her body that she ached from the near-death ordeal.

It could have ended in such tragedy. She could have been killed. She could have killed other innocent people. It was only by sheer luck she'd survived with only a concussion and various bumps and bruises.

He knew she was in good hands and was grateful that his mother had insisted Debra spend a few days recuperating at the estate. The thought of her all alone and hurting at her townhouse swelled a pain inside him.

He had a feeling from what little she'd shared of her past that she'd been alone for most of her life, that she'd never had anyone to depend on but herself.

Thank goodness she hadn't lost her baby. He could tell by the way she'd talked of her pregnancy that she was already invested in the baby she carried, was probably already making plans for the birth and life after.

It had been a little over two months since they'd slept together and if she already knew she was pregnant on that night, then she had to be approaching or already be in her second trimester.

It hadn't shown. As he thought of the vision she'd been the night before in that amazing spill of emerald green, there had been no hint of a baby bump or maybe he just hadn't noticed.

He kept busy until four when Rhonda announced the arrival of his brother. Thaddeus Winston was thirty-one years old and wore his light brown hair slightly shaggy. He was dressed in a pair of black slacks, a white shirt and a jacket that Trey knew hid his shoulder holster and gun. He was not just a crime-scene investigator, but had all the full capabilities and powers of a member of the Raleigh Police Department.

"How are you doing, brother?" Trey got up from behind his desk and shook Thad's hand. He then motioned him to the sitting area of the room. "On duty or would you like a drink?"

Thad sank down on the sofa. "Off duty and Scotch neat would be perfect," he said.

Trey went to the minibar at the back of the room and poured two glasses of Scotch. He handed one to

Thad and then sat in the chair opposite him. Thad took a sip of the drink, placed it on the coffee table in front of him and then leaned back, his hazel eyes filled with curiosity.

"What am I doing here? We don't exactly hang out on a regular basis."

"That was your choice," Trey replied. Thad had long ago turned his back on the family business and definitely didn't like anything that had to do with politics.

Thad nodded, accepting the fact. "You mentioned something on the phone about needing my skills as a crime-scene investigator. What's happened?"

Trey explained to his brother about the event the night before and Debra's car accident on the way home. As he spoke Thad listened attentively.

Trey knew his brother had a reputation for being an intelligent, valued asset to the police department. If anyone could get to the bottom of Debra's brake issue, it would be Thad and the strings he could pull with his police buddies.

"Alcohol not an issue?" Thad asked.

"Definitely not, and when her toxicology results come back they will prove that she wasn't drinking. She's pregnant, so she didn't even have wine with dinner."

"You know traffic issues and accidents really aren't my field," Thad said.

"But you know the people on the force that could launch an investigation into this. I just want to know if it was some sort of mechanical failure or something else."

Thad raised an eyebrow. "Something else? As in something nefarious?"

Trey shrugged. "It just seems odd that something like

that happened on the night I pretty much told everyone that I intend to run for senator."

Thad's frown deepened. "And what has Mom decided to do? Has she said anything about her own political future?"

"It's my personal opinion that she's going to run," Trey said truthfully. "Although officially she hasn't said anything yet, it's just a feeling I have."

Thad took another drink of his Scotch and then leaned back against the sofa. "To be honest with you, I hope she doesn't run. Politics has never done our family much good."

Trey knew his brother was thinking about their father. "Dad was a cheater first, a senator second," he said softly.

"It's not just that," Thad said, although Buck's cheating had taken a toll on their entire family. "It's also the idea of a national spotlight being on all of us again. It's bad enough that you've gone to the dark side," he said wryly.

"You know that Mom is going to do what she decides to do and she'll make her decision based on many factors, including the price we'll all have to pay if she decides to run for president."

"I know, but I also know that I intend to maintain some distance from all of it. You know I love you all, but I love my job and I don't want everyone else's ambition to screw around with my nice, quiet life."

"I understand that," Trey replied. "But as far as I'm concerned, running for public office isn't just a job for me, it's a calling."

"I get it, but I don't have to particularly like it. You

know you'll win the election. You always get what you go after."

Trey smiled. "I hope to win, but who knows what could happen between now and the day that people actually cast their votes." His smile faded as he thought of another subject. "Have you visited with Grandma Eunice lately?" he asked.

"Not lately enough," Thad admitted. "It's been a couple of weeks. Why? Is she sick?"

"I'm not sure what's going on with her," Trey replied and explained what had happened the last time he'd visited their grandmother. "Secrets and lies, that's all she kept saying before Sassy finally gave her a sedative. Do you know any deep dark secrets about our family that might come to the surface during a campaign?"

Thad shrugged. "Beats me. We all weathered the biggest secret in the family, that our father was a womanizer who didn't give a crap about his wife and kids. When Mom became vice president I'm sure there were people looking for secrets and lies to bring her down, but nothing ever came out."

Trey knew their father's betrayal was responsible for Thad deciding to remain a bachelor. He maintained he had no taste for family life given what they'd seen in their parents' marriage. Thad finished his drink and then stood. "I'll have to call in some markers but I'll get Debra's car from the impound lot to the police-station garage where a mechanic can take a close look at it."

"I really appreciate it, Thad."

His brother flashed him a smile. "You just appreciate the fact that I'm leaving here before five o'clock and you don't have to buy me dinner."

Trey laughed and walked his brother to the door. "If you want to hang around, I'll be glad to buy you dinner."

"Thanks, but I want to get right on this thing with Debra's car. Hopefully I'll have an answer for you by the end of the evening."

"That would be terrific," Trey replied.

Once Thad had left, Trey returned to his desk, his thoughts scattered like the seeds of a dandelion in a breeze. At least he'd set into motion obtaining some answers about what had happened to cause Debra's accident last night.

She might have blown a hose and the brake fluid had all drained out. Or the brakes might have failed for some other mechanical reason.

Trey admitted he knew a lot about business and politics, but he was fairly ignorant of the workings of a car. A trained mechanic at the police garage would know what to look for and in the meantime all Trey could do about that particular issue was wait.

He'd already spoken to Cecily first thing this morning, but he found himself wanting, needing to check in on the woman who was in the forefront of his mind.

He called the house and Maddie answered the phone. "Hi, Maddie. I just thought I'd call and check in on our patient."

"Do you want me to transfer the call to her room?"

"No, that's not necessary. I was just wondering how she's doing." He didn't want to bother her if she was sleeping, nor did he feel like it was a good idea to speak to her until he had something concrete to say. It wasn't enough that he just wanted to hear the sound of her voice.

"She's been sleeping most of the afternoon, poor

thing. Myra is getting ready to take her up some of her chicken soup and she'll probably go back to sleep after she eats. It's the best thing for her. Sleep heals, you know."

"I know," Trey said with a smile. "You've spent most of my early life telling me that."

"And that's because of you three boys you were always the most difficult to get to sleep each night," Maddie replied. "You always had a hard time winding down."

"I still do," he admitted. "Well, I just wanted to do a quick check in to see that Debra was resting comfortably," he replied.

"You know we're all taking good care of her."

Once he was finished with the conversation, he decided to call it a day and head home. Thad would contact him by cell phone and his work in the office was done for now.

It took him only twenty minutes on a Saturday late afternoon to get from the Adair Enterprises offices to his home just outside the Raleigh beltline.

The six-bedroom, eight-bathroom mansion wasn't as impressive as the Winston Estate, but it was more house than Trey had ever imagined for himself.

It had been his mother who had encouraged him to buy it when it had come on the market a year before. It still didn't feel like home and he knew what he was missing were the skills of a decorator and the company of a spouse.

Sooner or later he'd need to rectify that situation. There was no question that he would be a more appealing candidate with a wife by his side, especially given his father's reputation for being a cheating ladies' man.

As a single man, Trey knew the public might be more apt to tar him with the same brush. A wife was as important as a good campaign manager.

He frowned as he walked through the front door and threw his car keys on the nearby marble table in the foyer. When had he become the coldhearted soul who would make a decision as important as marriage simply because it was politically appealing?

The silence of the house thundered around him as he walked through the great room with its high ceilings and modern furnishings. There was just the minimum of furnishings, nothing decorative to add any warmth or personality.

He had a cleaning service who came in once a week, but other than that he had no house staff. Most days he ate all of his meals out so he didn't require a cook and he figured once the time was right his wife would staff the house with the help she thought was important and do the decorating that would make the house feel like a home.

He went into the kitchen and put on a pot of coffee and as he waited for it to percolate, he stood at the windows that overlooked a lush backyard and a large patio surrounding a swimming pool.

His head filled with a vision of a hot summer day, of the large brick barbecue pit spewing the smoky scent of cooking meat, of colorful umbrellas open against the shimmer of the sun and the taste of tart lemonade in his mouth.

He closed his eyes and allowed the vision to play out. There should be children in the pool, laughing and shouting as they splashed and swam from one end to the other... *His* children.

A sense of pride, of joy buoyed up in his chest as he thought of the children he would have, children who would carry on the Adair Winston legacy.

And in his vision he turned his head to smile at the woman who'd given him those children, the woman who was his wife. His eyes jerked open and he realized the woman he'd seen standing beside him in the vision wasn't Cecily at all, instead it was Debra.

Irritated with the capriciousness of his own mind, he poured himself a cup of coffee and went back into the great room where he sank into the accommodating comfort of his favorite chair.

Lust. That's all that it was, a lust that he felt for Debra that refused to go away. But he certainly wasn't willing to throw away all his hard work, all his aspirations, by following through on that particular emotion. That would make him like his father and that was completely unacceptable.

No matter what he felt toward Debra, she was the wrong woman for him. He had to follow his goals, his duty to pick the best woman possible to see him to his dreams, to the dreams his grandfather Walt had encouraged him to pursue.

Besides, it wasn't like he was in love with Debra. He liked her, he admired her, and he definitely desired her, but that wasn't love.

Debra inspired his lust, but Cecily inspired confidence and success and encouraged his ambition. If he used his brain there was really no choice. The lust would die a natural death, but his relationship with Cecily would only strengthen as they worked together for his success. At least that's what he needed to believe.

It was almost eight when his cell phone rang and he saw that it was Thad.

"Hey, bro," he said.

"Trey, Debra was telling the truth," Thad said. His voice held such a serious tone that Trey's heartbeat reacted, racing just a little bit faster.

"A malfunction of the brakes?" he asked.

"I'd say more like a case of attempted murder. The brake line was sliced clean through."

Chapter 10

Debra stared at Trey in stunned disbelief. He and his brother Thad had come into the bedroom just after breakfast to tell her the news that somebody had cut her brake lines. Somebody had obviously tried to kill her.

"But who? And why?" She was seated in a chair next to the bed, clad in her nightgown and robe. She raised a trembling hand to her head, where a pounding had begun. None of this made any sense. How could this be happening to her?

"That's what I want to talk about with you," Thad said. He remained standing with a small pad and pen in his hand as Trey eased down onto the foot of the bed. "We were hoping you might have some ideas for us."

She looked from Thad to Trey and then back again. "Ideas? Ideas about who would want to hurt me? Who might want to kill me? There's nothing for me to tell you. I can't imagine anyone doing something like this to me."

"You were lucky you weren't killed," Thad said, his hazel eyes hard and intent. "At the very least you could have been hurt badly."

"It has to be some sort of a mistake," Debra protested, her heart taking up the pounding rhythm of her head.

She felt as if she'd once again taken a plunge into the sea of insanity, like her items disappearing and then reappearing, like the guest list found in the freezer.

Somehow, someway, this was all part of her craziness because it felt impossible that Trey and Thad were here to tell her that somebody had intentionally tried to kill her by cutting her brake lines.

Maybe she should mention those other things to Thad? Perhaps she should tell him that she felt like somebody was trying to gaslight her, that she couldn't possibly be as absentminded as she'd been over the past couple of weeks.

She immediately dismissed the idea, certain that one thing had nothing to do with the other. Her absentmindedness didn't cut her brake lines and telling him about the other things might only manage to muddle the case.

"Have you had problems with anyone? Old boyfriends you've ticked off?" Thad asked. "People maybe you worked with on the event that you might have rubbed the wrong way?"

"No, nothing like that," she replied.

"There is an old boyfriend," Trey said and Thad looked at him and then gazed back at her expectantly.

"Barry. Barry Chambers. He owns Chambers Realty, but he wouldn't want to hurt me. We broke up weeks ago. He's old history and in any case he's not the type of man to do something like this."

"Who broke up with whom?" Thad asked.

"It was a mutual thing, but he broke up with me before I got a chance to kick him to the curb." Once again she raised a hand to her forehead, where she knew her bruise had already begun to take on the colors of green and yellow. "The breakup was quite civilized, done in a public place over dinner."

She steadfastly kept her gaze away from Trey, who had ended that night with her in a hotel bed where they'd had wild, passionate sex. "Trust me, Barry doesn't care enough about me to try to kill me or hurt me in any way," she added.

Thad frowned. "That brake line didn't just cut itself. Somebody had to have intentionally crawled under your car while you all were inside the hotel dining and dancing. That somebody had something sharp enough to cut the brake line." He looked at his brother. "Could this have anything to do with Mom or you?"

"I don't see how," Trey said slowly. "But I have no clue what to think."

"I'm just a glorified secretary, for God's sake," she exclaimed as horror washed over her. She dropped her hand from her forehead to her lap. "Maybe somebody got the wrong car?"

Trey's frown deepened. "What do you mean?"

"I drive a common type of car, nothing fancy or unusual. Probably half the staff at the hotel drives something similar to my car. This has to be about somebody else. It can't be about me. I can't imagine anyone wanting to hurt me for any reason." She swallowed hard against a rising hysteria.

Thad drew a hand through his hair. "If you think of somebody, no matter how crazy it sounds, you need to contact me." He reached into his coat pocket and withdrew a card. "Meanwhile, I'll check out the hotel and see if the answer lies with somebody there. In any case, it's possible somebody saw something that night that might help us find out who is responsible for this."

"Thank you, Thad," Debra said. He nodded and left the room. Trey remained seated at the foot of the bed, his gaze focused intently on her.

"How are you feeling?" he asked.

"A little shaken up, especially now that I've been told that somebody tried to kill me," she replied, her voice trembling slightly. "Honestly, Trey, I can't imagine anyone hating me enough to do something like this. I can't imagine anyone hating me at all."

"I can't either," he admitted with a soft tenderness that soothed every exposed nerve of her emotional chaos.

"Maybe it really was just a case of mistaken car identity and Thad will figure it all out. Maybe it has something to do with somebody who works at the hotel."

She shifted positions in the chair. "You know, there is one person who kind of creeps me out and keeps asking me out on dates. I turn him down all the time, but, I can't imagine him having anything to do with this."

Trey's eyes narrowed to blue slits. "And who is this person?"

She hesitated a moment and then replied. "Jerry Cahill."

One of Trey's eyebrows lifted in obvious surprise. "You mean Secret Service Jerry Cahill?"

She nodded and released an uncomfortable laugh.

"I'm sure it's nothing, that I'm just overreacting. It's just whenever he's on duty at the side entrance he always stops my car and wants to know why I don't want to go out with him."

"And what do you tell him?"

"That I don't have time to date and obviously I'll be having less time for personal relationships in the future." It was a backhanded reference to the fact that it wouldn't be too terribly long before she'd be juggling both her job and single parenthood.

"I'll check it out," Trey said, his voice filled with a simmering anger. "His job is to guard the house and my mother, not to make any of the staff feel uncomfortable."

"I don't want to get him into any trouble," Debra replied hurriedly. "He's never done anything to me except flirt, and one day I thought I saw him just standing outside my townhouse."

"Why didn't you mention this before?" Trey asked.

"Because I thought he was harmless. I mean, he's a Secret Service man. They go through all kinds of security and background tests to get their jobs. They can't be the bad guys."

Trey's jaw clenched. "Anyone can be a bad guy, Debra. Men have been known to do terrible things to women they feel have rejected them."

Wearied both physically and mentally, Debra sagged back in the chair. It all felt like too much... The accident that wasn't an accident, the crazy incidents of forgetfulness or whatever they were. She felt as if her brain was stuffed with too many strange things and she had somehow entered an alternate universe like the Twilight Zone.

Trey stood up and walked over to her. He held out his hand. "Come on, I think it's time for you to be back in bed. It's not even noon yet and you look exhausted."

"Attempted murder does that to a woman," she replied. She eyed his hand and hesitated a moment, almost afraid to touch him, afraid that a simple touch would force out all her emotions that she'd tried to keep in check.

She finally slipped her hand into his and he pulled her not just out of her chair, but into his arms. A sob caught in her throat as he held her against him, his hands lightly caressing up and down her back.

"It's going to be okay," he murmured, his breath a warm promise against her hair. "We aren't going to let anything happen to you."

She couldn't help it, she began to cry. All of the uncertainty of the past few weeks coupled with the accident and now the knowledge that somebody had deliberately tampered with her car mingled together in a roar of emotions she could no longer contain.

She hadn't realized until this moment how badly she'd needed to be held, how much she'd wanted strong arms wrapped around her, assuring her that she was okay.

She leaned into him, drawing in the comforting heat of his body, breathing in the familiar scent of his cologne. His heart beat against her own, a steady rhythm that slowly calmed the racing of her own heartbeat.

Her tears finally ebbed, leaving her spent and clinging with her arms around his neck, her face turned into the hollow of his throat. She wanted to kiss him, to tip her head up and feel his lips pressed against hers.

She felt loved. In his arms she felt loved as she'd

never felt in her entire life. She wanted to stay in this room, in this moment forever.

And for just a crazy instant she wanted to tell him that she was madly in love with him, she wanted to confess that the baby she carried was his.

Thankfully at that moment he released her and she got back into bed, her love for him shoved down and buried deep inside her as she pulled the sheet up to cover herself.

It was unusually warm for the last few days of January as Trey drove to his mother's mansion to take Debra home to her townhouse Wednesday morning.

He didn't want her to leave the safety of his mother's place, but Debra had insisted that she'd overstayed her time at the estate and needed to go home and get settled back into her usual routine.

She'd told him she was also ready to get back to work. Haley had stepped in to take her place while she'd been recuperating, but now it was time for Haley to step aside and let Debra resume her position.

So far nothing had come out of the investigation Thad was conducting in regard to the cut brake line. Nobody at the hotel had seen anything unusual the night of the dinner and Barry had an alibi for the evening.

Thad and Trey had spoken to Jerry Cahill together the day before. Trey had found the Secret Service man slightly arrogant and completely indignant that anyone would believe he would do anything to harm a member of the family or the staff.

He confessed that he liked to tease Debra, but Trey told him in no uncertain terms that his "teasing" wasn't welcomed and he should not bother Debra or anyone else on staff again. It was not only unbecoming, but it was unprofessional, as well.

Jerry had agreed, but Trey had seen a flash of anger in the man's eyes that he didn't like. Jerry didn't know it, but he was under investigation by his bosses to make sure he wasn't some loon who had managed to slide into the system where he didn't belong.

Trey pulled up to the front door of the mansion and got out, enjoying the fact that no coat was needed and the forecast for the next week mentioned highs in the upper sixties.

Thankfully the long-term forecast was for Raleigh to enjoy an unusually mild week or two. That was fine with Trey, he'd prefer not to battle the cold and ice or snow, although he doubted that winter was finished with them yet.

Spring was his favorite season, the time for rebirth and green grass and lush flower gardens. He reminded himself that he needed to hire a gardener so that he would have some flower beds when spring arrived.

Maddie let him into the house and told him that Debra was waiting for him in the sitting room. He walked in and couldn't help the way his heart lifted at the sight of her.

Her forehead bruise was still visible, although fading with each day that passed. She was seated on the sofa, clad in a pair of jeans and a pink sweater.

A medium-size pink duffel bag and her purse sat on the floor next to her. Her eyes lit up as she saw him and he didn't know if she was happy to see him or just happy to see her ride home.

"I still think you going home right now is a bad idea,"

he said as he sank down in the chair next to the sofa. "I'd prefer you stay here for a while longer."

"I'm feeling fine and I need to go home."

"If I were your boss, I'd insist that you stay here," he countered.

"Thankfully you aren't the boss of me," she replied, "and I've taken advantage of your mother and the staff's kindness long enough. It's time for me to get back to my own home and my own routine. Tomorrow I intend to be back at my desk here as usual."

She lifted her chin in a show of defiance, as if she expected Trey to give her more of a hard time. He knew that look of steely strength that arrowed from her eyes. He'd seen it when she'd been negotiating with the hotel. Sweet little Debra had a will of iron when necessary.

"Besides," she continued, "if I don't get back to work, Kate will hire Haley to take over my position permanently."

Trey laughed at the very idea. "Yeah, like that's ever going to happen. You know my mother is totally devoted to you. You don't have to worry about your job."

"All the more reason that I need to get back to work for her. I'm feeling much better, my bruises are going away and it's time to get back to my own life."

"That's what scares me," he replied. "We still don't know who was responsible for your accident."

"And we may never know, but that doesn't mean I have to suddenly stop my life." She stood and grabbed both the duffel and her purse. "My car was targeted, not me, and I still believe that somehow it was a crazy mistake and some creep cut the lines on the wrong car. Besides, why not target my house, smother me in my sleep or shoot me when I'm driving to work?"

She shook her head. "This was done in a public place. For all we know it was done by a couple of whacked-out teenagers looking to cause trouble."

Trey stood and took the duffel bag from her. He knew she was right in that she couldn't just stop living because of what had happened, but he still didn't like the idea of her being all alone in her townhouse when they couldn't be sure that she wasn't the target of the brake failure. He definitely didn't believe that it was the work of teenagers looking for a thrill.

"Do you really think Haley wants your job?" Trey asked when they were in his car and headed to her townhouse.

"Of course she would," Debra replied without hesitation. "She's bright and ambitious, but there's no way I think her desire to have my job led to her trying to kill me, if that's where you're going with this conversation. I still refuse to believe that anyone tried to kill me."

Trey hoped she was right, but just to be on the safe side he made a mental note to tell Thad to check out Haley and any of the other interns that worked for his mother.

"What are you going to do about a car?" Trey asked as he pulled up to the curb in front of her home. He knew her vehicle would be in police impound for quite some time.

"The insurance company has totaled mine out, so I'll be getting a check in a week or two. I'm going to call for a rental later this afternoon and then maybe when the insurance pays out I'll go car hunting. It was time for a new car anyway."

They got out of the car and as he grabbed the luggage, she dug her keys out of her purse. When they reached the front door she unlocked it and pushed it open, then turned to him and took the duffel bag from him.

"Thanks for the ride home, Trey. I really appreciate it."

"Not so fast," he said and slid inside the foyer. "I want to do a check of the locks on your doors to make sure you're secure when you're home."

While he did want to check her doors and windows, the honest truth was he wasn't ready to leave her company yet. He walked through her living room and into the kitchen where he knew she had a back door.

He was intensely aware of her trailing behind him, having dropped the duffel bag and her purse in the living room. "I'm sure my locks on my doors are more than adequate and, besides, nobody has ever tried to break into my house," she said.

He checked the dead bolt and lock on her back door and then turned to look at her. "While I'm here I wouldn't mind a cup of tea or maybe some of that special mint hot cocoa of yours."

Her beautiful eyes narrowed. "Why didn't you just ask me to invite you in for something to drink instead of making up some stupid pretense of looking at my locks?"

"I did want to look at your locks," he protested and then laughed as she gazed at him in disbelief. "Okay, you busted me. I just wanted to sit with you for a little while."

"Why?"

He looked at her in surprise. The simple question wasn't easily answered, at least not completely honestly. He wanted to tell her that he loved watching her, that she was charmingly uncomplicated and he found her lack of artifice refreshing. He wanted to tell her that he'd much rather spend time with her than the woman he intended to marry, but he didn't.

"I enjoy your company," he finally replied. "And I'm formally declaring my intentions to run at a press conference next week and I have a feeling the next couple of days are the last I'm going to see of any real peace and quiet."

She pointed to a chair at the table. "I'll make the hot cocoa."

She worked with a graceful efficiency that hadn't been present on the night he'd danced with her. He smiled to himself as he thought of how often her feet had knocked into his in the short period he'd held her in his arms. Okay, so she wasn't going to win a dance contest anytime soon, but he didn't intend to enter one anytime soon, either.

To be as far along in her pregnancy as she claimed she was, she didn't show at all. "Are you eating enough?" he asked.

She turned from the counter to look at him in surprise. "I'm eating fine.... Why?"

His gaze drifted down to her abdomen. "You don't have any baby bump."

A blush colored her cheeks and one hand fell to her stomach. "The baby is just fine. I'm eating fine and if you saw me without my clothes you'd be able to see the baby bump." She turned back to the cabinets to get some cups.

It was the worst thing she could have said to him, because a vision of her naked took hold of his brain and refused to shake loose. Even with a huge pregnant belly, she'd still be beautiful naked. He clenched his fists, his short nails digging into his palms. He couldn't think about her like that. He had no right to entertain such thoughts.

By the time she carried two cups of cocoa to the table and sat down across from him, he'd managed to banish the evocative vision from his brain.

"How are you going to manage it all?" he asked. "I mean being a single working mother?"

She took a sip of her drink and then lowered her cup. "The way hundreds of other women do it every day of their lives. I'm blessed that I make enough money that I'll be able to hire a good nanny to take care of the baby while I'm at work. I'm equally blessed that I work for your mother, who for all intents and purposes was a single mother herself while your father was a senator."

Trey had a difficult time arguing with her about that. When he was young, weeks would go by when his father wasn't in the house. Of course none of them knew about the mistresses that were a part of his life.

"Do you know whether you're having a boy or a girl? Isn't this about the time they can tell the sex of the baby?" It was ridiculous, the little rivulet of jealousy that tingled through him as he thought of her carrying another man's child.

"I don't want to know the sex ahead of time," she replied. She took another sip and then stared down into her cup, as if the topic of conversation was making her uncomfortable. But, when she looked back at him it was with a soft smile. "All I care about is having a healthy baby."

"If you don't know the sex of the baby then how will you know what color to paint a nursery?"

"There are more colors than pink and blue," she replied. "I'm planning to paint the guest bedroom a bright yellow with lots of bold primary color accents. I've heard using bright colors stimulates a baby and helps them learn."

Emotions rose up inside him as he gazed into her eyes, where the love for her unborn child radiated. "You're going to make a fantastic mother."

"I know I will," she replied with an easy confidence. "I know what it's like to grow up feeling unloved and unwanted. I know all the things I didn't have as a child and this baby is going to be the most important, beloved thing in my world. I intend to spend each and every moment of the day and night letting him or her know that."

He remembered the vision he'd had of children laughing in a swimming pool, the joy that had filled him as he'd experienced the love of his imaginary family.

He wanted to be part of Debra's family. He wanted to be as important to her as the child she carried. It was the very last thing in the world he should want. He took another drink, finding it suddenly bitter.

Pushing back from the table, he stood, needing to get out of there, needing to get away from her. "I should go and let you get settled back in here," he said.

An oppressive force pushed against his chest and he knew it was the ever-present desire he felt whenever she was near him. It wasn't just a desire to hold her in his arms. He wanted to hear the ring of her laughter, watch her as she cooked. He wanted to know her opinions about everything from the weather to religion, from baby diapers to politics.

She was dangerous to him. He knew it in his heart,

in his very soul. She was dangerous to everything he'd dreamed about, everything he wanted in his future.

He left the kitchen and didn't realize she'd followed him to the front door until she called his name. He turned back to face her.

"Did I say something wrong?" she asked, obviously confused by his abruptness.

"No…nothing like that."

"Then what? I can tell something is wrong," she said, her green eyes so soft, so inviting.

Something snapped inside him. He pushed her up against the foyer wall as his mouth captured hers. He'd lost his mind, given in to the raw driving need inside him. There was no right or wrong, just his desire for her.

She gasped in surprise and he plunged his tongue into her mouth as she wrapped her arms around his neck and pulled him close…closer.

His hands slid up under the back of her sweater, reveling in the feel of her silky bare skin. She moaned in pleasure as his fingers worked to unclasp her bra.

Wild. He was wild with the taste, the scent of her. Reason had left his mind as he moved his hands around to cup her bare breasts.

Trapped between the wall and him, Debra made no attempt to escape, but rather turned her face to break their kiss and then pulled her sweater over her head. It dropped to the floor, along with her bra and once again their lips met in a fiery kiss that filled the void in his soul, that stoked the flames of his passion for her even higher.

He wanted her naked and gasping beneath him. He wanted a repeat of the night they'd shared. He'd wanted it since he'd put her in the cab the morning after.

"I want you, Debra," he finally managed to gasp. "I've wanted you again ever since we spent that night together."

It was as if the sound of his voice shattered her, splintered the moment and harsh reality intruded. She shoved against his chest and quickly leaned down to grab her sweater to cover her nakedness.

"This is madness," she whispered, her eyes glowing an overbright green. "I won't lie, Trey. I want you, too. But we both know we can't do this. It would be a mistake for both of us."

He suddenly felt small and selfish. He backed away from her. "Of course you're right." He released a deep sigh, but he wasn't sure if it was a sigh of regret because she'd stopped him or one of relief because she had.

"I know your hopes and dreams and I want those for you, Trey. I also know that I'm a complication you don't need in your life." She remained leaning against the wall. "You will do great things, Trey, and you need the right woman by your side. We both know I'm not that woman."

She straightened and took a step back from him. "This…energy or chemistry or whatever you want to call it between us can't be allowed to flourish. I think it would be best if we see as little of each other as possible in the future. I understand that we'll run into each other at the estate, but there's no reason for you to come here anymore."

"You're right," he said. "Of course you're right. And now I'll just say goodbye."

He turned and lunged through the door. He didn't look back as he strode to his car. Once inside he stared at the front door, which was now closed.

Closed. Debra had to be a closed book in his life. Making love to Debra wasn't fair to her and it certainly wouldn't be fair to Cecily.

Duty versus passion, he thought as he drove away from her townhouse. Passion waned, but duty and dreams lived on and ultimately Trey knew that Debra was right. He would do the right thing and choose his duty over any crazy desire that was probably fleeting.

Chapter 11

It had been two days since Debra had almost lost her mind in Trey's arms, two days ago that they'd nearly made a terrible mistake.

She was back at her desk, although her thoughts weren't on her work and she forcefully kept them off Trey. Instead she wondered how much longer she could keep up the pretense that everything was just peachy in her personal life.

This morning when she'd driven through the side entrance to come to work, Jerry Cahill had been on duty. He'd motioned her on through and it was only when she parked and glanced in her rearview mirror that she'd seen him glaring at her.

Obviously he'd been questioned about her car accident and wasn't too happy about being called on the carpet. Still, he wasn't uppermost in her mind as she contemplated the past two days.

Things had begun disappearing again. Her favorite pink mug had been missing this morning when she'd gone to the cabinet to retrieve it for a morning cup of tea. Yesterday she'd been half-crazed when a throw pillow she normally placed in the center of her bed was found in the bottom of the clothes hamper.

She was obviously suffering some sort of a mental breakdown and it not only frightened her for herself, but also for her baby. Her hand fell to her lap and she rubbed her belly in a circular motion. Her slacks had felt tighter this morning. The baby was growing and she was losing her mind.

What if she cracked up altogether? What if she wound up in some mental institute? Then what would happen to her baby? If she gave birth would somebody hand the baby to Barry to raise because everyone thought the baby was his?

She shuddered at the very thought.

Despite her desire to keep Trey out of her thoughts, he kept intruding. She wasn't sure what caused her more stress: the thoughts of losing her mind or her overwhelming feelings for Trey.

He'd held an unexpected press conference the day before and had officially announced his decision to run for the office of state senator. Cecily had been at his side, as she should have been, as it was supposed to be. They had looked perfect together, poised and at ease in front of the cameras.

But, for the first time in her life, Debra understood why some women chose to be mistresses. It wasn't always about money or the thrill of forbidden fruit, sometimes it was just about love.

She loved Trey enough to want any piece of himself

that he could give to her. Fortunately she loved herself enough not to compromise her true wants and needs, her very soul, by becoming his mistress. And in any case, she knew the core of him, she knew who he was as a man and knew he would never take a mistress. It wasn't in his moral fiber to do such a thing.

Debra was an all-or-nothing kind of woman when it came to love and commitment. Besides, Trey hadn't spoken to her about love, he'd told her he wanted her, that he desired her, and that would never be enough for her.

The Friday morning flew by as she focused on the usual work that kept Kate's schedule running smoothly. At noon she stopped and went into the kitchen where Myra fixed her a sandwich and some coleslaw. She ate quickly, grateful that she didn't encounter any other members of the family, and then returned to her office.

She wasn't in the right frame of mind to put up with Sam's moodiness and although she'd spoken to Thad a couple of times over the past few days, he'd had no new information to give her as to who might have been responsible for her car accident, an accident she still refused to believe was a specific attack on her personally.

She'd just settled back at her desk when a knock fell on her door. Kate poked her head in. "How about we have a chat in my office?" she asked.

"Sure," Debra agreed. She picked up a memo pad.

"You don't need to bother with that. We won't be talking about anything that requires note-taking."

"Okay." Debra got up from her desk and followed Kate into her office. As Kate sat behind her desk Debra sank down into one of the chairs in front of her.

"I just wanted to check in with you and see how

you're doing. How you're feeling." Kate leaned back in her chair, obviously relaxed.

"To be honest, I think my pregnancy hormones are making me a little crazy," Debra replied. "I've been misplacing things and finding them in strange places. I'm having a little trouble concentrating, although it isn't affecting any of my work for you," she hurriedly added.

Kate smiled. "I wasn't concerned about that. I remember when I was pregnant with Sam I had the same kind of issues."

"Really?" Debra asked.

"Really. Of course, Trey was two at the time and he didn't help my sanity any. I remember one day I took him to the park to play and then an hour or so later I got into my car and realized I was about to drive off without him." She laughed and shook her head. "Thank goodness I had Maddie here to keep me at least partially sane."

Debra's relief was enormous. Maybe all of the strange things that had been happening to her really were due to hormones gone wild.

"One of the things I wanted to talk to you about was next Sunday I'd like to have a family continental breakfast on the patio. The weather has been so unusually lovely I thought it would be nice to get everyone together and discuss the ramifications of my running for president."

"Is there something you need me to do? Pastries to be ordered or anything like that?"

"No, Myra will take care of everything. I'm just telling you because Sunday is your day off and I'd really like for you to be there."

"I'd love to come," Debra replied, pleased to be included.

"My decision will affect you as well as the family," Kate continued, "so I want you to have a voice in the process. Are you planning on taking off time when the baby is born?"

"Maybe just a couple of weeks," Debra replied, although the idea of leaving the baby at all with anyone for anything was painful.

"You know, there's no reason for you to leave the baby while you work here. We can set up one of the bedrooms as a nursery and Maddie would love to take care of a little one again."

"Really? So I could bring the baby to work with me?" Debra's heart expanded with happiness.

"I don't see a problem at all." Kate grinned. "My goodness, we've been together so long, Debra, I feel like you're giving birth to my grandbaby. It will be nice to have a little one in the house once again."

Debra prayed the expression on her face didn't change, although the weight of her lies about the father of her baby slammed into the bottom of her heart. "Your family has always been like my own. You know I think of you as a surrogate mother."

A wash of pain flickered across Kate's face, gone so quickly Debra wondered if she'd imagined it. She stared at a family photo on her desk. "I always did want a little girl." She looked back at Debra. "But fate gave me three strapping boys who have been the joys of my life."

"And this baby will be the joy of my life," Debra replied, feeling terrible that Kate would never know that the child she carried *was* her first grandbaby. "But, you can count on me to juggle motherhood and work with no problem."

Kate gave her an affectionate smile. "It never occurred to me otherwise."

Minutes later back at her desk, Debra thought of the Sunday morning breakfast. She would have to see Trey again. It would be the first time she'd seen him since they'd practically attacked each other in her foyer.

He'd started it, but she'd desperately wanted him to finish it. She'd wanted him to drag her up the stairs to her bedroom and make love to her. It had only been a surprising flash of sanity that had saved them both from making another mistake. Whatever it was between them was strong and just a little bit frightening in that Debra had almost no control in her desire for him.

At least Kate had managed to put her at ease a bit as far as her forgetfulness was concerned. She smiled as she envisioned Kate getting into her car to leave a park and suddenly realizing the car seat where Trey should be was empty. Now that was the height of absentmindedness.

By the time six o'clock came she was ready to call it a day. She knew the unusual fatigue she suffered was from her pregnancy, a fatigue that hopefully would pass when she went into her second trimester in the next few weeks.

On her way home she thought about stopping in at some department store to pick up a few pairs of maternity pants and skirts. It wasn't going to be long before the clothes she owned would no longer fit her belly bump.

It was a fleeting thought. She was too tired to shop. She'd make plans tomorrow to take off an hour early and shop then. It would be nice to have something comfortable to wear to the breakfast on Sunday.

At the moment she just wanted to get home, eat some dinner and curl up on the sofa in front of the television where hopefully a good sitcom or crime drama would chase away thoughts of the man she loved, the man she was certain would be the next North Carolina senator... as long as she stayed out of his life.

Trey felt as if he were living some sort of weird double life. During the days he worked at Adair Enterprises and then in the past three evenings he'd had two business dinners to attend and had dined with Cecily the other night.

He hadn't slept with Cecily since the night he'd slept with Debra. He'd made a million excuses to Cecily about their lack of intimacy. Too busy, too tired, not good for his public image to be seen coming and going from her house before they were married, the excuses had fallen from his lips with a surprising ease.

He knew that Cecily was frustrated with him, but she took each of his excuses in stride, telling him coyly that they'd catch up on lost time once they were married.

The truth of the matter was that Trey couldn't imagine making love to Cecily when his passion and his emotions were still tied to Debra.

And it was emotion and fear for her that had him doing something crazy each night. When darkness fell he found himself parked across the street from Debra's townhouse where he'd remain until the wee hours of the morning.

He knew it was crazy, but he couldn't help himself. Even though there was no concrete evidence that somebody specific had targeted Debra by cutting her brake line, Trey believed danger had touched her and wasn't finished with her yet.

He was afraid for her, and so he had taken it upon himself to be her secret nighttime bodyguard. Anyone who got too close to her house while she slept peacefully inside would have him to deal with.

He had a conceal-and-carry permit and a 9 mm with him on these nightly surveillance details. He was dead serious about seeing that no harm came to Debra or the baby she carried.

The only downfall of these nightly visits was that each morning when he got to his office he directed Rhonda to hold all his calls for a couple of hours so he could catch up on his sleep.

Tonight was like the past two nights. It was just after midnight and although it was Saturday the neighborhood was quiet. Debra had turned off the light in the house around nine or so, letting him know she was having an early night.

He yawned and slumped down a bit in the seat, trying to find a more comfortable position to sustain for the next couple of hours.

Was he being foolish? Maybe, he conceded. But he'd rather be foolish than take a chance and have any harm come to Debra. Did he intend to do this nightly vigil every night for the rest of his life?

Definitely not, but he would be here until something or someone managed to make him believe that the cut brake lines had been as Debra had believed, an accident of the wrong car being targeted and not something personal against her. Only then would he stop this madness and get on with his life.

His life.

He stared unseeingly at the center of his steering wheel. He should be thrilled with the direction his life was traveling. Since the dinner party and the press conference the donation dollars had begun to pour in, Chad had put together a machine made of devoted people to work campaign headquarters, which was being set up in a downtown storefront.

Banners and signs had been made to hang on the outside of the building and it always jarred him just a bit to pull up and see his own face smiling from one of those signs.

Cecily was more than ready to step in as a supportive wife and partner and there was no question that she would be an asset to his career. She had money, connections and the personality that would serve him well.

Yes, everything was falling nicely into place. So, where was his happiness? He'd assumed he'd be euphoric at this point in the process, but his happiness seemed to be sadly absent.

He glanced back at Debra's house and frowned as he saw a faint red glow coming from someplace inside, a glow that hadn't been there minutes before.

Was Debra awake? Had she turned on some kind of light? If so, it was a strange red light. A lick of flame danced before the front window.

Fire! It was fire.

His mind screamed the word as he fumbled with his cell phone and called 911. As he gave Debra's address to the dispatcher he got out of the car and raced for the front door.

With the call made, he tossed his cell phone in the

grass and pounded on the door with his fists, calling her name at the top of his lungs.

The odor of smoke drifted through the door, making his blood freeze. Was she unconscious? Already overcome by smoke that had risen to her upstairs bedroom?

Panic seared through him as he rang the doorbell and then pounded once again, screaming her name as the flames at the window grew bigger and more intense.

Vaguely aware of lights going on in the houses around hers, conscious of the distant sound of sirens, he picked up a flowerpot that was on her stoop and raced around to the back of the townhouse.

His heart thumped painfully fast with every step. He finally made it to the kitchen windows where just inside he'd sat at the table and had coffee with her. He raised the heavy pot and threw it through one of the windows, shattering the glass and allowing him entry.

The air in the kitchen wasn't bad, but when he entered the living room the smoke tickled the back of his throat and obscured his vision.

The curtains at the windows blazed and dropped malicious imps of flames onto the carpet below. Although his first impulse was to race up the stairs to Debra's room, instead he ran to the front door, unlocked it and pulled it open so that the arriving firemen could easily access the house.

Swirling cherry-red lights announced the arrival of the emergency vehicles as Trey raced up the stairs, the smoke thicker now, causing him to pause as he was overcome with a spasm of coughing.

He clung to the banister until the spasm had passed and then continued upward. There were three doors upstairs and thankfully all of them were closed, hope-fully keeping most of the smoke in the narrow hallway.

A night-light shone in a wall socket, guiding him forward despite the thickening smoke. The first door proved to be the guest room.

Across the hall was a bathroom where he quickly wet a hand towel with cold water. He entered the door at the end of the hallway and saw Debra unmoving in the bed.

His heart stopped beating for a second. Was she dead? Overcome by smoke? But the smoke was only now just drifting faintly into the room.

"Debra?" He ran to the side of her bed, but she didn't move at the sound of her name. "Debra!" He shook her and gasped in relief as she roused.

"Trey?" She sat up in obvious confusion and shoved a tangle of hair off her face. "Trey, what's happening? Why are you in my bedroom?"

"Fire. There's a fire downstairs. We've got to get you out of here." He didn't wait for her to get out of the bed. He handed her the wet cloth. "Put this over your nose and mouth," he said and then he scooped her up in his arms and rushed down the hallway toward the stairs.

On the lower level he could hear the sound of fire-men at work and when he reached the living room the fire was out and only the smoke and soot remained.

Trey carried Debra directly out the front door, where emergency vehicles had been joined by news vans. It wasn't until he tried to lay her down in the grass that he realized she was crying.

"It's okay," he said, shouting to be heard above the din. He was aware of a familiar reporter standing nearby, but his focus was solely on Debra. "You're safe now," he said in an effort to comfort her.

She shook her head and clung to him, her sobs of fear breaking his heart. "You saved my life," she said, the words coming out in deep gasps. "You saved our baby's life."

In the glow of the headlights around them he saw the horror on her face as the words left her lips. Everything else faded away...the lights, the people and the sound. The entire world shrunk to just him and her and the words that had just fallen from her lips.

She released her hold on him and instead wrapped her arms around herself as she shivered, refusing to meet his gaze.

"*Our* baby?"

She looked up at him. Her tear-filled gaze held his as she slowly nodded her head and then began to weep once again. He stood, his head reeling with the information that the baby she carried was his. Not Barry's, but *his* baby.

He helped her to her bare feet as the fire chief approached them. "There's not a lot of damage," he said. "It looks worse than it is, mostly smoke. We didn't even have to use our hoses. We got it out with fire extinguishers. It was intentionally set, an accelerant used. I'm guessing gasoline by the smell of things," he said to Trey and then turned his attention to Debra. "We'll do a full investigation but I'm afraid you'll need to find someplace else to sleep tonight."

"I'll take you to Mom's," Trey said. He took Debra's arm and looked at the fire chief. "You'll see to it that a guard is posted for the duration? I broke a window in the back to get inside."

"A police officer is already standing by. We'll make sure everything is secure before we leave here."

"And you'll let us know what your investigation discovers?"

"Absolutely, Mr. Winston." He smiled sympathetically at Debra. "We should be finished with our documenting the crime scene by midday tomorrow. If you get a good cleaning crew in here you should be able to return home either tomorrow night or by Monday."

"Thank you," she replied, her voice barely audible among the other noise.

"Let's get out of here," Trey said. He found his cell phone where he'd tossed it in the grass and then they started for his car.

Before they could get there a bright beam of a camera light flashed in Trey's face and a microphone was thrust in his direction.

The reporter he'd seen earlier smiled like the cat that had swallowed the canary. "Mr. Winston, would you like to make a statement about Ms. Prentice's pregnancy?"

"No comment," Trey growled and grabbing Debra closer to his side, he hurried her to his car.

Once she was in the passenger seat, he slid behind the wheel and started the engine with a roar. He pulled away from the curb, a myriad of emotions racing through him and he was afraid to say anything to her until he'd sorted them all out.

She shivered and he didn't know if it was because she was clad only in a copper-colored short nightgown or if it was because she didn't know what to expect next.

Hell, he didn't know what to expect next. There was a part of him that was filled with great joy at the idea of her carrying his child and there was also a part of him that battled anger that she'd intended to keep the baby a secret from him, to pretend that the baby belonged to her old boyfriend.

He couldn't begin to think about the fact that somebody had gotten into her house without him seeing them. That person or persons had set her living room on fire. He hoped the initial assessment was wrong and that it had been faulty wiring or something other than a man-made flame.

For several long minutes they rode in silence and it was finally he who broke it. "You were never going to tell me the truth about the baby?"

"The last thing I wanted to do was screw things up for you," she replied. "I figured it would just be easier to pretend the baby was Barry's and then you get to have your shining future with Cecily and everyone would be happy."

The fact that she'd lied for him to keep his dream alive stole away any anger he might harbor against her. She was willing to sacrifice the Winston power and influence for his happiness, to assure that he reached his dreams.

She'd been willing to go through all the struggles and sacrifices as a single mother to allow him to reach his own goals.

Once again silence fell between them. His brain felt half-contused from bouncing around in his skull. Too many things had occurred in too short a time.

"I'll arrange a cleaning crew to come to your place as soon as the fire department releases it," he said. "I'll also see to it that a security system is installed." He didn't even want to acknowledge at this point that somebody had apparently entered her house and set fire to the curtains.

He pulled up to the side entrance of the estate but didn't turn off the car, nor did she make a move to leave. "That reporter, he heard what I said." Her voice was a whisper. "It will be all over the news tomorrow." She stared straight ahead, her face pale in the illumination from the dashboard. She finally turned to him, her eyes wide and holding a soft vulnerability. "What do you want me to do?"

"What do you mean?" He eyed her curiously.

"I could lie. I could say that the reporter misunderstood what I said, that I was confused by the fire and everything that was going on."

"That's definitely not going to happen," he replied. And it was at that moment he knew he wasn't going to marry Cecily. Even if he got to be where he wanted to be in the political arena, he didn't want the cool, absolutely perfect Cecily next to him.

"Marry me," he said.

Her eyes widened. "Don't talk crazy."

"It's not crazy," he responded. "You're the mother of my child. We'd make a family and you'd never have to worry about anything."

"That's a ridiculous idea and I won't marry you." She opened the car door and in the dome light she looked ghostly pale and exhausted. "Right now I'm going inside to sleep and in the morning I have to figure out who got into my house and tried to burn it down with me still inside. You deal with the press however you want to. I'll follow your lead. I just can't deal with anything else tonight."

She got out of the car and slammed the door. He remained sitting in the car long after she'd disappeared inside the house.

A baby...a fire... His head ached with the night's events. Cecily was going to be angry when he broke it off with her, but that was the least of his problems at the moment.

What concerned him more than anything was the fact that he believed twice now somebody had tried to kill not just Debra, but the child she carried, as well... His child.

Tomorrow he'd deal with Cecily. Tomorrow he'd also discuss his intention to be a huge part of the baby's life. He'd have to deal with whatever the news reports contained and he needed to speak to Thad about this newest threat against Debra.

The one thing he didn't care about at the moment was any ramifications this might have on his career. And the odd thing was that he wasn't sure he cared.

Chapter 12

"Marry me."

Debra awoke with the ring of Trey's words echoing in her head. She was in the same bedroom where she'd stayed following her car accident and as she thought of everything that had happened the night before she wanted to pull the blankets up over her head and never get up again.

A glance at the clock on the nightstand let her know it was after ten. Obscenely late for her to still be in bed. She should be at her desk, she thought and then realized it was Sunday. She should at least be at her house finding out what the fire marshal had learned. She should be anywhere but under the covers thinking about how often she'd fantasized Trey saying those two words to her.

"Marry me."

In her fantasies he'd spoken the words because he

loved her, because he couldn't imagine a life without her. In her dreams he'd held her in his arms and kissed her with love and commitment as they planned a future together.

In reality she knew he'd said the words in an effort to begin damage control and perhaps because he wanted to be a part of his baby's life. He'd proposed to the baby inside of her, but not to her.

There had been no love offered from him. If she'd agreed it would have been like a business deal to him, a merger to get accomplished for the best results possible.

She was worth more than that. The off-the-cuff proposal had stabbed through her loving heart like an arrow. She wouldn't be his lover and she refused to be an inconvenient wife to him.

Hopefully, despite her pregnancy, he could make things right with Cecily and continue on his way. Surely he could figure out a way to make Cecily forgive him for a single night's indiscretion. Of course eventually there would be custody issues to deal with, weekends and holidays when the child would be with him... With them, instead of with her.

She turned over on her back and stared up at the ceiling, reluctant to face any part of the day. Somebody had tried to kill her last night. Somebody had come into her home and started a fire in the wee hours of the morning. If Trey hadn't been there she probably would have died of smoke inhalation long before the flames reached her bedroom.

She frowned thoughtfully. What had Trey been doing at her house at that time of night? How had he managed to be at exactly the right place at exactly the right time when it should have been the last place he'd be? It didn't make sense, but then nothing about her life lately had made any sense at all.

Somebody had gotten into her house. Who? Who had crept in and started a fire that would have certainly been the death of her if Trey hadn't rescued her?

A knock fell on her door and Kate came in carrying a cup of hot tea. Debra wanted to hide her face in shame. Instead she pulled herself up to a sitting position and took the cup of tea that Kate offered her.

Kate sat on a tufted chair next to the bed. "Well, my dear, you've created quite a stir."

"Kate, I'm so sorry," she said miserably.

"Sorry about what?" Kate smiled at her kindly. "I should be angry with you for not telling me that you're carrying my first grandbaby, but I'm not. I understand why you lied about the father of the baby."

"I didn't want to mess things up for Trey and now I've ruined everything," she said, fighting back a wave of tears that threatened with every word. She set the tea on the nightstand, afraid of spilling it and making even more of a mess of everything.

"Nonsense," Kate said briskly. "Oh, there's no denying that some adjustments will need to be made, but Trey is intelligent and flexible. This won't stop him from getting where he wants to go."

She pursed her lips and held Debra's gaze. "You know, somehow I'm not surprised by the news. There is an energy between you and my son that I've noticed every time the two of you are in the same room."

"It was just one night. One crazy, stupid night," Debra replied. "Only I would be stupid enough not to think about birth control."

"Debra, darling, you aren't the first woman in the world to make a mistake where that's concerned."

"But...the press," Debra protested.

Kate gave her a look of distaste. "The news is out everywhere with such salacious headlines that one would think the two of you committed some heinous murder rather than slept together. Trey has a press conference this afternoon at four to address the issue."

Kate motioned to the cup on the nightstand. "Drink that before it gets cold." Debra grabbed the cup and raised it to her lips as Kate continued. "Trey spoke to Cecily this morning. He told her that under the circumstances he was breaking off their relationship for the time being. He told her he needed some time to figure out all the ways this will impact him."

Debra swallowed hard. "How did she take it?"

Kate leaned back in the chair. "According to Trey she was a bit upset, but in the end quite gracious about the whole thing. She said she still intended on being involved in his campaign and wished him well in his personal life if they didn't manage to reconnect. Cecily is a survivor, Kate. She's a barracuda who will find a mate based on criteria that will make her the most successful in the endgame."

"But surely she's terribly hurt and Trey has to make her understand that I don't mean anything to him, that it was all just a terrible mistake. Surely they can work through it. She is in love with him," Debra replied.

Kate smiled. "I seriously doubt that Cecily is in love with Trey. She is in love with who he will become and where that would take her. If they don't get back together she'll move on and will be quite fine, I'm sure."

She stood. "I'm not sure how you and Trey intend to

work things out between you, but I'll have you know that I intend to embrace that baby with all the love I have to give. And now, speaking of Trey, he and Thad are in the sitting room and want to talk to you."

She moved toward the doorway. "Haley happened to have a pair of sweats and a T-shirt that you can put on. Anything I own would be too short on you. The clothes are laid out in the bathroom. Once you're showered and dressed, we'll see you downstairs."

The minute she left the room Debra set her cup down and flopped her head back on the pillow. She didn't want to face Trey. She didn't want to talk to Thad. She just wanted to hide for the rest of her life.

But she couldn't hide. Reluctantly she got out of bed and carried her teacup with her into the bathroom and set it on the counter while she got into the shower.

She hadn't noticed the odor of smoke that had clung to her until it was washing away down the drain. She'd spent her morning thinking about Trey and all the ramifications of her secret unexpectedly being spilled. Now it was time to think about who had been in her house and who wanted her dead.

Haley's gray sweatpants fit comfortably and the navy T-shirt hid the fact that Debra didn't have on a bra. Trey had carried her out the night before in her nightgown and so she hadn't been wearing one. Kate had even provided a pair of flip-flops for her to wear.

She slid on the shoes and then walked down the stairs with dread weighing down each footstep. She dreaded seeing Trey again and she knew that Thad was here to talk about the fact that somebody had tried to kill her. The fire made the cut brake lines very personal and this thought chilled her to the bone. Two attempts on her life... Who could be behind them? And why would anyone go to such trouble to kill her?

Trey was seated on the sofa and Thad in a chair opposite him. Both of them stood as she entered the room. She motioned them back down and then sat on the opposite end of the sofa from Trey, carefully keeping her gaze away from him.

He probably hated her for spilling her secret at a place and a time where a reporter would overhear. He probably hated her for making him scramble to deflect any negativity that might come in his direction at this important time in his life. She was also the reason he'd had to break it off with Cecily. Such a mess she'd made of everything.

"How are you feeling?" he asked.

"I'm okay," she replied and finally forced herself to look at him. There was no anger shining from his eyes, there was nothing but a gentle caring. *For the baby,* she thought. He would put aside any anger he might feel toward her for the sake of the baby she carried.

"We need to talk about what happened last night," Thad said.

She nodded and then looked at Trey again. "Why were you there last night? How did you happen to be there at just the right time?"

She was surprised to see a faint color creep up his neck. "I'd been parked outside your house every night since you quit staying here. I just had a bad feeling after the car accident and so I was spending my nights parked outside your place, watching to make sure nobody bothered you."

She stared at him in stunned surprise. He'd been doing that for her and he hadn't even known yet that the baby was his. He'd been there each night, keeping vigil over her. Maybe he did care about her just a little bit.

"Thank goodness he was there," Thad said. "I touched base with the fire marshal this morning and the fire was definitely set at the foot of the curtains in the living room, probably with a pile of papers and gasoline."

"I just don't understand this," she replied. "I mean, if somebody wanted to kill me, then why set the fire? Why not just creep up the stairs and stab me while I slept? Why not shoot me with a gun and be done with it?"

"I'm guessing that whoever is behind all of this wants your death to look like an accident. The point of ignition in the living room was just beneath an outlet. If the fire department hadn't gotten there as quickly as they did because of Trey's phone call, then the fire chief might not have smelled the gasoline and it might have been written up as a tragic electrical fire."

Debra rubbed her hand across her forehead, where a small headache was forming. "I don't understand any of this."

"My team checked the house. Other than the window Trey broke to get inside and him unlocking the front door to enable the firemen to enter, there appeared to be no point of entry that wasn't a normal one, which leads me to believe somebody got in using a key. So, my question to you now is who has keys to your house?"

She stared at Thad. A key? Somebody had used a key to get into her home? The misplaced items, the guest list in the freezer... Was it possible somebody had been accessing her house all along? Was it possible she wasn't losing her mind after all, but rather was being made to believe she was going mad?

"Strange things have been happening for the last several weeks," she said. "Cups disappear and reappear in the cabinets, a paperweight on my desk vanished and then two days later was back where it belonged. I thought I was losing my mind. I believed I was going insane."

"Why didn't you say anything before now?" Trey asked in surprise.

"Because I thought it was me. I thought I was doing those things to myself." She slumped back on the sofa, horrified and yet relieved. "Keys, your mom has a key and Haley has one. I imagine several people on staff have a key to my house because occasionally they're sent to pick something up from there."

"What about Barry?" Trey asked.

She looked at him and slowly nodded. "Yes, Barry has a key. He never gave it back to me after we broke up." Her head reeled. Was it possible Barry had known she intended to break up with him and had pulled an end run by breaking up with her before she got a chance? Was it possible he was so angry with her that he could be behind these deadly assaults on her?

At this point she didn't know what to think. "Can I get into the house?"

"You won't want to stay there until some cleanup work is done," Trey replied. "I've got a crew in there now. They should be finished by sometime late this afternoon. I suggest you stay here for tonight and tomorrow you should be able to go back home."

"You'll have a new security system that Trey is having installed. It will alert you if anyone tries to get into a door or window in the house. He's also made sure that all the locks on the doors are being changed. Whoever has a key now will find that it doesn't work if they try to get in again." Thad looked down at the notes he'd taken and then back at her.

"Right now I'm going to see how many house keys I can retrieve from the people you've said have one and each person better hope they have good alibis for the night of the dinner and last night." He rose from the chair. "And on that note I'm out of here and will check in with both of you later."

Debra turned to look at Trey, unsure what to say to make anything better. "I'm sorry about you and Cecily. Hopefully you two can work things out despite everything that's happened. I never meant for any of this to get between the two of you. I hope you told her that I don't expect anything from you."

Trey held up a hand to halt her ramble. "Cecily is fine," he replied. "I told her I needed a break to figure things out, but right now I'm more worried about you than any other relationship. I think you need to take the day and rest. Later tonight if everything is ready and I know that the security is up and working, then, if you want, I can take you home."

"How bad is the damage?"

"Actually less than what I initially thought. The only area that was damaged was around the front windows. Your living room will need a new paint job, but the firemen got enough windows open quickly after putting out the flames that the smoke damage was minimal."

She nodded and stared at the coffee table. "I'm sure we'll have lots of things to discuss and work out in the future, but right now everything just seems too overwhelming."

"Which is why I would encourage you to eat a good

breakfast and then maybe go back to bed for some extra sleep." His voice was tender and filled with a caring that both soothed and somehow hurt at the same time.

He cared about her because of the baby, she reminded herself. As she thought about the car accident and the fire, she only hoped she managed to stay alive long enough to give birth to a healthy full-term baby.

Trey stood in Debra's living room, checking to make sure everything had been done that could be done to clean up the mess and secure her safety. The doorknobs had already been changed out and the security company was finishing up its work.

He'd even had a painting crew come in to Sheetrock and paint the wall that had been damaged. At least the house now smelled of new paint instead of smoke.

His press conference had gone as smoothly as he'd expected it to go. He'd made an announcement that Debra Prentice was carrying his child and while the two had no plans to marry he intended to be a loving, supportive father to his baby and a friend and support to Debra.

Surprisingly, in the world of political news it had made only a small splash. Both he and Debra were single, consenting adults and that fact took any salacious elements out of the situation.

Cecily had even made a statement of support for him, showing her to be a classy lady as she lauded the many good qualities he possessed and the fact that she and Trey had agreed to take their personal relationship one day at a time.

Trey knew she was giving a signal that she would stand by her man. But as much as Trey appreciated her loyalty, after speaking with her and telling her they needed to take a break from each other, he'd felt more relief than he'd expected.

He hadn't realized how much pressure everyone had been subtly putting on him to pop the question, make a formal announcement of an engagement. Now with that pressure off him, he realized whether good or bad for his campaign he wasn't ready to marry Cecily.

All in all, politically he'd weathered the storm, but that didn't mean all was well. There was no question he was frightened for Debra and he'd spent much of the day working names of people around in his mind, as if the guilty person would suddenly appear in his head like a magical vision.

At the moment his suspicions were on Haley, who had jokingly told Debra time and time again that she was after Debra's job.

As he thought of the sequence of events as he knew them it made a strange kind of sick sense. How better to undermine Debra's confidence in her ability to do her job than by gas-lighting her into thinking she was losing her mind?

Maybe the results of that hadn't worked as quickly as she'd hoped. Haley had known that Debra would be at the dinner party and Haley also knew Debra's car.

He didn't believe that Haley had actually crawled under the car herself, but she was young and pretty and probably had a male friend who could do it.

What he'd like to do was grab Haley by the scruff of her neck and force her to tell the truth one way or the other. But Thad had made it clear to Trey that he was to stay away from the investigation because it was now in the hands of the Raleigh Police Department.

Just when Trey had convinced himself that Haley was responsible, he'd change his mind and think about Jerry Cahill. The Secret Service agent had made it clear that he wanted to date Debra, and Debra had made it equally clear to him that she wasn't interested. Cahill would know how to cut brake lines. He probably even had the ability to break into a house and leave no trace behind.

And then there was the possibility of it being somebody not even on Trey's radar. The only thing he knew for certain was that Debra was in danger and he was doing everything he could to assure that her home was secure.

Although as a crime-scene investigator Thad wouldn't specifically be driving any investigation, Trey also knew his brother would make sure that things were being done right and that the people who needed to be interviewed and checked out would be.

Thad might not spend a lot of time with the family, but when anyone was threatened, he was definitely a Winston at heart, ready to jump in and protect them at any moment.

"Hey, thought you might be here."

Trey looked at Sam in surprise as he walked through Debra's front door where a technician from the security company was at work. "What are you doing here?"

Sam shrugged. "I got bored at home, so I figured I'd take a ride and I wound up here. I brought you a present."

He tossed a plastic bag to Trey, who looked inside and laughed as he saw a package of tiny diapers. "Thanks, I think we're going to need a lot of these."

Sam and Trey walked outside into the front yard

and away from the men working in the house. "Do you have any ideas about who was responsible for this?" Sam asked.

"Lots of ideas, but not a real clue," Trey replied.

"What about that guy Debra was dating before?"

"Barry Chambers. Debra insists he wouldn't be involved in anything like this."

"What about Cecily?"

Trey laughed. "Definitely not her style, besides what would be her motive?"

Sam raised an eyebrow. "Uh…you're having a baby with another woman?"

"The things happening to Debra started long before anyone knew that Debra was pregnant. In any case, Thad and the police are involved, so hopefully they'll figure things out."

Sam pointed to the cameras located on each corner of the house and above the front door. "It's going to be easier to break into Fort Knox than this house when you get finished with it."

"That's the idea," Trey told him.

"Why don't you just marry her and put her in that secured mansion you bought?" Sam asked.

"I asked her and she said no."

Sam's eyebrows rose. "That's a surprise. I didn't think anyone had ever told you no," Sam said with a touch of dry humor.

Trey smiled with affection at his brother. Sam's calm moods came so rarely and when they did he remembered how much he loved Sam, how much he wished for better things for the brother who had served his country with honor and come home damaged. "I can't believe I'm going to be a father."

"You'll be good at it," Sam assured him. "I'll tell you one thing, I like Debra a hell of a lot better than I ever liked Cecily."

Trey looked at Sam in surprise. "Why don't you like Cecily?" He'd thought the entire family was happy when he'd started dating the beautiful, wealthy socialite.

Sam scowled. "Cecily has eyes like a shark… Cold and dead. She smiles prettily, but the smiles never quite reach her eyes. She reminds me of…" His voice trailed off and he shook his head. "Never mind," he said, tension in his voice.

"What, Sam? She reminds you of what?"

"Nothing. I've got to get out of here. I just wanted to deliver the baby's first gift to you."

"Sam?" Trey called after his brother as he turned on his heels and headed for his car. Sam didn't look back or acknowledge Trey again. He got into his car and drove off.

Trey couldn't begin to imagine what demons chased his brother since his imprisonment and torture at enemy hands. Apparently he saw something in Cecily's dark eyes that brought back those terrible demons to his head.

He wondered if Sam would feel the same way about Cecily if she had blue or green eyes. He just wished that somehow, someway, his little brother could find some help and ultimately peace in his heart.

He checked his watch. He had a seven-o'clock meeting with Chad to discuss any further ramifications of Debra's pregnancy and Trey's impending fatherhood and how it might affect the campaign going forward.

As far as Trey was concerned, his press conference had addressed the issue and now it would be a nonissue.

He still wanted his dreams of becoming a state senator, but he also wanted to be the best father in the world.

When he'd asked Debra to marry him and she'd turned him down, there was no question that he'd been hurt and that had made him realize he cared about her more than he wanted to admit to himself.

But it was obvious she didn't feel the same way about him. There had been no hesitation when she'd told him no. Her firm reply had left no room to even discuss the matter.

She didn't love him. It was as simple as that. They'd had a night of passion and it was a passion that still simmered inside him, still boiled between them, but ultimately she didn't love him.

And he wasn't sure why that fact ached in his heart. While he cared about Debra deeply, surely he wasn't in love with her?

He thought of how she'd looked the night of the dinner dance, with that spill of emerald-green silk clinging to her curves. Despite her lack of dancing skills, she'd felt so right in his arms.

He remembered how much he enjoyed sitting in her cozy kitchen, talking about anything and everything except politics. He'd felt relaxed and at home. Was it the surroundings or was it the woman herself?

Cecily had seen him as a candidate, as a means to an end—her end. And he'd accepted that as being enough because he knew that ultimately they would make a good team.

But was being a good team enough for him? Why had he so easily accepted a relationship without love? He was fairly certain the answer was in his own childhood, where it was clear his mother and father didn't love one another but had stayed together because of an understanding between them.

He stared back at Debra's house and remembered that hot, sexy moment when they'd almost made love in her foyer. She'd said they couldn't do that anymore, that they couldn't allow themselves to lose control, but that was before he and Cecily had called it quits.

Debra might not love him, but she definitely felt passion for him. Why couldn't they follow through on that again? Every muscle in his body tensed and his blood flowed hot through his veins as he thought of making love to her once more.

He'd like that. He'd like the pleasure of stroking her smooth skin once again, hearing her soft moans of pleasure as he took possession of her.

Now all he had to do was somehow convince her that she wanted him again, too.

Chapter 13

It was Sunday night and Trey was on his way to the estate to take Debra back home. It was almost nine o'clock and while she knew she should be growing tired, she'd already spent most of the day in bed resting.

From what Trey had told her on the phone, he'd spent most of his day making sure her townhouse was ready for her return. She didn't know how she would ever repay him for everything he'd accomplished in such a short amount of time.

She knew he'd probably pulled all kinds of strings to get the place clean and secure in a single day so that she could get back where she belonged.

Maybe she should be afraid to go home since it had only been the night before that somebody had crept into her house and tried to kill her. But Thad was hunting down anyone who might have had a key to her place, new doorknobs and locks had been installed and according to Trey if a squirrel managed to so much as brush against a door or window the police would arrive within minutes.

Besides, she knew that Trey would never allow her to return to a place that wasn't safe, not as long as she carried his baby.

She absently caressed her stomach as she sat in the family sitting room waiting for Trey's arrival. Kate had left earlier for a charity event and Sam had gone to his room. Maddie had retired for the night and the house held an uncharacteristic silence.

It wouldn't be quiet for long. She had a feeling in the weeks and months to come the estate would be a buzz of activity as both Trey and Kate began campaigning in earnest.

Although Kate had yet to make an announcement that she intended to run for president, Debra had a feeling next Sunday's morning breakfast would be her time to hear any concerns that the family might have to say and then she'd let them know that she'd decided to run.

Kate was as much a political animal as her husband before her and now her son. Debra knew she had a steely will and was not just ambitious but truly believed she would be the best choice for the country. Ultimately, Kate would be driven by a sense of duty.

She jumped as Trey suddenly appeared in the doorway.

"You startled me. I didn't hear you come in." She tried not to notice how handsome, how sexy he looked in his jeans and a blue button-up shirt.

"Sorry, I didn't mean to startle you." His gaze was dark and unreadable. "Are you ready to go?"

"I'm definitely ready." She rose from the sofa, feeling strange not to have a suitcase or a purse. But she'd arrived here with nothing but the nightgown she'd been wearing when Trey had pulled her out of the townhouse. She'd thrown the nightgown away, not wanting any memories of the night somebody had gotten inside her home and set a fire in an attempt to kill her.

"I can't believe everything you got accomplished today," she said when they were in her car.

He flashed a smile. "It helps to be a Winston when you want to get things done. People tend to jump through hoops in an effort to please."

"Even on a Sunday?"

"Even on a Sunday," he replied.

She imagined he'd paid extra dollars to get the work done on a Sunday. She wasn't sure she would ever be able to pay him back, but she was determined to do so even if it took years.

"Sam got me a present for the baby," she said. "It's a cute bib that says I Love Mommy." Her heart expanded as she thought of the unexpectedness of the gift.

"He brought me a present for the baby, too. Diapers." Trey laughed. "I guess he figures you get feeding duty and I'm going to get diaper duty."

"It works for me," Debra joked. But of course she knew that separation of baby duties would never work. They'd be living in different homes, leading separate lives. He would be a busy state senator while the child was growing up, but no matter how busy his life would become, Debra knew he'd be a fabulous father.

She knew that if you stripped away the political aspirations, the trappings of the shrewd businessman, what would be left was a caring, giving man. He was a loving grandson to his grandmother, a role model for his younger brothers, and a help and support to his mother.

He had a good sense of humor and a large streak of kindness. That was who Trey Winston was at his very core. And those qualities were what would make him a loving, caring father and what made her love him.

"You know I'd never let you return home if I didn't think it was safe," he said, interrupting her contemplations.

"I know that," she affirmed. "Have you spoken to Thad today about the investigation?"

"Officially the investigation is being headed by Lieutenant Al Chase, but unofficially Thad is working on it as much as he can. He called me about an hour ago and said they had interviewed Barry, who indicated that on the nights of both incidents he was working late with his secretary. Apparently his secretary confirmed his alibis."

Debra released a dry, humorless laugh. "Well, of course she would. They've been sleeping together for years. That's why I wanted out of the relationship with him. He's had a relationship with his secretary, who is married and has kids, since he opened the real estate office."

"From what Thad said, Lieutenant Chase wasn't impressed with the alibi so Barry isn't home free."

Debra frowned thoughtfully. "Barry is a slimeball, but I just can't see him being behind any of this. He has no motive to hurt me."

"He has no motive that you know about," Trey countered. "If there's one thing I've learned in big business and politics, it's that there are some crazy-ass people out there."

"And it's so comforting to think that one of them is after me," she replied.

Trey reached out and placed his palm on her thigh. It wasn't a sexual touch, but rather meant to soothe her. "We're not going to let anyone hurt you, Debra. Thad and the police will be able to figure this out and put the guilty party behind bars." He removed his hand from her leg and returned it to the steering wheel in time to park by the curb in front of her house.

She knew he'd be coming inside. He needed to show her the new security system and how to work it. She gasped in surprise as she walked into the living room. It smelled of new paint and carpet cleaning, of washed walls, and showed no sign of the life-threatening event of the fire.

She shuddered to think of what might have happened if Trey hadn't been parked outside, if he hadn't seen the first flames and jumped into action. Consciously she shoved those thoughts away and continued to look around. The curtains that had hung in the window were gone, but wood-slatted blinds were in their place.

"I didn't want to buy new curtains for you. My mother has always told me all my decorating taste is in my mouth, but I thought the blinds would be fine until you can shop for something else," he said.

"They're perfect," she replied. "Everything looks perfect. I don't know how to thank you. We'll set up some sort of payment plan so that I can pay you back for everything this has cost you."

He waved a hand to dismiss her offer. "I'm not worried about that now. Let me show you how to work the new security system."

As he showed her the monitor next to the front door

and how to switch it to views of different areas from the cameras mounted outside, she tried not to smell his cologne, not to revel in the warmth of his nearness.

"If the alarm goes off, you'll immediately be contacted by the security company. If there is no danger, then you're to answer that everything is fine. If there's somebody with you and you're in danger, then you're supposed to say that everything is okay. Fine is safe. Okay is danger."

Debra nodded, taking in the information that might save her life. "When you enter the house you'll have two minutes to punch in a code that will reset the security behind you. I set up the code and I've got it right here." His gaze held hers intently as he handed her a small piece of paper he pulled from his pocket. "You and I are the only ones who know the code. Don't share it with anyone on staff at the estate or friends or neighbors," he said.

"Trust me, I intend to memorize the number and then I should probably eat this piece of paper to assure nobody finds it," she kidded.

He grinned. "I'm not sure that's necessary."

"After everything I've been through I think it is." She wrapped her arms around herself, suddenly chilled as she thought of everything she'd endured. "Would you like something to drink?" she asked, not sure if she wanted to be alone just yet. "I think I might have some orange juice in the fridge."

"I'll tell you what, why don't you get the juice and I'll build you a nice fire."

"That sounds perfect." He started work on the fire and she went into the kitchen. By the time he had the fire crackling in the fireplace, she had two tall glasses of juice waiting.

"We can take it into the living room," she said.

"Sounds perfect," he agreed. Together they went back into the living room with their glasses and sank down on the sofa.

"What a difference a day makes," she said, and released a pent-up sigh. "I feel like I've ruined things for you."

"You haven't ruined anything, Debra. You've given me a great gift. Your pregnancy will be old news within a couple of days, but for me it's the beginning of a wonderful event that will last the rest of my life."

Debra took a sip of her drink. "I was so afraid, I mean it wasn't exactly like we planned this. I was so worried that if you found out, if anyone found out that the baby was yours, then it would ruin all of the dreams you had for yourself and I didn't want to do that to you."

"As far as I'm concerned nothing has changed my dreams. The only thing you have done is added to the dreams I have for myself."

"But, I totally messed things up between you and Cecily," she replied.

He shrugged. "Cecily and I made a great political team. But I wasn't in love with her and I'm sure she wasn't in love with me. You probably did me a favor, because had we gotten married based on mutual ambition alone, we may have ended up two bitter, unhappy people and in the end that's what I experienced with my own parents. I don't want that for myself."

Debra shook her head in amazement. "You Winstons have always managed to turn any negative into a positive."

"That's because we don't see negatives, we only see opportunities. You're giving me the opportunity to be a dad." His eyes darkened with emotion. "And I didn't realize how badly I wanted that until you told me you were pregnant with my baby."

He turned his head and stared at the fire. "I don't know what the future holds, but I can tell you what I want at this very minute." He turned back to look at her. "I want you to know that I haven't had sex with Cecily since the night you and I spent together and what I want right now is to make love to the mother of my child on that red rug in front of the fire."

Debra paused with her glass halfway to her mouth, stunned by his words and by the heat of desire that pulsed in his eyes, desire that instantly pulsed through her.

Part of the reason she'd stopped their near lovemaking in her foyer was because she knew he was going to marry Cecily, because she didn't want to be that woman who cheated with a man who was already taken.

She'd made that mistake on the night they'd been together, and had refused to make it yet again when they'd almost lost it in her entryway.

She set her glass down, her hand trembling slightly. "I won't be your mistress, Trey. I won't be your baby mama who you occasionally stop by to have sex with. I want better than that. I deserve more than that." She drew a tremulous breath. "But I won't lie. I want you again. I want you tonight and then we're never going to be together intimately again."

One last night with him to remember, she told herself. One final time to be held in his arms, to feel his body against hers. A final chance to love him without inhibition, without restraint, surely after all she'd been through she deserved that.

"Are you sure? I don't want to talk you into doing something you aren't comfortable with."

"The only thing that is making me uncomfortable is how long it's taking you to kiss me," she replied.

He shot across the small space between them on the sofa and wrapped her in his arms as his mouth covered hers in a fiery kiss that stole her breath away. Her heartbeat responded by rapidly fluttering in her chest.

It was almost frightening how easily he could take her from zero to a hundred on the desire scale. Although she would never speak of her love for him aloud, she could show him in her kiss, in the intimacy that was about to follow.

The last time they'd had sex, it had been hot and wild and completely spontaneous. Now she wasn't having sex with him, she was making love with him…for the first and the very last time.

They kissed for some time before he broke the contact and stood. He held out his hand and she took it as he led her to the soft throw rug in front of the fireplace.

He lowered her to the floor as if she were a fine piece of china and then he stretched out next to her and took her in his arms once again.

As their lips met, Debra fought against the wild emotion that rose up in her heart. Love. She felt as if she'd loved Trey Winston forever.

Despite the fact that she knew he loved her because she carried his baby, at the moment it didn't matter what he felt for her. She just wanted to give to him everything her heart had to give. It didn't matter if he couldn't give her back what she wanted from him.

The fire warmed her, but not as much as Trey's mouth plying hers with heat, not as much as the love that burned hot in her soul.

As they continued to kiss, she began to unfasten the buttons of his shirt, wanting, needing to feel his bare, muscled chest, the strength of his naked shoulders.

Once she had his shirt unbuttoned, he threw it off and reached for the bottom of her T-shirt. He pulled it over her head and tossed it across the room and then he drew her against him, their nakedness melded together as her breasts rubbed his naked chest.

His lips once again captured hers and she tried not to think about the fact that after tonight they would both be going cold turkey in their addiction to each other.

It didn't take long before kissing and hugging wasn't enough. He kicked off his shoes and tore off his socks, then shucked his jeans and navy briefs in a hot minute. At the same time she shimmied out of the sweatpants and her panties.

For several sweet moments he hovered just above her, his gaze sweeping the length of her. "You are so beautiful," he whispered.

He was beautiful as well, with the light of the fire illuminating his muscles and emphasizing his handsome features. "Don't talk…. Kiss," she said breathlessly.

He complied, once again slanting his mouth down to hers where their tongues swirled as their bodies fell together like two pieces of a puzzle.

His hands were everywhere, cupping her sensitive breasts, sliding down her stomach, running across her back. It was as if his fingers, his palms hungered for the feel of her skin and she couldn't halt the small moan of pleasure that escaped her.

She, too, loved the feel of his skin and ran her fingers down the length his back and then up to grip his shoulders and then the biceps that were like rocks.

He tore his mouth from hers and trailed kisses down her jawline, into the soft hollow of her throat and then licked one of her nipples, creating an electric current that raced through her from head to toe.

He toyed with first one nipple and then the other and she could feel his turgid manhood against her thigh, letting her know he was fully aroused.

His mouth left her breasts and dragged down to her lower stomach, lingering there as if he were kissing the baby she carried inside. She squeezed her eyes tightly closed as once again emotion welled up from deep inside her.

Love my baby, love me, a little voice whispered in the back of her head. The voice was silenced as his hands slid down her stomach, lightly touched her inner thigh and then caressed the center of her that throbbed with need.

Rational thought left her as she raised her hips to meet the intimate touch, as the build-up of sexual tension climbed higher and higher.

He moved his fingers faster and then slowed as he teased and tormented her. She dug her fingers into the rug on either side of her as his fingers once again worked faster and she gave in to the waves of pleasure that washed over her, leaving her gasping, crying and laughing all at the same time.

"Again," he whispered, his eyes filled with the joy of her pleasure. Once again his fingers found the same spot and began to move…slowly, sensually rubbing and caressing as she struggled to catch her breath.

He seemed to know exactly what she needed, what she wanted and then she was there again, crying out his name as her body shuddered with a second release.

She grabbed his hand to stop him from touching her again. She needed to catch her breath, she wanted to give back to him a little of the sheer pleasure that he'd just given to her.

She sat up and pushed him onto his back, determined that if this was the last time they were going to be together, she would make sure he had as much trouble forgetting it as she would.

He lay perfectly still as she leaned over him and kissed him on the lips. Her kiss was soft and light, just a promise and then she began to trail kisses down the length of his chest and stomach.

Light and teasing, she kissed and licked his skin, loving the taste of him on her tongue, loving the way he groaned her name as she made her way down his lower abdomen.

His body held a tension that she reveled in as his hands tangled in her hair and he once again moaned her name. She licked first one inner thigh and then the other as she took him in her hand. Hard and throbbing, his arousal was magnificent and she loved the fact that it was her he wanted.

"Debra." Her name escaped him in a husky, strangled protest. "I need to be in you now. If you touch me anymore I'll lose it."

"We wouldn't want that," she replied, surprised by the husky want in her own voice.

He sat up and laid her down and she opened herself to receive him as he moved into position on top of her. As he eased into her, his mouth sought hers. The kiss was achingly tender and brought tears to her eyes once again.

Love my baby. Love me.

The words reverberated around in her head as he moved his hips against her in a slow, long stroke and she gasped at the sheer pleasure that soared through her. He broke the kiss and cradled her against his chest as his hips moved faster against her, into her.

She was vaguely aware of the crackling fire nearby, but the real fire was inside her, burning a forever impression onto her heart and into her soul as he took her to the heights of pleasure once again.

He tensed and whispered her name as he found his own release and then collapsed, holding the bulk of his weight off her and onto his elbows on either side of her.

He stared down at her, his features relaxed, yet his eyes dark and fathomless. She had no idea what he was thinking. She wasn't even sure he was thinking.

She only knew that this was a kind of goodbye for her, that she would never compromise herself again with him, no matter how much she loved him, because she loved him.

He finally rolled over to his back beside her. "It was even more amazing than I'd remembered."

She sat up, feeling too naked, too vulnerable as he gazed at her. "It's just sex, Trey, and it's never going to happen between us again."

She got up and pulled a red-and-yellow-striped blanket from the back of her sofa and wrapped it around herself. He sat up and reached for his briefs, as if he, too, suddenly felt too naked.

"We'll be great at co-parenting," she continued.

He finished dressing without saying a word. Had she

made him mad? Had he really thought he could maybe convince her to continue a sexual relationship with him?

She'd be an easy sex fix throughout the stresses of a campaign, a quick drive-by physical relief whenever he stopped by to see the baby.

No way, no how, she thought firmly. She'd compromised herself enough tonight. She'd sworn she'd never settle for a piece of a man's heart instead of the entire thing. She'd determined long ago that when it came to love, for her it was all or nothing.

When he was fully dressed he stepped over to her and pulled her into his arms. She allowed the embrace, even leaned into him, knowing that if nothing else she could always trust him to have her safety and her welfare in his heart.

"I won't let you down, Debra," he said, his voice a whisper against her ear. "Anything you need, at any time, I'm just a phone call away. We're tied for life now through our baby and all I want for you is happiness." He released her and stepped back.

She followed him to the front door, emotion a tight knot in the center of her chest. "I'll see you next Sunday at your mother's place," she said as he reached the door.

He turned back to face her. "I can't say that I'm not sorry we aren't going to be intimate again. I love making love to you, but I have to respect your wishes. Everything is going to work out fine. If nothing else, we'll parent our child and be good friends."

"I'd like that," she replied, but of course it was a lie. At the moment she couldn't imagine loving Trey the way she did and settling for a friendship. Hopefully, eventually she would be able to do just that.

"Then I'll see you Sunday morning."

Her tears began the minute she punched in the code to reset the security after he'd left. Hot and burning, they trekked down her cheeks as her chest grew more and more tight.

She should just go to bed and forget about tonight, forget about Trey Winston. Instead she curled up back on the hearth and wrapped the blanket more firmly around her, chilled despite the warmth of the fire.

She stared into the flickering flames and remembered the gentleness of his kiss on her belly, a kiss she'd believed was meant for the baby growing inside her.

Her child would always have a place in the Winston family. Trey would make sure that his son or daughter was loved and accepted without question.

A sob escaped her, followed by another and another. She curled up on her side on the rug where she could still smell the scent of his cologne and she wept.

She cried because somebody was trying to kill her and she had no idea who or why. Finally she cried because despite what Trey had just said to her, she'd never felt so alone. Everything had changed and she no longer knew where she belonged.

Chapter 14

Trey slept little the night after making love with Debra again. He'd tossed and turned with thoughts rioting in his head, creating a chaos of visions that had made sleep next to impossible.

The week had flown by since then. He'd kept himself busy at work and had given a couple of speeches to local businessmen and at a lunch for the fire department. He'd spoken to Debra on the phone each day, but hadn't gone by the townhouse to see her.

The investigation into both the cutting of her brake lines and the fire in her house had stalled out despite Thad's working hard to find the guilty party in any spare time he had. But there was always another crime scene for him to investigate, always a new mystery to be solved.

Trey had also stayed away from the estate for the

past week. He had no reason to go by there and didn't want to make Debra feel uncomfortable.

It had been a long week for him. He felt as if he was in withdrawal... Debra withdrawal. The idea of never making love with her again was downright depressing. But, he knew it was time to think of her only as the mother of his child, a woman who intended to go on living her life without him in it other than as the father of her firstborn child.

She would probably eventually marry somebody and perhaps have other children. Trey would make sure that whatever man she chose would be a stellar stepfather to his child. This thought also depressed him.

He was ridiculously glad when Sunday morning came and he knew at least he'd see Debra at the breakfast his mother had arranged.

It was a perfect Sunday morning as he left his home to head to the estate. The sun shone brightly and although it was only just before ten the temperature had risen to the mid-sixties as the area enjoyed an unusual streak of mild temperatures that, unfortunately, wasn't going to last. Still, right now it was perfect for breakfast outside by the pool.

He'd chosen a lightweight black-and-gray-patterned sweater with a pair of black jeans for the casual family breakfast that morning.

Hopefully the weather would stay decent through the next weekend, when his mother was the keynote speaker for the chamber of commerce Valentine's Day celebration.

During the past week he'd spoken to his mother several times and knew how she was looking forward to the Valentine Ball, but more importantly to the speech she would be giving at the event.

He had a list of things he wanted to accomplish in the next week that had nothing to do with either Adair Enterprises or his campaign. He wanted to visit his grandmother again. It had already been too long since his last troubling visit with her.

Secrets and lies. He hadn't been able to forget how upset his grandmother had become during his last visit, and he hadn't been completely satisfied by his mother's explanation. Secrets and lies. Hopefully it was just the meaningless ramblings of an old woman whose mind was starting to slip.

He knew things were going to start to go crazy with his schedule in the next weeks and it was important that he get out to the nursing home to see how she was doing. His last visit had been so unsettling, but he hoped his next one would be better, that she'd be better.

He also wanted to find a contractor who could paint one of his bedrooms in yellow with primary colors as trim to sort of match what Debra would be doing in her guest room for a nursery.

He'd use the guest room closest to his master suite and turn it into a baby wonderland. He planned on being a hands-on father in a way his own dad had never been. He loved that baby already and, like Debra, he intended to let the child know that he or she was both wanted and loved.

Buck had been too busy being an important senator and sleeping with other women to be much of a parent to his three sons. Trey wanted to be a better kind of father even though he and Debra wouldn't be together.

And it had been that which had kept him tossing and

turning all night. He was so confused about his feelings toward Debra. He'd somehow hoped that in making love with her one last time his constant, overwhelming desire for her would wane or disappear altogether.

But that hadn't happened. Even now, driving to his mother's home for breakfast as he thought of Debra a fresh wave of physical desire punched him in the gut.

His feelings for her didn't stop with the simple, uncomplicated emotion of physical lust. He wanted her safe from harm, he wanted to say things that caused her eyes to twinkle and laughter to spill from her lips.

He not only wanted to talk to her about his campaign, but he also wanted to share with her his worry about his grandmother. He wanted to confess the fact that he loved to watch old John Wayne movies and he liked his popcorn with extra butter, that some country songs could bring tears to his eyes.

He wanted to tell her that he and his brothers had once played cowboys and he and Sam had tied Thad to a tree so tightly they hadn't been able to untie him. Thankfully a gardener had been working nearby and had used a pair of gardening shears to cut the ropes.

For an hour afterward, Thad had chased them with a big stick, threatening to whip them if he managed to catch them. He tightened his hands on the steering wheel as the happy memory played out in his head.

He had so many memories of home and his brothers. Growing up they had been almost inseparable. But adulthood had brought so many changes. Sam had closed himself off mentally after coming home from overseas and Thad had removed himself both emotionally and physically from the core of the family.

For the first time in his life Trey realized he was

lonely. He was thirty-five years old and had nobody in his life who saw the essence of the man he was at his very core. Everyone only saw the top layer, the successful businessman, the new candidate for senator.

He could be something different with Debra. He thought of the peace of just sitting with her in her kitchen, of how relaxed he felt when it was just the two of them together and he didn't have to put on any kind of a public facade.

Was it possible he was in love with Debra? The thought shot through his head so forcefully, it momentarily took his breath away.

Was this what love felt like? This need to see her face, to make her happy? This desire to keep her safe and see no harm ever came to her? This passion to hold her in his arms, not just while making love but through the night while she slept?

Even if he did love her, it didn't matter. He'd asked her to marry him and she'd told him no. It was obvious she wanted him in a physical sense, but she wasn't in love with him.

Funny that the first thing he would fail at in his life was love. Although he wasn't laughing. He pulled through the side entrance of the estate and as he parked his car it was with an aching heart that felt somehow bruised.

He glanced at his watch as he got out of his car. He was early and from the lack of cars in the side parking area none of his siblings had arrived yet.

He knew that Debra had been invited to attend his mother's breakfast also. With the realization of the depths of his feelings for her, he felt unusually vulnerable.

Somehow, someway, he had to get over it. They had a lifetime of working together as partners to raise their child. He couldn't let unwanted emotions get in the way.

He walked into the kitchen where it was obvious Myra had been busy since early this morning as the fragrances of a variety of foods mingled together to make a heavenly scent.

"Don't you go touching anything in here, Trey Winston," Myra said sternly as she hurried into the kitchen from another area of the house. At her heels was Tiffany Burgess, one of the kitchen helpers.

Trey held his hands up in innocence. "I was just thinking about maybe pouring myself a cup of coffee, that's all."

"Everything is already set up out back by the pool. We just have a few more things to finish up to get the food out there. Now go on with you, coffee is there and your mother should be downstairs anytime now."

He left the kitchen, walking past Debra's and then his mother's office. Just off the foyer was a large ballroom that his mother used when giving charity balls or other such events. It had been a while since she'd used it.

He passed it, as well, and went on to the family sitting room where double doors led out to the pool area. The staff had been busy.

A long glass-top table had been set up with bright turquoise placemats and white plates. Turquoise-and-white-patterned cloth napkins were neatly folded by each place and the silverware gleamed in the sunshine. It looked both inviting and like a signal of the summer to come.

A second table held the beginnings of a buffet. A silver coffeepot and cups took up one end along with a pitcher of orange juice and a tiered serving platter that held a variety of sweet rolls and plump muffins. On the other side of the table hot electric servers awaited food to be placed into their bins.

Trey served himself a cup of coffee and then carried it to a chair away from the table and closer to the pool. In the springtime the beauty of his mother's backyard was breathtaking, with flowerbeds splashing color and a waterfall that spilled over rocks and then disappeared into a large decorative urn.

In the distance a tree line stood outside the black wrought-iron fence. The trees were far enough away that they couldn't be used to help anyone scale the fence, but in the springtime when in full leaf, provided a beautiful green backdrop to the large yard.

Looking around the yard and pool area, Trey made a mental note that it was past time for him to do something about his own property. He'd talk to his mother about her landscaping services and see if he could borrow somebody to tell him what would be best to plant.

It was impossible to miss the men who were stationed at the four corners of the yard. The Secret Service would never allow Kate to sit in her own backyard without them present. He doubted that his mother even thought about their presence anymore. They had been a constant in her life since she'd served as vice president.

He sat up straighter in his chair as Thad walked outside. Clad in a pair of black slacks and a white shirt and jacket, he looked more like a businessman than a cop. But Trey knew the slight bulge beneath his sport coat indicated a shoulder holster and gun.

The two brothers had been on the phone to each other several times a day throughout the week as Trey checked in to see if there had been any new information about the attacks on Debra.

He raised a hand in greeting to Trey and then poured himself a cup of coffee and walked over to where Trey sat. "Don't ask," he said in greeting. "Because if you ask I'll have to tell you we have nothing new."

"You still haven't been able to identify any real person of interest?" Trey asked.

"We have a couple persons of interest, but no evidence to tie them to any of the crimes. Everyone we've spoken to has an alibi that so far we've been unable to break."

"What about Haley?" Trey asked in a low voice, even though he knew the intern wasn't at the house on Sundays.

"We spoke to her. Her alibi for the nights in question was that she was at her place alone." Thad shrugged. "We haven't been able to absolutely place her at home, but we also haven't been able to disprove that she was there. The motive that you've come up with, that somehow she wants to get rid of Debra so that she can have Debra's job is a bit weak."

"It's the only motive I could come up with given that Debra isn't the type of woman who makes enemies."

"I know you've got her all locked down in that townhouse of hers, but she still needs to watch her back when she's out of the house," Thad said. "Since we have no real motive and no real suspects, we can't warn her in advance should something else happen."

Trey nodded, a new little hole ripping in his heart as he thought of something bad happening to Debra. "I'm thinking about talking to Mom about maybe getting her some full-time security. Maybe one of the Secret Service men knows somebody who wants to moonlight and shadow Debra to make sure she stays safe when she's away from home."

"Might not be a bad idea," Thad agreed. "At least until we can get a break on the case." He took a sip of his coffee and eyed Trey with open speculation. "Why do you want to run for the Senate?" he asked.

Trey looked at him in surprise. "Because I think I can make a real difference for the state of North Carolina, because I see problems and issues that I believe I can help to fix. Why?"

Thad raked a hand through his hair and released a deep sigh. "I just feel like politics is what screwed up our whole family life and I can't imagine why you'd want to put yourself out there like that."

"Thad, I know you love what you do. I know you feel a true calling in your work. That's the way I feel about politics. That's the way mom feels about politics. It's not just a job—it's a true calling, a real passion and a need and desire to make things better in the world."

At that moment Debra stepped outside. Clad in a pair of leg-hugging jeans and a blue-and-green-patterned sweater, she looked more beautiful than ever.

She paused just outside the door and offered a smile to the two brothers. It was at that moment, with her hair gleaming in the sunshine and her smile warming him from head to toe that Trey knew without a doubt that he was madly in love with Debra Prentice.

That crazy anxious jangle of nerves accompanied an acceleration of her heartbeat at the sight of Trey. She turned and poured herself a glass of orange juice, grateful that at least her hands remained steady.

She had to get used to seeing him and not loving him. She had to transform her love to a friendship for the sake of their baby. She had to figure out how to stop being in love with him and just love him as the father of her child.

"Good morning," she said as she carried her cup to where the two men were located near the pool.

"Back at you," Thad said with a smile.

At least he was here to serve as buffer, she thought as Trey murmured a greeting, his blue eyes far too intense as his gaze remained on her.

Was he thinking about their last moments together, a flickering fire, a red throw rug and desire spiraled out of control? Certainly she'd been thinking about it since then, every single day for the last week.

But, she refused to think about it now. It was done. They were finished, and this morning's breakfast was all about Kate. "Where is the lady of the hour?" she asked.

"She hasn't made an appearance yet," Thad replied.

"Neither has Sam," Trey added.

They all turned to look as Myra and Tiffany came back outside, each carrying metal baking pans that they placed in the awaiting electric warmer.

"Your mother and Sam should be out here any minute," Myra said as she and Tiffany disappeared back into the house.

"I have a fairly good idea that I'm not going to like what I hear here this morning," Thad said.

"I'm sure you're probably right," Trey agreed.

Debra sipped her orange juice, wishing Sam and Kate would come outside so things could get underway and she could get back home.

She wasn't even sure why Kate had included her in this family gathering. It wasn't like Debra was really a part of the family.

Sam was the next one outside and once he'd joined them with a cup of coffee in hand, he pointed to the glass of juice Debra held.

"I'm glad my niece or nephew is getting a dose of vitamin C this morning instead of a cup of caffeine," he said.

The shadows that always darkened his blue eyes were gone for now and Debra was grateful that he appeared to be in a fairly good mood. Hopefully nothing that occurred during the breakfast would bring the terrible darkness back into his eyes.

"What are you all doing over there when I have this lovely table set beautifully for everyone?" Kate's voice pulled everyone's attention toward her as she stepped out of the back doors and onto the patio.

"We were making plans to overthrow the monarchy," Thad said with a wicked grin.

Kate laughed. "I know Debra isn't a part of such a plan and it would take far more than three big men to get the job done right."

She looked stunning in a pair of tailored black slacks and a red blouse with a black cardigan sweater flung over her shoulders. "Come on, come on. Let's fill our plates and get this party started."

It took some time for all of them to serve themselves and then get seated. Debra was grateful to find herself across the table from Trey rather than seated next to him. Instead she sat next to Thad with Sam across the table next to Trey, and Kate at the head of the table.

The conversation remained light and easy as they ate.

Debra was pleased to discover that it was late enough in the day that the food tasted delicious and she suffered no nausea or belly rolling.

As the conversation turned to the brothers' childhood, stories began to roll out that had Debra both relaxing and laughing. The stories of brotherly antics and love also made her realize how much she'd missed out on by being the only child of an alcoholic mother.

She also realized that she didn't want her baby to be an only child. Siblings weren't just brothers and sisters; they were also friends and support systems for lifetimes.

But she couldn't be sure what the future held. Right now she just wanted to have a healthy pregnancy and baby, deal with the co-parenting issues with Trey and figure out what the next step in her personal life might be.

The breakfast talk went from old memories to the mildness of the weather and finally to Kate's upcoming speech for the chamber of commerce event the following Saturday night on Valentine's Day.

It seemed ironic to Debra that she was pregnant and yet had nobody to send her flowers or chocolates for the special lovers' day. But she'd never gotten flowers or anything from a man on Valentine's Day.

Barry had been one of few men she had dated in her lifetime and they hadn't even known each other last Valentine's Day.

Throughout the meal she was acutely conscious of Trey's gaze lingering on her. Dark and unreadable, something about his unwavering attention made her uncomfortable.

What was he thinking? Was it possible that he might fight her for full custody when the baby was born? Certainly with the Winston power, influence and money, it would be a battle she'd lose.

Her hand fell to her stomach, as if to somehow protect her baby from such a confrontation. Surely that couldn't be what he was thinking. They'd spoken about co-parenting. But what might happen when he married? Once he had a wife, might not he want his child to live with them full-time?

Stop borrowing trouble, she reprimanded herself. Without a magical crystal ball there was no way to see what the future might hold, and she'd just have to deal with everything one day at a time from here on out.

She definitely didn't want to think about the fact that the investigations into the attacks on her had yielded nothing. At least with her new security in the townhouse she felt completely safe when she was there.

It wasn't until they had all finished eating, their plates had been removed and their coffee and juice refilled that Kate raised a hand to get everyone's attention.

"I'm sure you're all wondering why I asked you to come here for breakfast this morning," she began.

"Not really," Thad muttered under his breath.

"Before I make my final decision about what my future is going to hold, I wanted to give you all a chance to talk about your concerns," she said.

Debra stared over Trey's shoulder to the distant tree line, knowing that she didn't have a pony in this show. Kate needed to hear from her sons, not from one of her son's baby mama. Besides, Kate already knew that Debra was up for whatever she decided.

"I'm considering announcing formally my decision to run for president of the United States next Saturday night at the chamber of commerce event." She looked at her sons expectantly.

Debra focused her attention back to the table. "You know I'll support that decision," Trey said.

"You're going to do what you want to do anyway," Sam added, his voice holding resignation.

Thad frowned. "I just don't understand why you'd want to do this given what politics has done to our family in the past."

"If you're talking about when you were young and your father was a senator, the only thing I can tell you is that our family fell apart because of your father's bad choices, not because he was in the Senate," Kate replied.

"You should have left the bastard," Sam said, his eyes taking on the darkness that they held far too often.

"I did what I needed to do to keep the family together," Kate replied with a steely note. "Things weren't so terrible for all of you when I served as vice president and as an ambassador."

"That's because nobody ever cares that much about the vice president," Thad said. "But as President of the United States every move you make will be in the spotlight and a lot of that spotlight is going to bleed over onto us." He raked a hand through his shaggy brown hair. "But I guess we can all handle that if this is what you really want."

"Sam?" Kate looked at her middle child with affection.

He shrugged. "I know you want to do this and I'm not going to be the one who stops you from pursuing what you want."

"So I have tentative blessings from everyone?" Kate asked.

"I think you can say that you have complete blessings from everyone," Trey replied.

Kate turned and motioned to Myra, who stood just inside the door and held a silver tray with flutes of champagne. "Then this calls for a celebratory toast."

Thad laughed dryly. "You've already got the champagne poured. You weren't worried a bit about getting our blessings."

Kate beamed a smile around the table as Myra stepped outside. "I knew my boys would only want my happiness and this is something I feel destined to do."

Myra went around the table, handing each of them a glass of champagne. "No bubbly for you," she said when she got to Debra. "You have a flute of nice white grape juice."

"Thank you, Myra," Debra said as she accepted the delicate, thin glass.

Kate stood and held up her glass. "Bear with me, I have a rather long toast to make."

Debra smiled inwardly as she saw all three of her sons roll their eyes, as if they were accustomed to "bearing with" their strong, assertive mother.

The rest of them remained seated, giving Kate her moment to shine even at a family breakfast.

"First of all to Debra, who will forever be a part of this family and hopefully continue to play an important role in my professional life as well as my personal one." Kate smiled at Debra and then looked at Sam.

"To my middle son, Sam. You awe me with your bravery, with your honor and duty you showed by serving your country. I only pray that your heart and soul eventually heal as your body does. I love you, Sam."

Debra felt herself getting a bit teary as Kate honored each of her children.

"Thaddeus," Kate continued. "I'm so proud of the life you've made for yourself as a part of law enforcement. You honor the family name with your work as a public servant. I love you, Thad."

She turned her attention to Trey. "And to my first-born, who has not only driven the family business to new heights, but is also about to discover the insane world of politics and parenthood. I love you, Trey, and wish only good things for my boys in the future."

She raised her glass. "Cheers."

"Gun!" Thad suddenly screamed and pointed to the trees in the distance.

And then the world exploded.

Chapter 15

A thousand things occurred almost simultaneously, creating wild chaos. A shot sounded. The glass table shattered, cups and glasses crashing to the ground. Trey dove across the broken table to reach Debra who sat in her chair stunned.

He scrambled to her, yanked her from the chair and pulled her to the ground. Sam grabbed his mother's hand and pulled her down also as Thad and half a dozen Secret Service men raced in all directions. Thad and a couple of men ran to the side entrance gate and out of the backyard.

Two other agents rushed to stand next to the shattered table, their backs to each other and their weapons drawn as they protected everyone on the ground. Several more agents raced to the back of the yard, their guns pointed up at the tree where the shooter was no longer visible.

"Are you okay?" Trey asked as he covered Debra's body with his on the hard concrete near the pool.

Around them chaos continued to reign as men yelled to each other and another gunshot split the air. Trey could feel the frantic beat of Debra's heart against his own.

Her breath came in gasps of terror against his collarbone and his brain worked to try to make sense of what had just happened, what was still happening. "Yes," she replied, her voice small and scared.

There was no question that somebody had been in those trees, that Thad had spied what apparently had been a man with a gun. The gun had been fired, shattering the table, but had the bullet been meant for his mother or for Debra?

His body shuddered at the thought of either woman being shot. He looked over at Sam, who had their mother down against the concrete, a look of anguish on his face.

Trey knew his brother was probably wishing he had his weapon on him, but Sam had been deemed unfit for duty and all of his weapons had been taken from him by the army brass who had released him.

Trey's body jerked as another gunshot exploded and then Thad's voice rose in the distance. It had a triumphant tone and Trey felt the muscles in his body begin to relax a bit.

One of the Secret Service men standing near them talked into his radio, listened a moment and then turned to face everyone on the ground. "They've got the shooter in custody."

The two agents remained on guard as both Trey and Sam rose and helped Debra and Kate to their feet. It was only as he saw Debra's terror-filled eyes that he recognized the bottomless depth of his love for her.

He pulled her to him and she willingly huddled in the secure embrace of his arms. Love. It flowed through him, unmistakable and undeniable. But he didn't know what to do about it, knew there was nothing to be done about it.

"Well, that's the way to end a toast with a bang," Kate said in a slightly shaky voice as Sam helped her to her feet.

"We'd like all of you to move as quickly as possible into the house," Secret Service Agent Daniel Henderson said as he took Kate by the arm. "It's for your own safety. We don't know who else might be out here somewhere."

As Daniel ushered Kate back into the house, Trey did the same with Debra, still unsure who the ultimate target had been. They all took seats in the sitting room and waited, the silence in the room growing more and more tense with each minute that passed.

Had there been more than one shooter? Had this been some sort of an organized attack? Trey's mind raced to make sense of what had just occurred.

Thad, Jerry Cahill and Robert D'Angelis appeared at the back door. Between Thad and Robert was a thin man in scruffy jeans and a black jacket. His hands were cuffed behind him and Robert held a high-powered rifle with a scope in his hand.

"Ms. Winston, do you know this person?"

Trey stared at the man. He was small and slender and wore a black sweatshirt and jeans. His eyes were dark and a smirk formed on his thin lips as if everyone else was in handcuffs and he was free.

Sam lunged toward him. "Who are you and why were you shooting at my mother?" he yelled. Kate stopped him from advancing by grabbing his arm.

"I don't have to talk to you," the man said with a scowl. "I don't have to talk to any of you. I know my rights. Besides, if I don't talk then I get some time in prison. If I do talk then I get a bullet to the back of my head. It's a no-brainer. I don't have nothing to say to nobody."

"I've never seen him before in my life," Kate finally said.

"Get him out of here," Sam growled. "Get him the hell out of here."

Thad and Cahill took the man back out the door where Trey assumed he'd be handed over to Secret Service agents and other authorities to deal with.

Sam turned his wrath on Daniel Henderson and Robert D'Angelis. "How in the hell did this happen? How did that little creep manage to get up in a tree with a rifle without any of the agents noticing? I want to know who didn't do their job."

"I don't know how this happened, but I promise you by the end of the day we'll have some answers," Robert replied, his gray eyes cold and narrowed. "Now if you'll excuse me, I'll go find out as much information as I can right now."

He headed through the house, toward the kitchen and the side door that would bring him out by the guesthouse where the security operations and agents worked from.

Trey turned to look at Debra, who stood beside him, frozen like a deer in headlights. It was only then that he saw a trickle of blood seeping from her hairline down the side of her face.

His heartbeat spiked as he grabbed her by the arm. Had one of the bullets grazed her? "Debra, you're hurt," he said. Had a piece of shattered glass from the table ricocheted to her?

"What?" She looked at him with blank eyes.

"Your head… You're bleeding." He dropped his hand from her arm.

She raised a hand up and touched the area and then stared at the blood on her hand and then back at him. "It must be glass from the table."

"We need to get you cleaned up," Kate said briskly, back in control despite the horror of what had just happened.

Somewhere in the back of his mind Trey knew it was this very trait, the ability to function with a cool head in a crisis, that would benefit the country if Kate was elected.

"Maddie," Kate turned to the housekeeper who hovered in the doorway. "Take Debra into one of the bathrooms and clean up her face and check to make sure she doesn't have any glass in her hair or on her clothes. I'm going upstairs where Birdie can help me do the same thing. Sam and Trey, you both need to make sure there isn't any glass in your clothing or hair."

"Come on, honey," Maddie said to Debra as she walked across the room and gently took Debra's hand in hers. "Let's go get you all cleaned up."

The two women left the sitting room and Kate turned to Daniel Henderson, the last agent left in the room. "You can go, Daniel. We're good now. Just please keep me informed of anything you hear about the investigation into what just happened."

Daniel gave Kate a stiff half bow. "You know I'll do whatever I can to get to the bottom of this, but I imagine by now all kinds of agencies will be moving in to take over the investigation. Of course the Secret Service will be doing most of the work."

"Just keep me informed." Kate headed out of the sitting room while Daniel left by the back doors.

Sam remained in place, his hands in fists at his sides and angry frustration evident in every muscle in his body. "I should have seen that guy in the tree. I should have been paying more attention. I was trained to watch out for snipers."

"Cut yourself a break, Sam," Trey replied. "You weren't trained to look for snipers in our backyard at a breakfast. But I'd like to know who hired that guy. From what he said he was definitely a hired gun."

Sam's hands relaxed. "Either that or he was just a thug trying to make a name for himself and he just added in that bit about a bullet to the head business to make us believe he was nothing more than a hired gun."

Sam threw himself into one of the nearby chairs. "Hell, she hasn't even formally declared yet and already somebody is trying to kill her."

"At this point we can't be sure exactly who the target was," Trey replied, also sitting down in a chair near Sam.

"Who else would the target be?" Sam asked, looking at Trey as if he'd lost his mind.

"Maybe rumor had gotten out that you've been a real cranky ass to live with and Mom actually hired that man to put you out of your own misery," Trey said with a teasing tone.

"Ha ha, very funny," Sam replied.

"Okay, then Thad could have been the target because of his police work, or me because I've declared my intentions to run for senator." He paused a moment, his chest burning with anxiety. "Or the target could have been Debra. She's already been targeted by somebody twice. Maybe this was a final attempt to get rid of her."

Sam drew a deep breath and fell back into the chair. "What a mess."

"I suggest we both do what Mom said and head into bathrooms to check ourselves for glass," Trey replied.

Definitely a mess, Trey thought as he went in one direction and Sam disappeared in another. Somebody had just missed being shot and even though they had the shooter in custody Trey wasn't feeling optimistic that any agency would be able to get any real information out of the creep.

Was it possible that this would make his mother change her mind about running for president? Somehow Trey believed that if anything this would make her more resolute to follow through on her plans.

Trey knew that beneath Kate's pleasant exterior beat the heart of a warrior and a will of steel. She knew the dangers the office held and he had a feeling she would still be just as determined to make a run for the White House.

What he needed to do was talk to Thad and bring up the fact that it was possible the target wasn't Kate at all, but rather Debra.

Debra.

His heart filled with the newly realized love he felt

for her. Yes, everything was a mess. A man had just shot to kill somebody seated at the table and he was in love with a woman who apparently didn't love him back, a woman who might have been the intended victim of the shooting.

Debra sat on the toilet lid as Maddie used tweezers to pick pieces of glass from her hair and off her sweater. Maddie had already cleaned the blood off her face and Debra had sat like a child being ministered to by a loving mother.

She knew that she was in a little bit of shock because everything felt surreal. Her heart had finally found a normal rhythm after having beat nearly right out of her chest.

Everything that had happened to her—the mad drive in the middle of the night with no brakes, the fire that had occurred in her house—both seemed like mere nuisances when compared to what had just happened.

Somebody had shot a gun with the intent to kill. It was only by chance that Thad had seen the man in the tree and his warning shout had apparently made the gunman lose his aim.

Who had he been aiming at?

Who had been his target?

The logical answer would be Kate, but Debra couldn't stop the idea that kept coming back into her head, the idea that the target had been her. A shiver worked through her.

"Are you cold?" Maddie asked with concern. "Would you like a blanket or something around your shoulders while I finish up?"

"No, I'm fine. I'm just suffering from a little bit of

post-traumatic stress. I don't think I've ever been quite so frightened."

"You just need to relax now. You're safe and at least they caught the man. Besides, it's not good for your baby for you to be so stressed out."

Debra nearly laughed. Her baby wouldn't know how to exist without stress. Debra had been mentally frazzled since the moment she'd taken those three pregnancy tests. God, that felt like years ago. So much had happened in the past four weeks.

The thought that she was losing her mind, the crash of her car, the fire in her house... The only good thing that had happened was that since the new security system had been installed nothing in her home had disappeared only to reappear later.

Still, the idea that somebody had enjoyed free access to her home to try to drive her crazy and then had moved to more deadly means of getting rid of her would haunt her until somebody had been caught and jailed for the offenses.

"There, I think we got them all," Maddie said as she stepped back from Debra. On the vanity counter on a paper towel were about a dozen slivers of glass in various sizes.

Maddie took Debra's chin and raised her face so that she could look into Debra's eyes. "Are you sure you're okay, honey? Maybe a nice hot cup of tea would help calm you down a bit."

"That sounds wonderful," Debra agreed as she got up from her sitting position. "And thank you, Maddie, for taking such good care of me."

Maddie smiled. "That's what I do. I take care of

Winstons." She swept up the paper with the glass in her hands and then left the bathroom.

But I'm not a Winston, Debra thought as she stared at her reflection in the mirror over the sink. She looked shell-shocked, her hair a mess, her eyes too big and still filled with the terror that had momentarily made it impossible to move away from the shattered table.

Trey had virtually thrown himself across what was left of the table to get to her and pulled her to the ground where he'd covered her body with his, protecting her from harm.

No, not her, but their baby. He'd been protecting his baby from harm. She just happened to be carrying that baby. She left the bathroom, unsure if she wanted the cup of tea or not.

What she really wanted was to be at the townhouse, safe within the walls of her highly secured home. What she wanted was to know who was behind the attacks on her, who was responsible for wanting her to believe that she was going crazy.

Trey met her in the hall, his eyes dark and his expression radiating concern. "Are you sure you're okay?" he asked.

She nodded. "It was just a small cut. Maddie got it to stop bleeding and I'm perfectly fine." She raised a hand to tuck her hair behind her ear and knew the tremble of her hand belied her words.

"Okay, so I'm not so fine," she admitted. "I'm definitely shaken up and Maddie is making me a cup of tea to calm my nerves."

"Then let's go to the kitchen and have a cup of tea." He took her by the elbow, his touch gentle and warm.

They entered the huge kitchen and went directly to

the small table where Sam often sat to have his morning coffee.

"Just in time. Maddie told me you would be in for a nice cup of tea," Myra said, and set a cup in front of Debra. "Do you want sugar? Lemon? And do you want a cup, too, Trey?"

"No, thanks, I'm good."

"And this is fine for me. Thanks, Myra." Debra wrapped her hands around the heat of the cup in an attempt to warm the cold places that had found a home inside her during the past thirty minutes.

For a few moments she and Trey sat in silence. Debra sipped her tea and looked out the window where a number of security agents were gathered in front of the guesthouse.

Somebody's head would roll for the breach in security, she thought. "I wouldn't want to be the agent in charge of security for that quadrant of the yard."

Trey followed her gaze and then looked back at her. "Somebody will figure it out. I just thank God that Thad saw the guy before he managed to hurt somebody."

Debra took a sip of her tea and then returned the cup to the saucer. "You know it's possible it wasn't about your mother."

He held her gaze and in the depths of his troubled eyes she realized the thought had already crossed his mind. "We can't jump the gun. We don't know who the target was supposed to be right now."

"But you understand that given everything that has happened to this point in time, it's very possible I was the target." Just saying the words out loud leeched any warmth she might have gained back out of her body.

She shoved the cup of tea aside. "What I'd really like

to do right now is go home." Tears burned at her eyes and blurred her vision as she stared down at the table. "I just want to go home," she repeated softly.

"Then I'll take you home." Trey stood and touched her shoulder.

"But my car is here."

"Debra, I'd feel better under the circumstances if I drive you home. You're still upset and I can always bring you back here for work in the morning and you'll have your car here to drive home tomorrow night."

She nodded and stood. She was grateful that he was taking charge, that she didn't have to drive herself. Sometimes it was better to allow somebody else to take care of things and this was definitely one of those times. She'd been taking care of herself for her entire life and just for a little while she wanted to abdicate control.

They were escorted to Trey's car by two agents with guns drawn and gazes narrowed and focused on their surroundings. Debra felt as if she had entered an action film set. Surreal. How had her life gotten so dramatic, so intense?

She breathed a sigh of relief as Trey pulled out of the driveway and away from the estate. "I have to say, Kate sure knows how to put on an exciting breakfast."

"Let's hope we never have one as exciting as this one again," Trey replied. "The shooter, you didn't recognize him, did you?"

"No, I'm fairly sure I've never seen him before in my life, but that doesn't mean he wasn't hired by somebody to kill me." The words created an almost physical pain inside her. The idea that somebody hated her so much was unbelievable.

"Keep in mind that we don't know that this attack was about you," Trey said.

"I understand that. I get that your mother might have political enemies, but we both know I have an enemy, too, and maybe that person has given up trying to kill me and make it look like an accident."

"Thad will be checking it out along with the Secret Service," he replied. "I intend to talk to Thad about the fact that this might have been an attempt on you and not on Mom."

Debra stared out the side window. "It just all feels so horrible, to know that there's somebody out there who wants me dead. I've never done anything to anyone. I've never harmed anyone. Who could have such hatred for me?"

"I wish I knew, Debra."

They were silent for the remainder of the ride and she was grateful for the quiet. She still was trying to process what had happened, how quickly a lovely family toast could have turned into a complete and utter tragedy.

When Trey pulled up to the curb in front of her townhouse, he shut off the engine and then turned to look at her. "Stay put," he said.

She watched as he got out of the driver side and then came around to her side of the car and opened her door. He instantly pulled her out of the seat and surrounded her with his own body.

Awkwardly they made their way to the front door, him like a shield wrapped around her back. She was tense, expecting a gunshot at any moment or a knife-wielding maniac to jump out of the bushes nearby.

She didn't relax until they were safely inside the house with the security on. She collapsed onto the sofa and Trey sank down next to her. It only took a simple touch from him and she was in his arms, crying out the stress and fear as he held her tight and murmured words of comfort.

Her crying jag lasted only a couple of minutes and then she sat up and wiped the tears from her face. "I'm okay now. I just needed to get that out."

He smiled at her. "My mother always said that a good cry never hurt anyone." He leaned back against the sofa cushion. "So I guess there's no Sunday specialty cooking planned for today."

"I'm thinking dinner is going to be something nice and easy," she replied.

"Maybe you should put something in your stomach now," he suggested. "I noticed you didn't eat much earlier."

It was obvious he was in no hurry to leave and she wasn't sure she wanted him to go just yet. Nerves still jangled through her and the horror of the morning lingered.

"A bowl of soup might be good," she replied. She pulled herself up from the sofa and he followed suit.

"Why don't you just go into the kitchen and sit at the table and I can handle the soup," he said.

She thought about protesting, but instead merely nodded. "Thank you, I appreciate it. I'm still feeling just a little bit shaky."

Together they went into the kitchen where Debra took a seat at the table and Trey moved to the pantry where she stored her canned goods.

"I see chicken noodle, tomato and split pea." He looked back at her and made a face. "You don't really eat that split-pea stuff, do you?"

She laughed, unable to help herself at his look of utter disgust. "Actually I do and I love it. But I think a bowl of chicken noodle will be just fine, and open two cans if you'd like some, too."

"Maybe I'll just do that," he replied as he grabbed a saucepan from the baker's rack.

"Wouldn't you rather be back at the estate checking on the investigation instead of here babysitting me?" she asked, suddenly feeling guilty for taking up his time.

"The Secret Service will take over any investigation so there's really nothing I can do there. Thad will have his nose in things and will let me know of any breaking news."

He paused to use the can opener and poured the contents of the two soup cans into the saucepan. "Besides, I can't think of anyplace else I'd rather be right now than here with you eating canned soup."

He placed the saucepan on a stove burner and turned it on and then dug into her silverware drawer for a big spoon. She stared out the window and wished he wouldn't say things like that to her. He shouldn't be so nice to her. He made her want more than what he'd ever be able to offer to her.

She shouldn't have even let him come inside. This whole scene was a little too domestic for her taste. It brought up the yearning for it to be real, for them to be together as a true couple.

As he stirred the soup, Debra found her gaze wandering around the room, looking everywhere but at him. It was bad enough that she could smell his familiar cologne, a scent she thought she'd never get out of her mind.

She frowned as she spied something under the edge

of one of her lower cabinets. Had she dropped something that had rolled there? She couldn't imagine what it was, but it appeared to hold a touch of sparkle.

"What are you doing?" he asked as she got up from her chair.

"There's something here on the floor under the cabinet." She bent down and grabbed it, then stood and opened her hand. It was an earring. A diamond and ruby earring that she'd never seen before in her life.

"What is it?"

"It's an earring, but it isn't mine." She looked at him in confusion.

Trey stepped away from the stove to see what she held. His face paled and he stumbled backward a step.

"Trey? What's wrong?" Debra's heart began to pound as she saw the odd look on his face as he stared at the piece of jewelry.

"I know that earring. I bought a pair of them for Cecily."

Debra frowned. "How would one of Cecily's earrings get into my kitchen?" She gasped in stunned surprise as the realization of who was behind the attacks on her became apparent by the piece of expensive jewelry she held in her hand.

Chapter 16

Trey stared at Debra for a long moment, trying to make sense of the earring she held in her hand. They were an unusual design and unmistakable. He specifically remembered purchasing them five months before and surprising Cecily with them over dinner at La Palace. Since that time she had worn them often.

Had she worn them when she'd set the fire in this house? Had they adorned her ears when she'd been moving cups and shifting around items to make Debra doubt her own sanity?

Cecily?

His mind boggled with the irrefutable evidence that she'd been inside Debra's home. Cecily had been behind everything. He couldn't seem to wrap his mind around it.

"I understand if she was angry when she found out

I was pregnant with your child, but most of the terrible things that happened occurred before anyone knew I was pregnant by you," Debra said thoughtfully. "Why would she try to hurt me when she didn't know anything about us?"

"I need to call Thad," Trey said as he fumbled his phone out of his pocket. "If she's responsible for everything that's happened to you then she needs to be arrested and charged."

As he punched in the number to connect him with his brother, Debra moved the saucepan and turned off the stove. "Thad." He was surprised that his voice shook with tension as he heard his brother answer the phone. "Can you get over to Debra's townhouse? I think we've found the source of the attacks on her."

With Thad's assurance that he'd be right over, Trey sank down at the table, still stunned by this new development. Debra sat down next to him, the earring on the table between them.

"I'm sorry, Trey," she said softly.

He looked at her incredulously. "Why are you sorry?"

"Because I know you cared about her, that you had intended to make her your wife. I'm sorry because I know that if what we believe is true you have to be hurting."

"Hurting?" He stood and slammed his hands down on the table. "I'm so angry right now she's lucky she isn't here in front of me. I knew she had a cold streak inside her, but I had no idea the evil that she has to possess to do what she's apparently done."

"She must have known about that night we spent together," Debra said.

Trey drew a deep breath and once again sat down

at the table. "I don't see how she could have known. I certainly never said anything about it to anyone and I'm sure you didn't, either. It was spontaneous, neither of us planned for it to happen. How could she have known about it?"

He closed his eyes, trying to recreate that night in his mind. He'd called Cecily and had invited her to join him in his celebration, but she'd been at a charity event and had told him she really couldn't get away.

Was it possible she had decided to show up at the restaurant anyway? Had she seen him and Debra and watched them as they left together to get the room in the nearby hotel?

Why hadn't she confronted him at the time? Why hadn't she told him that she knew about his tryst with Debra?

The doorbell rang and Trey got up, indicating that Debra should stay seated while he let his brother in. "I figured you'd be tied up with the shooting at the house," he said as Thad stepped inside.

"Right now the Secret Service is in charge of the crime scene and investigation, but if they think I'm going to leave it to them, then they don't know me," Thad said grimly. "So what's this about you believing you know who is behind the attacks on Debra?"

"Come on into the kitchen," Trey said. As Thad followed him Trey realized the stunned surprise he'd initially felt had transformed into a cold hard knot of anger in his chest.

Cecily had tried to kill the woman he loved, the woman who carried his baby. He'd sat across the table from her a hundred times at special events and in restaurants. He'd held her in his arms and gazed into her eyes and considered a future with her and yet he'd never seen the evil that had to dwell inside her.

As he and his brother entered the kitchen, the sight of Debra seated at the table made him realize just how superficial his feelings had been for Cecily.

The woman he truly loved sat in the chair with big green eyes and a touch of worry on her face. Debra might not love him, but he knew without a doubt she cared about the man he was, not the man he might someday become.

It took only minutes for Trey to explain about the earring that Debra had found beneath the lower cabinet. Thad immediately called Lieutenant Al Chase, who agreed to meet them at Debra's house and then Thad placed the earring inside a small plastic bag and joined them at the table as they waited for Al to arrive.

"I have no idea how she might have gotten a key to my house," Debra said.

Thad gave her a rueful smile. "I've got news for you, Debra. There are key rings all over the estate that somebody could have plucked up and brought to your house, found the appropriate key, had a copy of it made and then returned the original to the key ring."

"And she could have hired some thug to crawl beneath my car on the night of the dinner and cut my brake lines." Debra shook her head as she stared at the earring encased in plastic on her table. "She smiled at me that night, thanked me for everything I'd done for Trey. She was so nice and all the while she'd plotted my death."

Trey reached across and covered one of Debra's hands with his. "It will be over soon," he said. If Thad hadn't been present he would have told Debra what was in his heart, that obviously Cecily had seen her as a threat because somehow Cecily had known Trey was deeply in love with Debra.

"It's definitely possible that sniper in the tree this morning had nothing to do with Mom, but was somebody Cecily hired to kill Debra," he said instead.

Thad frowned thoughtfully. "That would definitely be nice for the Secret Service who are not only investigating but pointing fingers at each other as to who was responsible for that area."

At that moment the doorbell rang again and Lieutenant Chase arrived. Once again Trey told the story of the earring and everything he now suspected Cecily of being responsible for, including the possibility of her being behind the shooting that morning at the estate.

"Sounds to me like we need to speak to Cecily," Al said. "Do you know if she's home?"

Trey pulled his cell phone from his pocket. "I can find out." He punched the number he'd dialed a hundred times before and when she answered he was pleased that his voice betrayed none of the rage that had built up inside him with each moment that passed.

"Cecily, it's me," he said when she answered.

"Trey!" She was obviously surprised.

"I was wondering if you were going to be around for a little while this morning. There's something I'd like to talk to you about."

"Yes, certainly I'll be here. What time do you want to come by?"

"Right now."

"Oh, okay. I'll be waiting for you."

He could tell by the slight purr in her voice that she was expecting a reconciliation.

He was looking for reconciliation, too. He hoped that

by the time they finished talking to her they would finally have the answers as to who had been behind the attacks on Debra.

And once he knew she was safe, despite the intense love he felt for her, it would be time for him to give her the space to go on with her life, a life that would include him only as the father of their child, not as the husband, the lover, the life mate he wished he could be.

Debra knew that neither Al nor Thad were particularly happy that she had insisted she go with them to Cecily's house, but she wanted to be there, she wanted to look into Cecily's eyes as she attempted to deny what Debra knew in her heart she had tried to do.

Trey and Debra were in his car, followed by Thad and Al in a police car behind them. They drove in silence and Debra absently rubbed her lower abdomen as she stared out the passenger window and thought about the coming confrontation.

Even if Cecily lied about having done anything, the evidence of her earring in Debra's kitchen at least indicated that she'd been in Debra's house without an invitation.

She wasn't sure why a little bit of anxiety dwelled within her, but it was there, along with a huge hope that this truly was the end of all the madness for her.

She just wanted to get back to her work, back to a normal life. She wanted to focus on the baby, on transforming her guest room into a nursery and interviewing potential nannies.

She just wanted her life back—a normal, sane life that made sense. Was that too much to ask?

Her anxiety mounted as Trey drove up the long driveway to Cecily's large home.

Cecily had been born wealthy and it showed in the house she lived in. Although not as grand as the Winston Estate or Trey's home, it was a two-story colonial with massive columns and a sweeping veranda.

It was a perfect backdrop for a beautiful Southern socialite who spent most of her time attending charity events and getting her photo in the society pages.

It had already been agreed that Trey would greet Cecily at the front door and then the others would follow him inside. It would be a surprise attack that would hopefully catch the woman off guard and allow her to make a mistake.

When Trey knocked on the front door, Thad, Al and Debra stood out of sight on one side. Debra's heart thudded rapidly in her chest. Was she about to come face-to-face with the woman who had tried more than once to orchestrate her death?

The door opened and Cecily's voice drifted out on the cool air. "Trey, darling. Come in."

Thad and Al stepped up behind Trey. "Oh, I didn't realize you'd brought company with you." Her voice remained pleasant until Debra showed herself. "What's she doing here? Trey, what on earth is going on?"

"We need to talk to you, Cecily. May we all come inside?" Trey asked.

Cecily was dressed in a chocolate-brown dressing gown with jeweled buttons running from her breasts to the floor. Her hair and makeup were perfect and Debra would guess that she'd expected something far more intimate to happen when Trey had called to visit her.

"Of course," she replied with a new coolness in her

voice. She ushered them all into a formal living room that was a mix of white furniture and mirrored coffee tables.

Debra's discomfort level immediately increased. The room was cold, almost sterile, the only color coming from a large painting of a younger Cecily that hung on the wall.

Introductions were made between Al and Cecily, who had never met, and then Debra and Trey sat on the sofa while Cecily sank down in a nearby chair. Al and Thad remained standing. "So what's this all about?" Cecily asked. "I don't believe I've ever had one of Raleigh's finest in my home before, although I contribute heavily to the Wives of Fallen Officers charity."

"And we appreciate that," Al replied. "But I have some questions to ask you that have nothing to do with your charitable contributions," Al said.

"Questions about what?" Cecily's gaze met Trey's, Thad's and then Al's, but she refused to acknowledge Debra by even glancing at her.

"We'd like to know where you were on the night that Debra's living room was set on fire," Thad said.

Cecily released a tinkling laugh. "I have no idea. I'm not even sure what night she had the fire." Al told her the date. "I'd have to check my social calendar," she answered. "I stay so busy, off the top of my head I can't remember that specific night."

"We'll wait for you to get your calendar," Al replied, his deep voice filled with a firm resolve.

The pleasant smile that had curved Cecily's lips fell as she rose from her chair. "My secretary usually takes care of this, but I have a copy of my calendar on my notebook. I'll just go get it."

She left the room and as she did Trey reached over and lightly touched Debra's hand, as if to offer silent support, a hint of protection against the woman everyone had thought he would one day marry.

Cecily returned with her electronic notepad in hand. She sat back down and touched the screen to flip pages until she came to the one that held her calendar. "Ah, that night I was at a birthday party for a girlfriend."

"And what time did this birthday party end?" Al asked.

She frowned. "I think it broke up around ten."

"And then what did you do?" Al asked.

"I came home and went to bed…alone." She shot a quick glance at Trey and her brown eyes darkened to black. "Just tell me what this is all about. I'm an important woman and I have things to do. I have no idea why you're asking me such silly questions." There was a definite edge to her voice. "And I still don't understand what Debra is doing here. She's nothing but Kate's assistant and if you're here on some sort of official police business, then she has no place here."

Debra opened her mouth to respond, but Trey once again placed a hand on hers to halt anything she might be going to say. "Debra wanted to be here because she doesn't understand what you were doing in her home when she didn't know you were there," Trey said.

"I don't know what you're talking about. I've never been in Debra's house before. I don't even know exactly where she lives," Cecily protested.

"Then maybe you could explain how this got beneath her kitchen cabinet." Al pulled the earring in the clear plastic bag out of his pocket.

Cecily stared at it and then looked at Al. "I've never seen that earring before in my life."

"I have," Trey replied and got up from the sofa. "I bought them for you. I still have the sales receipt for them and I distinctly remember you wearing them when we went to the Christmas ball. I'm sure we can dig up a photo from that night."

When Cecily looked at Trey her lips twisted into an ugly sneer. "I came to the restaurant that night. I was late and saw the two of you together... You and that slut leaving the restaurant and going to the hotel. I sat in my car all night at the hotel and then I saw you put her in a taxi the next morning."

Debra gasped. "It was just a stupid mistake, Cecily. It would have never happened again, and you and Trey could have stayed together."

"You're having his baby!" Cecily's voice was a near screech of outrage.

"And I didn't intend for him to ever know about the baby," Debra replied.

"He's in love with you, you stupid cow." Cecily jumped up from her chair, the notepad falling to the floor and she glared at Trey.

"You think I didn't know? You think I didn't see the way you looked at her? The way you look at her now? You were supposed to love me. I was the woman who was going to help you achieve greatness. She's nothing, and yet you even stopped sleeping with me after you had her that night in the hotel room."

"So you tried to kill her," Trey said flatly as he stood to face her.

Cecily appeared to have lost all consciousness of the presence of anyone else in the room except herself and Trey. She took a step closer to him. "I did what was best for you…for us, Trey. At first, I just wanted her to think she was going crazy, believe that she was no longer capable of doing her job with Kate. I thought it would protect you if she decided to go public. Who would believe a crazy woman who couldn't even keep track of things in her own house?"

"But that didn't work." Trey's voice was emotionless.

"I had to do something. I couldn't just let all of your dreams and all of mine slip away." Cecily gazed at him as if she didn't understand why he would be upset with her.

"And so you hired somebody to tamper with her brakes."

Cecily stepped closer to him, her gaze softening as she toyed with one of the jewel buttons on her gown. "Don't you understand, Trey? She had to go." Her eyes took on a pleading look. "You might think you love her, but she isn't right for you. I'm what you need to get you where you want to go. She was nothing more than an obstacle that had to be removed so that we could build your future together, the way it is supposed to be."

She's insane, Debra thought. She's crazy as a loon, first in believing that Trey was in love with Debra and secondly in believing that by killing Debra she was assuring him the bright future Cecily saw herself in with him.

Debra held her breath as Cecily placed a hand over Trey's heart. "Don't you understand?" Cecily said. "The brakes…the fire… Everything I did was for you, for us. We want the same things; we are the same kind of people."

Trey grabbed her hand by the wrist and threw it off

him. "We aren't the same, Cecily. We aren't the same at all. At the very least the difference between us is that I have a conscience."

Cecily stared at him and then threw back her head and laughed. "A conscience? You stupid fool, you'll never make it in the world of politics if you have a conscience."

"Cecily McKenna, you are under arrest for the attempted murder of Debra Prentice," Al said, ending the confrontation.

Cecily gasped as he pulled her hands behind her and cuffed them. "I was only doing what had to be done," she replied and then laughed again. "You have no real proof that I've done anything wrong. I have a reputation as a charitable, law-abiding citizen. I'll hire the best defense attorney in the United States!" She screamed the words as Al led her out of the house.

"You haven't seen the last of me, Trey. We were destined for greatness. We're the power couple and you belong to me."

"Shut up." Al's voice could be heard just before the slam of his squad car silenced Cecily's voice.

"Is that earring enough to build a solid case against her?" Debra asked worriedly as she got up from the sofa.

Thad smiled at her. "Don't worry, Debra. They'll build a rock-solid case against her, and you and Trey will never have to worry about her again. Can I catch a ride back to your place with you guys? It appears Al forgot that I rode with him. He's already gone."

They locked Cecily's front door and minutes later were on the road back to Debra's place. As Thad and Trey talked about the case they would build against Cecily, Debra stared out the window and thought about what Cecily had said about Trey loving her.

How ironic was it that she'd nearly been killed by a woman who was under the mistaken impression that Trey loved her when nothing could be further from the truth. Trey cared about her as the mother of his child and he certainly loved the baby she carried, but Cecily had been twisted by knowing about the night Trey and Debra had shared together, a night that had just been a terrible mistake.

Then how do you explain the second night? The question whirled around in Debra's head, but she dismissed it as they pulled to the curb in front of her house.

It was over now. Cecily was arrested, the threat was finally gone and it was time for her to get back to living a new kind of normal life and planning for a baby and shared custody.

Her momentary worry that Trey would want to fight her for full custody seemed silly now. She knew Trey's heart and she knew there was no way he would do anything like that to hurt her.

They would co-parent well together because despite the fact that he didn't love her, they respected and genuinely liked each other and that's what was important.

Trey parked in front of her house and they all got out of the car. If felt like it had been a lifetime ago that they'd all been seated at the table in the Winston backyard about to celebrate with a toast when the gunfire had erupted.

"She never said anything about hiring somebody to shoot me," Debra said as they all got out of the car.

"We'll figure it all out, Debra," Thad assured her. "As it stands right now we can't be sure if she was responsible for the shooter or if somebody else was, but we won't stop digging until we have all of the answers. We know for sure she was in your house and she admitted to being responsible for the cut brake lines and the fire. That's enough to hold her on attempted murder charges even without what happened this morning at the breakfast. I'm out of here." With a lift of his hand in a wave, he hurried toward his car.

Trey walked with her to her front door. "Can I come in?" he asked. "As I remember, there's soup meant for the two of us waiting."

She smiled at him, her heart filled with both love and relief. "I think I could even rustle up a couple of grilled cheese sandwiches to go with that soup."

"Sounds good to me."

It felt far too comfortable, him following her into the kitchen. "I still can't believe she did everything she did because she thought you loved me," Debra said as she opened the refrigerator door to get out slices of cheese.

"I do love you."

She ignored the slightly faster beat of her heart as she closed the fridge door. "You love me because I'm the mother of your baby."

"No, I'm in love with you, Debra." His blue eyes held her gaze. "I would be in love with you whether you were carrying my baby or not, but I know you don't love me. When I proposed to you, you made it clear you weren't interested in me in that way."

The slices of cheese slipped from Debra's fingers and fell to the floor. "I thought you were proposing to the baby... I mean, I thought you were proposing to me because you thought it was the right thing to do and you always do the right thing."

"Then let me make it perfectly clear to you," he said as he took a step closer to her, his eyes lit up with a warmth, with a promise as he reached out and placed his hands on her shoulders. "I'm in love with you, Debra Prentice, and I can't imagine living the rest of my life without you by my side."

"But I'm not good material to be a politician's wife," she protested, finding it hard to think, to concentrate as she stared up into the bottomless depths of his eyes. "I don't know how to help you make your dreams come true. I don't know how to dance and sometimes I can be quite clumsy…"

His hands squeezed her shoulders with gentle pressure. "Just love me, Debra. I don't need you to work my campaign for me. I have Chad to do that. I don't need you to be the perfect political asset. I just need you to be my wife, to cook me special meals on Sundays and listen to everything that's in my heart. I just need you to love me and no matter what else happens in my future, my dreams will come true."

Debra's heart swelled so big in her chest she couldn't speak. She could only nod like a bobblehead doll. He seemed to understand as he pulled her tight against his chest and captured her lips with his in a kiss that stole her breath and lifted her heart to a place it had never been before.

Love my baby. Love me.

"I love you, Trey," she finally said as his lips left hers. "I've loved you since the moment I first met you. I don't care if you're a senator or you empty the garbage pails at the Senate. I just want to be your wife, to be a soft place for you to fall after a long day. I want to sit in front of a fire snuggled in your arms and watch our baby play."

"Babies," he replied and took her mouth once again in a kiss that banished loneliness, healed wounds and promised a lifetime of passion and love.

Chapter 17

The ballroom at the Capital Hotel was magnificent, with five-story, floor to ceiling windows on three sides, and chandeliers that appeared to be sparkling stars against the deep blue high ceiling; it would have been impressive empty.

But tonight it wasn't empty. White-clothed tables surrounded the large polished dance floor, each table decorated with a red-and-pink floral arrangement in the center. Tiny red glittering hearts had been scattered around the arrangements, an instant reminder that it was Valentine's Day.

Debra felt as if it had been Valentine's Day for the past week, ever since she had accepted Trey's proposal. That morning she'd awakened to him serving her breakfast in bed and along with the bacon and eggs and orange juice had been a blue velvet ring box. As the server took their plates away from one of the front tables where they all sat, she admired the sparkle of the two-carat solitaire.

"Wishing it were bigger?" Trey asked her as he leaned closer to her.

She smiled at him, as always her heart expanding at the very sight of his handsome face. "Not at all. As it is now I have trouble lifting my hand."

He laughed and settled back in his chair and looked around the table with the expression of a contented man. For the past week they'd shared many long talks about their future, deciding on two children but keeping the possibility of a third open.

He'd taken her to his house where she'd declared that she absolutely hated it and that she'd need a big budget to transform the cold, beautiful house into a warm, inviting home. He'd taken her into his arms and assured her that it would be warm and inviting as long as she was there with him.

The plan was for her to put her townhouse on the market and within the coming weeks move into Trey's home. She wanted to be settled and married before the birth of the baby and she knew Trey felt the same way.

Every night of the past week he'd slept at the townhouse, snuggled with her in her bed. They'd made love each night and she wondered if she'd ever tire of the feel of his arms holding her tight, the taste of his lips against her own. He rubbed her belly each night and told the baby a ridiculous made-up bedtime story that always ended in her laughing.

No, she would never tire of Trey Winston. They would be together through good times and bad, through thick and thin, with their mutual love for each other to shelter them from each and every storm.

It had definitely been a magical week. Cecily was still in jail. Surprisingly, the wealthy socialite hadn't been so wealthy after all. She'd been living on credit and had been on the verge of bankruptcy. She had been unable to make the huge bail the judge had set.

It was obvious that Trey had not only been her dream man because he wanted to be a senator, but also because he was wealthy enough to save her from her own financial ruin.

Debra released a sigh of happiness. They shared the table with Kate, Sam, Thad and the president of the chamber of commerce, Bob Duke, and his wife, Sherri.

Dinner had been a pleasant affair, with everyone in the festive mood of the evening. All of the men wore tuxes and the ladies were visions in ball gowns, the prevailing colors red and white and pink.

Debra and Trey had gone shopping for her dress, a bright pink with a fitted bodice with tiers of white and vivid pink that went from her waist to the floor. The tiers effectively hid the baby bump that was now clearly visible.

The guest of honor for the night, Kate, was a vision in white with ruby bling in a gorgeous necklace and matching earrings to add color to the sophisticated, simple white gown.

Dinner had been entertaining, a bit of political chatter at first, but then the conversation had changed to the weather forecasting cold and snow possibilities in the next week. Bob had shared disastrous Valentine's Days he'd spent with his wife, Sherri, in the thirty years they had been married.

"Men just don't always get it right." Sherri had laughed after Bob had tried to justify that a new garden tractor was a perfectly acceptable Valentine's Day gift to his wife.

There had been plenty of laughter, but Debra would have been perfectly happy if it had just been her and Trey alone in front of her fireplace.

Trey leaned closer to her once again. "It won't be long now and I'll have you in my arms on the dance floor."

"Be afraid…be very afraid," she replied in mock soberness.

She got the expected result she'd wanted. He laughed, that low, rich laughter that she desired to hear every day and every night for the rest of her life.

When the last table had been cleared, Bob turned and whispered something to Kate. She nodded and smiled around the table at all of her family as Bob got up from his seat and approached the podium at the front of the room.

He tapped the end of the microphone, testing to make sure it was turned on and then began to speak. "I'd like to welcome you all to the Chamber of Commerce Valentine's Day Charity Ball. I hope you've enjoyed your dinner and I also hope you've all had an opportunity to check out the room next door where we have a silent auction taking place. Pull out your checkbooks, men, there's plenty of jewelry and goodies over there that the ladies will want."

Everyone laughed and Trey's hand found Debra's beneath the table, radiating his love, his happiness through their physical contact.

"And don't forget to stick around for the dancing,"

Bob continued. "We have a terrific band standing by for your dancing pleasure. But now, it's my great pleasure to introduce our speaker for the night, although she scarcely needs an introduction. Kate Adair Winston is one of our own who has served not only the city of Raleigh with her charitable work, but also has served the United States as former vice president and former ambassador to France. Her family business, Adair Enterprises, has brought jobs and revenue to our fair city. Kate, we welcome you."

Applause filled the room as Kate rose from the table and took her place behind the podium. She had no notes. Debra had helped her work on the speech over the past couple of days and she'd heard it a dozen times as Kate had practiced it over and over again so that she would have it fully memorized.

Trey released her hand and relaxed back in his chair as Debra rubbed her lower stomach, caressing the baby who would be born into love, a child who would grow up in an intact family.

The room was utterly silent as Kate reached the podium, an indication of the respect she commanded. She turned to thank Bob and there was a distinctive ping sound.

"No!" Sam erupted and lunged from the table in an attempt to reach his mother.

Everything happened at the same time. The center of Kate's white dress exploded in red as Secret Service agent Dan Henderson reached her before Sam, took her down to the floor and covered her body with his. Two more pings resounded, followed by the crackling of glass at one of the huge windows.

Screaming filled the ballroom, along with the sound

of running feet and Secret Service swarming the area. Thad was on his phone, and then raced for the exit as Trey tugged Debra under the table.

Gunshots, Debra thought in horror. Kate had been shot. She squeezed her eyes tightly closed as she thought of the red stain that had suddenly appeared on Kate's stomach. Was Kate dead? Debra's heart pounded with dreadful intensity.

As Trey huddled next to her, his arm tightly around her shoulders, she was able to pick out familiar voices among the din. Sam sobbing and screaming in agony, somebody else shouting about a lockdown and finally the scream of sirens as emergency vehicles and local law-enforcement officials began to arrive.

Jerry Cahill leaned down beneath the table, his eyes cold and hard. "We need to get the family out of here right now," he said. "We're clearing the ballroom. All the guests are being moved to other areas of the hotel, but we have a car waiting for you two and Sam to head to the hospital where your mother is being taken."

Trey nodded and as he pulled Debra from beneath the table, he motioned to the distraught Sam to come with them. Two ambulance stretchers had already arrived in the room and it looked like both Kate and Dan Henderson were being loaded.

"I should have seen this coming," Sam sobbed as Trey threw an arm around his shaking shoulders and they all followed Jerry out of the ballroom. "I should have been able to save her. There were so many I couldn't save, but I should have saved her." Sam appeared to be shattering, his words indicating some sort of post-traumatic stress in addition to his fear for his mother.

Jerry led them to a back entrance of the hotel, all the while talking and listening on his radio. He stopped them at the door, appeared to get some sort of confirmation, and then with his gun in his hand, opened the door.

Directly ahead of them was a black sedan that Debra knew probably had bulletproof windows. Sam got into the front seat and she and Trey in the back and then Jerry slammed the doors, gave the top a thump and the driver pulled away.

The driver was Secret Service man Jeff Benton and as Sam managed to pull himself together, Jeff told them everything he knew, that from the direction that Kate had been shot, apparently the gunman had been in one of the darkened high-rise buildings on the left side of the street from the hotel ballroom and both local and federal agents were clearing those buildings now.

He couldn't tell them the condition of either Kate or Dan Henderson, who apparently had been shot also. He was driving them to Duke University Hospital where both Kate and Dan would be taken and were already in transport.

It was only then that Debra's brain began to process the horror. She leaned into Trey and began to silently weep, her heart aching for the entire Winston family. What should have been a night of triumph for Kate and her sons had become a night of sheer terror.

The ride to the hospital seemed to take forever. Was Kate still alive? *Please, don't take Kate,* Debra prayed as Trey held her tightly against his side. Sam, Thad and Trey needed their mother and Debra needed Kate, too. Her baby needed a grandmother. *Please, let Kate be okay.* It was a mantra that echoed over and over again in her head.

What about Dan Henderson? Had he sacrificed his life in doing his duty tonight? Four shots. There had been four bullets. One of them had hit Kate, but had the others hit Dan?

And where was Thad? Why wasn't he safely in this car with them? They should all be together right now, praying that Kate wasn't badly hurt, that nobody had been critically injured. They should all be praying that the gunman was captured and somebody could make sense of what had just happened.

She gazed down at the glittering ring on her finger and cuddled closer to the man who would be her husband. She told herself that no matter what happened tonight, she and Trey would get through the future together.

By the time they reached the hospital Trey was frantic and trying hard to hide it not just from Debra but also from Sam, who appeared to be on the very edge of his sanity.

They were led into a private waiting room with Jeff Benton stationed just outside the door. Thad was already there and he stood from the loveseat where he'd been sitting as they all entered the room. Thad looked haggard, as if the past forty-five minutes or so had sucked the very life out of him.

"What do you know?" Trey asked.

Thad gestured for Trey and Debra to sit on the loveseat and then he and Sam sank down into two straight-back chairs. "Nothing, other than the two victims have arrived and are with the doctors or whoever. I just got here a few minutes ago myself." Thad sat only a moment and then jumped up to begin to pace the small confines. Thad was tightly wound, his movements jerky with tension, his jaw taut.

Trey noted the fact that Thad had referred to their mother and Dan Henderson as the victims as if in an effort to completely divorce his emotions from the situation.

Sam had grown silent, his eyes staring unseeingly at the wall in front of him with his hands clasped together tightly in his lap.

As the oldest and the unofficial leader of the family, Trey felt helpless to do anything to help his brothers through this horrifying time. As he thought of that moment when his mother's white dress had turned red and she'd fallen, his heart felt like it stopped beating.

How could he help his brothers when he felt the open hand of utter despair attempting to grab him around the throat? The only thing keeping him partially grounded was the warmth of Debra's body next to his, the feel of her small hand gripping his so tightly and the baby that would make them a family.

Thad stopped pacing and stared at the doorway that they all knew somebody would eventually come through to give them an update. He looked as if he wanted to tear through the door to find some answers right now.

"You know, Cecily never confessed to hiring a gunman to shoot at Debra at the breakfast last week," Trey said, trying to gain Thad's attention.

"And the gunman has continued to refuse to talk about who hired him," Thad replied. "There's no way he wasn't a hired gun. His rap sheet shows him as a low-rent thug with charges of robbery and check fraud. He's not bright enough to mastermind his way out of a paper bag."

"But, after tonight, I believe his target was Mom that

day and not Debra." Trey tightened his arm around the woman he loved, remembering how frightened he'd been for her even before he'd acknowledged the love he had in his heart for her.

Thad turned back to stare at the doorway, as if he could will somebody to show up to give them some kind of a report as to what was happening with their mother.

"I wonder what's going on back at the hotel. I wonder if they've caught the shooter," Sam finally spoke, his hands curled into tight fists in his lap.

Thad looked at his brother. "I'm cut out of the loop for obvious reasons. I guess at some point we'll get an update from the Secret Service when they have something to share with us."

At that moment the door opened and a nurse stepped inside. Trey immediately recognized her as the same pretty nurse who had tended to Debra after her car accident. Lucy, that was her name. Lucy Sinclair.

"I just want to let you all know that your mother and Agent Dan Henderson are being attended to by our trauma team. Unfortunately, that's really all I can tell you at this point," she said sympathetically.

Thad took a step closer to her. "Well, that's not good enough," he said tersely. "Do you have any idea who my mother is?"

Lucy's green eyes widened a bit and then narrowed. "At the moment your mother is nothing more than a patient who needs immediate medical treatment."

"I demand to speak to the doctor in charge," Thad replied. "I'm Officer Thad Winston of the Raleigh Police Department and I want to speak to the doctor right now."

"Right now every trauma doctor we have on staff is desperately working to keep your mother and Agent

Henderson alive. They are both in critical condition." She took a step closer to Thad, her eyes flaming in aggravation. "You need to stand down, Officer Winston."

She stood toe-to-toe with him until Thad stepped back and fell back on the chair, his features crumbled in with defeat and fear.

As Lucy left the room, Trey looked at his family. Shell-shocked, that's what they were and yet despite the trauma that they were now experiencing, Trey's commitment to continue in politics only surged stronger inside him.

The bad guys didn't get to win. No matter what the outcome of tonight was, Trey intended to be on the ballot when it came time to elect the next senator of North Carolina.

One way or the other they would all survive this night. They carried Adair Winston blood inside them—they were strong and would carry on.

Debra took his hand and held tight, as if knowing what he was thinking and silently telling him that she would be right at his side.

* * * * *

Join Britain's BIGGEST Romance Book Club

- **EXCLUSIVE offers every month**
- **FREE delivery direct to your door**
- **NEVER MISS a title**
- **EARN Bonus Book points**

Call Customer Services

0844 844 1358*

or visit
hillsandboon.co.uk/subscriptions

MILLS & BOON®

Why shop at millsandboon.co.uk?

Each year, thousands of romance readers
find their perfect read at millsandboon.co.uk.
That's because we're passionate about
bringing you the very best romantic fiction.
Here are some of the advantages of
shopping at www.millsandboon.co.uk:

* **Get new books first**—you'll be able to buy
  your favourite books one month before they
  hit the shops

* **Get exclusive discounts**—you'll also be
  able to buy our specially created monthly
  collections, with up to 50% off the RRP

* **Find your favourite authors**—latest news,
  interviews and new releases for all your
  favourite authors and series on our website,
  plus ideas for what to try next

* **Join in**—once you've bought your favourite
  books, don't forget to register with us to rate,
  review and join in the discussions

Visit **www.millsandboon.co.uk**
for all this and more today!